T0144246

A Modern Lover

A Modern Lover
George Moore

MINT EDITIONS

A Modern Lover was first published in 1883.

This edition published by Mint Editions 2021.

ISBN 9781513291017 | E-ISBN 9781513293868

Published by Mint Editions®

 MINT
EDITIONS

minteditionbooks.com

Publishing Director: Jennifer Newens
Design & Production: Rachel Lopez Metzger
Project Manager: Micaela Clark
Typesetting: Westchester Publishing Services

Contents

I

A Picture Collector

I'll let you have it for fifteen shillings."

"I dare say you will, but I don't intend to buy anymore water-colours of you."

"I am very hard up; give me ten shillings."

"No, I really can't; I have at least a hundred and odd drawings by you, and half of them aren't even numbered: it will take me a week to get through them."

"I'm nearly starving."

"So you have often said before."

The last speaker was an old, wizened little creature, with a grizzled white beard; the other was a young man of exquisite beauty, his feminine grace seemed like a relic of ancient Greece, saved by some miracle through the wreck and ruin of ages. He leaned against an oak bureau, placed under a high, narrow window, and the pose defined his too developed hips, always, in a man, the sign of a weak and lascivious nature. His companion looked nervously through a pile of drawings, holding them up for a moment to the light, then instantly throwing them back into the heap which lay before him. He was evidently not examining them with a view to ascertaining their relative value, nor was he searching for any particular one; he was obviously pretending to be busy, so that he might get rid of his visitor.

The day died gloomily, and the lateral lines of the houses faded into a dun-coloured sky; but against the window the profiles of both men came out sharply, like the silhouettes of fifty years ago.

Pictures of all sizes and kinds covered and were piled against the walls; screens had been put up to hang them on, but even then the space did not suffice.

Pictures had gradually thrust almost everything else in the way of furniture out of the room; the sofas and chairs had been taken away to make place for them. The curtains had been pulled down to gain more light, only the heavy gold cornices remained, and the richness of these precluded the idea that the place was the shop of a vendor of cheap lodging-house art. Besides, the work, although as bad, was not of that kind. It was rather the lumber of studios, heads done after the model posing for a class, landscapes painted for some particular bit, regardless of composition. And what confusion! Next to an admirable landscape you would find a Virgin in red and blue draperies, of the crudest description; then came a horrible fruit piece, placed over an interesting attempt to reproduce the art of the fourteenth century; and this was followed by a whole line of racing sketches, of the very vulgarest kind. Yet in the midst of this heterogeneous collection there was a series of pictures whose curious originality could not fail to attract the eye.

Before them the Philistine might shake with laughter, but the connoisseur would pause puzzled, for he would see that they were the work of a new school that had broken with the traditions of all time and country, and was striving to formulate a new art. Bar girls, railway trains, and tennis players flared in the gayest colours, and, in the hope of interesting the old man, Lewis examined and rapturously praised a flight of ballet girls which hung on the opposite wall. The ruse was so far successful that Mr. Bendish joined eagerly in the conversation, and explained that if the new school who called themselves "The moderns" ever succeeded in gaining the public taste, the Fitzroy Square collection would excite the envy of the *dilettante* of Europe. As he spoke, his little wizen face lightened up, and his eyes sparkled with enthusiasm.

Lewis looked at him and wondered. Here was a man who talked of a new artistic movement, and at the same time bought every conceivable kind of rubbish that was brought to him, provided the seller came down to his price. London is a strange fashioner of tastes, and Bendish was a curious example of what she had done in this respect. Being utterly ignorant, not knowing a *Millet* from a *Corot*, a Raphael from a Rubens, he bought pictures as an old clothes man buys second-hand pocket-handkerchiefs. He spoke volubly, and predicted the millenium in art, when the traditions, of which he knew nothing, would be overthrown, and Mr. Bendish would possess the finest collection in the world. Lewis listened, patiently awaiting an occasion of getting back to the subject of his water-colour drawings. At last his chance came: in the course of conversation, the old man asked him why he had deserted the new school? This, Lewis explained, was not so; and to prove his case he referred to his drawings. But immediately Mr. Bendish relapsed into silence, and showed that he took no further interest in the question. He evidently was determined not to buy anything more that day. His fancies were as varying as the wind; and there were times when he would look at nothing, and would turn away from the most tempting bait like a sulky trout.

This was one of his worst humours; and even Lewis, with his soft, winning ways, could not get him to give fifteen shillings for a pretty water-colour.

From Lewis's hesitating manner, it was clear that he saw that there was not much hope of getting anything out of the old man. But his necessities were so pressing—he had only a shilling in the world—that they forced him to try again.

"I am very hard up; I don't know how I shall get through next week; give me a few shillings for it, say five!—three!"

"I really can't," returned the old man, peevishly. "I have over a hundred of your water-colours, half of which are not framed, the rest not even numbered. I sha'n't buy anymore at present; call another day."

A look of fear and helplessness passed over the young man's face; he said nothing, but took up his drawings, and, leaving the old man still fumbling through his portfolios in the failing light, he walked down the bleak stone staircase into Fitzroy Square.

A slight rain was falling. The wet dripped from the tall trees slowly; occasionally a leaf fluttered down into the dirty gutter. The air was quite still; a soft smell of mud hung over the windless streets; and in the night, which grew darker, Lewis thought he saw an image of the fatality which pursued him.

"I can bear it no longer," he muttered; "anything is preferable to this bitter struggle for life, for bread, yes, for mere bread! for at the best I cannot hope to make more, with my wretched little drawings that no one cares about, not even old Bendish."

For two days he had not left his miserable room, but had sat working at the drawings that Bendish now refused to buy at any price. He had lived on a few crusts and a little tea, afraid to spend his last shilling. And now, as he walked wearily, he took it out of his pocket and looked at it: it was all that remained between him and starvation. But black as were his prospects, he shuddered when he thought of the past, and he remembered that death was preferable to such a life, even if he could continue it. But his resources were exhausted, his clothes were pawned, and he did not know who would lend him a sixpence; all his acquaintance were wearied of him.

As he approached the Strand, the passersby grew more frequent, but he only saw them as phantoms, their voices sounded in his ears like a murmur of distant waters, and out of his soul there rose from time to time a mute protestation against Providence and God.

He walked on like one in a desert until he came to Drury Lane; then the light, which the flaring windows of half-a-dozen public-houses threw over the wet pavement, awoke him from the torpor into which he had fallen, and he realised again, and more bitterly, that he was lost, without a hope to guide. Like a torn flag in a battle, portions of his past life floated through his mind. He remembered how he had come only two years ago to London, expecting pleasure and fame, and he had found, what? Despair, stifled cries, and vanishing dreams. He remembered how the very first night he had wandered through the self-same Strand, and how exultingly he had thought of the great city that extended around him. The crowds that passed him, men and women, the shop windows, rich with a million treasures, carriages, monuments, the turmoil, feasts, beautiful dresses, acclamations, triumphs, all had turned in his head—a golden nightmare, that had tempted and tortured him for a while. But now all was over; he had neither courage nor desire for anything. It astonished him to see people pressing onwards, all having apparently some end in view. To him the world seemed to have come to an end. He was like a corpse over whose grave the city that had robbed and ravished him was holding a revelling carnival.

As he turned into the Strand, he was caught in a crowd that poured through the entrance of a fashionable theatre, and the clear voices of two young men sounded shrill in his ears.

They were in evening dress, and the white cravats and patent leather shoes brought back to him the dream of the life of pleasure and luxury he so ardently desired.

"My dear fellow," said one, "there is no use your going to her ball, you will bore yourself horribly; come into the theatre, and we'll go to supper afterwards."

The ball-goer, however, was not easily persuaded, and his friend proceeded to tell him of the ladies he intended to invite, appending to each name an anecdote, over which both laughed boisterously. Lewis listened, and soon losing sight of his own personality, saw the scene as an independent observer, and dreamed of a picture to be called "Suicide." In the foreground, just out of the way of a fashionable crowd going into a theatre, two young men discussed whether they would seek amusement there or elsewhere, whilst a wretched wight stood reading a notice posted on the walls—

TWO POUNDS REWARD

Yesterday, at nine o'clock, a young man drowned himself from the parapet of Waterloo Bridge. The above reward will be paid to anyone giving such information as will lead to the recovery of the body.

The idea fascinated him, and he wondered if it would be possible to explain by the expression, that the poor devil reading the notice recognised the fact that dead he was worth two pounds, but alive he was merely an outcast, in whom no one took the least interest. He continued to think of his picture until he actually began to consider the advisability of painting it. Then his face winced as if with a sudden pain. He remembered that there were no more dreams for him to dream, no more glad or sorry hours for him to live. He must steal away into the eternal silence of the grave, and leave London to laugh above him. Then a cry for mercy, for life, went up from the bottom of his heart, like a shrill voice heard in the vastitude of night.

"Surely," he asked, "I am not going to die, like a rat, of starvation in the middle of this enormous city?"

Then again his thoughts drifted, and looking at the women as they went wrapped up in silk, the rose colour of their feet visible through the open lace stockings as they stepped from their broughams, he grew dizzy with envious rage, that none of their elegant life, so artistically fashionable, was for him. Carriages came up every minute. All were filled with people who had money, who had come forth to spend it in the night, and in his madness he fancied he heard the shower of gold and kisses that fell over the city.

Then, again, a cry for life and its enjoyments arose out of his feeble heart, and he moaned at his own helplessness. What was there for him to do? he asked himself, again and again. He could not sell his drawings. What was there for him to do? Everything, except the women that passed before him so deliciously beautiful, seemed to advise him to die; but in the silken rustle of their skirts, and the faint odour they left, he heard a thousand secret voices, that seemed to whisper of a vision of perfumed lace, in which one day he would be enwrapped at rest, on the bosom of the siren city which now so cruelly cast him aside.

The crowd round the theatre-door had grown denser, and Lewis still stood looking vacantly before him, lost in an utter sense of abandonment. He had fallen into that state of torpid meditation so common to criminals on their way to the scaffold. The crowd jostled him, but he paid no heed, until he was at last hustled into the street, and then, waking up suddenly, he found he had to cross it to avoid a series of passing cabs. The accident, trivial in itself, seemed to him like an omen, for he was now nearer the Thames than before. The vision of wealth and beauty he had seen had darkened for him even the darkness of death; he now feared the water as a woman fears the tempter that whispers in her ear; had he not been obliged to cross the bridge to get home he would not have ventured to walk down Wellington Street, so gloomy did it look, with its shadows and vast background of cold sky.

Picking his way out of the crowd, he walked until he came to the middle of the bridge, then, leaning his arms on the parapet, he examined the countless crustations of the stone which sparkled in the rays of the electric light. But in a moment remembering himself, and thinking his conduct unworthy of a man who contemplated committing suicide, he looked mournfully at the wide flood of ink that swirled through the piers of the bridge.

All was fantastically unreal, all seemed symbolical of something that was not. Along the embankment, turning in a half circle, the electric lights beamed like great silver moons, behind which, scattered in inextricable confusion, the thousand gaslights burned softly like night-lights in some gigantic dormitory. On the Surrey side an immense curtain of shadow stretched across the sky, out of which a red light watched him with the haggard gaze of a bleeding eye.

But the mystery of the dark wandering waters suggested peace, and in the solemn silence he longed for the beatitude that death only can give, as in the glitter and turmoil of the Strand he had yearned for the pleasures of living. Then a dream of those who had ended their troubles from where he stood arose before his eyes; in a febrile and vacillating way he thought of emulating the courage of his predecessors, and he mused long on the melancholy poetry of suicide. A story he had heard of two lovers who had drowned themselves together, profoundly interested him. Before they threw themselves into the water, the woman had bound herself to the man with a scarf taken from her shoulders, so that they might not even be separated in death. He dwelt on the idea, thinking it a beautiful one, and he said to himself, "Tomorrow or today, what matters since death is the sure end of all we see or feel?"

Then the fluid magnetism of the water took possession of him, and he felt his nature dissolving slowly; his thoughts swayed and flowed with the tide, and he saw monuments, bridges, and lights in a mist that seemed to descend, and in turn to pass into the river. He could resist the temptation no longer, and clutching the parapet, sought to climb over, but as he did so, memories flitted across his mind, among which a girl's name and face came foremost; the face was one of an ordinary work girl, the name was Gwynnie Lloyd. He remembered that it was Friday, tomorrow she would have fifteen shillings, and thinking that she would not refuse to share it with him, he stood irresolute, leaning against the bridge.

"After all," he thought, "Bendish told me to call another day"; and feeling much relieved at the respite, although somewhat disappointed at the common-place *dénouement* of his magnificent project, he walked to his lodging in the Waterloo Road, where he had come to hide from a few creditors.

Threading his way through the crowds of girls and boys who filled the roadway and collected round the stalls, he moodily wondered if this passer and that were more unfortunate than he, until he stopped at a house taller, but not less grimy, than the rest. The bottom part formed a shop, where the landlord sold common delf and tin ware. At the present time he was bargaining with an old woman who would not give the price he asked for a copper kettle. Lauding its merits, he held the article up to the light of a paraffin lamp, that cast a lurid glare over the large white and blue china basins, jugs, and tin saucepans, which were piled and hung on stands outside.

As Lewis passed through the shop to his room, the landlady's little daughter ran forward, tottering under the weight of an enormous yellow cat, which she held in her chubby arms.

"When are 'ou doing to paint my picture wid pussy, Mr. Seymour?"

"Tomorrow, perhaps, if you are a good girl," said Lewis, stooping to kiss the child, much to the large, stout mother's delight, who stood holding in her hand a string of kettles, which she had lifted down from a peg at the back of the shop.

Lewis owed three weeks' rent, and he hoped to persuade Mrs. Cross to let him pay it with a sketch of the child; anyhow, a kiss on Dinah's fair hair was not unpleasant, and might soften the mother's impatience.

With a nod to Mrs. Cross, he went up the dirty staircase, and on the top floor struck a match. The sudden light showed two doors almost facing each other. As he unlocked one, the other opened, and a clear voice asked:

"Is that you, Lewis?"

"Yes; come in."

Shading the match with his hand from the draughts, he eventually succeeded in lighting the tallow candle which stood on a table covered with paints and brushes.

Gwynnie Lloyd was a charming specimen of the English work girl. She was only sixteen, and under the little black dress, her tiny figure, half a girl's, half a woman's, swelled like a rose-bud in its leaves. Her face was fresh, but pale from overwork; her eyes, although almost destitute of brows or lashes, had a delicious look of confidence and candour that made them beautiful through sheer force of truth; her hair was the colour of fine dust; her hands were those of her class, stout and rather coarse.

"So you have been waiting for me, Gwynnie?" he said, passionately. His whole heart was in the words, for apparently her affection was the only thing he possessed in the world.

"Yes, I expected you earlier," she answered, timorously, for she guessed from his manner that he had not sold his sketches.

"I loitered by the river, and if it hadn't been for you, Gwynnie, I think I should have drowned myself; I can stand this misery no longer."

"Oh, Lewis, how can you say such a thing! Do you not know that God forbids us to destroy ourselves?"

In her life she had never heard anyone say so wicked a thing, and as she clung to him, she mentally prayed for him.

"Ah!" he exclaimed, despairingly, "how happy we might be if we had a little money! You are a dear good girl, and I love you better than anything in the world; but all is useless for the want of a few pounds."

"Have a little patience," said Gwynnie, trembling at the idea of losing her lover.

"That's all very well," replied Lewis, sinking into a chair, and sobbing bitterly; "but what shall I do? They won't let me remain even here another week if I don't pay my rent. I have only a shilling left."

Gwynnie would have liked to have cried, but she felt it was her duty to support him.

"Never mind," she said, trying to assume a cheerful voice; "I shall have fifteen shillings tomorrow; that will keep us alive, and you are sure to sell something soon."

Lewis could not answer her at once for sobbing, but he drew her closer with one arm.

"And now," she said, restraining her tears with difficulty, "you will promise me never to say such a wicked thing again; besides, you say you are fond of me, and you talk of drowning yourself; what should I do without you?"

Then Lewis dried his eyes, and said he would do some more sketches; Gwynnie promised to sit to him for a head on Sunday morning, and for a long half-hour they talked of their little affairs.

He had seen a good deal of her since he came to live in the house. They had made acquaintance by rendering each other little services, and he had easily persuaded her to come into his room to see his pictures. Once or twice she had been out to walk with him on the wide London Road; clinging to his arm, she had looked at the stars, and had thought of the infinite goodness of God. Then the conversation turned on her early life, and she told him how her father was a Methodist carpenter, but her mother, who was a Roman Catholic, had brought her up in that religion.

Seeing that the subject interested her, Lewis told how his mother had also brought him up a Roman Catholic, but that his father was an atheist. She didn't know what an atheist meant, and was so shocked when she heard, that she refused to believe that his father had been so wicked. Lewis listened, amused at her pious chatter, till at last, to change the subject which began to bore him, he asked her if she were happier now than when she lived in the country. She did not answer, but involuntarily pressed his arm. The tenderness of that evening was not to be forgotten; it perfumed her life like a grain of scented salts fallen by accident into an empty wardrobe. Lewis knew that she loved him, and he returned her affection because it cheered his loneliness to do so.

As she was about to wish him goodnight, a shuffling step was heard on the stairs, then a knock came at the door; on their frightened faces was plainly written the word landlord.

Without waiting for an answer, the stranger pushed the door open and entered.

"I have something for you—a commission," he said, distorting his long mouth into a laugh, and showing one solitary tooth.

"I am very glad to hear it, Mr. Jacobs," said Lewis, trying to conceal his joy. "What is it?"

Mr. Jacobs was an old Jew, who undertook commissions of all sorts, but his chief business lay in pictures. He knew every dealer and every artist in London, and he trotted about from one to the other, buying and selling for them, supplying information, finding addresses, arranging meetings of all kinds, in fact, carrying on underhand commerce of the most complicated description.

"I called in at Mr. Carver's today, you know, in Pall Mall," said the old man, in a husky voice, "and I found him in an awful fix; he has an order to supply some decorative panels; he promised that one should be ready by Monday—in fact, it will be of no use if it isn't—and the gentleman he relied on to do them is ill, another is out of town, and the third—I forget what happened to the third—anyhow, I thought of you, and I have brought you the panel, and I'm going to pay you liberal, and if it suits, you will have more to do."

"How much?" asked Lewis, excitedly.

"Well, this is what I want done," said Jacobs, taking the panel from out a piece of paper, "I want you to paint me a Venus rising from the sea, with a few Cupids, and it must be at Mr. Carver's on Monday by twelve."

"How much is it to be, a fiver?"

"A fiver!" repeated Mr. Jacobs, as if horrified; "you are joking." Eventually it was arranged that three pounds was to be the price, and Mr. Jacobs was about to go, when Lewis said:

"Could you let me have a trifle in advance; I am very hard up?"

"I really couldn't; I have only a few coppers on me; besides, it is Mr. Carver who will pay you; but I am sorry not to be able."

"Couldn't you manage half a sovereign?"

"No, no," cried the old man, testily; "I'd sooner give the panel to someone else."

Seeing that he would not give him anything, Lewis fetched the light to show him downstairs.

"On Monday morning at twelve; no mistakes; it will be no use later."

"Don't be afraid, Mr. Jacobs; it will be all right."

"And mind you make it look 'fetching;' it is for a gentleman who is very particular," said Mr. Jacobs, as he shuffled downstairs. When Lewis came back, Gwynnie took hold of his hands and wrung them.

"Now, Lewis," she exclaimed, "did I not tell you it would all come right? Three pounds and prospects of more work, isn't it fine?"

"Three pounds isn't much, he ought to have given me five; but never mind, let's have some supper on the strength of it."

"'Tis foolish to be extravagant just because you have had a bit of luck; that is what gets you into such trouble."

"Oh, nonsense! I have a shilling tonight, and you will have fifteen tomorrow, and I shall have three pounds on Monday; it is all right, we can have a couple of sausages and a pint of porter."

"Very well," replied the little girl, "I will run and fetch them."

He gave her a shilling and she ran off.

When she was gone he took up the panel, and, drawing in the air, began to calculate, but suddenly a grey cloud passed over his bright face.

"Good heavens!" he said, "I have no money to pay for a model! What shall I do? I had quite forgotten."

Then he thought of some drawings of which he would be able to make use, for it was only a decorative panel, and the gloom faded from his face.

In a few minutes Gwynnie returned with the eatables; she added a couple of baked potatoes to the sausages; there was no cloth to lay, and they had only to push aside the paints and brushes.

As they supped he tried to explain to her what the picture would be, but she did not like the conversation, and he laughed at her scruples. They had often discussed the subject before, particularly on one occasion, when he took her to the National Gallery. Many of the pictures had shocked her, and he failed to convince her that it was not sinful to paint such things, until he told her that many had been painted in Rome, and had received the approbation of the most pious popes.

But how delightful was that supper! Lewis watched Gwynnie trying to eat the too hot potatoes, and she pressed him to drink the porter, with a sense of complete happiness: until the candle burnt low in the socket they chattered of their future prospects, and how happy they were going to be.

Then he remembered that they both had to be up in the morning early, that it was time to go to bed.

Lewis conducted her to the door and waited till she fetched her candle, which she lit from his. They wished each other goodnight affectionately, and shut their garret doors.

II

Painting from Imagination

At eight o'clock next morning Gwynnie and Lewis bade each other goodbye. The former went off to the shop in Regent Street, where she was employed, the latter sat down to his easel.

After hunting a long time through his academy studies, he found two which he thought would suit him. He would fit the legs of one on to the other, and patch his picture up in that way.

He had nearly all he required, but the action of one arm and shoulder bothered him; somehow he couldn't get them to fit. He wanted to represent Venus tossing a cloud of hair round her body, but, try as he would, the arm did not seem to come right. He looked again through the portfolio, but could find nothing to guide him; however, he slaved away at his drawing till twelve, and at last, after much rubbing out, thought he had got the movement he was seeking for. The Loves were easily done; he had a big engraving from one of Boucher's pictures, and he could take the Cupids from it, arranging them differently, of course.

Then, confident in himself, he set to work to rub in the sea and sky. All went well until he began to mould the figure, and then the faultiness of the drawing became apparent. He shifted the arms, raising and lowering them, thinking every minute he was getting it right. But no, it would not come right. He continued to change and alter until the light began to fade; the panel was thick in paint, and the drawing seemed to be worse instead of better.

At last, in deep despair, he changed the entire pose of the arms; walked backwards and forwards, and tried to think what the action of the figure would be, but nothing would do: at last, half mad with fear and disappointment, he took his palette knife and scraped the panel clean.

There was no use in trying anymore, he could not do it without a model, and he had no money to pay for one, so there was an end of it. Leaning back in his chair, he hid his face in his hands, and his thoughts reverted to the question of suicide. He regretted that he hadn't drowned himself the previous night. If he had only had the courage to have taken the plunge it would be all over now.

What was the use of trying to live? He had been clearly blackballed out of life; he had nothing, not a hope, not a love but one, and that was a poor little work-girl. But as he thought of her his face brightened; she would have fifteen shillings: he would borrow five to hire a model. For a moment he thought of asking her to sit, and he regretted that it would be impossible to persuade her that it was a mere question of art. However, this did not much matter; she would give him her earnings to pay for the model, and there was the difficulty solved. He would be able to find a girl tonight, anyone would do, and by working all tomorrow and getting up early on Monday, he would he able to finish it.

His large, tender, blue eyes grew bright with hope, and he walked up and down, waiting for Gwynnie to return. He looked around the room and prayed fervidly that he might get some more panels to do. It is torture to remain here, he thought, and a look of loathing passed over his face.

Truly it was a miserable place. In the far corner was a narrow iron bed covered with some discoloured blankets. Hanging on some pegs by the door were the rags of clothes that remained to him; a pair of trousers, a waistcoat, and a flannel shirt. By the wall stood three chairs, one broken, and a few canvases.

About six o'clock a blithe voice came singing up the staircase, and a moment after Gwynnie bounced into the room. Her face was rippling with smiles, but they disappeared as her eyes fell on the bare panel.

"Why," she exclaimed, "what have you been doing today, Lewis? Where's the picture?"

"I spoilt it; it wouldn't do; I wiped it out."

"Oh, Lewis, how could you!" said Gwynnie, her clear eyes filling with tears.

"Dear Gwynnie, don't cry; I am as much cut up about it as you; but it is no good, I can't do it without a model."

"What's that? What, a real woman?" she said, with a frightened expression of face, "to sit like those drawings?"

"My dear," returned Lewis, "I was thinking of asking you to lend me a few shillings to pay a model; you know there are lots of girls who make their living by sitting to artists."

"But of course I will," she answered, putting her hand in her pocket; a weight of indefinite apprehension was taken off her mind; she fancied he was going to ask her to sit. But suddenly she withdrew her hand from her pocket, her purse was not there, and, pale with fright, she said, trembling, "I am afraid my pocket has been picked."

A dull, death-like look passed over his face; it was beautiful in gladness, but grief caricatured the features strangely.

In an instant, divining his thoughts, Gwynnie flung her arms on his shoulders and exclaimed, sobbing, "Oh, Lewis! did you not promise me never to think of anything so wicked again?"

"My dear child," he said, putting her arms aside, "I am thinking of nothing."

"Oh, yes, you are, and you have made up your mind to kill yourself."

"Well, what if I have? I can't wait till starvation finishes me."

"Oh, Lewis, Lewis, how can you!" cried the girl, almost frantic with fear. "What should I do without you?"

"It is no use making this fuss," he explained, brutally; "will you sit for this picture? Otherwise, even if I don't drown myself, I shall starve!"

"No, Lewis, don't ask me; I would do anything in the world for you but that."

"Yes, anything but what will save me; I did not think you were so heartless, Gwynnie."

"Don't speak so; I would do anything in the world for you; I will beg for you."

"You know," he said, taking her hand, "I love you, Gwynnie, and that I would not ask you to do anything I thought wrong. I assure you it is only a question of art, nothing more; surely it can't be wrong to save our lives. Remember, neither you nor I have any money, and you heard what Jacobs said, that this would bring other orders, and then we shall have lots of money, and shall be able to get married, for you know I love you better than anybody in the world. You won't sacrifice everything, will you; you won't see me starve?"

At the word married, a bright look passed through her tears over the girl's face, and she said:

"How do you mean I must sit, Lewis, like those drawings?"

He appreciated the sacrifice she was making for him, and his voice trembled with love and gratitude.

"There is no use in mincing matters, Gwynnie," he said, after a pause; "there are, if you refuse, only a few days between us and starvation. It is no good to talk about begging; if you can beg, I can't, and won't. No painter ever painted a nude figure without a model; there is really no harm; will you or will you not save me from starvation? But I won't starve; I have borne up against this poverty long enough, there is always the river," he added, trying to decide her.

Gwynnie sobbed hysterically; she longed to lock herself into her own room, but knowing that that would determine nothing, she resisted the impulse. Lewis let her have her cry out. He had seen the same scene in the studios often before, and it had always ended by the girl giving way. He thought, considering the terrible necessity, that it was rather unreasonable for her to make such a fuss about it. Besides, there was really no harm, for he knew a perfectly good girl who sat for a shilling an hour. Lewis watched her; he was pale with anxiety; for should she refuse, he did not see what there was for him to do. Gwynnie sobbed heavily; she felt sure that if she said, no, Lewis would drown himself, and to say, yes, was beyond her strength.

The two months she had spent in London had scarcely sullied her pure little mind. She had closed her ears to the low talk in the London shop, and was nearly as simple-minded as when she used to walk three miles every Sunday to hear mass.

Religion had been laid so carefully about her early life that it was the soil to which tended the roots of all her thoughts. If her father had not taught her his faith, there was one word he had engraven on her mind, which was *Duty;* therefore, if Lewis could persuade her that it was her duty to save his life at the cost of her modesty, she would do so, as Lady Godiva saved Coventry. Still, of all the virtues, modesty is the dearest to the Methodists, and her struggle was the bitterest; and, decided either way, would infallibly influence the rest of her life. If she refused, and so caused her lover's death, remorse would cloud her life; if she consented, pure as might be her intentions, she would have lost her modesty, and then, what shield would she have to keep her from sin and ruin?

But still, on the other hand, the sacrifice of all she held dear to save not only the temporal but the spiritual life of the man she loved, might so poetise and etherealise her nature that it would be able to withstand all temptations which might otherwise have attended it, and enable her to live in the past as a saint lives in the future. This transfiguration would undoubtedly be the result of subjecting so fervid a nature as hers to so fearful a test, but would it endure through her whole life, or for a time only? Would the struggle for existence which she would be engaged in, slowly but surely grind away the beautiful structure of feminine devotion she had raised, and leave her neither good nor wicked in the end, but only sordidly common-place? These were the different issues which her decision involved, and which it is one of the objects of this story to trace.

Gwynnie continued to sob until at last the poignancy of her grief became so acute that Lewis felt he would rather die a hundred deaths than ask her to sit.

"For goodness sake don't cry like that, Gwynnie," he said, with tears in his eyes. "I am sorry I asked you; let's say no more about it."

At the sound of his voice the girl stopped crying, and, looking up at him, said:

"I will sit for you, Lewis, since it is necessary; but I am not a bad girl, nor do I wish to be, but it cannot be right to see you starve or drown yourself, when I can save you."

Lewis did not speak, he felt that words were out of place. He knew that she suffered, although he didn't exactly know why. His was a soft, sensuous nature, that instinctively took the easiest road to walk in, without a thought whether it was the right or the wrong one.

Gwynnie Lloyd, on the contrary, might hesitate a long while before deciding, but once convinced which was the right path, she would follow it, no matter how thorny it might prove.

The silence became each moment more irritating, but Lewis left her to break it, feeling himself unequal to the effort.

"When do you want me to sit?" said Gwynnie, resolutely.

"I am afraid I shall have to ask you to sit nearly all day," he answered, timidly, afraid that she would draw back. "Do you think you will mind?"

She looked at him surprised; her only excuse was to do what was wanted of her, efficiently.

"Certainly not; I will sit for you as long as you require me."

"Well, then, suppose we begin at eight; but I am afraid you will not be able to sit without a fire. Have you any money? I will buy a little wood and coal."

The mention of these details produced the same effect on her as the first sight of a guillotine will, even on those most prepared to die.

Luckily, she had two shillings, which had escaped the pickpocket's fingers, and she gave them to him, saying:

"I suppose you have had nothing to eat:" then her thoughts wandered, and she added, absently, "I don't know what we shall do if you don't sell this picture. I wonder how I lost my money!"

"I have been at work all day," said Lewis; "I haven't had time to feel hungry; will you come, and we'll have some supper together?"

"No, thank you, I had some dinner with one of the girls; I am tired, and I think I shall go to bed."

Then she got up and bade him goodnight, and went towards the door in a hesitating way, as if she had left something unsaid.

"I do this, Lewis," she explained, holding the door open, "because we are nearly starving, because I believe I am saving your life; but you'll not think worse of me; you will respect me, will you not?"

Lewis raised his hands in mute protest while he sought for words, but before he could speak she had bid him goodnight, and slipped out of the room.

III

Painting a Venus

He was heaping some more coals on the fire when Gwynnie entered the studio-garret next morning. With one hand she clasped round her shoulders a coarse woollen shawl, with the other she held up her skirts which hung loosely about her. Her feet were bare.

She had slept feverishly and fitfully. All night she had been awakened and startled by dreams. Each half hour's sleep had been followed by a long vigil, full of the ardours of plighted and enfeebled by the lassitudes of broken promises. She would have had no difficulty in acting rightly had she known where her duty lay. But there was no one to whom she could turn for a word of advice, and she often got out of bed and prayed in the clear moonlight on her knees for grace.

Often she seemed to see her father's face, but it told her little; sometimes it seemed to frown, sometimes to smile, but she found comfort nowhere, save in a voice that told her that we do right when we believe what we are doing is right.

"How good of you to come," said Lewis; "I was afraid that you would change your mind."

"Why should we change our minds when we think we are doing right?" she answered, unaffectedly, but with a desire to excuse her conduct.

Both were very much embarrassed. He, even more than she, dreaded the first step, and cowardly tried to put it off by suggesting that she had better wait till the room was warmer; she, on the other hand, having come for a certain purpose, did not understand why it should be delayed.

"I think the room is quite warm; I am ready when you are," she answered, with the faintest tremble in her voice.

Lewis placed her in the centre of the room where the light would fall directly upon her, then he arranged his easel in front of her, and stood waiting:

Bravely she threw her shawl away, and showed her arms and bosom. Then there was a pause. She held her skirts irresolutely about her, until at last, with a supreme effort, she threw them aside.

If she could have stood as she was the worst would have been over, but Lewis had to tell her how to stand, to place her arms, her legs, her head, and she was so nervous she could scarcely understand what he said. Then she felt a faint sickness come over her, mixed with an aching detestation of her own person, and an infinite desire to beat herself against the walls, to be crushed out of sight. Twenty times she thought she was going to faint, it was only her pluck that saved her.

However, at last the pose was found, and Lewis commenced his drawing. The knowledge of the sacrifice she was making for him intensified his powers of concentration, and in an hour he had made a very excellent drawing; he had caught the whole spirit of the pose.

Gwynnie stood posing admirably; but those who are not professional models will stand still for a quarter of an hour or so, and then fall suddenly from their full height without a word of warning. Lewis, being aware of this, watched carefully, and at the first quivering of the muscles of her face, threw her shawl over her shoulders, and helped her to a chair. When the faintness had passed off she cried a little, but was consoled at hearing the drawing was getting on beautifully.

The ten minutes' rest went by rather awkwardly, and when he asked her to resume the pose, she did so a little reluctantly.

It caused her perhaps a bitterer pang than before; the uncertainty was gone and the humiliation remained; but knowing that it would not do now to draw back, she bravely returned to her place.

Having assured himself by measuring that his drawing was in proportion, he took up his palette and began to paint. Everything went right as if by magic, and if Gwynnie had been able to hold out till three o'clock, he could have finished it all from nature, but although she took long rests of twenty minutes, she began to feel so dreadfully tired, that after two o'clock she had to go to her room and lie down. Luckily this did not matter. Lewis had it all well laid in, and could complete it from memory.

He had still to paint in the sky, sea, and the Cupids; he worked till the light first reddened the windows, until he began to fear he might spoil his picture if he went on.

Then he carried his easel, with the picture on it, to the lightest part of the room, and surrendered himself to the pleasure of looking at it. It was, he thought, certainly one of the best he had done. The figure was graceful, pretty in colour; the Cupids were well grouped. There was no doubt Mr. Carver would not only be enchanted with it, but would give him other orders. He would undertake to do some more panels at the same price, and then he would ask for an increase: this would be only fair; there was no doubt that Carver, or whatever his name might be, would not be able to get them half so well done for twice the money.

He looked at it from the right and then from the left, and thought what a pity it was he couldn't have another sitting. The drawing was all there—it only wanted a little finishing; he wondered if he would be able to persuade Gwynnie to get up early, and give him half-an-hour tomorrow morning; but, remembering how much she had suffered for him, he began to grow sentimental, and determined not to ask her.

The morality of the question interested him profoundly. How different girls were! To think that there are thousands who do the very same thing everyday of their lives, for one-and-sixpence an hour, and some of them quite good girls; whereas Gwynnie, he did not suppose anything in the world would have induced her to do what she did, but the conviction that she was saving himself from suicide.

He wondered if he would really have gone and drowned himself if she had not sat for him. There was no doubt that he was in the worst fix he had ever been in in his life. Everything pawned, and not a shilling in the house—lots of men had done away with themselves for less cause. It was very probable that he would not have been able to have borne up any longer; but it was all right now.

Then his thoughts went back to Gwynnie, and he had not much difficulty in working himself up to the point of believing that he loved her quite perfectly, and above all, unselfishly. There was no doubt she had done him a very great service, and, vowing that she should be compensated, he began to consider his project of marrying her. The idea fascinated him, and he turned it over in his mind until the room became quite dark, and his stomach told him sharply that he had only eaten a crust of bread all the day long.

Gwynnie, too, had eaten nothing, so he resolved that they should go out together and have some supper.

He went into the passage and listened, but, not hearing her stir, he pushed the door open. She lay fast asleep on the bed. She slept so soundly that he feared to awaken her, and, not knowing how long he might have to wait for her, he determined, after some hesitation, to go out alone, have something to eat, and come back in half-an-hour to see how she was getting on.

But Lewis' half-hour was a long one; and before he came back, Gwynnie awoke—partly from cold, partly from hunger; she had not eaten anything for nearly twenty hours. She got up and drank a little water: it relieved her; then she groped her way into the studio. It was in complete darkness; she called, but, receiving no answer, began to fear that he had spoilt his work, and gone out in despair. Trembling, she sought for the matches: at length she found them, and, by the light of one, which flared and went out, caught a glimpse of the picture on the easel. Reassured, she struck a second, and lighted a bit of candle, curious to see what she had sat for.

During the rests, she had had no heart for anything but to escape from her dreadful situation. Lewis had asked her to look at his painting, but she had turned away her head. It seemed to her that to cast but a glance at it would be unendurable shame. Now, however, that he was gone, she approached it timidly, terrified, yet with a feeling of compulsion upon her. She must know the worst.

When the light of the candle fell on the panel, she started back in horror. The white woman who rose out of the sea, and, as she threw back a heavy fleece of golden hair, seemed to exult in her nakedness, was she. She recognised herself; the arms, the legs, the hair, were hers, even the face was like hers.

Her first impulse was to dash the vile thing to the ground, and seek some place where she might hide herself. She felt as if she would never dare to encounter human eyes again; she recalled every moment of that terrible day, and she asked herself, half mad with fear, how she would ever be able to meet Lewis.

She glanced round hurriedly, and remembered that he might return at any moment. She felt that she would sooner die than look him in the face. No, they must not meet now; the word "never" was on her lips, but she loved him too well for that. She would see him in a few weeks, in a month; but now she must fly from him. But why? He could not despise her for what she had done: it is impossible to despise those who save our lives. But he might ask her to sit again, and that she would never do. Then she remembered that he had spoken to her of marriage. But her pride tempted her, and she said to herself, that she would never let him marry her out of gratitude. She loved him truly; and, if he returned her love, they would be happy together, but not otherwise. Clearly the best thing would be to leave him. Her resolution was hurriedly taken. At first she did not know where to go, but remembering that a girl who worked in the same shop had often asked her to share her room, she resolved to go to her.

Preparation she had little to make; her few bits of clothes could be rolled into a little bundle, and, acting on the impulse of the moment, she packed up her things.

She came back once or twice to bid goodbye to the studio, where she had found all the happiness and bitterness her life had known. It cost her many a cruel pang to go, but she felt that if she stayed, other temptations would result from what she had done, and, fearful of her own strength to resist, she sought safety in flight.

IV

A Picture Dealer

At the public house close by Lewis had something to eat; and then, being a little elated by his luck, and tired by his long day's work, he thought he would not return home just yet, but would take a turn in the Strand, and see what was going on. There he met some friends whom he had not seen for a long while, and they pressed him to come and have drinks with them in a bar-room where they could sit and talk.

Drink succeeded drink, and it was not till half past twelve, still explaining their artistic sympathies, that the friends bade each other goodnight on the pavement.

About ten o'clock the next morning he jumped hastily off his bed and rushed to see his picture.

When he had admired the drawing, the colour, the composition, he remembered last night's spree. Then he wondered where Gwynnie was; he hoped she would not be angry with him for having gone out without her. Casting a last look at his picture, he went to look for her.

Not finding her in her room, he supposed that she had gone to work. From a lodger he learnt it was half-past ten, so he had just time to clean himself up a bit before going to Mr. Carver's. He bought a paper collar, brushed his clothes, tied his necktie so as to conceal its shabbiness, and started for Pall Mall, with his picture under his arm.

After having explained his business to the shop assistant, he was told that Mr. Carver would see him when disengaged.

At present he was, as Lewis could see, showing some pictures to a tall, aristocratic looking woman, who, judging from the dealer's obsequious politeness, was a well-known customer.

She was well, but a little carelessly dressed; there was not that elegance and exactitude in her toilette which betokens the merely fashionable woman. A shrewd judge of character would tell you that she was a woman of the world, spoiled with artistic tastes. After examining the crows' feet, which were beginning to crawl about the intelligent eyes, he would tell you that she was some years over thirty, and he would add, if he were very sharp, that she was probably a woman who had missed her vocation in life, and was trying to create for herself new interests. There was about her a peculiar air of dissatisfaction.

As she raised her arm to point out some merits or defects in the picture before her, the movement dragged the long, sleeveless, grey cashmere mantle closer to her figure, and showed the shape of her broad shoulders and delicate waist: the fox fur border made the hand look smaller even than it really was.

Her rather square face was handsome and intelligent, but not pretty. The mouth was large and sensual; the nose was very small and well shaped, but the nostrils were prominent, like those of negress; the forehead was broad and white, but the black hair was tied up hastily, and slipped from under the dark velvet bonnet.

Lewis watched her attentively: she was the kind of woman who would attract a man like him. He wondered if she loved anyone, and he tried to imagine what this mythical person was like. She looked so aristocratic and dignified, that it seemed to him impossible that anyone could exist whose right was to kiss her lips and call her by her Christian name.

The picture dealer was very busy trying to sell a magnificent mirror in old Saxony, which hung on the wall opposite to which Lewis was sitting.

The lady examined it so attentively that Lewis thought she was going to buy it, but, as he looked from her to the mirror itself, he saw with surprise that she was examining him, and not the red and white flowers. Their eyes met for a moment, then she turned to ask Mr. Carver some questions anent a small picture which stood on a tall Chinese vase in the far corner.

What with an enormous stand laden with china, and the pictures in the window, the back of the shop was in perpetual twilight. Mr. Carver was therefore obliged to take the little picture which interested the lady over to where Lewis was sitting, so that she might admire it thoroughly. Mr. Carver asked Lewis politely to move a little on one side, and then, holding the picture under the lights, began to explain its beauties.

"Yes, Mrs. Bentham, this is a very sweet landscape, by Corot; I can guarantee it; I had it of a man who bought it from the artist himself, you know his signature?"

She made some casual remarks, and then her eyes wandered from the picture to Lewis. Some women would have thought him mawkish, said that his hands were too long and white, his eyes of too soft a blue. The languid poses that his limbs naturally fell into rivalled the sweet dreamful attitudes of Greek statues modelled by Roman sculptors; and all this harmony of body showed the epicene abandon of the man. The beautifully turned temples pointed to the sensual intelligence of the girl, not to the virile intelligence of the male; there was nothing there that fixed the regard, all was transitory all was mobile. So Lewis's face had the rare charm of touching the imagination; it was as suggestive as a picture by Leonardo da Vinci, and already Mrs. Bentham felt singularly curious to know who he was. He looked so poor, so wretched, and yet so gentlemanly, that, involuntarily, she saw him the hero of a series of romantic misfortunes, and was burning with curiosity to know him.

The occasion was ready at hand. She had seen him unpacking his picture; it was there before her.

"Oh, what a charming panel!" she said, after a moment's hesitation; "and how prettily the Cupids are grouped round the Venus! Is it an expensive picture, Mr. Carver?"

"It is a commission I had from a gentleman; he ordered it to fit the corner of a smoking-room," replied Mr. Carver.

Mr. Carver was a large, stout man, and he wore huge bushy whiskers; his face was a rich brown tint, and his fat fingers played perpetually with a heavy gold chain which hung across his portly stomach. Like most men of his calling, he was observant, and having caught Mrs. Bentham more than once looking at the young painter, suspected that she was interested in Mr. Seymour.

Afraid to introduce him because of his shabby appearance, he resolved, seeing that Mrs. Bentham still continued to look at Lewis, to adopt a middle course.

"You see, Mr. Seymour," he said, in his pompous way, "that listeners do sometimes hear good of themselves."

Lewis blushed violently, and Mrs. Bentham pretended to look a little confused.

"I am sure I think the picture charming," she said, half to Lewis, half to the dealer.

Lewis' heart was in his mouth, and he nervously tried to button his collar.

"I should like to buy this very much," said Mrs. Bentham, as she advanced to examine the Cupids more minutely; "but don't you think there's too much sea and sky for the size of the panel?"

Lewis blushed red, and answered her awkwardly and abruptly. He felt so ashamed of his clothes that he could scarcely say a word.

Mrs. Bentham was disappointed. She had imagined him painting frescoes worthy of Michael Angelo in a garret; had expected to hear him denounce the tyranny of wealth, and by a chance word or two give her an idea of the grandeur of his soul and the austerity of his life. Instead of this he murmured something vague and common-place between his teeth; and after another attempt to get him into conversation, she turned away, thinking him a very uninteresting young man. But at this moment Lewis caught Mr. Carver's eyes upon him as a gleam of sunlight awakens a bird, he recovered himself, and commenced talking on decorative art.

The spell being broken, Lewis chattered away pleasantly, and Mr. Carver, with the tact that always distinguished him, walked away under the pretext of give an order at the other end of the shop.

"Ha, ha!" thought the picture dealer, as he played pleasantly with his watch-chain, "so, Mrs. Bentham, you like my painters better than my pictures; well, never mind, I daresay I shall be able to turn your tastes to my advantage, no matter how they lie."

For a moment his face wore the expression of a man who has done a good action, but as he talked to his shopman it grew gradually more reflective. An idea had struck him. He remembered that sometime ago—some six months ago, but that didn't matter—Mrs. Bentham had asked him if he knew an artist who would, under her direction, decorate her drawing-room from a series of drawings she had colleted for the purpose. The commission had somehow fallen to the ground, but he now felt that the time had arrived to remind her that she had never put her delightful scheme for the decoration of her ball-room into execution. Charmed with his ingenuity, Mr. Carver came forward and joined in the conversation.

After a few prefatory remarks on art, he introduced the subject of the drawings, and suggested Mr. Seymour as just the person to whom such a work might be confidently entrusted.

Lewis had aroused Mrs. Bentham's sympathy, and the idea that she might help him was already stirring in her heart. But she was not prepared for so swift a transition from her dream of possibilities to an actual opportunity. The vague desire, in which she had found pleasure a moment earlier, frightened her when it took shape in Mr. Carver's suggestion, and she received it with silent astonishment. If she should give this commission to the young man, she must ask him as a visitor to Claremont House, and her look of surprise told the dealer that in proposing it he had gone too far. His thoughts had outstripped hers, but, nevertheless, they were travelling on the same road.

He was ready enough to let the question rest, and to talk about the Corot. But the idea of the decorations seemed to sing in Mrs. Bentham's ears, and she feared that her silence might have wounded Lewis. She tried to return to the subject; she glanced at him, she hesitated, and eventually, not knowing well what to do, she promised to call again in the course of the afternoon, and wishing them both good-morning, got into her carriage and vanished like a good fairy.

Lewis stood looking after her in amazement, until Mr. Carver tapped him on the shoulder.

"Well, my young friend," he said, affecting an American accent, "I guess you are in good luck, you have only to play your cards well"; then, pulling his long whiskers, he leaned and whispered, "she has seven thousand a year, and has been separated from her husband for the last ten years."

Lewis did not answer, he did not quite understand what the dealer meant.

After watching him for a few moments, his head thrown back in the fashion of a picture he had once possessed, of Napoleon surveying the field of Austerlitz, he said:

"I am afraid you are too green, but if you weren't—"

He did not finish his phrase, but he seemed to see a conquered world at his feet. At last, awaking from his reverie, the dealer said, surveying Lewis, attentively:

"You owe me a big debt of gratitude."

"And which I will repay you one of these days, if I get on as well as you seem to think I shall. But do you think she will give me the work to do that you and she were speaking about?"

"Oh, that I can't say," said Mr. Carver, murmuring like one waiting for an inspiration; "but I think it quite possible that she may interest herself in you, that is to say, if I speak of you as perhaps I may be tempted to do."

Lewis ventured to hope that Mr. Carver would be so tempted.

Mr. Carver did not answer, but continued to look into space, with the deep gaze of his favourite picture; at last he went over to the till, and taking out three sovereigns, gave them to Lewis.

"This is what I owe you; call here tomorrow morning; I shall see her this afternoon, and will speak to her on the subject."

Lewis thanked him humbly for his kind intentions, and asked him if he were satisfied with the panel.

"Oh, perfectly, perfectly; it is very satisfactory indeed."

"Then, will you give me another to do?"

"Certainly; I shall have two ready for you tomorrow, that is to say, if nothing comes of the matter in hand," replied Mr. Carver, with the air of a man who wants to be left alone to his reflections.

Stunned with the shake the sudden turn of Fortune's wheel had given him, Lewis walked towards the Strand, wondering how it was that Mr. Carver knew so well what Mrs. Bentham would do. As he turned into Pall Mall, he met Frazer, and the two went together. Frazer's face was wofully ascetic; he lived for art, and for art only. He existed on a shilling a day, and made his wife live on less, whilst he dreamed of a new ideal. He belonged to the group of painters who styled themselves "The moderns," and sold their pictures to Mr. Bendish. Having the least talent of the lot, he was the most fanatical.

Rapidly Lewis told Frazer the story of his success, and forgetting that his friend took no more interest in women than in cab horses, gave him a minute account of Mrs. Bentham's personal appearance.

"Isn't it an extraordinary story, and what a delightful time I shall have in Sussex with her, if what Carver says is true, that—" but noticing that Frazer was absorbed in contemplating the lights and shadows in the streets, he stopped.

The day was sloppy, but the sun shone between the showers; the violet roof of Waterloo Place glittered intensely, and scattered around reflections of their vivid colour. A strip of sky, of a lighter blue than the slates, passed behind the dome of the National Gallery, the top of which came out black against a black cloud that held the approaching downpour.

"You say that my sunset effects are too violet in tone; look there!" exclaimed the enthusiast; "isn't everything violet? walls, pools, and carriages, I can see nothing that isn't violet."

Lewis admitted that there were some violet tones in the effect; but denied that it was composed exclusively of that colour, as Frazer wanted to make out.

As they walked along, the question was argued passionately. Frazer's whole soul was in the discussion; Lewis thought how he should spend the afternoon. It was only two o'clock; he could not sit at home with three pounds in his pocket, so he invited his friend to come with him to a bar-room, and have something to eat.

GEORGE MOORE

Frazer, who had eaten nothing all day, and only had had a dried herring at a fish-stand for dinner the night before, assented. He wished to continue the conversation, for he hoped to bring back Lewis to the fold. Lewis had once been a "Modern."

Pushing through the doors, bright with varnish and polished brass, they stood in the twilight, warm with tobacco smoke, of the bar-room. The place was full of people, they lolled in groups and couples along the counter: behind it stood a line of girls, whose clear voices, as they gave an order, rang above the long murmur of the conversation. An odour of liquor drifted upwards, escaping slowly by the high windows. Edging their way through the crowd of betting-men, artists, journalists, and actors, they at last got to a table in one of the crescent-shaped nooks which ran along one side of the room under the cathedral windows.

Lewis ordered a copious lunch, and much whiskey and water, the sight of which attracted some academy students who were talking to the barmaids.

At this time "The moderns" were terribly laughed at; Thompson, the head of the school, was admitted to have some talent, but the rest were considered fools and madmen. So, with whiskey to drink, and Frazer to chaff, the academy students got on capitally, and when they got the enthusiast to say that the only painting of any interest was what "The moderns" did, they fairly shook with laughter. Frazer never lost his temper; and he continued to pour forth his aphorisms, unconscious of the mirth they occasioned. At last the hilarity was cut short by the arrival of Thompson; he was with Harding, the novelist, whose books were vigorously denounced by the press, as being both immoral and cynical. Places were made for the two leaders of the modern movement. Lewis knew them both, so he at once set to work to tell them about his luck.

Thompson looked bored; Harding listened sneeringly, his face was that of the intellectual sensualist.

"So you are going to decorate the walls," said Thompson, drily, "with the extract of Boucher, and you are going to do it together? Well, I hope the collaboration will succeed."

"I suppose you would like me to paint ballet girls and housemaids over Greek walls. If the room is Greek, the decorations must be Greek, at least it seems to me so."

"Naturally," replied Thompson, languidly (he had not much belief in Lewis's artistic future), "but don't you think there is a way of giving a modernized version of Greek subjects, that would be quite as archæologically correct as the Greek seen through Boucher and Poussin? Do what they did, take an old form and colour it with the spirit of the age you live in."

The remark awakened a hundred thoughts in Lewis's mind, and he remained thinking.

"But what is the use of arguing," said Harding. "Leave him alone, he will succeed much better by joining the women artists with their school of namby-pamby idealism, than by working with us. The age is dying of false morality and sentimentality, and neither you nor I can do anything to help it, nor a host like us. These confounded women, with their poetry, their art, their aspirations, have devoured everything, like a plague of locusts; they have conquered the nineteenth century as the Vandals did Europe in the sixth. Later on, I dare say they will arrive at something; at present they are a new race, and have not yet had time to thoroughly digest what they have learned, much less to create anything new."

"Not created anything new!" exclaimed an academy student: "what do you say to George Sand, George Eliot, and Rosa Bonheur?"

"That you have chosen the three that I would have chosen myself to exemplify what I say. If they have created anything new how is it that their art is exactly like our own? I defy anyone to say that George Eliot's novels are a woman's writing, or that "The Horse Fair" was not painted by a man. I defy you to show me a trace of feminality in anything they ever did, that is the point I raise. I say that women as yet have not been able to transfuse into art a trace of their sex; in other words, unable to assume a point of view of their own they have adopted ours. For instance, no one will deny that woman's love must be different from a man's. Well, does George Sand, in one single instance, paint woman's love as seen differently from how we see it ourselves? And what splendid chances they miss! Female emotion in art is an unknown quantity, but to analyse it would require an original talent and that is what they have not, and I am afraid never will have. They arrange, explain, but they do not create; they do not even develop a formula; they merely vulgarise it, fit it for common use. No, not only are they not fathers, but in art are not even mothers."

"Quite so," exclaimed Frazer; "and if all modern art is based on love, it is owing to their influence. The fault I find with Shelley is that he can't write ten lines without talking of love;—it is quite sickening."

Frazer could get no further, but with a grimace as if he were really feeling ill, he buried his long nose in a tumbler of whiskey and water.

"But don't you think love beautiful?" asked Lewis, perfectly horrified; "how could anyone write poetry without it? It is the soul of poetry: even Swinburne, whom you so much admire, writes constantly about love."

"Never!" said Frazer, energetically; "he respects himself too much. I defy you to show me anywhere a trace of sentiment in his poetry. Ah, yes, I forgot, he does in the case of the leper; but then it was a leper who was sentimental, which renders it far less repulsive."

This startling paradox obtained a laugh, and all wondered how far Frazer was serious in what he said. The conversation then turned on women, and everyone, including the academy students, who spoke to each other, explained to his neighbour what his individual opinions were upon the subject. Lewis believed in passion, eternal devotion, and, above all, fidelity; he could not understand the sin of unfaithfulness, in any shape or form; without truth there could not be love, and how any man could make love to his friend's wife, passed his comprehension. Frazer declared that in that respect only he had never feared his friends. Thompson said that an artist's best love affair is to marry his cook, for in that way he not only makes sure of his servant's honesty, but secures himself against all invitations to dinner parties.

Frazer endorsed that opinion cordially. Lewis combated it resolutely, and cited a number of successful painters and authors who had devoted their lives to love as well as to art. This drew forth a long discussion, to which everybody contributed something, on the rival merits of Michael Angelo and Raphael, Wordsworth and Shelley: at last the conversation returned to its starting point, and the possibility of creating a new æstheticism was again passionately discussed.

"I'm sick of the argument," said Thompson; "people won't understand, or can't understand, and yet the whole question is as simple as A B C."

"Well, what is your A B C?" asked an academy student.

"This," replied Thompson, "ancient art was not, and modern art is, based upon logic. Our age is a logical one, and our art will not be able to hold aloof any longer from the general movement. Already the revolution is visible everywhere. It accomplishes nothing in music that it does not do in literature; nothing in literature that it does not in painting. The novelist is gaining the day for the study of the surroundings; the painter for atmospheric effects; and the musician will carry the day for melodious uninterrupted deductions, for free harmony which is the atmosphere of music."

This profession of faith touched the heart of a musician who had joined them, and he exclaimed: "Just so, and yet it is impossible to explain to people that that is Wagner's whole principle. Take a symphony or a sonata, and ask a dozen writers to describe what it means, and you will get ten different theories. But if music, by itself, does not go further than to express generalities, once you join it to literature it becomes an instrument of the most extraordinary precision, for the sensibility of the listener is awakened to that particular emotion, to that particular shade of sentiment. The idea is completed by the suggestion, and in this way you obtain what is, perhaps, the most perfect of all the arts, an art that speaks at once to the ear, the soul, to the heart, and to the eyes. The dramatist gives the visible, the musician the invisible. The musician is the Pygmalion, the dramatist is Galatea."

There being no other musician present, the conversation went back to the novel, and someone asked Harding why he always chose such unpleasant subjects.

"We do not always choose what you call unpleasant subjects, but we try to go to the roots of things; and the basis of life, being material and not spiritual, the analyst inevitably finds himself, sooner or later, handling what this sentimental age calls coarse. But, like Thompson, I am sick of the discussion. If your stomach will not stand the crudities of the moral dissecting room read verse; but don't try to distort an art into something it is not, and cannot be. The novel, if it be anything, is contemporary history, an exact and complete reproduction of social surroundings of the age we live in. The poem, on the other hand, is an idealisation, and bears the same relation to the novel as the roast beef does to the rich, ripe fruit which you savour when your hunger is satisfied."

"Believe before it is too late," exclaimed Mr. Frazer, warmly, to the academy students; "the die has been cast; what has to come will come. It will not be Mr. Hilton's Venus, nor Mr. Baring's pretty mothers, that will retard the coming of the modern art. A bombshell is about to break, and you open your umbrellas; but have a care, oh, you who are academicians, the bombshell will destroy without mercy all things, both the small and heavy, that oppose it. I say this as much for Mr. Hilton as for Mr. Baring, as much for Mr. Channel, as much for Mr. John Wright and Mr. Arthur Hollwood, I say it for all who aspire to live in the future."

GEORGE MOORE

This speech, which was given with all the vigour of a prophecy, threw a chill on the conversation. Some tittered at the enthusiast's vehemence; Thompson and Harding testified in a few words their approval of the opinions expressed. Lewis, who had only half understood, and who had a strong prejudice against all sudden events, felt uneasy at the prospect of bombshells against whose fury umbrellas would prove of no avail. Gradually, however, everybody began to speak quietly to his neighbour of the quality of the whiskey and the disagreeableness of the weather, until the conversation turned on Mr. Bendish. He was both criticised and defended, and it was declared that he was uncommonly useful when a sovereign or half a one was indispensable. But Lewis, who only remembered his last futile visit to Fitzroy Square, was of a different opinion; he wished Frazer would leave off propounding theories, and allow him to ask Thompson what his opinion really was about Mrs. Bentham and the decorations. He waited impatiently for sometime, but seeing that the chances of finding a sympathetic listener were becoming smaller and smaller, he began to think of going. It was just seven o'clock, Gwynnie would be due at half-past; he would just manage to get home in time to meet her. So, bidding his friends goodbye, he started off at a sharp pace.

As he passed along the Waterloo Road he looked up at the grimy windows. Three days ago there was not one of the many inhabitants in that long line of dismal chambers with whom he would not have exchanged places; now he almost pited them as he exultingly remembered that he alone knew *her*. Never had the shop, with the old iron and china piled about the walls, appeared so hateful; and when he entered he forgot to speak to Dinah, who ran forward to meet him. Mrs. Cross told him that Miss Lloyd had not yet come in. This was strange and annoying, but there was nothing to do but to wait.

The evening being fine, he opened his windows, and, resting his arms on the wall, sat down to enjoy his dreams. He wondered if it were really possible that he was going to stay with a fashionable lady in her country house, meet grand people, and be introduced to them as an equal.

He thought of what he should say, what they would say to him, and his life became as sweet with dreams as a cup with wine until he remembers his poverty. He had but three shirts, a couple of pairs of old trousers, and the cracked shoes he wore. It was obviously impossible for him to go without a complete fit out—and he had only two pounds ten. His dreams fell down like card houses, but they rose again in rose-coloured wreaths when he thought of Mr. Carver—he, of course, would advance him the necessary money. Yes, on the whole, his life's sky appeared to be quite clear, and his thoughts hovered about surveying the horizon for a cloud, until they alighted on Gwynnie. He regretted he had not been able to paint his picture without having asked her to sit for it. People who make sacrifices for you always live with the idea that you are going to make sacrifices for them.

She was, he assured himself, a dear, good girl who had done a great deal for him, and he hoped that she would not in anyway try to mar his future prospects. Then his face darkened a little, and he felt annoyed with himself when he recalled the fact that he had promised to marry her. Fervidly he hoped she would not make a scene: he hated scenes; nor cry when he told her he was going away. It would be perfectly ridiculous if she did; for, surely, she did not expect him to live in a filthy room all his life? And so his thoughts wandered until the excitement of waiting became too intense, and he found himself at last obliged to go out to get rid of his troubles.

V

MR. VICOME

On leaving Pall Mall, Mrs. Bentham drove to see her father. Mr. Vicome had been for many years completely bed-ridden: he lay helpless in a large bleak house in the neighbourhood of Cavendish Square. Mrs. Bentham was the only person he ever saw. She managed the Claremont House property for him, gave him what money he required, and did what she liked with the rest. He never interfered; she did as she pleased, regarding the Sussex estates as her own, for being his only child, she would inherit them at his death. But although he could never leave Cavendish Square, he was interested in everything concerning Claremont House, even to the dismissal of a gardener. It was he who had given her the first idea of the ball-room, and he questioned her on every detail, as the work proceeded, as impatiently as if he were going to preside over the balls given there for the next fifty years.

After having questioned the servant as to Mr. Vicome's health, Mrs. Bentham passed along the dreary stone passage to the dining-room, where he generally sat in the afternoon. On a small table next to his wheeled chair lay his wig, sunk into a packet of black clothes; the white face and head lolled feebly; a napkin covered his lap, and he was trying to eat something out of a cup.

On seeing his daughter, he put on his wig, and called to the servant to take away what he was eating.

Mrs. Bentham sat down by him, and they talked in short phrases of Claremont House. She told him all she could think of, how the old people whom he had himself known were getting on; how so-and-so's grand-daughter had gone away to service and hadn't written home; how so-and-so's son intended to get married next spring.

He listened delighted to all she had to say, and asked innumerable questions. Suddenly he recollected that the ballroom was not yet finished.

"I wonder, my dear Lucy," he said, pettishly, "you don't find some artist to do those decorations; you know I want to have that room finished."

It seemed to Mrs. Bentham like a coincidence that he should speak to her on the subject, and forgetting that he rarely failed to do so, in a constrained way that surprised her, she explained that it was difficult to find an artist to whom the work might be entrusted. The room was quite beautiful since the walls had been painted in light blue and straw colour.

"I told you," said the old man, joyfully, "that that was the right colour, and you would not believe me. I hope it is a light blue turning to mauve."

Having been assured on that point, he continued:

"I tell you I want the room finished. If you have carried out my idea, it will be the prettiest room in Sussex. I shall make an effort and try and get down there when the decorations are done; but you must see about an artist to do the pictures; why, there are dozens of clever young men starving about London who would do it splendidly. Can't that man Mr. Carver, whom you are always talking about, find you one?"

"'Tis curious," answered Mrs. Bentham, reflectively, "you should speak of it, for not half-an-hour ago Mr. Carver introduced me to a young man who he said would do the work splendidly."

"Then why don't you have him down to do it?" asked the old man. "I may go off any day, and I want to see that room finished before I die; it is really very selfish of you."

Mrs. Bentham assured him that there was not the slightest chance of his dying for many a year, and that she would be very glad to have the young man down to do the decorations; but, as she was staying there at present, she did not see how it was to be done, unless, indeed, she asked him as a visitor. On this point Mr. Vicome offered no opinion nor suggestion, but declared energetically that she should be there to superintend the work.

The conversation then turned upon other matters, but from time to time the old gentleman continued querulously to allude to the subject, until Mrs. Bentham, as she got up to go, promised definitely to see to it.

As she left the dark house she thought rapidly of Lewis; his face came back to her with singular persistency, and she could not help noticing that fate seemed to force her to do what in her heart of hearts she desired.

There was no doubt she had, in her father's commands, an excellent reason for asking him to Claremont House, one which her prudish cousin Mrs. Thorpe would find it hard to gainsay, but then there were the county people to be taken into consideration; and when she thought of Lewis' compromising face, she heard a thousand disagreeable remarks and petty sarcasms ringing in her ears. She changed her position nervously in the brougham, and apostrophized the injustice of the world's opinion, and the falseness of a woman's position in modern society. As she leaned back on the cushions she turned the subject over in her mind, finding, every instant, a new reason for taking her father's advice. She remembered how nicely Mr. Seymour talked, and the suspicion came upon her that he might be a gentleman born to the same position as herself. The stories she had heard of young men who die for the want of a friend, of a helping hand, unknown, on the bosom as it were of a million beings, in the middle of a crowd weary of the gold they do not know what to do with, thronged across her mind; and, irritated by the thought that he might be one of those miserable ones who starve while the person who wishes to succour them is considering the most proper way of extending his or her friendly hand, she told her coachman to drive to Pall Mall, resolved, if the references were satisfactory, to give him the decorations to do.

Mr. Carver received her in his large and unctuous manner; he overwhelmed Mrs. Bentham, dazzled her with an impromptu sketch of what Lewis' future would be, "if he only got a chance," soon. On this point she no longer had a doubt; she was convinced that he would some day blossom into a Raphael. Nevertheless, for the moment, she found herself obliged to consider the more prosaic question of his past life, and after some beating about the bush, she asked Mr. Carver if he would tell her who this young painter was.

Mr. Carver had, on this subject, little information to supply, but he threw himself at once into the Napoleonic pose, and talked just as if he had known Lewis in his cradle. He told Mrs. Bentham that Lewis was the son of a country doctor in Essex, who had died, leaving his widow in bad circumstances; that, on his mother's death, Lewis had found himself obliged to come to London to seek his fortune. So much Mr. Carver had found out, for he found out something concerning everyone he had ever been brought in contact with; and he embroidered ingeniously on this slight material until he brought tears into Mrs. Bentham's eyes.

A few more words sufficed to settle the matter: it was decided that Lewis should be sent down next Thursday to Sussex, Mr. Carver charging himself with all the arrangements.

VI

DESERTION

Lewis slept very badly on Monday night; Gwynnie's pale face kept him awake. She had not returned, and he feared that she, overcome with shame, had committed the crime that she had saved him from.

In the morning the landlady brought him up a letter; he looked at it hastily. It was from Mr. Carver, asking him to call about eleven. Having assured himself that his own affairs were all right, he asked Mrs. Cross if she had heard anything of Miss Lloyd. No, she hadn't, and what's more, she thought it very strange: Miss Lloyd, as long as she had been in the house, had never done such a thing before.

Lewis was frightened—so much so that he determined to go off at once to her shop and make inquiries. But when he got downstairs he found it was twenty minutes to eleven. By taking a hansom he would only be able to get to Mr. Carver's in time, and it never would do to miss that appointment. Besides, Pall Mall was on the way, and he would go on to Regent Street afterwards, it was only a question of five minutes' difference; Mr. Carver would not keep him longer, and he must know his fate.

Mr. Carver received him very affably, told him that it was all arranged, that he was to go down to Claremont House the day after tomorrow, and stop there until he had finished the decorations, a three months' job, for which he would receive two hundred pounds. Lewis was dazed at his good fortune, and the dear dreams of the night before seemed all to have grown into beautiful realities.

Mr. Carver, in the Napoleonic pose, watched his astonishment with a tender interest akin to that which an inventor takes in his new patent.

"But who is Mrs. Bentham? You say that she is separated from her husband?" asked Lewis, emboldened a little by his success.

"One of the biggest swells in London, my dear boy. I can tell you 'twas a lucky day for you when you put your nose into my shop."

Mr. Carver had no doubt that in the course of this adventure something would occur which would enable him to turn the weaknesses of human nature to his profit. He did not know what, but he was sure that something would happen. Something always did; at least that was his experience of life. The only thing of which he was uncertain was Lewis's power of restraint, of conducting himself properly at Claremont House. Therefore, with the air of one who has never spoken to anything less than a baronet, Mr. Carver proceeded to give Lewis what he considered many useful hints as to how he should behave himself. He told him that he would meet all the best people, who would tear him to pieces as monkeys would a newspaper; but to be forewarned is to be forearmed, and Mr. Carver advised him to be very reserved, and, above all, very polite to everybody—from the lap-dog upwards.

It was part of Lewis's nature to believe that women were in love with him, and cautiously he tried to find out what opinion Mr. Carver held on the matter of Mrs. Bentham's affections. But Mr. Carver only eyed him sharply and advised him to be very careful, to look before he leaped, and, better still, not to leap at all, but to let things untie themselves gradually. Mr. Carver seemed to enjoy the conversation immensely, and, as a trainer gives the jockey the final instructions, he explained to Lewis the perils he must avoid, and the circumstances he must take advantage of.

As he told him of the grand people he would meet at Claremont House, Lewis looked in despair at his broken boots and stained trousers. At last, interrupting the list of grand names with which the dealer was apparently baptizing him, he asked boldly for a small advance of money.

"Of course, of course; you are in a piteous plight, I see," replied Mr. Carver, looking him up and down.

Lewis thought the inspection rude, but forgave it when he was handed five ten-pound notes.

Then, in his turn, Lewis looked Mr. Carver up and down, from the large plaid trousers to the red cravat, an attention which put the dealer in a good temper for the rest of the day, it not occurring to him that the painter might be looking to see what to avoid rather than what to copy.

Then, after having signed a bill, and listened to a little advice on the subject of dress, Lewis was free to go and look after Gwynnie. He took another hansom and drove to her shop, where he was gratified to hear that she had been at work all the day before. He drew a deep breath of relief; there was no longer any reason for supposing she had committed suicide. Still, it was extraordinary she had not returned home; and he continued to question the forewoman until she would listen to him no longer: all she knew was that Miss Lloyd had been there yesterday, and had gone away with a lady friend.

"But do you know her friend's address?" insisted Lewis; "I shall be so much obliged—"

"I assure you I haven't the least idea, but if you will leave a message or a letter, it shall be given to Miss Lloyd."

Lewis asked her to say he had called, and, with a sense of of having done his duty, drove off to buy his clothes. Pettishly he assured himself that he could do no more, unless, indeed, he put the matter in the hands of the police, and to do that would be ridiculous. She was her own mistress, and had a right to hide herself if she pleased. He turned the subject over in his mind, but could think of no reason why she had not returned home, unless, indeed, it was because she was angry with him for not having waited for her. Anyhow, he was sure of one thing: that she had not committed suicide, and, comforting himself with the assurance, he drove to a tailor's.

All that day and the next he spent buying shirts, coats, trousers, collars, neckties, and boots. As he walked along the streets he looked to see how the upper ten thousand were dressed. He observed how their coats were buttoned, and the kind of scarfs they wore, and tried to find out what the differences were that distinguished them from the middle classes.

It was absolutely necessary for him to know these things, for he felt he would be seriously compromising his position if he went down to Mrs. Bentham's dressed like a shop boy.

He fancied that Mr. Carver had hinted that it was not merely his talents as an artist that had induced Mrs. Bentham to give him the commission to decorate the ball-room, and it afforded him much pleasure to think that she was interested in him.

The time at his disposal neccssitated orders to Mr. Halet instead of to Mr. Johnson; but, his figure being perfectly-proportioned, he was easy to fit, and the clothes, with a few alterations, almost satisfied him. He bought two suits of country clothes, short jackets and coloured trousers, to which he added a velvet coat for painting in. Dress clothes were indispensable, and these, at least, he would have liked to have had from a first-class tailor, but it was not possible—he had to start the following day. Having to buy everything, from a portmanteau to a tooth-brush, he had not a minute to spare, and every now and then, when he had fancied he had ordered all he would require, he found himself obliged to start off again to buy some pocket-handkerchiefs, collars, or silk socks. Instinctively he was attracted by what was soft and delicate. Some silk shirts with cords tempted him so much that he was restless until he possessed them.

A great deal of money was also spent in scent, powder, nail-polishers. Although he had had but little opportunity in his life of becoming acquainted with such luxuries, he divined their uses as if by instinct, and his white, feminine hands as they strayed over the shop counters seemed to love the touch of all things connected with the toilette-table.

Yet, notwithstanding his occupations, he found time to inquire again at the shop in Regent Street after Gwynnie. She had not returned, nor had her friend, and Lewis went away, wondering what was the reason of this disappearance.

He felt that he ought to take more trouble to find her, but he assured himself that he hadn't the time, his hours were numbered. Of course it was very unfortunate, it seemed perfectly abominable to go away without seeing her; but then, what was he to do? Over and over again he asked himself the question. At last he resolved to write her a letter.

In his excited state, it was a matter of no small difficulty to explain satisfactorily the story of his luck, to express fear for her safety, and abuse her affectionately for having gone away without leaving him word to say where she had gone to. Lewis found the letter horribly difficult to write; he often felt inclined to throw it aside, but he struggled on to the end, and he finished it just before he had to start to catch the three o'clock train.

As he drove away, Mrs. Cross stood at the door and followed the hansom with her eyes.

"I am sure, 'Arry, that young gentleman was someone great, or will become someone great."

'Arry did not answer; he went on arranging the jugs and basins and tin saucepans in his window, so as to attract his customers, evidently thinking that his wife's prediction did not call for reply.

Dinah, however, left off teasing the yellow cat, and hiding her golden curls in her mother's coarse apron began to cry.

VII

Lewis Seymour's Early Life

B ehind his mother's death, Lewis's early life extended like a wide grey cloud. In the hurry and trouble of London life he had forgotten the past, but as he leaned back in the comfort of a first-class carriage, he complacently amused himself by picking out some portions of the obliterated picture. In '43 his father, whom he just remembered, had been appointed dispensary doctor, in the little town of Santry. He had been elected in the face of much opposition, for an inkling of his gravity and sternness had got wind, and the inhabitants of Santry disliked above all things an unsociable doctor. The women worked heaven and earth against him; but his splendid testimonials for hospital service carried the day against his rival's reputation for dancing and croquet playing.

On his arrival at Santry, Mr. Seymour took a house, built a laboratory, declined an invitation to a dance.

This curious behaviour excited much comment; and as the days went by, the good people of Santry came to the conclusion that Mr. Seymour in no way belied the character that had preceded him. He was found to be an excellent doctor, but he did not care for society. He neither drank nor gambled, but he lived, as a wag said, buried in a lot of saucepans. In other words, Mr. Seymour was a chemist, and for his favourite pursuit he neglected everything except his patients. The townspeople used to say, when the thick smoke issuing from the chimney of his laboratory attracted their notice, that Seymour was burning away hundreds of pounds in his crucibles. But what he spent or saved was problematic. He took no one into his confidence; he lived in himself, avoiding as much as possible the garrulous society of the place. He paid his visits, took his fees, and shirked dancing and dinner parties.

This continued for years, until one day the smoke ceased to issue from the tall chimney, and then the doctor manifested a desire to become more cordial.

The society of Santry hailed this conversion with delight, and the matrons soon discovered that Mr. Seymour was on the look out for a wife. The young girls made faces when their mammas spoke of him;

he was far too serious for their tastes, but they were overruled by their elders.

For two months everyone was on the tiptoe of expectation, and it was then perceived that the doctor's choice had fallen on Miss Oyler, the daughter of a rich corn merchant.

May Oyler was a soft, fair girl, with a receding chin. She liked her father's clerk far better than the doctor; and when it was found out that Mr. Seymour had spent several thousands in chemicals, and that it would take more than half her fortune to pay off these debts, she hoped ardently that this would suffice to break off the engagement. But Mr. Seymour's practice was large; for, notwithstanding his unsociable disposition, his undoubted abilities had enabled him to maintain the position of fashionable doctor. Mr. Oyler was, therefore, ready to consent to anything, provided Mr. Seymour promised to give up chemistry.

This was agreed upon, and May Oyler became Mrs. Seymour.

For a year Mr. Seymour tried to do his duty, tried to be affectionate to his wife, tried to bring his nature down to hers; for a year he went with her into society, and let her receive the friends she liked. Had she possessed a little resolution, she might have easily weaned him from his vice; but, unfortunately, her nature was so tepid, so incapable of an effort, that to escape from the horrible *ennui* of her company he soon began to pay fugitive visits to his laboratory.

Mrs. Seymour cried meekly in secret, she went to church to pray, and that was all she did or could do.

Lewis was the only child born of this ill-sorted match. He was his mother's darling, but his beautiful blue eyes had in them a silly look, which horrified the father. The mother's dullness seemed to have fallen on the son, and Mr. Seymour shut himself up more than ever in his studies. What Mr. Seymour's studies were no one ever knew exactly.

Dr. Brown, who was the only person who could boast of much intimacy with Mr. Seymour, said that he believed in the future of electricity, and was making experiments with that view.

"A very able man indeed, but something of a dreamer," Doctor Brown often said. Had he finished his remarks there he would have been saved regret, but, on being pressed for details, he added that Mr. Seymour had declared electricity to be the modern god that would revolutionise the world. Everybody was shocked. A suspicion of atheism was all that was wanted, and imperceptibly Mr. Seymour's practice slipped away from him.

Writs came down from London, but Mr. Seymour paid no attention, he continued to work harder than ever in his laboratory, and the smoke poured more lustily than ever out of the tall chimney. Some said that he was on the eve of a successful experiment; and they were not wrong: on the day the bailiffs came to seize he was found dead: the jury returned a verdict of accidental death from an overdose of chloral, but it was generally supposed he had committed suicide.

Mrs. Seymour's whole fortune on her husband's death consisted in an interest to the extent of two hundred pounds a year in her father's corn business, which, the old man being now dead, was now carried on by her brother.

On this modest competence she determined, not only to live, but if possible to save money. She took a very small house at the end of the town, and devoted the rest of her wretched life to her son's welfare.

Mother and son lived quite alone, seeing nobody but a few relations. Mr. Seymour's suspected atheistical opinions and manner of life had alienated them during his lifetime from the society of the place, and now she felt herself incapable of making new friends: those of her youth were dispersed.

Poverty also lent its hand to complete Mrs. Seymour's isolation, but she did not complain, she accepted life as it came.

Lewis grew up by her side a shy, timid lad. She taught him how to read and write, and what she remembered of French. But she did not succeed very well, and the silent tears would often stream down her cheeks on to the books. Her only consolation, and it was a supreme one, was that her son seemed to be content to be with her.

He shrunk from the rough play of boys, and the only acquaintances he made were women. He had quite a circle of admirers, whom he used to visit, with whom he used to spend long dreamy afternoons, full of infinite tenderness, feminine sympathies and affinities, which he knew so well how to savour and appreciate, but which husbands, and even lovers, pass their lives in ignoring, or misunderstanding. And to sit and look into women's eyes as they talked, or to lie down alone in a quiet woodland place, was all he seemed to care for. His intelligence dawned slowly; and it was not till he was over fifteen that his mind began to brighten, and he asked to be allowed to attend a school. There he dawdled away his time learning something vaguely in a desultory way, evincing no taste for anything except dreaming. Sometimes he would take a volume of verse to the woods, and strive to read it, but it soon fell from his hand, and he would lie for hours like a plant, conscious of nothing but the air he breathed. These endless langours continued until instinctively he began to draw on the margin of the paper the landscape before him. This last fancy developed itself daily, and the whole of his seventeenth year was spent brush in hand. Little bits of green underwood, pleasant places where the shadows were soft and soothing, were what he loved best to depict, and as he used to wander about, painting whatever caught his fancy, he soon became a conspicuous person in the place.

He made the acquaintance of Mrs.——, who belonged to one of the first of the county families, through a sketch he was making near her house. He looked so poetical, with his long curls hanging round his neck, that she made her husband go and speak to him; the conversation ended in his being asked to lunch.

After this success he was made quite a lion of; he was asked out everywhere, and everybody was of the opinion that one day or another he would become a great artist. Mrs. Seymour was not invited, nor did she want to follow Lewis into society: she was content to sit at home and wait for him to return, and tell her of his successes, and these last years were about the happiest of her life.

But as Lewis got on with his painting he began to think of going to London to study; and he was advised to do so by everybody he knew. Mrs. Seymour was prepared to sell up her home, and sacrifice herself for her son's welfare; but her health, which had for sometime been in a declining state, so suddenly gave way, that the project had to be given over. Then followed a year full of wearying anxiety, of ominous hours, of whispered words. Mrs. Seymour died slowly; one month she appeared to be recovering, the next she seemed to be sinking. In the end, she died, as she had lived, feebly.

Lewis watched and waited, fretted, grew wearied, and was sorrowful. The house, always dark, grew more oppressive as the livid shadows of death crept through the rooms; the neighbours came and went, and pitied the young man.

But at length the last night arrived. Lewis was sitting in the little drawing-room, trying to read as he waited for the doctor. The lamp burned on the table, and the clock ticked on the chimney-piece, and the hours grew darker and more silent. Feverish with apprehension, he threw open the window, and stood looking into the moonlit street.

Then he heard a rapping at the door, and the nurse entered: her grave face told him what had happened.

If all had gone well, his mother's death would have put him in possession of a very nice little fortune. The house and furniture would have fetched at least two hundred pounds, and after paying all the funeral expenses, there would still be a balance of one hundred and fifty pounds. With this to use as ready money, and two hundred a year of fixed income, he would have been able to study art in all the countries in Europe, if it so pleased him. But his life's current had to run through many sudden shoals and eddies before it swelled into a wide stream of prosperity.

The first of the shipwrecking reefs he had to pass was his uncle's failure. This occurred almost immediately after Mrs. Seymour's death. Mr. Oyler had not only failed, but his failure was a fraudulent one, and he had fled the country.

The two hundred a year to which Lewis was entitled out of the business was utterly lost, and he found himself obliged to face the world with something like three hundred and fifty pounds, instead of a comfortable competence.

This was a terrible reverse to receive at the very start; but Lewis's temperament was an enthusiastic one, and knowing nothing, he feared nothing, and he thought London would fall at the first sound of his clarion.

His pictures had been admired by Mr. So-and-so and so-and-so; he had been received by Mrs.——, and the *Essex Telegraph* had said he was a promising young artist. So, like many a one before him, he thought that because he had succeeded in the country he would succeed in London. He had done lots of drawings at the training school at Santry, anyone of which he was sure would get him admitted into the Academy in London, and on his three hundred and fifty pounds he could live until the golden ducats came tumbling in.

In this manner he read the sign of the horoscope, and one morning he took a last look at his native place. His eyes were full of tears as he bade his friends goodbye; they had all been very good to him.

He was full of confidence. He had two suits of clothes and nearly a dozen shirts in his portmanteau; his three hundred and fifty pounds were safely deposited in a bank, and the master of the training school had given him a letter of introduction to a Mr. Thompson, a very clever fellow, the head of a new school who styled themselves "The moderns."

The drawing master had not been able to tell him anything about "The moderns," and very little about Thompson; he had not seen him for years. He had only heard that he was at the head of this movement, which was supposed to be very much opposed to classics.

All the way up to London Lewis tried to fill up the scanty outline; he wondered what Thompson was like, and he tried vainly to imagine what the painting of "The moderns" was like. Of art he had seen nothing but the plaster casts in the training school, the pictures in the country houses he visited, and some photographs of a new school, which, in a kind of early Italian form, gave expression to much ephemeral languor. These Lewis thought the *beau idéal* of all that life could desire, and he wondered if that was what Thompson did; it seemed to him impossible to desire more.

On arriving in London he drove to the hotel he had been recommended; and next morning, at an early hour, went off to see Thompson.

He had never been in a studio in his life, and he was full of apprehensions and surmises. After a great deal of hunting through Chelsea he found the address. He was received kindly, but his first feeling on looking round was one of complete bewilderment.

He had expected to see graceful nymphs languishing on green banks, either nude or in classical draperies, and, instead, he was regaled with housemaids in print dresses, leaning out of windows, or bar girls serving drinks to beery looking clerks. In fact, the walls were covered, not with the softness of ancient, but with the crudities of modern life.

He turned his eyes to the right and left dumbfounded. At the end of the room there was a picture of two acrobats in their pink fleshings; Lewis looked at it in amazement. The strong odour of life it exhaled was too much for him. So extraordinary did the pictures appear to him, that at first he felt as if he were the victim of some monstrous joke. Yet, on examining it, he recognised exquisite bits of drawing and colour, but the form of expression was so strange.

"I see you are astonished," said Thompson, laughing; "you know we don't care for the modernised versions of the early Italians, so popular now-a-days, but we will talk about that later on; you will get to understand what we mean by-and-bye; whether you'll agree with us or no is another question. Let me see your work."

Lewis unrolled a quantity of drawings he had done from the antique in the training school, and he tried to read in Thompson's face what he thought of them. They were fairly well done, and showed dexterity of hand.

When Thompson had gone carefully through them, he asked to see Lewis's original sketches; with these he was less satisfied, but he knew it would be vain to expect much individuality from one who had been taught in a country training school.

"So you have come up to London to learn to be an artist," said Thompson, eyeing Lewis severely.

Thompson was a stout, short man; he wore a red beard, and spoke with a strong Scotch accent.

"Yes, I wanted to enter the academy; but you don't care for Greek art," replied Lewis, who began to feel very miserable; he had expected that Thompson would go into raptures over his drawings, and he had only looked at them as he would at a child's copy book.

"I didn't say I didn't like Greek art, but I make a difference between the pseudo Greek and Italian of the nineteenth century, to that of Pericles and Innocent III; but you will hear all about that soon enough. At present you want to get into the Academy; well, on the whole, I think it is the best thing for you to do, and I think one of these drawings will get you in."

He then asked Lewis some questions as to his money arrangements, and appeared to think three hundred and fifty pounds was plenty to start in life with. He told him where he could get a room for seven shillings a week, and where he would be able to dine for tenpence, and explained how in that way he would be able to live for more than three years on the money he had, and by that time, if he had anything in him, he would be able to get along.

Although Thompson loathed the Academy system of training, he could not think of anything better that Lewis could do than to join the schools. He was a country boy, alone in London, and it would take him sometime to learn even what people in the London art world were thinking about.

A year in the schools would do him no harm. He would meet there some of the "Moderns," whose counsels would counteract those of the Mediævalists, and Lewis would be able to choose between the two.

Under the general title of "The moderns" were united all the artists, painters, musicians and writers, who believed that the arts are the issue of the manners and customs of the day, and change with those manners according to a general law. Of such elements the group was really composed, but the title was most commonly applied to the painters, of whom Thompson was the leader.

Wearied of the art that only tried to echo the beauty of the Apollo and the Venus de Medici, and loathing that which distorted the early Italian formula to make it available as a means of expressing the sexless hysteria of our age, they longed for a new art racy of the nineteenth century. They declared that a new æstheticism was to be discovered; that the materials were everywhere around them; that only the form had to be found.

This was what they sought; the new formula which would enable them to render modern life in all its poignancy and fulness. They maintained that the world has seen four perfectly distinct artistic methods. The first on the list is the Egyptian; the second, the Greek; the third, the Italian; and the fourth, the Japanese; and they declared that the absolute originality of the Japanese in art could only be accounted for by the fact, that they had been fortunate enough never to have seen a Greek statue. It was a favourite subject of joke amongst them to imagine what would have been the result if a ship-load of the Elgin marbles had been cast on the shores of Yeso, in the year of our Lord—

Thompson was the leader of this little band. He fortified them in their faith that nature is not limited to these four formulas, and he encouraged them to seek for a fifth in the seething mass of human life, one as comprehensive of our civilisation as the art of the Egyptians was of theirs. He forced them to love art for its own sake, and prevented them from prostituting their talents to the pay of the cheap dealers, who demand the vile and the worthless. It was Thompson who served them as a sort of centre; he rallied them, theorised their confused aspirations, and gave to many, if not the clue to the problem, at least strength to believe that they were following the light of the truth.

In a month from the time Lewis arrived in London, he entered the Academy as a student, and every Saturday he brought his week's work to Thompson's studio.

He lived in a room in Chelsea, which cost him seven shillings a week; he spent sixpence on his breakfast, which his landlady supplied, and with a shilling he dined comfortably in one of the cheap eating houses where the joint is fourpence.

Living in this way, the necessaries of life would cost him about forty-five pounds a year; adding twenty-five pounds to that for clothes, paints, brushes, and occasional expenses; the total would come to seventy pounds; consequently, he would be able to work in perfect security and calm for the next five years, and by that time he hoped to sell his pictures.

As Thompson expected, it took sometime before Lewis fell in with the ideas of the new artistic movement. For a long time he could not understand why academical drawings, where every muscle is beautifully modelled, belong to no species of art; for a long time he could not understand Frazer's sunset effects in deep violet, or why Cassell painted black hair blue: but before the end of the year he was one of the most ardent disciples of the new faith.

An ardent disciple in theory, but only faintly in practice; for he was never able to shake himself free of the conventional prettiness of things.

One evening a week they met in Thompson's room, and those were the hours they all looked forward to; there they smoked and argued and encouraged each other.

He had fallen in with a clique of strong-minded fellows; they soon grew to like him, and it was owing to their influence that for over a year he struggled against his natural proclivities, and worked steadily. He made rapid progress, he learned to draw intelligently and correctly, and if it had not been for one of those million chances of which our lives are composed, he might have lived to have conquered his passions, and to have done good work for art's own sake.

Thompson would not allow him to paint pictures, but made him stick to his drawing. On Sundays, however, he used to go into the country to sketch, and one day, happening to do a bit of river scenery which pleased Thompson, he thought he would have it framed, and present it to his friend.

But the picture dealer and frame maker to whom he went was struck with the sketch, and offered him fifteen shillings for it. At first Lewis refused to part with it; but thinking that he could do another better, he ended by taking the money.

Up to that time his expenses had been so regulated that every penny that passed through his hands had had a purpose, but now there came fifteen shillings which he could not account for—that is to say, which he could spend as the fancy prompted him.

He jingled the money as he went along, and, remembering that his neck-tie was very soiled, he entered a shop and bought a new one. As he walked towards the coffee-house where he dined habitually, he passed a cheap *café*, and he could not resist the temptation of dining there;

he had a cup of coffee and a cigar after dinner. These little luxuries, coming after so much steady privation, were very soothing and flesh satisfying, and the fifteen shillings enabled him during the whole week to make little additions to his dinner; but to continue them necessitated purloining hours from regular study to do drawings for the frame maker.

At prices varying from five to fifteen shillings, Mr.—— consented to buy his sketches, and Lewis found that an extra ten shillings a week made his life much more comfortable. But this slight change in his way of living involved him in many temptations. Having a few shillings in his pocket made him care less for his lonely chamber and more for bar-rooms; he was enabled to go out with students whom he had before avoided because he had no money to spend, and these causes, acting together, quickly produced a change in him; it was not long before he began to shirk his daily work at the Academy.

This hesitation between duty and pleasure continued for over three months, and then came the old story, the old stumbling block, over which, curiously enough, he had not till now tripped, at least to any appreciable extent. Even now it was only a half-hearted affair; there was very little of the Sardanapalus about it; it was not a passionate love for which he sacrificed everything; it was merely weak sensuality that led him to spend a little more money on gloves, to dine on three instead of two shillings, to idle a little more than before, and in six months all his money was gone. Then he lived on credit and his friends; occasionally he sold trifles, which staved off the evil days, but soon, he was pawning his clothes, and would have starved long ago, had it not been for old Bendish.

VIII

In the Country

Claremont House was in Sussex, and from the terrace in front of the house you could see the sea.

At the station a footman, in the majesty of a grey livery, asked Lewis if he were Mr. Seymour.

On being answered in the affirmative, he went to look after the luggage, and in a quarter of an hour after, from the cosy cushions of a brougham, Lewis saw the lodge-keeper open a large white gate, and the carriage entered the avenue. It ran straight through two hedge-like lines of thin beech trees, and on both sides rolled great seas of green pasture land.

During the whole journey down, Lewis had played with his dreams like a child with a box full of new toys; delighted, he had examined one after the other, and then laid them aside timidly; but now, sitting in the brougham, where so often her skirts had rustled, the intoxicating odour of his future life rose to his head like the perfume of a flower crushed and smelt in the hollow of the hand.

After passing a bridge, the avenue took a turn, and for some distance skirted along the river. The trees were here large, and a group of tall elms, growing on a swampy island, extended their huge masculine arms as if to embrace the feminine foliage of beeches that coquettishly leaned towards them. Under this natural archway, the carriage turned and rapidly approached the house. It was a long, narrow, grey building, pierced with innumerable windows. It stood like a Noah's ark at the end of a long terrace, and the blue slates melted into the deep green foliage of the silver firs, which were the pride of the domain.

The original house had been destroyed a century ago by fire; the present one had been fashioned out of the stables, which accounted for the elongated shape and its many gables.

On the left, the terrace was bounded by a high wall entirely concealed by laurels, which, growing from a distance of fifty feet, formed an immense sloping bank. On the right, facing the sea, there was a huge flight of steps leading to the second terrace, under which the river rippled round the laurel-covered islands down to the sea, which lay motionless and dim in the far distance.

The beauty of the landscape was exceeding, and the day died amorously. A crimson sun sank slowly out of a rose sky into a grey sea, and out of the blue heights of the heavens there fell the sweet satiety that marks the end of an August day. Trembling floods of violet shadow heaved and rolled up from the distant strand along the hill sides, and the two ladies who were leaning on the balustrade, watching the sun setting, came out black in the soft dissolution of light.

The carriage drew up at the hall door: a small, unpretending entrance, unapproached by steps, and opening into a passage rather than a hall. The footman took down Lewis's portmanteau, and the butler unpacked it for him, putting his morning suits, shirts, collars, and pocket handkerchiefs, away in a large mahogany wardrobe, and laying out his evening clothes with wonderful precision on the clear-curtained, iron bed. While he did so, Lewis sat at the window and watched. The ladies were walking across the solitary terrace towards the house. The evening had grown chilly, and they had drawn their shawls more tightly round their shoulders. Lewis recognised one as Mrs. Bentham—he thought she looked up once at his window.

Then the servant brought him some hot water, and told him that dinner would be ready in half-an-hour. Lewis could not realise his position, and as he dressed for dinner he was conscious of nothing but a clinging sensation of pleasure, of expectant happiness.

Determined to enjoy himself, he washed himself elaborately: there was nothing this young man loved like looking after his body. Then he dried, powdered, and scented himself with care, and, full of misgiving, tried on the evening clothes. The trousers he thought too wide, the waistcoat seemed to him vulgar, but he could only hope that no one would suspect they were ready made. It was a long time since he had enjoyed the comfort of fresh clothes, and it was with an exquisite sense of real delight that he drew on his silk socks, tied his white neck-tie, and brushed—standing before the tall glass—his rich brown hair.

At last he got dressed, and the footman showed him into the drawing-room. There he found Mrs. Bentham. She received him with a large white smile, and introduced him to Mrs. Thorpe, her cousin. Mrs. Thorpe bowed, and continued to knit in the chimney corner. Lewis was more than timid: he was positively frightened, and his new clothes made him feel very awkward.

But Mrs. Bentham thought he looked divinely handsome, and she remembered how wretchedly poor he looked when she met him at Mr. Carver's shop.

At last dinner was announced, and Mrs. Bentham asked him to take in Mrs. Thorpe. He did it very stupidly, scarcely knowing if he had to offer her his hand or his arm: the women exchanged looks; one was of annoyance, the other of reproof. Dinner went by in a slow and irritating manner; everybody was ill at ease. Lewis, who had never been anywhere except to a few luncheon parties in Essex, was so pre-occupied thinking how he should eat and act, that he could not say a word. He was conscious that Mrs. Thorpe was watching him, and he fancied that she would make use of any little slip to his disadvantage; consequently, he did not take the bread out of his napkin until he had seen Mrs. Bentham take hers, and during the whole meal he ate and drank after first observing one of the ladies.

But he was wrong in supposing that Mrs. Thorpe was his enemy. The old lady was merely a little alarmed at what she could not consider other than excessively eccentric behaviour. Mrs. Bentham had told her how anxious Mr. Vicome was to have the decorations finished; but this failed to strike Mrs. Thorpe as a very valid reason for picking up a young man, and bringing him down to stay with them. If it were really necessary to have all these paintings done—and on that matter she did not venture an opinion—she thought it should have been put into the hands of a respectable firm, who would see that they were executed properly. But with regard to Mr. Vicome's eagerness in the matter, it was preposterous.

"What did the poor old gentleman want with decorations?" she asked, pityingly. "He could not even come and see them when they were done," and now, all she hoped was, that the county people would not misinterpret Mrs. Bentham's motives, and that this young man's good looks, which were startling, would not create any scandal. Such were Mrs. Thorpe's opinions, and she had expressed them in a no less explicit way, when her cousin told her all she could tell her—which was very little—of the young man she was expecting from London.

The old lady belonged to a long past time, and could neither feel nor understand anything of the fashions of today. For over thirty years she had lived in a little country house, mourning the loss of a husband she had loved devotedly, and her grief had known no change until it was doubled by the loss of her only son. Her life had been made up of two great loves and two great griefs; of all other passions and desires she knew as little as a child; and the falseness of fashionable life was so repugnant to her nature that she only remained with Mrs. Bentham because she had undertaken to do so—because she felt her presence was necessary.

When the ladies rose from the table, Lewis scarcely knew how to act; he had heard that gentlemen stopped behind, but did not know if the rule applied when there was but one.

Mrs. Bentham divined his embarrassment, and asked him to follow them into the drawing-room, unless he wished to smoke. He did, but was delighted to say he didn't, for he dreaded the eye of the butler, knowing that that functionary would read him like a book.

All three went into the drawing-room. Mrs. Thorpe sat silently down in her wicker-work chair behind a Japanese screen, which protected her from the draught; and Lewis, with that feminine tact which was part of his nature, endeavoured to talk to her. At first she tried to resist his advances, and answered him in brief phrases. From a little distance, Mrs. Bentham watched the comedy.

Mrs. Thorpe was dressed entirely in black cashmere, which fell loosely about her spare figure. She wore a white cap, under which appeared some thin white hair, suggestive of baldness. The arms were long and bony, and the brown hands were contracted and crooked from her incessant knitting—in fact, they seemed like a knitting machine perpetually in motion; it was the exception to see them still.

As she took from time to time a needle out of her cap, she would look from Lewis to her cousin, and then her eyes would return to her stocking. But at last her curiosity to know who Lewis was tempted her out of her silence, and as an opportunity presented itself, she asked him some questions about his early life.

Lewis knew well it would be dangerous to tell lies, so he gave only a pleasant version of the truth. He told her about the straits his father's improvidence had reduced them to, and how he had lived all alone with his mother till she died; how his uncle had failed at the same time, and how he, Lewis, an orphan, had found himself obliged to face the world with three hundred and fifty pounds.

The picture he gave of how he had lived all alone with his mother recalled to Mrs. Thorpe her son's childhood and early manhood, and her eyes filled with tears of pity for Lewis's loneliness.

Mrs. Bentham listened to the sad story dreamily, only interrupting it to ask a question from time to time. Her attitude gradually grew more abandoned, and the intervals of her silence became longer as she let her thoughts drift through the melancholy land of reverie. Her life had not been a successful one. She had married a man whose vices had so horrified and frightened her that in the third year she asked for a separation. She might have had a divorce, for her husband had on more than one occasion used violence towards her, but as she never expected to wish to marry again, and as separation was more favourably viewed by society at large, she had accepted the equivocal position of living apart from her husband. This necessitated a companion, and after some difficulty, she persuaded Mrs. Thorpe to leave her home in the north of England, and come and live with her.

And, believing that she was asked to share, not relinquish, the quietude she cherished, Mrs. Thorpe had consented to come and live with her heart-broken cousin.

But it is only age that can enjoy solitude; youth can but coquette with it, and as the memories of her past life faded, Mrs. Bentham commenced to weary of the retirement. She was grateful to her cousin for the sacrifice she had made in coming to live with her, but she had not found in her the moral support she had hoped for, which she needed in her moments of lassitude; and her days were barren for want of appreciative sympathy.

These inward desires to return to society were hastened by outward events. Her father, two years after the court had granted her separation, had given her over the control of the Claremont House property, and on her uncle's death, which occurred about the same time, she had inherited five thousand a year, strictly tied up, and independent of her husband's control. She was therefore a rich woman, whose life's duty seemed to be simply to abandon herself to the current of fashionable life; to interest herself as well as she could in small flirtations, still-born loves, meaningless smiles, and causeless dislikes. She had striven to do so, like many another, but year after year she grew more wearied of this eternal chase not even after pleasure but merely amusement. Instinctively she longed for a large sweet affection wherein she could plunge her whole soul, as the trout on the warm grass longs for the cool stream that ripples in sight.

Lewis continued to tell of how he arrived in London; he drew a graphic picture of the work he had done, and hinted of the misery he had endured. Mrs. Thorpe had stopped knitting, her hands had fallen on her knees, and she looked at him, blankly, quite carried away by his eloquence.

Lewis talked well, as do all whom nature destines to be amateurs, or, in other words, the proclaimers of an artistic truth. He could explain, formulate, and theorise, far better than he could execute; what talent he had was more of an appreciative than a creative one. The artist, like the mother, has to undergo the throes and labour of child-bearing, long months of solitude and suffering; whilst the amateur, like the father, unweighed by a struggling infant in the womb, is free to explain and criticise at ease.

Lewis drew an interesting picture of modern London, seething in the heat of a new artistic movement, and awakening in the auroral light of a new period of renaissance; and elated, he ventured to prophesy the success that awaited him who could formularise the cravings of this new generation. There was nothing definite in what he said, but suggestiveness is a far more seductive quality than mere precision, and Mrs. Bentham, whose artistic studies just enabled her to understand him, thought she had never heard anyone speak so beautifully.

We have all a spectre thought, a thought that peeps and mocks at us from behind the happiest moment. Mrs. Bentham's spectre thought was that she was wasting her life; therefore, it is not extraordinary that she felt an immense desire rise up in her mind to protect, to help, to watch and to guide him towards that success of which he spoke so eloquently; it would be part of herself, part of her work, and she would not have lived in vain. She did not reflect that she was a young and handsome woman, that even if she could content herself with this quasi-maternal feeling, he, who was only ten or eleven years her junior, would not accept what must seem to him either too much or too little.

Mrs. Thorpe, who had understood little of the art conversation, returned with interest to the story of his early life, and asked him to tell her more about his mother.

The room they were sitting in was both long and narrow. There were three windows, two of which looked out on the wide grey and laurel-surrounded sweep; the third faced the sea. In the choice and arrangement of the furniture the influence of the artistic movement, known afterwards as the aesthetic, was just visible. The heavy red curtains still remained, but between the windows there were some exquisite renaissance cabinets; on each side of the fire-place stood two Japanese vases of fantastical design; and from the middle of the ceiling, over a vulgar divan, hung a beautiful Louis XVI chandelier.

Mrs. Bentham was too much oppressed with her thoughts to listen very attentively to the details of the story which she already knew in outline, so she let them talk as they would. The room was very still, and the light of the reading lamp did not touch the gold frames of the innumerable pictures which lined the walls. It fell principally on her arm, which was raised to her head, reflecting it deep in the mirror-like surface of an ebony table; the hand was in half-tint, the face was lost in shadow, but delicately modelled by wandering reflected lights. Outside, the moon gleamed with a graveyard whiteness on the level sward, and every now and then the curtains blew out, filled with a rose-imperfumed breeze.

She thought of her childhood, of the time when she used to cry for loneliness as she played with her toys in the echoing stone passages. She considered the difference it must make in a girl's existence to have a mother to see, to love, to confide in. She recalled a hundred details of her early life; her governesses, her aunt's reprimands: how she used to appeal to her father in the melancholy room where he sat in his wheel-chair. Then her thoughts drifted, and she passed on to the time when she was taken to her first ball, and she remembered how different it had been to what she had expected. They had few friends; their relations were all old people, at whose dinner-parties her blue frocks and bright smiles had often seemed strangely out of place. It was at one of these dismal soirées that she had met Mr. Bentham. She now remembered bitterly how he had fascinated her; how she had mistaken him for all that was noble and brilliant, how she had married him, dreaming a girl's gay dream of life-long purity and love.

Then her thoughts turned from the hideous memory of her married life, darkened with wrecked hopes and sullied illusions, towards the years since she had been separated from her husband: and they passed before her, a train of conventionalities seen through a haze of vapid sentiment and much squandered emotion. Not one had brought the fulfilment of a hope, the assuagement of a single desire. But, as she stared into the rich shadows which struggled for mastery with the moonlight, she felt herself falling into a delicious torpor; and dreams of what might have been floated softly through her life's gloom. An immense temptation seemed to float about the purple gloaming; a thousand little wishes passed through her mind; but, as she tried to define them, disappeared into the darkness, until the sound of Lewis's voice addressing her broke the current of her thoughts. Seeing that he had completed the conquest of Mrs. Thorpe he turned to Mrs. Bentham; he tried to speak to her of indifferent things. But the conversation flagged until it became painful.

Ill at ease, Mrs. Bentham went to the piano; the music of Faust lay on the stand. Feverishly and rapidly she played the waltz, she passed from piece to piece till she came to the page's song. Then, irritated to a last degree by the suggestive vagueness of the music, she asked Lewis if he sang. He had a light tenor voice, and, breathing the perfume of her hair and neck, he sang song after song, until the Dresden clock, amid its porcelain flowers, struck half-past ten, and Mrs. Thorpe put away her knitting.

Mrs. Bentham had to accompany her cousin; but, when she bade Lewis goodnight, their fingers lingered interlocked, she told him that breakfast would be at nine, and that afterwards she would show him the studio, and explain her intentions as regards the decorations.

Then both women went up to their rooms to tell each other what they thought, or part of what they thought, of the young painter.

IX

The Decorations

With a boiling brain during many dark and solemn hours, Lewis asked himself if Mrs. Bentham was in love with him. The abandonment of her manner during the evening had not escaped his notice; and, not knowing enough of human nature to recognise that her lassitude was merely an outward manifestation of that feeling of nervous discouragement so common to all who have missed their vocation in life, he dreamed wildly of persuading her to seek a divorce, so that she might bestow on him her heart and her wealth.

Early the next morning the warmth, the tenderness of the ample white sheets which lay about, awoke him, and he opened his eyes with a glimmering feeling of passive enjoyment.

The windows shone with sunlight, and the clear, luxurious room was so different from the dark, dusty garret he had left, that he closed his eyes, conscious only of an exquisite sense of living, and a faint dream, which came and went, of Mrs. Bentham.

Once he thought of Gwynnie: the thought startled him. Already he had begun to see her as one who sails away sees a friend standing on the fast receding shore; but, unable to associate her with his present life, he satisfied himself with a resolution to "look her up when he returned to town," then lazily closing his eyes, he sought for a pleasanter dream. But soon he was interrupted by the servant, who brought in his hot water, and told him his breakfast would be ready in half-an-hour.

Never had he been attended upon by a man-servant before, and the dignity of the proceeding enchanted him. It seemed to him that he was the hero of a fairy tale; his brain swam with pleasure, and distracted with a hundred plans for winning Mrs. Bentham's heart, he dressed quickly, and went down stairs.

He found the ladies in the breakfast-room; a room bright with mahogany and Brussels carpet, and green from the glare of the terrace which encircled the three windows. Mrs. Thorpe was scattering out of her crooked hands some bread-crumbs to the pigeons that flew from the gables and eaves: the light of their wings fell upon Mrs. Bentham and flying shadow darkened for moments the glittering sward.

All the heat and languor of the night before were gone; and Mrs. Bentham smiled gaily. She was full of the decorations, and chatted volubly. As they talked, lifting their cups of tea to their mouths, Lewis grew thoughtful. He wanted to speak of last night; he wanted to ask Mrs. Bentham some questions about Faust, but he failed in all his endeavours to lead up to the subject.

He did not care to introduce it suddenly, and, several times, some accidental phrase had turned the conversation, just as the words were on his lips.

They were talking about tennis, and now Mrs. Bentham announced that the Sussex County Club were going to play the last ties for the championship at Claremont House; she had agreed to lend them the terrace. This provoked a discussion, and Mrs. Thorpe denounced the game as one of the most meretricious of modern fashions, and wearied Lewis with appeals as to whether he thought it proper for young ladies to run about as they did when they played the game. When this was over, Mrs. Bentham asked him some questions on decoration in general; so he gave up all hopes of speaking about Faust, resolving to reserve the subject until he found himself alone with her: this, on consideration, he thought would be the better plan. At last breakfast drew to an end; and Mrs. Bentham asked him to come with her, and she would show him the ballroom; she explained she had been forced to build it, for the old rooms were so small that it was impossible for her to give a large party in them.

The new room was at the other end of the house, and accessible only through the dining-room, the gravity of whose oak wainscoting was calculated to form a charming contrast with the frivolity of the saloon, the clear walls of which were as bright as a ball-dress.

There all the cornices and mouldings were Greek; plaster of Paris supplying the place of white marble. The walls were divided into large panels, varying in size according to the exigencies of space, and painted a light straw-colour, the frames a pale mauve, the beading being picked out in brighter tints. The room had not been furnished, but the windows were draped with mauve satin curtains to match the walls. There was one large couch littered with portfolios, containing drawings; a few cane chairs and two easels stood in the middle of the French parqueted floor.

Lewis was enthusiastic about both rooms, particularly the one he was to decorate; and it pleased him not a little to see that there was at least four if not five months' work before him.

"You think, then, that the colours are not too badly chosen?"

"They could not be better; but are the walls prepared to receive paint?"

"Oh, yes, that's all right," she said, as they walked round the room. "And this is my idea: I want a small figure painted in the centre of each panel, with an appropriate arrangement of leaves and flowers encircling it: do you think that would be in good taste?"

Lewis replied enthusiastically that that was just what was required; but his desire to speak of the music of Faust made him a little absent-minded. Nothing prevented him from rushing into the subject but Mrs. Bentham's manner: she seemed so changed.

All the undetermined affection, the nervous and vaporous reverie, was replaced by light gaiety of manner, which seemed to say, "I haven't a desire in my heart; I am perfectly satisfied with everything." During the night she had thought a good deal; she remembered how she had picked up Lewis in a most casual way—and that he was only just a gentleman.

She had brought him down to paint pictures, not to make love to him; and when she reflected how she had languished over the piano, she tossed on her pillow: she quarrelled tediously, and was disgusted with herself. Finally, she made up her mind never again to so forget herself, to treat him coldly, to reassert her dignity. Therefore, the more Lewis spoke of the evening before, the more coldly did Mrs. Bentham return to the subject of the decorations; and she did so somewhat as if she wished to remind him that they were wasting time. She looked so stately in her black dress, and so inaccessible, that Lewis despaired, and cursed himself as an idiot forever having dreamed of making love to her.

They had walked round the room two or three times, discussed each panel, and looked out of the window: it was obvious that they were neglecting the work they had proposed to get through.

"Shall I show you the drawings I have collected for the decorations?" said Mrs. Bentham, at last.

"I shall be delighted if you will," Lewis replied, feeling as if a weight had been lifted off his shoulders.

They went over to the couch and untied the portfolios. There was plenty of material to go upon. Mrs. Bentham had bought all the engravings of the decorative work of the seventeenth century. There were Venuses and Cupids to no end; flowers, tendrils, grapes—all kinds of fruit in profusion; and Mrs. Bentham proposed to select from this stock and compose something suitable to each panel. The whole morning they sat side by side looking at Bouchers and Watteaus.

Sometimes they would turn a lot over, bestowing on them merely a glance; sometimes they would linger over and admire a bit of drawing or a lucky bit of composition; sometimes they would alight on a picture that contained matter so suitable to their purpose, that Lewis with a pencil would make a hasty arrangement, and then Mrs. Bentham would go into raptures at his dexterity. But she did not allow him the slightest intimacy. Now and then, a somewhat too coarse revel of nymphs and satyrs would embarrass them; but Lewis had the tact to go quickly on to something else.

The morning passed away delightfully. Before lunch, Mrs. Bentham had fully explained her ideas, and they made a rough choice of the drawings he considered would be most serviceable to him.

A scheme of decoration was now fermenting in his head, and he was almost glad when Mrs. Bentham told him that she and Mrs. Thorpe were going out to drive, and that he would have the whole afternoon to consider his projects.

The dignified familiarity with which Mrs. Bentham begirt herself, and the artistic interest of the drawings, had led Lewis away from his love-dreams, and now he thought of the high white walls as ardently as he had of the languor of her hands and the raptures of her lips.

Although nature meant him more for the lover than the artist, she had not denied him a certain amount of enthusiasm, and he forgot everything as he looked at the great blond panels, and his fingers itched to cover them with his fruit, flowers, and cupid fancies.

He worked all the afternoon, till the light went, composing nymphs in shady bowers, and cupids encircling garlands of blossoms. He did not leave off till the dressing-bell sounded.

That evening, Mrs. Bentham, had company. She had invited to dinner Lord Senton, a near neighbour, and his friend Mr. Day, a Scotch farmer, who, on sufferance, was received into county society.

Lord Senton was a lank young man with bad teeth, his thin fair hair was brushed closely down on both sides. Mr. Day was a scraggy young man: he had a wild, vicious look on his dark face. He held a farm from Lord Senton; the two were inseparable friends.

Lord Senton seemed somewhat perplexed as he looked at Lewis, as if he were trying to conjecture by what combination of circumstances the young artist had been prevented from getting his hair cut. When he was told that Lewis was a painter, he talked at the earliest opportunity with Day, who laughed viciously.

After dinner, when the ladies left the room, Lewis knew the tug of war had come. He was conscious that Lord Senton was undressing him with a look, and already knew that his clothes had come from Halet's. He saw with dismay that his coat was a waiter's, and he looked enviously at Lord Senton, who smiled in his white and black elegance, and showed his decayed teeth.

With much condescension, Lord Senton spoke about art, evidently thinking that he was expected to do so, for it was not to be supposed that a painter could speak on any other subject.

Frightened lest his lordship should sneer at him to Mrs. Bentham, Lewis humiliated himself. He agreed with him, tried to help him out of his stupid observations, threw conciliatory words to Mr. Day; but when their cigars were finished, and Lord Senton rose to go upstairs, he let Lewis pass out first.

"Well, he's a silly kind of a fool, old chappie," he said, when Lewis was out of hearing. "Did you notice how he was dressed?"

"He's not bad looking though," replied Day, with an apprehensive air.

"You surely don't think that Mrs. Bentham allows him to make up to her."

"I can't say, but I'll keep a look out upstairs."

Lord Senton's sole passion was to play the part of a Lovelace, a *role* for which nature had in no wise fitted him: and he judged of a man's worth in proportion to the number of women he supposed him to be able to compromise.

In his silly way he flirted with Mrs. Bentham, she accepted his compliments, his presents of flowers and game, because it was as well to take as to refuse them. She was at the present time the absorbing topic of his life, and he used to discuss perpetually with Day what he should say to her, how he should push his suit. It was wearying, sometimes, to be called upon fifty times during dinner to determine whether Mrs. Bentham had squeezed Lord Senton's hand in a certain quadrille accidentally or otherwise; but Mr. Day was Lord Senton's tenant, and he found that patient attention to his lordship's amours facilitated rent-paying.

When the two friends entered the drawing-room, Lewis was talking to Mrs. Bentham; she could not help looking at him a little tenderly, for Lord Senton had been boring her all the afternoon; she had been enervated by the memory of insufficient years, and harassed by the menacing monotony of those to come.

For some moments nothing was heard but the click, click of Mrs. Thorpe's knitting needles; the three men looked at each other. Then Lord Senton talked about the county people, particularly of Lady Granderville and her daughter Lady Helen, who were coming to stop with Lady Marion Lindell, Lord Granderville remaining at St. Petersburg, where he was ambassador.

The interest in the conversation centred in Lady Helen, who was a great beauty, and till tea-time her personal appearance was passionately discussed.

Not knowing anything of the people whose names were mentioned, Lewis remained silent. He was very ill at ease; Mrs. Bentham did not take any notice of him, and evening passed away slowly and wearily. An ominous something seemed to float in the air; everyone felt as if something was going to happen, but nothing did happen, and when they bade each other goodnight, their five different smiles indicated the measure of their *ennuis*.

X

An Interlude

For the next four or five days Lewis saw very little of Mrs. Bentham. She did not come into the ball-room in the morning, she had been out to dine twice. Once she had remained in her room the whole evening with a sick headache: in the afternoons Lord Senton took her out to ride.

Still, for Lewis the mornings passed delightfully, whether Mrs. Bentham was there or not. His work interested him beyond measure; it was exactly what he could do best. His talent was neither original nor a profound one, but it was graceful and fanciful; and he thoroughly enjoyed scattering nymphs, cupids, and flowers, over the great clear-coloured walls. At the end of his third week he had finished his compositions for the principal panels, and made out a scheme of colour, which met with Mrs. Bentham's entire approval. A scaffolding had been put up, and she declared that she was ready to superintend.

Latterly, she had been to fewer dinner parties, and had not been out to ride with Lord Senton for some days. When Mrs. Thorpe asked why, she laughed, and said that the most vigorous constitution could not stand more than a fortnight of him at a time; and that, under no pretext whatever, would she see him again till the end of the year. Mrs. Thorpe raised her eyes from her knitting, and declared that she was delighted at the news.

"For, my dear Lucy, I have been wondering what was the matter with you; never have I known you so irritable as you have been for the last fortnight. When I used to meet you on the stairs, going off to a dinner party, one would have thought it was to a funeral you were going, so discontented did you look."

"Have I really been out of humour? I didn't notice it," said Mrs. Bentham, laughing. "Well, that young man is very dispiriting."

Although she scarcely knew it, the real cause of Mrs. Bentham's gloom was that she had been for the last fifteen days vainly trying to persuade herself that she preferred going out riding with Lord Senton to sitting in the studio with Lewis. She argued that she had always liked riding, and with this for plea, she continued to accept Lord Senton's invitations. But after some days he began to weary her so intolerably that one afternoon she passionately decided that no one could be expected to allow themselves to be bored to death, and wrote to him on the spot asking him to excuse her. He was, she said to herself, dull—oh, deadly dull; and, what was worse, he made love to her more obviously everyday. Last Wednesday she had had all the difficulty in the world to prevent him from proposing that they should run away together. If he had said such a thing she would have been obliged to quarrel with him, which, with a next door neighbour, would be more than disagreeable, so the best thing to do was clearly to drop him for a bit.

Besides these excellent reasons, Mrs. Bentham remembered that she had always intended to go back to her drawing; and here was an occasion to do so, which it would be folly to miss. She had an artist in the house who would teach her, and under his guidance she would soon pick up again what she had forgotten.

After this little change in Mrs. Bentham's opinions, the domestic life of Claremont House became quite idyllic. The mornings were sweet beyond measure. Mrs. Bentham drew at her easel, and Lewis talked to her from his scaffolding. All the dignity of the *grande dame* was thrown aside, and a most delicious *cameraderie* was established in its place. She chatted, and laughed, and told stories; it amused her to talk to him as he sat painting. Sometimes he would turn his back on the great white wall, and sit facing her, smoking a cigarette, whilst she told him some ridiculous story about Lord Senton, or asked him for advice about her drawing. The brown curls, the soft sensual face, and the loose velvet coat coming out on the straw-coloured background, recalled a picture by Andrea del Sarto. She thought him very handsome.

Everyday she grew more interested in him, and she often hoped that when the decorations were finished, she would still be able to find the means of helping him. All her dreams came back to her, of being the benefactress of one whom she would lead to success; who would, in the hour of his triumph, come to her, and taking her hand, say, "I owe it all to you."

She did not know that she was, she did not suppose she was ever likely, to fall in love with Lewis, and as an ostrich buries its head in the sand, she hid her heart in a vague maternal sentiment, without caring to look into the future.

At first, her kindnesses raised his hopes to the highest pitch, but, as before, he had to renounce his expectations, for on the slightest advance, she drew away with so much mechanical grace that he was uneasily unhappy for the rest of the day. Sometimes he tried to punish her by exaggerating his position as paid decorator; but it mattered little, natural or affected, Mrs. Bentham remained his superior.

Besides, her humours were so subtle and various that he utterly failed to understand her. She had put him so often back in his place, and for the merest nothings, and afterwards so evidently appeared to regret what she had done, that he fairly lost his head. Then he strove to accord himself to her fancies, as a dog does to its string.

They often spoke of what love is, and is not, and it was oftenest Mrs. Bentham that introduced the subject; but whenever the conversation seemed likely to take a serious turn, or become in the least degree personal, she dexterously changed the subject. They were like friends who dared not venture on the slightest liberty, but who showed by a thousand little things that they longed to be less reserved with each other.

But if the mornings were pleasant, the evenings were delightful; Lewis and Mrs. Bentham sometimes sang together, sometimes discussed art, and as they argued, with the lamp light streaming over their faces, Mrs. Thorpe would let her knitting fall on her black dress, and look at them with kind, affectionate eyes.

Five or six days passed, and Mrs. Bentham savoured slowly the pleasures of this life of unreserved intimacy, and it was with reluctance that one afternoon she took Mrs. Thorpe with her and went to pay a round of visits. Lewis, however, was not displeased; he had that morning completed a drawing, and was going to attack another panel with paint.

He watched the carriage drive away, and then returned with a full heart to his work.

The panel over the chimney-piece, although not nearly the largest, was by position one of the most important: he had therefore arranged for it a somewhat complex composition. It represented a nymph seated high in a bower, made of a few tendrils and roses, with a ring of merry Cupids dancing round her to the music of a reed flute which she played.

Rather nervous, Lewis set to work to lay in the face, shoulders, and hair of the nymph, taking care to keep it very light in tone. He worked steadily, modelling the blown out cheeks carefully from his preparatory sketch, till the sun sank behind the western wolds. He then got down from the scaffolding, lit a cigarette, and began to think of Gwynnie Lloyd. He wondered why she had not answered his letters, hoped that nothing had happened to her, and then went out for a stroll on the terrace, quite satisfied with his day's work.

That evening the ladies had a great deal to say, they had been quite a round of visits, and to their surprise, the whole county knew about the decorations, and were dying to see them, and hoped that Mrs. Bentham would give a ball to show them off when they were completed. They had been to call on the Frenchs, where they had met all the tennis players in the couuty, and it had been settled that the last ties of the tournament were to be at Claremont House, the day after tomorrow.

"So you will make the acquaintance of the whole county, Mr. Seymour," said Mrs. Bentham, laughing; "everybody has heard about you, and is dying to see you. Lord Senton has, I think, been abusing you to Lady Marion; at least she told me that he said he didn't like you; so Lady Marion is dying to see you, for she says that there must be something nice about anything that Lord Senton dislikes."

"But who is Lady Marion?" asked Lewis, a little perplexed.

"Oh, the dearest old lady in the world, but awfully learned, and interested in everything, particularly art. She is dying to ask you some questions about French decorative painting."

Then Mrs. Bentham told Mrs. Thorpe to be sure to remind her to tell the gardeners to pass the mowing machine over the ground. There was an immense discussion with the housekeeper about the luncheon, and the things they would be obliged to send to Brighton for.

Every minute Mrs. Bentham remembered something, or Mrs. Thorpe would remind her of something; between times, everybody in the county was discussed.

"But, my dear," said the old lady, suddenly stopping her knitting, "we have forgotten to tell him about Lady Helen. Do you know, Mr. Seymour, that you will see one of the most beautiful girls in the world. All St. Petersburg went mad about her last season. You are sure to fall in love with her."

Lewis declared that he would be enchanted to see the beauty, but hoped he would not fall in love with her.

Then, after a pause, Mrs. Thorpe, who seemed to have Lady Helen and Lewis terribly mixed up in her head, said:

"Do you know, Lucy, I am thinking what a pretty picture Mr. Seymour could make of Lady Helen. You ought to ask her to sit to him."

"I shall be delighted to do so, but I don't know that Lady Helen will have time to sit; she is going away, you know, very soon," replied Mrs. Bentham, slightly embarrassed.

"But I really have no time to begin a portrait," said Lewis. "I am too much occupied with the decorations." In reply Mrs. Bentham smiled pleasantly, and asked him to come and sing at the piano.

XI

A Tennis Party

A little after two o'clock, before either Mrs. Bentham or Mrs. Thorpe had finished dressing, Lord Senton and Mr. Day drove up in a dog-cart. They were both in tennis suits. The footman showed them into the drawing-room, saying that Mrs. Bentham would be downstairs in a few minutes.

"I can't understand it," said Lord Senton; "she has put me off three times; I am certain that she will never go out to ride with me again."

The prophecy was uttered in a thin whine, expressive of misery. Day did not speak at once, but continued to caress his chin.

"Now tell me exactly what you said to her the last time you saw her," he asked, with the air and voice of a doctor prescribing.

"Well, I can't remember the exact words," replied Lord Senton, brightening up like a patient who expects to be told he is likely to recover; "but we were riding along a road, trees grew on both sides, and the sun was setting, and I said something about—well, about holding her hand."

"But were you holding her hand?" exclaimed Mr. Day, looking up anxiously.

"No, no, how could I? we were out riding; but I leaned my hand on the pommel of her saddle."

At this moment a carriage passed round the sweep to the hall door. It contained an old lady in mauve and two young girls in pink dresses, who shaded their faces with blue and cream-coloured sunshades.

"Here are the French girls; what bores they are!" said Day, as he looked out of the window.

Sussex society consisted of three distinct elements: the aristocracy, the landed gentry, and the people connected with, but who did not belong to, the county. This last class may be termed the hangers-on; they included the gentlemen farmers who held land from either the gentry or the aristocracy, the parson, the curates, the doctor, and the people who leased shooting or hunting lodges in the county. At the head of the county the Marquis of Worthing was throned like a fixed star, and for radiance he had scattered his sisters in marriage to the right and left. He was a grave man, who was always spoken of with great respect. When he came to spend his annual three months at Westland Manor, everyone was invited either to dinner or on a visit of a few days; and the position of the fag end of the landed gentry was determined by the length of their visit, and that of the hangers-on by the number of luncheons and dinners they had eaten at Westland Manor. The Marquis' eldest sister, Lady Marion, had married a Mr. Lindell, a county gentleman, who had died many years ago. She was an old, childless woman, but rejoiced in a great reputation for learning. As Mr. Day said, she was a "regular treasure trove to a young man seeking for information"; she represented the erudition of the county.

Lady Alice, the second sister, had married a Sir Richard Sedgewick, who had a large property, but who lived very little in the county. The third sister, Lady Henrietta, had married a diplomatist, Lord Granderville, who was now ambassador at St. Petersburg.

Lord Senton and Sir John Archer were the two great catches; but the former's vain efforts to play at Don Juan, and the latter's passion for racing, preserved them both from hymeneal influences.

The landed gentry were more numerous than the aristocracy. Mrs. Bentham had five thousand a year; she represented modern fashion. Mr. Swannell, whose rent-roll was about the same, was the politician; he had contested the county at the last election in the Conservative interest. Then came Mr. Vyner, whose income was about the same as Mr. Swannell's; his daughter was desperately in love with Sir John Archer. The Frenchs and Fanshaws were remarkable principally on account of their numbers, and the two Miss Davidsons were much spoken of in connection with matrimony; they had a little fortune of eight hundred a year between them.

Of the hangers-on, Dr. Morgan and Mr. Day alone occupied much of the attention of the county families. The former was very popular, the latter very much disliked; yet both were seen everywhere; no party was complete without them.

Dr. Morgan's flirtation with Mrs. French's governess, and an enumeration of the ladies who would and who would not marry Mr. Day, were he to ask them, were subjects that never failed to provoke an interesting discussion.

When a few of the guests had assembled, the conversation flitted from tennis to the weather, from the weather to tennis. Then Mrs. Bentham asked Mrs. French, who simmered in her mauve dress, how her husband's health had been lately.

"Thank you, pretty well; indeed, he is very anxious for the shooting to commence, and I am afraid he will lay himself up with rheumatism as he did last year. He forgets he was sixty-five last birthday, and wants to do what he did at twenty."

"We find it difficult to remember that we are no longer as young as we used to be," said Mrs. Bentham, smiling vacantly.

"Lady Marion Lendell, Lady Granderville, and Lady Helen Trevor," shouted the footman. Mrs. Bentham got up to receive them.

Cursing his luck and the footman, Lord Senton went over and spoke to the eldest Miss French.

In the meanwhile, Lady Granderville sat on a sofa and whined; the heat of the drive had made her feel faint. Her daughter, the great beauty, was beautiful in a clear, flower-embroidered dress; and Lady Marion, anxious to find a listener, fidgeted a little.

"And how is Mr. Seymour getting on with the decorations? I want you to show me what he has done," she said, at last, getting near Mrs. Bentham; "you didn't tell me how you met the young man."

"I should be very glad, but I am under a promise not to show what he is doing to anybody," said Mrs. Bentham, preferring to answer the first part of Lady Marion's phrase rather than the second.

Lord Senton had gone to speak to Lady Helen; and the Miss Frenchs, finding themselves alone, had commenced to whisper together; the elder said to the younger:

"I wonder she lets him come out; I hear he is just too handsome."

"How much she must regret being married," said the younger sister, reflectively: and then both went into a little smothered fit of laughter.

Carriages now drove up in quick succession, and emptied their cargoes of pink muslin and jersey-dressed young ladies at the hall-door. The word tennis was heard all over the drawing-room, and Mrs. Bentham, observing a great desire on the part of the younger people to commence the serious part of the day's pleasure, proposed that they should go out on the terrace.

Everything had been prepared; the gardeners had done nothing since six in the morning but pass the machine over the ground; the turf was like velvet, and the white chalk lines glittered in the sun. The tennis players felt the ground with their feet; they could complain of nothing but a want of shade. There were trees on the north, south and east, but on the valley side the terrace was exposed, and the sinking sun overspread it with light till the end of the day. It only, however, affected the players, for at the far end three splendid silver firs and some spreading beeches formed a tent, in whose shade the white cloth of the luncheon table glittered like a bank of snow. It was there the company collected and talked as they watched the game.

The terrace was large enough for three courts, so it was hoped that they would be able to play off the last ties of the ladies' and gentlemen's doubles. The tossing for sides took some few minutes, and then the games began in real earnest.

The girls looked charming in their tennis aprons; they forgot the heat, and their light shadows flitted o'er the green sward.

Mrs. Bentham walked with Lord Senton up and down the terrace. She had a vague notion that people had already commenced to connect her name with Lewis, and was glad, therefore, to pretend to flirt with Lord Senton. He was delighted, for since the beginning of the week, he had resolved on a plan which would bring matters to a conclusion.

All this while the matches were progressing; some of the ladies and gentlemen waiting their turn, wandered, racquets in hand, through the pleasure grounds. Under the shade of the silver firs next to the laurel-covered garden-wall, sat a group of chaperones dressed in dark colours, in the middle of which Mrs. French's mauve silk made a crude stain. Lady Marion sat talking to her sister about Lord Granderville. Miss Vyner, who had at last secured Sir John, walked across the terrace, and Mr. Vyner, under cover of listening to Mrs. French's description of her husband's gout, kept his eyes on his daughter and her companion.

"My dear Marion," said Lady Granderville, who, as usual, was boring herself almost as much as she bored her sister, "I always thought Mrs. Bentham a charming woman, though a little fast; but, really, this young man—I hear that he is perfectly beautiful."

"I cannot understand you, Henrietta; surely the woman must have her room decorated, and I hear that this man has a great deal of talent. It is not Mrs. Bentham's fault if he is good-looking, anymore than it is that her friend Lord Senton is very ugly."

Lady Granderville, who was disposed to consider Lord Senton as a very possible husband for her daughter, raised her eyes to see if Lady Helen, who was standing a few yards away talking to two sisters in white, had heard Lady Marion's ill-advised remark.

The light filled Lady Helen's saffron-coloured hair with strange flames, and the red poppies in her straw hat echoed, in a higher key, the flowers embroidered on her dress. She was quite five feet seven, and very slender. She was the type of all that is elegant, but in her elegance there was a certain hardness; her face seemed to have been squeezed between two doors. Lady Helen was very pale, and in the immaculate whiteness of her skin there was scarcely a trace of colour; it was pure as the white of an egg, only around the clear eyes it darkened to the liquid, velvety tint, which announces a passionate nature. The head beautifully placed on a long, thin neck, fell into ever varying attitudes; the waist, which you could span with your hands, swayed deliciously, and the slight hips recalled more those of the Bacchus than the Venus de Milo. Her figure, if the expression be permitted, was beautifully decorative, and could not but attract the eye of a painter.

"Lord Senton says that he doesn't think him a bit good-looking, and that he is awfully silly," said one of the girls in white.

"Lord Senton thinks everybody silly who doesn't drink brandies and sodas, and tell beastly stories," replied Lady Helen, with indifference.

"How do you know that Lord Senton tells beastly stories?"

"My brother told me that his conversation is simply abominable; and if William thinks so—"

The sisters looked up at each other slyly, but Lady Helen intercepted the look, and replied:

"Oh, you needn't look, I know that everybody knows that my mother wants to make a match between Lord Senton and me, but I wouldn't have him; no, not if—"

At that moment, fortunately for Mrs. Bentham, her *tete-à-tete* with Lord Senton had been propitiously interrupted by the arrival of Mr. and Mrs. Swannell.

As Mr. Swannell approached, everybody instinctively tried to think of what they had read that morning in the *Times*, for Mr. Swannell never spoke on any subject but politics.

Lady Marion turned away to speak to Mrs. Bentham; a political conversation with Mr. Swannell would be as great a loss as a domestic one with Lady Granderville; but Mr. Swannell, encouraged by a group of young men who crowded to listen, addressed himself to Lady Marion as he would to the speaker of the House of Commons.

But suddenly, in the middle of a fine period, a fine rolling sentence, he noticed that he had lost the attention of everyone. The ladies looked towards the house, and a feminine look went round.

"I am sure it is he," whispered the elder girl in white; "did you ever see anything so peculiar in your life?"

As Lewis walked down the gravel walk, the sun turned the brown hair that fell on his neck to gold; the weak but delicately featured face was beautiful: the too developed hips gave a feminine swing to his walk.

There was a momentary lull in the tennis playing as he walked down the terrace with Mrs. Thorpe. Even Miss French stopped to look, and she said to her partner that she should like to see him play tennis.

Mrs. Bentham waited to introduce Lewis to Lady Marion, for she knew that half the county took their opinions from the old lady.

What with Lady Granderville's whining stories of her little worries, Mr. Swannell's political common-placeness, and the young men who assailed her from time to time with their stupid questions, Lady Marion was not in too critical a humour, and was disposed to hail anyone as a redeemer.

"I hear that you are decorating Mrs. Bentham's ball-room," said the old lady, by way of leading up to more serious matter.

"I have not yet finished my first panel; but all my sketches are done," said Lewis, very timidly, not knowing whether he should address Lady Marion as Lady Marion or your ladyship.

"Are your sketches original drawings?" asked Lady Marion, meaning to get on the subject of modern French decorative art.

"They are original. . . that is to say that I take a cupid from one engraving, and a nymph from another, and put them together."

Lewis was so pre-occupied, trying to catch how the gentleman who was speaking to Lady Granderville addressed her, that he could scarcely explain to Lady Marion that Mrs. Bentham had a very large collection of engravings and photographs, which she wished him to arrange into suitable pictures for the panels.

The footmen were handing round ices, tea, and claret cups; and in groups and single figures, ladies and gentlemen stood eating pastry and ices, and talking of tennis.

Lady Marion was quite satisfied with Lewis, and they were deeply engaged in discussing modern French art, at least Lady Marion was; Lewis knowing nothing about the subject, listened.

There was but one opinion among the ladies, that he was very good looking, although a little effeminate. Mrs. Bentham looked the picture of happiness as she watched her *protégé's* triumph over Lord Senton, who, with his usual want of tact, had been abusing him to everybody.

Lewis had asked Lady Marion, with very good manner, if she would come to the refreshment table, whether he could get her some tea or an ice. Having overheard how these phrases were used, he made use of them in the same way. As they got up he saw Lady Helen for the first time; she was talking to Lord Senton, and their eyes met.

He was startled by her decorative gracefulness; she was a beautiful motive for a picture, as she stood against a clump of flowering rhododendrons. The blossoms on her dress mixed with those in the trees, and the whole was drowned in light mellow shadow; her clear face and dress standing out against the green dark leaves. Seeing that Lady Helen was being bored, and thinking that Lewis might amuse her, Lady Marion introduced them.

Lady Granderville, who saw the introduction, said to herself, "Dear me, what a fool Marion is; she introduces that man to Helen simply because he can gabble about pictures; and now Helen's chances of being agreeable to Lord Senton are done for: that fellow won't leave her the whole afternoon. Really, Marion is too thoughtless."

At this moment a carriage drove up, and a murmur went round that it was Miss Fanshaw, last year's champion, who was to play with Miss French for the gold bracelet. She stopped the carriage and got out without going to the house, and stood to see her rival play.

She was a thin, wee girl, dressed in blue silk, and she looked as active as a flea.

The last games were won easily by Miss French and partner, and Miss Fanshaw came forward, and, coquettishly swinging her racquet, congratulated her rival, and the two girls went to have tea together.

The arrival of the two famous players invested the entire attention of the company in tennis, and the different points of their play were discussed passionately. It was contended that Miss Fanshaw, although a more brilliant, was not so sure a player as Miss French, and that she often lost a set by trying to kill every ball. But the Fanshaw supporters declared that Miss French would never be able to do anything with the champion's returns; they declared that she had improved very much lately, and that her service was now simply terrific.

But they all agreed that Miss French had been very foolish to tire herself in the double, and that she had prejudiced her chance very considerably. She, however, insisted that when it was time to begin she would be quite fresh, and she ate an ice, and talked blithely with Miss Fanshaw. The match had been arranged for half-past, and it was now four. The sun had passed over the trees and hung at an angle of forty-five over the sea. The breasts of the silver clouds that filled the great blue hollow of the sky were just faintly touched with crimson, and the violent heat was beginning to soften to the persuasive languor of evening.

Everyone was at their ease, and a murmur of intimate voices rippled through the sleeping shadows of the firs. Mr. Vyner watched his daughter, who still held fast to Sir John.

Mrs. Bentham was surrounded by her guests; she tried to listen to what they were saying, but she was visibly a little pre-occupied; every now and then she looked in the direction where Lewis was sitting with Lady Helen. They had now been talking for sometime together, and had done with the generalities and common-places with which we are all forced to open our conversations, and were now eagerly discussing their sympathies and antipathies. Lewis was lost in admiration. If Mrs. Bentham had appealed to him as a vision of comforting love, Lady Helen enchanted him like a beautiful poem of exquisite whiteness and rhythmical grace.

One was like a perfectly served dinner in a perfectly appointed dining-room, full of silver, fruit, and bordeaux; the other was like the ecstacy of the dance, when the scent of flowers and hair mingle and sing an odorous accompaniment to the languorous melody of the waltz.

Lewis spoke to Lady Helen of his artistic aspirations, and his idealization of materialism awoke many unknown sentiments in her heart. It was the first time in her life she had met with anyone whose ideas did not seem to her coarse and vulgar, and in talking to him she fancied she saw her own soul reflected in the mirror of his mind.

Lady Helen was as wayward a young lady as it is possible to imagine. From her earliest childhood the love of the *bizarre* was, as it were, the subsoil of her thoughts. She used to choose her dolls rather on account of their strangeness than their prettiness, and they became endeared to her in proportion as the other children did not like them. She loved people whose peculiarities singled them out from the rest, and she ever felt impelled to say unexpected things, things that would startle if they did not annoy those around her. These fancies developed and took a firmer hold of her as she grew up. She hated all that was ordinary, and preferred an equivocal success to straightforward admiration. Although only nineteen, her great beauty had won for her two proposals, which she declind, for no reasons, at least none that were intelligible to Lady Granderville.

To her the idea of accepting the position she had been born to, and fulfilling the duties of wife and mother, was utterly distasteful. Unlike Mrs. Bentham, who was as fitted to bear as she was to love children,

Lady Helen saw few joys in domesticity, and had little sympathy for the traffic in maternity. To be married and deprived of children might have rendered her unhappy; yet she wished for freedom, to be or not to be a mother as she pleased. She sighed for love, perhaps, as ardently as Mrs. Bentham, but whilst the latter knew instinctively what she desired and what would complete her happiness, Lady Helen lost herself in vague conjectures, in strange oceans of sentiment, where the islands of delight floated and disappeared in a thousand indescribable ways, sometimes enwrapped in the hundred hued golden sunset of desire, sometimes bathed and veiled in the rosy mists of poetical imaginings.

Mrs. Bentham felt, Lady Helen judged, or rather felt and judged simultaneously. She observed men when other women see but one, and if her first flirtations touched her heart, the later ones taught her how to recognise the lie that lurked in the compliment. But it was more the dry narrowness of the imagination than the falseness of the men she was surrounded with that discouraged her from striving to love them.

She loved love for love's own sake, and she knew that those who had proposed to her saw in it nothing but children, dinner parties, and a general settling down. Of the deep, womanly, trusting love, which was so distinctly a part of Mrs. Bentham's nature, Lady Helen could feel nothing, and finding herself misunderstood by those around her, she turned to art for sympathy, and daily the desire for the correction of form grew stronger in her soul.

She read all the poets with avidity; burned with the fire of yearning she soon began to seek for words, and in rhyme and metre sought to give expression to her aspirations. Her father read her sonnets with complacence, much to her mother's annoyance, who thought that such tastes should not be encouraged in young girls.

On all such occasions she would leave the room, declaring that she would interfere no more in her daughter's education.

It is therefore easy to understand how passionately and how suddenly Lady Helen was drawn towards Lewis.

The very similitude there was between their natures completed the charm; for self-love being the basis of life, we love best a wavering image of ourselves. He was softer and feebler than she; but, otherwise, their natures were moulded much after the same fashion.

They talked, conscious of nothing but each other. The sun sank momentarily lower in the sky, until the long fir branches no longer cast a shade over the seat where Lady Helen and Lewis were sitting.

The match between Miss French and Miss Fanshaw was just going to begin, and the company crowded on to the terrace to see the play.

To avoid the friends in whom she had no interest, and the rays of the sun which were stealing under her long fringed parasol, Lady Helen got up and walked through the pleasure grounds with Lewis.

Lady Granderville watched her daughter, Mrs. Bentham her lover, and the two women's faces told with what uneasiness they saw what was happening.

Lady Helen's position and beauty made her noticeable, and there was a movement among the girls; they exchanged glances, and tried to express in looks what they intended to discuss minutely afterwards; Lord Senton looked foolishly annoyed, and tried to make love to Mrs. Bentham.

Instinctively seeking solitude, Lewis and Lady Helen took the walk that led towards the river.

The woods were intersected with gravel walks, and under the bright boughs floated a deep sea-like silence.

On every slope the flowering rhododendrons filled the air with colour, and overhead the screening leaves were sprinkled with the azure of the sky.

Lady Helen spoke to him of her poetry, and of her interest in art, until they slipped into the theme, the oldest and most common-place, yet ever the most interesting between the sexes, the theme that every man must be able to discuss with *esprit* if he wishes to be liked by women.

A turn brought them to the river; to a dreamy, calm place, where a large elm had fallen into the stream, and the beeches cast everywhere cool and diaphanous shadows. Without knowing why, she stopped, and, sitting on the elm, drew listlessly with her parasol on the ground. She felt as persuasively interested in him. She longed to know who he was, what his past had been, how he had lived; she wished to penetrate into his most private life, into his most secret thoughts; and the young girl now felt an irresistible desire to ask him if he had ever been in love. At last, mustering up courage, she said:

"From the way you speak, Mr. Seymour, one would think that you could not live without love."

"Is that extraordinary? We must live on the hope of being loved, or the memory of having been loved; for, after all, it is the only interesting part of life; the rest counts for little."

"And do you look forwards, or backwards?"

"If you knew what my life has been, you could not ask me. As yet I have only dreamed, hoping that some day I might be able to realise my dream."

The words were uttered in a half melancholy way, which gave to them, above their meaning, that charm of regretful sadness so dear to youthful hearts. And yet they were not calculated; Lewis said to Lady Helen what we would have said to a hundred other women; he could not speak otherwise; the delicate rose-coloured sentiment contained in the words was the essence of his whole soul.

For a moment neither spoke, and their emotion was akin to the soft silence and light summer shade that floated around them. But had they looked up they would have seen that they were watched. Mrs. Bentham, pale as death, stood in the pathway by a large laurel. Her hands plucked nervously at the shining leaves, and the expression of her eyes grew fixed in its intensity. The meaning of her gaze and her attitude could not be mistaken, her very heart was laid bare in its jealous agony. But the possibility that the two by the river side might raise their eyes, and see her where she stood, never once crossed her mind. Perhaps it was her bitterest pang that she had no fear that they would think of her.

She was like an animal robbed of its young. She saw the lamb that she had found starving on the hill side, that she had taken home and fed, about to be stolen from her, and she writhed in angry despair beneath the cruel injustice. Why should Lady Helen, with all the world to choose from, rob her who had so little? For it was robbery; he was hers; she loved him. Out of the vague sweet sentiment that had filled her heart during the summer days which she had spent with him, was crushed the concentrated strength of a life's passion. She saw that in him lay her present and her future, that without him there could be nothing for her. And it was doubly cruel that she was not a free woman, that she could not even enter the lists on equal terms with the girl who was drawing him away.

The sound of approaching footsteps aroused her. She turned hastily and encountered Mrs. Thorpe, who, struck with her frightened face, asked her what was the matter.

"Oh, nothing, you only startled me," she said, with difficulty, "you came so suddenly round the turn."

"Then I beg your pardon," Mrs. Thorpe answered, smiling; "but Lady Marion is looking everywhere for Lady Helen; have you seen her?"

"No, I have not"; and Mrs. Bentham, anxious to conceal her trouble, took her friend's arm to return to the house. But they had not taken half-a-dozen steps before all such anxiety vanished in the feeling that to leave the pair together was unendurable, impossible.

"She might be walking by the river with someone," she exclaimed, turning back; "since we are here perhaps we had better make sure."

The two women had not gone many yards down the pathway when the lovers, hearing their footsteps, looked up; Lewis was embarrassed, he felt he had been guilty of an indiscretion, and Lady Helen's white face flushed red—she looked at Mrs. Bentham.

Nature had not made them rivals. Under ordinary circumstances they could not have been matched against each other. One was a delicate lily, the other was a sumptuous poppy.

Lady Helen was annoyed when she heard that her mother was waiting for her; she knew that it meant not only a lecture but a struggle as to whether she should choose, or let her mother choose for her, and she was determined she would have her way. Lewis interested her as no other man had, and her febrile and excitable nature allowed her to think of nothing but the immediate gratification of her fancies. She had been interrupted in an interesting part of her conversation; she would have liked to have walked up the pathway with Lewis, but to her vexation he lagged a little behind with Mrs. Bentham, and Mrs. Thorpe began a series of questions and remarks that forced her to keep in advance.

Lewis and Mrs. Bentham went slowly up the rhododendron covered slopes together. The evening air tasted of flowers and fruit, and the pearly laughs of several nightingales rippled over the tepid silence of the woods. But the delights of the evening affected not Mrs. Bentham; her mind was occupied by one burning thought: was she going to keep or lose her lover?

Stopping suddenly as they approached the terrace, she said:

"I suppose you admire her very much; have you been making love to her?"

"We were only talking about painting and poetry; she writes poetry, and wanted to know my opinion," he answered timidly, "and she said she would like to have some lessons in painting."

"Then give her the lessons she wants; you'll have plenty of time, for I don't think I shall take anymore of you."

Lewis trembled with fear; he saw how he had jeopardised his future, and his dirty garret loomed before his eyes. Speaking like a child, he said:

"I don't love her at all; you know I love you, and only you."

The words fell on Mrs. Bentham's ears as softly as dew on a flower, and her eyes grow full of tenderness. Perceiving his advantage, Lewis continued more confidently:

"Besides how could you suspect me of caring for her. We admire a lily, but we love a rose."

Instinctively she leaned towards him, and, carried away by her passion, he took her hands into his. She remembered not in the intoxication of the moment how she was compromising herself, how near they were to the tennis ground; for an instant they stood looking into the vaporous langours of each other's eyes. She bent her face and would have kissed him, but a sound of footsteps startled them: Lewis had only just time to let go her hands when Mrs. Thorpe appeared. After having left Lady Helen with her mother, she had returned to ask if anyone had been asked to stay to dinner; the cook wanted to know. Mrs. Bentham said she had asked no one, then the three walked up to the terrace, Mrs. Bentham thoughtfully, Lewis mortified at the interruption, but visibly elated at his success.

Everybody was collected round the tennis court watching the match. On a vast plain of gold sky, the group came out in black, like a huge picture painted in silhouette.

Lewis and the two ladies stopped as they left the wood, to gaze on the flaming garden of colours that stretched along the horizon. In the valley below, reflecting all the stillness of the reeds, the river glided like a white dream between the two hills, through the glittering reaches down to the shimmering sea. Drowned little by little in a bath of gold, the sun sank, and rays went up on every side, piercing some fluffy white clouds high up in the blue immensity, deluging the landscape with light, awakening the half-sleeping insects, and revealing every outline of the distant trees which stood against the sky.

But the sunset was lost sight of in the superior excitement of the tennis match. Every stroke was watched with almost breathless interest. Miss Fanshaw had won the first set easily; for the second there had been a fight, but Miss French had got it in the end; in the third set Miss Fanshaw was five games to Miss French's four. The play on both sides had been magnificent, but fatigue was beginning to tell on Miss French. Her hair had fallen down her back; her face was streaming with perspiration; Miss Fanshaw had run her about the court a great deal. Still, she was a plucky girl, and was determined to win the bracelet.

Throwing the ball in the air, she raised herself high on her toes, and hit it with all the force of her body. It cleared the net by about six inches, and came down upon Miss Fanshaw like lightning; she missed it, and, amid much applause, the marker called the game, "forty all, deuce."

Crossing to the right-hand court, Miss French made a still better serve, the ball went sliding out of the corner of the court; it was impossible to get at it: vantage, Miss French. As she crossed over to the left, her brothers whispered words of encouragement; but she looked very weak and tired; it was impossible she could last much longer. The excitement as she prepared to serve the third time was intense. Even Lady Marion grew interested, and attempted to explain the game to Lewis, who, to escape from Lady Helen, had taken refuge at her side. Mrs. Bentham tried to listen to Lord Senton's platitudes, but she heard and saw scarcely anything, so filled was her mind with the memory of Lewis's eyes, and the pressure of his hands.

Miss French's next serve did not come off so successfully as the last two; she banged it into the net, and had therefore to lob it over the second time. Miss Fanshaw very eleverly cut it down the lines, and it was only by a tremendous run that Miss French reached it; she returned it but feebly, and Miss Fanshaw volleyed it, and gave her another run; still she managed to get it up; this time Miss Fanshaw very nearly missed it: she hit it with the wood of her racquet, and it only just went over and dropped under the net, and Miss French killed it easily. They were now five all, and would have to play deuce and vantage games: this was against Miss French, who was terribly done up.

The sun had now slipped below the horizon: two large bands of purple-backed and crimson-bellied clouds stole forward from both sides, and the yellow evening faded to a dim russet colour. The rays that still played about the fantastic outlines of the rocks and cliffs of the further hills grew fainter, and at last the last light went out on the highest point, leaving the shadows to work their will.

Blue mists trailed up the valley from the sea, and the trees that crowned the summit of the hill facing the terrace, became a mass of violet colour seen against a background of cold crimson clouds.

There would be but another half hour of light, but to finish the match only five minutes were required. Miss Fanshaw had won the vantage game, and the score was "love, thirty." Miss French could no longer serve, she trembled as she walked across the court, and her face was perfectly haggard; it was clear she must soon give way. Her mother was whining that poor Fanny looked tired, that she was afraid she would be laid up; but Mr. French, a fat, country squire, said that that was of no consequence, and, calling on her to play up, he offered to bet an even fiver on the result.

In the left hand corner she made two faults, and her father and brothers, who were all standing together, swore simultaneously under their breath. It was now a hundred to one against her, but she still fought on with the tenacity of a bull-dog. She scored the next point with a serve and the next with a splendid return, and the marker called the game "thirty, forty." Could she pull off the next point they would be at "deuce." She threw the ball high, and, raising herself with her last shred of strength, she hit it with a straight bat, but unfortunately, it was a fault; then, trembling for fear, she lobbed the ball timidly. . . it fell into the net. There was a great pause; the lookers on would have liked it to have ended in a tremendous rally and not in this somewhat ignoble fashion. But nevertheless, it was all over: the bracelet was lost and won.

Loud applause went up through the still air, and, deadly pale, Miss French walked over to her father and mother. Her head seemed empty, and she realised nothing definitely. Had she not been so terribly exhausted, she would probably have burst out crying, for she had set her heart on the championship. Her father looked awfully cut up, and her brother began to abuse her for having made so many faults, but she neither saw nor heard; her eyes grew full of mist, the ground seemed to slide away from under her feet. She struggled for an instant, and then fell in a dead swoon into her father's arms.

The company, who were wandering up towards the house, came all running back, the clear dresses fluttering in the grey twilight. A cry passed here and there zig-zag through the group for salts and pocket handkerchiefs, and towards the pale skies a lament went up from the matrons, who in chorus deplored the evil effects of the new game.

The father and the brother carried the girl up to the house; two young men ran off to fetch Dr. Morgan. All seemed to have lost sight of their own little affairs in the excitement caused by Miss Freuch's fainting fit, except Mr. Vyner and Lady Helen.

Mr. Vyner, like a black ghost, watched from the far end of the terrace; his daughter, leaning against the balustrade, still talked with Sir John; but Lady Helen walked, excited and irritated, with her mother, Lady Marion, and Mrs. Thorpe. Lady Helen wanted to speak to Lewis. Seeing him coming from the house with Dr. Morgan, she slipped away from her mother on the pretext of asking after Miss French; but Lewis, seeing her in time, escaped by joining a group of ladies, leaving the doctor to explain to Lady Helen that Miss French was now quite recovered: she had over-exerted herself, and must be careful in the future. When this became generally known, the ladies took up their conversations at the point where they had left them off.

Lady Helen's flirtation with Lewis, the little walk by the river-side, had not passed unnoticed, and now, on the great wide steps leading to the lower terrace, there was quite a little conclave of girls discussing the matter. Lady Granderville reproached her daughter for having been so foolish as to have walked about the woods with Mr. Seymour; but Lady Helen was too intent on planning how she could manage to see him again to listen to her mother.

At last she saw a chance; Lewis and Mrs. Thorpe were talking together, and, regardless of her mother's voice that called her, she went towards them.

Lewis would have liked to have spoken to her, but seeing Mrs. Bentham on the steps, he saved himself by pretending that he had forgotten something. Lady Helen not divining the real reason, put it down to some unfortunate chance, and trembled with irritation. However, there was no help for it; the carriage came round, and she was obliged to content herself by squeezing his hand, and saying what she could with her eyes.

As they drove away, Lady Granderville thanked heaven that they were going back to London in eight or nine days; that, in three months they would be back in St. Petersburg, consequently nothing could result from this absurd adventure.

But Lady Helen had resolved that she would see Lewis before she went back to Russia; and she continued to think of him as they drove through the shadows of the park.

Carriage after carriage passed into the dusty twilight; and as the occupants drew together, covering their knees with rugs, some discussed Lady Helen's flirtation, some condemned the way that Miss Vyner was throwing herself at Sir John, some talked of how Miss French had lost the match, and the hubbub of the voices awoke the sleeping birds on the branches.

Lord Senton was the last to go; almost speechless with rage he bade Mrs. Bentham goodbye, and got into his dog-cart with Mr. Day.

Lewis had joined Mrs. Bentham on the steps, and together they stood watching the pale, passionless stars, insorbed by the magnetic charm of space and love.

Lord Senton saw them, and as he hit his horse heavily with the whip, he said to Day, between a couple of oaths, that he would give a hundred to kick that d——long-haired painter into a cocked hat.

XII

LOVE AND ART

Next morning Lewis could not eat anything at breakfast. He was haggard with excitement, and pale with want of sleep. All night long he had sat at his window, listening to the tall silver firs sighing in the breeze, and watching the river shining deep down in its shadowy-laden valley.

He had sat at his window till the chill dawn had brought sleep to his eyes, kissing his hands to the landscape, already believing it to be his own. He was delirious; and when at last he fell asleep, it was only to dream strange dreams, in which marriage, divorce, and duels, were mixed up in the most preposterous confusion.

He didn't know what would happen, but he knew something would, and was mad with expectation. He wanted to be with her alone; to tell her how he loved her, and to hear her say that their marriage was only a question of months, of weeks, of when she would obtain her divorce.

Generally, on rising from the breakfast-table, she accompanied him to the ball-room; but today she declared she had business with the housekeeper, and left him to go there alone. It seemed to him, after the plans he had made for sitting the whole morning by her side, bitterly cruel; and, sick with disappointment, he put his paint out on his palette, mounted the scaffolding, and set to work to lay in a cupid's head. But it was impossible to work; a thousand thoughts crossed from a thousand different sides, and passed through his brain like ants through a nest that some accident had overthrown.

Every moment he stopped to listen; his face brightened at the sound of footsteps, and darkened when they died away. He could do nothing; the great clear walls irritated him. Excited, he lit a cigarette, and walked up and down the room. The minutes passed like hours, until at last, when he had ceased to expect her, the door opened, and Mrs. Bentham entered.

His face lighted up with pleasure, and he said, with a nervous smile:

"Well, have you done ordering dinners?"

"Oh, yes," she replied, constrainedly; "but I am afraid I shall not be able to stay long this morning. I have a hundred things to do."

Lewis asked her to sit down, but she would not, giving as an excuse that she really hadn't time, that she really must be going.

It was an awkward interval. They walked up and down the room, they looked out of the windows vacantly. Lewis hinted at the events yesternight, and strove to speak of his love; but his courage dribbled out at his finger tips, and he talked with her now just as he had done the day after his arrival at Claremont House. As they were then they were now, nervous and embarrassed. The same scene was repeated, only with this difference—now the combatants were more evenly matched. No longer was he in doubt as to what her feelings were towards him—she had shown him what her heart was. As before, she wished to reassert her dignity, but this time it was less easy. She could no longer express surprise, nor could she forbid him to speak to her of love; and it was the knowledge that her defences were gone that made her so afraid of seeing him alone.

Her excuse that she had housekeeping to do was but a wretched subterfuge to gain time; and she thought, as she tried to bring her attention to bear on the bills, of a way of retreat out of the position into which a moment of passion had put her.

But she found it impossible to make up her mind as to what tone she should assume should Lewis make love to her. She hoped that he would not attempt any such thing, and at the same time trusted that he would not appear either cold or indifferent. At present she wanted to be a dear friend to him; to help him, to speak kind words, to be something sweeter than a friend; for she wished him to love her, that is to say, to like her better than anyone else; to think of her when she was not there, and when she came back she desired that their eyes should meet and say a thousand things their lips might not.

Such was the state of Mrs. Bentham's mind, and she did not care to look into the future, to think out logically what must be the end of such a friendship. She was *à vau l'eau;* she wished to let herself drift, to let things take their chance; and it was fear lest Lewis might think differently that made her dread meeting him. But, delay it as she might, sooner or later she would be bound to find herself alone with him; and having gradually come to that conclusion, she resolved to see him, and strike, if possible, the exact note of friendship she wished for. She had asserted her dignity before, and was determined to do so again, but in a different way.

Such were the plans Mrs. Bentham hoped to put into execution as she walked up and down the white room sketched all over with half-finished nymphs and cupids; but to explain her intentions adequately, it was necessary that Lewis should first make love to her in a somewhat marked manner, and this he did not seem inclined to do; and the vague allusions he made as to the state of his heart could not be used as a pretext for introducing the little sermon she had carefully prepared.

They tried several times to talk about the decorations, but she listened badly, and he was too excited to be able to sustain a conversation. His head was filled with vague schemes, all of which he rejected one after the other. He dared not try to kiss her; and to tell her that he loved her, in the middle of some trivial phrase, seemed to him ridiculous. Both were embarrassed, for each expected the other to act differently. At last Mrs. Bentham alluded to Lady Helen, and that gave Lewis the chance he was waiting for, and he immediately reproached her with having suspected him of caring for anyone but her.

They were standing by the window. Lewis was getting enthusiastic, and he leaned his arm against the shutter.

As she listened to his passionate declaration of love, she turned towards him. She had forgotten all her resolutions, and, perceiving his advantage, he let his arm pass round her waist.

The movement awoke her from her dream, and her face showed him that she resented the liberty. Then he grew frightened, and regretted his rashness; but it was too late, he had to go on; and he continued to tell her in short, vehement phrases how much he loved her—how useless his life would be without her.

At first she would not hear; but she gradually forgot herself and listened to him tenderly. He took her by the hands—she allowed him to do so, and they sat down on the sofa side by side.

Then, again remembering her good intentions, she spoke with dignity, and told him how she wished to help him. Lewis listened, forgetful of everything but the softness of her voice and the sweetness of her presence. His arm fell round her, and he drew her towards him. She could not resist; but as her head rested on his shoulder, a firm step was heard in the dining-room. They started, and looked at each in alarm, and Lewis had only just time to pretend to be turning over a portfolio of drawings when the butler entered. He handed a telegram, and said that Lord Senton was in the drawing-room, that he was going to London by the two o'clock train, and wanted to know if he could do anything for her.

She read the paper through hurriedly.

GEORGE MOORE

"Tell Phillips," she said, "to pack up what I shall require for a week, and tell the coachman that I am going to London by the next train, and to have the carriage round in time. By the way, which is the next train?"

"The two o'clock train is the next; shall I say you are at home to Lord Senton?"

"Certainly; say that I shall be with him in a minute."

"What on earth is the matter? Why on earth are you going with Lord Senton?" asked Lewis, as soon as the servant had left the room.

"This is a telegram, saying that my father is dangerously ill; I must go at once; I hope it is nothing very serious."

Lewis remained silent; he knew nothing about her father and cared less; but he cursed him, whoever he was, for having chosen this time, of all others, to get ill. In his mind there was no longer a shadow of doubt but that Mrs. Bentham loved him—Lewis Seymour; and he now felt sure of being able to persuade her to get a divorce and marry him; that is to say, if Fate would only accord him a fair chance.

Mrs. Bentham still sat beside him, but the love scene had been broken through, its spirit had fled, and he saw that it would be useless to try to urge her now to take any decisive step, when her mind was harassed by fears for her father's life. Yet, notwithstanding this *contretemps*, they talked for some minutes very affectionately together. She promised to write to him, and he called her once or twice by her Christian name, which he thought was a great point gained. She admitted that she liked him, and spoke with great tenderness of how she hoped to help him towards success, and what pleasure it would give her if, one of these days, he became a great artist.

They talked dreamily for some minutes, till suddenly she remembered that Lord Senton was waiting. This occasioned a little scene of jealousy, which forged another link in the chain which was being bound around their lives. Mrs. Bentham insisted that the young man bored her to death; that it was a most unfortunate coincidence, that she had to travel up to London with him; and she declared that if he were not her next door neighbour, she would refuse to see him once and forever.

Lewis accepted the assurance, but would not come into the drawing-room to see him, and bidding Mrs. Bentham goodbye for the present, he mounted his scaffolding and went on with the cupid's head.

Both were pretty well satisfied with themselves. Mrs. Bentham certainly had to admit that she had gone a little further than she had intended; but she comforted herself with the belief that she had, in the last part of the conversation, established the groundwork of the friendship she so ardently coveted; and she hoped that in future, without loving her less, Lewis would accept what she gave him, and that their lives would be as pleasant as possible.

Lewis, on his side, was forced to admit, as he sat cramped up on his low stool, right in front of the straw-coloured panel rimmed with mauve, that although everything had not turned out as he had expected, still he had no reason to complain.

He cursed her father's illness as a beastly piece of bad luck; but he assured himself that absence makes the heart grow fonder, and consoled himself with the prospect of continuing his courtship with increased vigour when she came back.

After Mrs. Bentham's departure, the house fell into a state of absolute quiet. Mrs. Thorpe never received visitors, and those who called after the tennis party left their cards, and went away disappointed.

For the first couple of days, Lewis thought of nothing but the letter he expected to receive from Mrs. Bentham, and he asked himself twenty times a day whether she would address him as, "My dear Lewis," "Dear Lewis," or, "My dear Mr. Seymour." Then he passionately regretted having missed kissing her; for he argued that if he had done so she would have been obliged to call him, Lewis. At last the letter came, and a grey cloud passed over his face as he read: "My dear Mr. Seymour"; however, it was very kind, charming, in every other respect, and obtained the consolatory news that Mr. Vicome, her father, was better, and that Lord Senton was boring her to death.

Mrs. Thorpe had also received a letter, and she kept Lewis till nearly eleven o'clock telling him about the poor old gentleman, and how anxious he was to have the ball-room finished.

Henceforth the days went by with the methodical monotony of an eight-day clock, and the periodical winding up took the form of a letter from Mrs. Bentham, saying that her father was better, or that he worse, and that for the present she could not leave London. Every morning after breakfast Lewis went to his decorations, and Mrs. Thorpe to talk with the gardener, the steward or the housekeeper, and had it not been for his painting, Lewis would have died of *ennui*. But as calm, dry weather will produce the best crop in a marshy soil, so the solitude of Claremont House forced him to concentrate his whole attention on his work, and he got on capitally.

The job of decorating all the panels proved a longer one than he had suspected. It is true that in the first month he had completed his sketches, but as he worked on he found that many of them did not please him; sometimes it was the composition that was not up to the mark; sometimes they did not suit the scheme of colour he had adopted.

They were, in all, six large panels, twelve feet by six, and a similar number of small ones; and although the decorations were, not to destroy the lightness of the room, of the very slightest description, they still took a long time to execute on account of their size.

Fearful of failing in the work which had been entrusted to him, he had very carefully made his compositions according to scale, so that they might be enlarged by means of squares on the panels. It was impossible to do this alone, but a country carpenter helped him with the measurements, and the page boy held the strings. Lewis worked very hard, and towards evening his arm ached, for the manual labour of rubbing paint over so large a surface was considerable. At seven he and Mrs. Thorpe dined together, and he told her new anecdotes about his father's laboratory chimney, how he (Lewis) had lived with his poor mother for so many years, and of his terrible struggle for existence in the wilds of London. Never till half-past ten did the old lady grow tired, but then, even in the middle of a touching bit of description, she would put up her knitting and wish him goodnight.

His gentle manner had quite won the old lady's heart, and she regarded him as one of the family, quite forgetting that when the decorations were finished he would go away, and that they would then see him only at the rarest intervals.

For nearly six weeks nothing except an occasional letter from Mrs. Bentham broke the calm regularity of his life, until, one day, the footman handed him Mr. Day's card.

Lewis looked at it for a moment, and wondering what the farmer had come to say to him, told the servant to show him in. It was scarcely singular that Lewis could not imagine what Mr. Day had come for; it had taken that gentleman two days' hard thinking to invent a legitimate excuse for his visit. Even now he had found nothing more ingenious than a request that Lewis would paint him a picture of a horse he was very fond of.

Mr. Day suspected that Lewis would be surprised to see him, but it could not be helped. Lord Senton had insisted on an interview, and at that moment Mr. Day had two letters on the subject, which had both come by the same post, and had to be answered at once. Poor Mr. Day detested letter-writing, and latterly he had done nothing else but cover reams of paper, trying to solve the most abstruse psychological problems.

He now absolutely dreaded the hour of the post, for it never failed to bring him letters from Lord Senton, asking the most complicated questions.

What did Mrs. Bentham mean by telling him (Lord Senton) that she did not like London, and would like to get back to the country? Did it mean that she liked the long-haired painter? Would it be advisable for him (Lord Senton) to ask her to go to the theatre with him, after having been refused half-a-dozen times? Would it be right for him to go on sending her bouquets? Up to now he had not missed a day; and what did Mr. Day think of the advisability of slipping a nice diamond ring into one and sending it anonymously.

Lord Senton's want of success rendered him irritable, and he now reproached Day bitterly for not being able to tell him if the long-haired painter was or was not Mrs. Bentham's lover. Day declared in many letters that, after having carefully examined the evidence for and against, he was inclined to think that Mr. Seymour was not Mrs. Bentham's lover; but that it was impossible for him, under the circumstances, to speak definitely. Yet this did not satisfy Lord Senton, and he had, in his last letters, so strongly insisted on a personal interview, that Day no longer ventured to resist his chief's commands, although he really did not know how he was going to question Mr. Seymour on the subject.

However, he was not a man to be embarrassed, and, armed with the picture of the favourite horse as an excuse, he tried to make friends with Lewis. Lewis told him, as he expected, that he could not undertake the commission, but thanked him very much for the offer.

"You paint figures, not animals?" said Day, as he examined a nymph and some cupids.

"I do anything I get an order to do, when I have time," replied Lewis laughing.

Then farmer and painter walked round the great clear walls, and Mr. Day made many facetious remarks about the scantiness of the draperies, and suggested that Mrs. Bentham's portrait should be painted on to one of the nymphs; Lewis did not like this, and resented the familiarity, which made Day prick up his ears.

"Heigh ho! you are so particular as that!" he said to himself.

Nevertheless, the men made friends, lit cigarettes, and began to talk quite affably.

"Remarkably fine woman, Mrs. Bentham," said Day; "I wonder she doesn't get married."

This was put out as a feeler, for Day was obliged to write something to Lord Senton.

Lewis looked at him, surprised, and said:

"But you know she is only separated from her husband; she is not a free woman."

"You are sharper than I fancied you were," thought Day, and then he said, aloud: "Yes, I know, but then she might easily get a divorce."

"How?" asked Lewis innocently.

Day looked at him admiringly. "Capitally parried, my friend," he said, to himself, and then a moment after continues, aloud: "Oh, very easily; if she ran away with anyone, then her husband would be entitled to a divorce; and I can tell you he's a lucky man who gets her; she has seven thousand a year, if she has a penny."

On the point of Mrs. Bentham's fortune Lewis was quite satisfied; but as regarded Mrs. Bentham's private character, he was anxious for information; so, hoping her name would be mentioned, he questioned Day on the morality of the county families. Day entered into the discussion with zest, but he looked at Lewis, as much as to say: "I'll talk with you, and tell you what I know, because the subject interests me, but you don't take me in with your innocence; a nice kind of young gentleman Senton has sent me down to pump; if I don't take care it will be you who will pump me."

After this discovery, Day seemed to see Lewis in quite a different light, and studiously tried to be civil to him.

He fancied he recognised in him a man of marvellous tact, and he came to the conclusion that of all the suitors, Lewis was by far the most likely to persuade Mrs. Bentham into marrying him. He admitted to himself that it was not a likely thing to happen, but it seemed to him to be distinctly on the cards; and as the possible owner of Claremont House, Lewis appeared to Mr. Day to be worth making up to, particularly as the doing so compromised him in no way with Lord Senton. Mr. Day made it a rule never to lose a chance; and there were plenty of farms to let on the Claremont House property that he would much rather have than the one he leased from Lord Senton; and as it is always worth taking a thousand to nothing, he asked Lewis to come over to his farm and lunch with him any day he liked, but just to drop a line. With this expression of goodwill, Mr. Day took his leave, and rode home to write a long account of the interview to Lord Senton.

Then some more uneventful days went by, and at last the welcome letter came, saying that Mr. Vicome was out of danger and that Mrs. Bentham expected to return home in a day or two.

At the news Lewis's illusions awoke like a summer garden, when the first grey gleams chase the trembling shadows out of the thickets. He had now forgotten Lady Helen as he had forgotten Gwynnie Lloyd, and the present passion of his soul was centred in Mrs. Bentham. She had always appeared to him as the type of worldly enjoyment, but now, in his solitude, having no other image to distract his attention, he had tried to surround her with the halo of all the poetry his nature was capable of perceiving. He grew tired of his work, and spent his days dreaming. Like one under the influence of a narcotic, he saw deep into the future; saw himself in turn rich, poor, successful, unsuccessful, but always loving and being loved by Mrs. Bentham. His tepid nature warmed up to something like enthusiasm, and under the influence of his love he began to discriminate and draw nice distinctions between certain questions of right and wrong; he became noble-minded, and suffered from outbursts of generosity; he recognised how badly he had behaved to poor Gwynnie, and he resolved to make reparation. Then, in the evenings, he went in for long conversations with Mrs. Thorpe, and they discussed the necessity of doing one's duty, and living up to a high and grand standard of morality.

These discussions interested him profoundly; and when he bade the old lady goodnight, he would linger on the staircase annoyed that he had not made himself clearer on certain points.

The days that separated him from Mrs. Bentham passed slowly; but when he thought of how she had spoken of assisting him, and of the desire she had expressed to see him a great artist, he became tenderly sentimental, and mused long on the solicitude of woman's nature. Then, suddenly remembering something Day had said, he grew indignant, and he asked himself if it would not be shameful for him to own any man as a friend who spoke of women as Day did; of course it would, and he resolved to see as little of him as possible in the future. These bursts of enthusiasm were often followed by fits of despondency; for when he remembered the women his mother had told him of—women who had flirted to the last with men, and then left them, laughing at their misery—he grew so angry that he frequently found himself borrowing from Mr. Day's vocabulary, and had to pick himself up.

But Mrs. Bentham, he reassured himself, was not one of these monsters; the worst that could happen was that she, in her angelic goodness, might not consent to get a divorce from her husband and marry him. This was a serious consideration, and a cloud seemed to have tarnished the burnished mirror in which he had been lately viewing the immaculate virtue of the sex, and he was forced to admit that you could lay down no hard and steadfast rule of conduct. It was impossible, he thought, that Mrs. Bentham would, for the sake of a few miserable prejudices, willingly ruin everything they had to hope for of happiness in life. As for himself, he felt that death would be infinitely preferable to life without her, and his thoughts wandered insensibly to the question of suicide.

He remembered, with horror, how near he had been to drowning himself over Waterloo Bridge, but now, it would be different; he was no longer a homeless vagabond, but a young man of talent, adored by women, and to die for love would exalt him to the position of a modern Romeo; and he thought of all the paragraphs there would be in the newspapers, and how, probably, the novelists would use him as a type of youth, beauty, and love. "Today or tomorrow, what matter, since we have to die?" he said to himself; "and who could wish a more poetic death?"

With such a strange mixture of doubts, desires, hopes, and fears, Lewis amused himself, until Mrs. Bentham's return threw him from his dreamland into the more satisfactory country of reality.

Doctors, nurses, anxiety for her father's recovery, and the thousand worries of a sick-room, had so occupied her mind during the past six weeks, that she came back to Lewis with almost the same thoughts as when she left him. Her intentions had not changed, and she hoped to be able to establish a sweet and lasting friendship between Lewis and herself, and it was with satisfaction she remembered that their parting words had been those of dear friends.

They were undisguisedly glad to see each other, but it was in doubt that she went to see him in the ball-room. "Why would he," she asked herself, "insist on making love to her? why could he not be content with what she gave him? Yet, notwithstanding her appreheusions, he proved very tractable, and they had the longest and sweetest conversation possible, sitting side-by-side on the sofa. She had to tell him all about her stay in London: how she missed her drawing-lessons, how she had to nurse her father, and how Lord Senton bored her. And there were the decorations to examine; for, like every artist, he could not resist explaining his intentions and showing off his work, and this was especially delightful to do, as Mrs. Bentham was perfectly enchanted with all he did.

Then they had to speak tenderly; to say how glad they were to see each other. Lewis took her hands, she let him do so, but soon withdrew them, and he, not anticipating another six weeks' interruption to his courtship, did not try to press matters.

For nearly a week their flirtation flowed as softly as the sweetest summer stream, until one morning, and they never knew whose fault it was, one love word led to another, until Lewis told her how passionately he loved her, and that it was impossible for him to live without her.

Passing his arm around her waist, he drew her down towards him, and endeavoured to kiss her. She resisted formally for a while, and then, with the phrase, sublime in its simplicity, "I can't help myself," she surrendered herself to him, and for a moment allowed him to lay his soft, large lips upon hers. But it was only for a moment, disengaging herself from his arms she stood vacantly looking at him, apparently regretting what had passed. But he, thinking that there was no longer doubt as to his success, rapidly explained that they should run away together, and when her husband got a divorce, why that they would get married.

"Oh!" she said, looking at him tenderly as she held his hand, "you do not know what you ask me; it is impossible; you don't know my husband; to punish me he would not ask for a divorce."

Lewis argued with her vehemently, in short brief phrases, but without being able to alter her opinion. She listened almost as if she did not hear him, until, suddenly withdrawing her hands from his, she said, with the voice of a woman who has recovered herself, who has got the better of her weakness:

"No, no, what you propose is impossible; let us never speak on this subject again, otherwise we cannot remain friends."

Lewis turned ghastly pale, and his lips twitched nervously; he looked at her fiercely, hating her for her cold words, and then, with a sense of having being vilely deceived, his rage overcame him. He looked round the room as if for a weapon; there was nothing within his reach but the tin palette knife, and so great was his passion that he only just saw in time the absurdity of his intention.

"Be friends!" he exclaimed, forgetful of everything; "you think that you can buy me with your money, but you are mistaken. I will leave you and your decorations tonight!"

Mrs. Bentham looked at him bewildered; but before she could reply he had rushed out of the room. The whole scene did not take five minutes; the explanation and the *denouement* came after each other with a rattle that would have delighted the heart of a modern stage manager.

Mrs. Bentham, like one who has received a blow on the head, looked round vacantly, her attention diffused. The wide, empty room, where she had spent so many charming hours, stared blankly at her; she looked at the great clear walls everywhere covered with nymphs, cupids, flowers, and tendrils; some were completed, some were barely indicated with a few black lines. Here a group of cupids quarrelled over some masks and arrows; some had disguised themselves with the former; some had wounded themselves with the latter. Forgetful of her grief, Mrs. Bentham tried to decipher the allegory. Each panel contained a picture illustrating an episode in the comedy of love. But there was little done, it was only a blurred and blotted dream, sad with the grievous grief of incompleted things.

Silently large tears rolled down her cheeks as she read all around her the story of her life, until at last, unable to restrain herself any longer, she sobbed passionately, hiding her face in her hands. She wept bitterly, but her tears brought neither counsel nor relief. She had won Lewis from Lady Helen, but how vain the victory now appeared; for with passionate despair she saw that she would have either to become his mistress, ruin herself in the eyes of the whole world, or give him up.

Give him up, oh, how the words burned in her soul! No, she could not do that, it would be worse than giving up her life; she had fought hard for him, and must keep him. But, oh! why had he put her in so difficult a position? why had he not been content to wait? Then she remembered that he said he was going, and with eyes bright with excitement, she thought of what she should do to prevent his leaving her. No, it must not be; she would implore him, she would beg of him to stay; no, he must not go, anything but that; to lose him would be more cruel than death.

Harassed by doubt, and irresolute from fear, she sat listening to the cold December wind and rain that beat against the window. She thought of him with infinite tenderness, mistaking his faults for good qualities, never for a moment suspecting that under no circumstances would he have the courage to turn his back on pleasure and comfortable ease. She did not know that he already bitterly regretted his folly, that in the solitude of his room his passion had rapidly cooled down, and that he was even now striving to mature some scheme wherewith to obtain her forgiveness.

His first impulse was to run downstairs and beg for pardon, but he remembered that he could always do that, and that it would be foolish to play his best card first. He cursed himself for having risked his all in one throw; she had offered him her friendship, he had refused it, like an idiot, and for no reason that he could see; for, after all, there was no hurry; he might have waited for months. Besides, even if she did refuse eventually, it would not make matters any better by quarrelling with her.

Shaking with fear, he walked about his room, trying to compose a definite plan of action; but Gwynnie and the garret in Waterloo Road so terrified him that he could think of nothing; his reason deserted him, and his instinct urged him to go down on his knees and beg forgiveness.

At last the lunch bell rang, and he went downstairs. The conversation turned on Mr. Vicome, and Mrs. Thorpe, not knowing that anything had happened, talked volubly of the old gentleman's recovery. Lewis watched Mrs. Bentham, and when he saw that she had been crying, he plucked up courage, and tried to allude to the time when the decorations would be finished. But Mrs. Thorpe was interested in Mr. Vicome's health, and it seemed impossible to speak of anything else. The meal seemed to him interminable, but when they got up from the table, he noticed with delight that Mrs. Thorpe stopped behind to put the wine away. This was the chance he wanted, and he followed Mrs. Bentham, who walked slowly down the passage.

Catching her up at the foot of the stairs, he called her softly by her name; she stopped, and took the hand he held to her, and it was made up in a look and a few words.

That afternoon the ladies went out to drive, and Lewis worked hard at his painting; he was in a high state of delight, for Mrs. Bentham had accepted the flag of truce which he had held out to her with such a show of gratitude, that he had not failed to perceive how indispensable his friendship was to her; and as he sat painting his cupids he carefully analysed the situation. He saw now that the mistake he had made was not in threatening, but in the way he threatened her; and having no longer anything to fear, he determined to see what the effect of the announcement that he intended to go to Paris to study art as soon as he had finished the decorations, would produce.

Lewis was not wanting in cunning, and he took care not to speak of his trip to the continent until Mrs. Bentham had forgotten all about their little quarrel. He chose his time carefully; and one evening, in the drawing-room after dinner, when the conversation flagged, he spoke carelessly of going to France.

Mrs. Bentham started, and tried to murmur something to the effect that she hoped they would not lose him so soon. As for Mrs. Thorpe, she dropped her knitting into the grate; if a bombshell had exploded she could not have been more astonished.

Perceiving how his ruse had succeeded, he proceeded, with much feigned composure, to explain that he only intended to stay away a year, guessing that it would sound in their ears like a century. Mrs. Bentham dared not say anything, but Mrs. Thorpe opposed his plan vigorously. She warned him of the moral dangers of the French capital; she tried to prove to him that he would not be able to learn painting because he did not know French; and with slight interruptions the discussion occupied the evening.

Mrs. Thorpe appeared to take it so to heart that Mrs. Bentham, under pretext of consoling her, ventured to hint that it was quite possible that they might take a trip over there, and then they would see how he was getting on.

The old lady took very kindly to the idea; she had never seen Paris, and admitted that, if Mrs. Bentham were going there, she would not mind accompanying her.

For the next week, during the long morning hours in the ball-room, Lewis and Mrs. Bentham talked the matter over, and they agreed that if they could persuade Mrs. Thorpe into chaperoning them, they would spend six months in Paris together.

It would take him another month to finish the decorations; that would bring them into February, and Mrs. Bentham proposed that Lewis should accompany them to London, where she would introduce him to people who would be of use to him.

But, partly because he wished to spite her for what he, in his secret mind, termed her intense selfishness, and partly because he had a vague notion that all he had to do to become a great artist was to go to Paris; he remained firm in his original purpose of going abroad as soon as the ball-room was finished.

The subject was discussed over and over again, sometimes *à deux*, sometimes before Mrs. Thorpe, to whom they both appealed as to a presiding judge.

Eventually it was agreed that he should proceed to Paris at the end of February, get admitted as a student to the "Beaux-Arts," and that after the London season, Mrs. Bentham and Mrs. Thorpe should come and see him. Before, it was impossible, for as she explained when alone to him that it would compromise her too much not to be seen in London during the season, but that once it was over, she could do as she liked.

Paris brought back a crowd of remembrances to Mrs. Bentham. It was there she had spent the first months of her married life. Mr. Bentham was of that horrible race, the Parisian English, which race seems to have the virtues of neither country and the vices of both.

She rarely heard of him now; when the court had granted her her judicial separation, he had left England for his favourite city. Sometimes curious stories about him reached her ears, fantastic duels, in which actresses' names were mentioned, but that was all. She gradually had learned to forgive him. In her heart she believed him mad, but when talking of him she could not always repress a shudder.

XIII

ENFIN

When the decorations were finished, Mrs. Bentham gave a ball. The whole county was asked, aristocracy, gentry, and hangers-on; a great many guests came from London, and for a week the house was full of people.

A dazzling white lustre hung from the middle of the ceiling; and, in the clear flames of its twenty-five wax candles, the vast straw-coloured walls took the appearance of a gigantic ball-dress—a dress embroidered with joyous cupids, and sleeping, singing, and revelling nymphs. Up and down the glittering parqueted floor, full of reflected skirts, and patent leather shoes, groups and couples walked and discussed the designs.

Sometimes they would form into masses before a particular panel, and then the pale tints of the women's shoulders were curious to compare with the rose skins of the nymphs.

Lewis was enchanted; the workmen had only that day finished hanging the chandelier, and it was therefore the first time he had seen his room lighted up.

What particularly pleased him was the way in which the long tendrils and delicate leaves encircled the pictures, and how their dead green harmonised with the mauve frames. His triumph was complete. A rippling sound of complimentary words came from wherever he went. When these reached Lord Senton's ears, he started; and, with a pained expression of face, strove to get out of hearing.

Everybody looked at Lewis, and was anxious to be introduced to him. Lady Marion talked with him, and gave him much advice about Paris, where he was going next week.

The artistic element was, however, wanting. Its sole representative was Mr. Ripple, a young man who wrote paragraphs in the society papers. He had made great friends with Lewis, and was now explaining to a group of ladies the signification of some of the allegories, and at the same time threatening them that he would mention their names in the world, an announcement which caused them to flutter with excitement.

No ball ever passed off more satisfactorily; everybody ate, drank, danced as much as they liked, and some had afterwards the ineffable pleasure of reading an account of their dresses, with their names appended, in omnibus language of a society print.

But it was Lewis who came out beautifully. He was described both physically and morally, and his decorations were declared to have been conceived in the best spirit of the seventeenth century. It was the first time he had ever seen his name in type: he shook Ripple's hand, and vowed friendship.

But the young man, who had this time contributed nearly half a column, declared that he lived by literature, and was only too glad to make known to the world any new talent it was his good fortune to meet with.

A fortnight afterwards Lewis started for Paris with twenty-five pounds in his pocket, and three hundred and fifty to his credit at the bank; for not only had Mrs. Bentham insisted on paying a hundred more than was agreed on for the decorations, but she had, as an excuse for giving him money, sat to him for a full-length portrait, which, alas! he had not been able to complete.

First, the drawing did not come right, then he had not been able to get it like; eventually he found himself obliged to put it aside, and say he would go on with it next year. The failure mortified his vanity; but it proved to him conclusively that he had much to learn, and he went to Paris burning with enthusiasm for work. But when he was gone, Mrs. Bentham became so restless that her life was a burden to her. The long, solitary evenings were intolerable, and even Mrs. Thorpe had to admit that the house was very lonely in his absence.

The only relief in Mrs. Bentham's life was when she got a letter from him; he was a good correspondent, and every week he wrote, telling her how he was getting on—how he would owe it all to her if he ever became a great artist.

She loved these letters, and the mornings they came she was always late for breakfast: she remained dreaming over them in bed.

With him her life seemed to have ended; nothing amused, nothing interested her, and she spent her days bitterly watching the spring rain dripping on the saturated terraces, until, weary as a Mariana, she determined to seek relief in the excitement of the London season. She went to many balls, but they, too, bored her, and the men who tried to make love to her only annoyed her. She thought this time of waiting would never come to an end.

At last, however, the 12th of July came, and, dusty and travel-stained,

Mrs. Bentham and Mrs. Thorpe stepped out of the sea-sick smelling railway carriage on to the dark grey and desolate Gare du Nord.

Next morning, in the gaudy hotel sitting-room of the Hotel Meurice, Mrs. Thorpe sat knitting next the fire-place; Mrs. Bentham, on the red sofa, tried to read the *Figaro*. The breakfast was laid for three. Both women waited impatiently. At last a footstep was heard, and Lewis rushed into the room, his bright face beaming with smiles.

Mrs. Bentham said little, but from time to time she raised her eyes and looked at him earnestly. Mrs. Thorpe wanted to hear the details of his daily life.

They were delighted to see each other, but the afternoon passed by full of uneasy silences, until the servant announced that the carriage was at the door, and Mrs. Bentham asked him if he would like to come with her for a drive. Lewis was delighted. He was dying to talk with her alone; and as they drove round the fashionable lake, leaning back on the comfortable cushions of the victoria, he spoke to her of their long separation, and passionately pressed her to say that she had regretted him.

She equivocated and they quarrelled, but were reconciled on her finally admitting that the London season had bored her dreadfully, and that she was perfectly happy now.

It was sweet to her to find that Lewis knew nothing of Paris; but he explained that he had done nothing but work; and when he told her he had only spent a hundred pounds, she pressed his hands in recognition. They appeared to have grown more intimate. With lazy little laughs, and whispered words, they talked of the past, and looked dreamily into the future. Every now and then Mrs. Bentham fell into reveries. She gazed distrustfully on the cafés, theatres, and gardens: a vision of a new life seemed to float seductively out of the soft evening air, and the beautiful city wore the pale sunset skies like a garment befitting her light pleasures and ephemeral loves.

About half-past six they got home. Both were in high spirits, and Mrs. Bentham insisted that they should dine at a restaurant. Mrs. Thorpe consented.

But it took a long time to decide which café to go to. Lewis could of course offer no suggestion; he knew of nothing but a quantity of "estaminets." At last they settled on the "Doyen"; but it was with difficulty they persuaded Mrs. Thorpe to dine out in the open air. She declared she had never heard of such a thing; and it was only on seeing how disappointed they would be if she refused, that she consented to take a seat, as she put it, out in the middle of a field. But once there it was all right; and, before she had finished her soup, she was forced to admit that she was very comfortable, although a little bewildered. Everything seemed to her so strange.

But Lewis, who loved the fantastic, was enchanted with the little white tables scattered over the green sward, encircled with bright foliage, that came out like lace-work upon the pale sky. The hurry of the quick waiters, the fresh faces, the endless novelty, amused him beyond measure. The "sole à la Normande," and the "caille aux feuilles de vigne," tasted a thousand times better than they had ever done in England, and the "Pommard" had in it some of the sunlight which glowed in their faces. Lewis and Mrs. Bentham laughed at Mrs. Thorpe's astonishment, for when the long garlands of lamps, which filled the foliage, began to light up, she said that it appeared to her like fairy land. As they sipped their coffee they heard the rollicking strains of a quadrille played in a neighbouring "café-chantant." Lewis proposed to take them there; but Mrs. Thorpe was a little tired, and they drove back to the hotel. When he left the ladies for the night, he stood on the Pont-Neuf. The city seemed to him like some voluptuous siren, dreaming to the strains of amorous music, and, following the simile out, he longed to place his hand on hers and lay his head a while to rest on the beautiful bosom she held to him.

Since he had been in Paris he had worked very hard. He had lived an abstemious life, and had not missed a morning at the "Beaux-Arts." In these four months of steady application he had made much progress. His fingers were clever, and learned easily what can be taught. But he now felt that he had earned his right to a holiday, and without a regret he shut up his paint box, and resolved to amuse himself.

Never, he thought, would so opportune an occasion present itself. He was in Paris, the city of pleasure, with a beautiful and fashionable woman for his friend. The word friend caused a feeling of regret and disappointment to rise through the current of his thoughts; but he consoled himself with the reflection that nobody but he knew the truth, and that the world would be more likely to take the most uncharitable view of Mrs. Bentham's conduct. The possibility of her motives being thus wrongly interpreted profoundly interested him, for the suspicion constantly haunted him, that many people fancied that he was the screen used to shelter an unknown and more favoured lover. Such false shame was essentially a part of his nature; he forgot all his benefactress had done for him, and railed against her, as deceitful, cruel, and weak minded, until at last his rambling thoughts would knock against some pleasant memory, and he would regret his baseness. Then the veil of ingratitude in which he had enveloped himself would fall from him, his eyes would fill with tears, his mind with tender souvenirs, and he would helplessly abandon himself to the poetry of his dreams.

These naturally were of the time when Mrs. Bentham would love him with a love that would be more than love, and having no work now to distract his attention, his desire took the possession of his life that water does of a sponge. It rendered him weak and inert; and, when not with her, his sole enjoyment was to wander listless about the streets, finding solitude in the most crowded places. For hours he would lean over the parapet of the Pont-Neuf watching the long line of boats slowly being hauled up with the chain, or under the green foliage, full of cooing pigeons, of the Tuileries Gardens, watch the children playing with the gravel, and the white-cuffed nurserymaids passing to and fro.

But although the past extensively occupied his thoughts, and he recalled with a sense of exquisite delight each tender word he had spoken, every kiss he had snatched, the possibility of her giving him a love more perfect, more complete, opened on his way a vision of a Paradise as infinite and delightful as ever soothed the sleep of a voluptuous lotus-eater. And the ruses he would have to employ, the pleadings he would have to make, absorbed him in an indefinite calculation where pleasure *versus* weariness, love *versus* virtue, prejudice *versus* truth, were successively pitted and loquaciously argued from their respective stand points.

They had been now just a week in Paris, but the seven days had appeared to him as seven centuries. It was not what he had expected. He had not yet found an occasion to tell Mrs. Bentham that he loved her. The word chance exasperated him, and he inwardly cursed Mrs. Thorpe—she always appeared to be with them, and asked himself feverishly, what was the use of Mrs. Bentham coming to see him in Paris if they were never to be alone. The intimacies of the first day, the drive round the lake, an involuntary pressure of hands, and a certain unconscious freedom and tenderness in the conversation, had frightened Mrs. Bentham, and while Lewis had been dreaming of his love, she had been making good resolutions and arranging a line of conduct to be pursued during the rest of their stay in Paris.

The first idea that occurred to her was to keep well behind Mrs. Thorpe, and give Lewis no opportunity of speaking with her alone. She did not reflect that this was now impossible, that three people could not spend their days together without some chance occurring which would divide them. Mrs. Bentham thought merely of saving herself, and grasped at Mrs. Thorpe's presence as the exhausted swimmer will at an overhanging willow twig. She had not been able to resist coming to Paris, but she was determined to frustrate all further temptations. It was a game of cat and mouse, and at last the turn of the latter came.

Mrs. Thorpe was confined to her room with a cold, which she declared she had caught the evening they had dined out on the grass. Mrs. Bentham had been attending to her all the afternoon, and had just come down to the drawing-room to fetch a book. She stood with it in her hand by the window. The beauty of the evening attracted her. In clear black outlines, as sharp as a dry point etching, the trees of the Orangerie and those of the Champs-Elysées were drawn upon a lemon-coloured sky, the highest points only indicated, the lower parts filled in with masses of violet shadow: the foreground of the picture was made of the grey spaces of the Place de la Concorde.

Mrs. Bentham yielded herself up to the persuasiveness of the scene, and its loveliness brought to her vague thoughts of love. Before many minutes she was thinking of Lewis: she then suddenly remembered that if she wished to act up to her resolutions, she would have to write to him at once, saying that Mrs. Thorpe was ill, and that they would not be able to dine together that day. As she was hesitating how to act, Lewis entered. Their eyes met, and not catching sight of Mrs. Thorpe, he looked round the room to assure himself of his good fortune. With a slight hesitation in his voice he asked after the old lady. Mrs. Bentham, in answer to his question, replied that Mrs. Thorpe was laid up with a cold; then the conversation awkwardly fell to the ground. After a long pause, Mrs. Bentham added:

"So you see we shall have to put up this evening with each other's company." The phrase fell from her involuntarily, although before the words had passed her lips she had an instantaneous and instinctive presentiment that she herself was leading up to the point which for the last three or four days she had been so carefully trying to avoid. But it was not her fault. For suddenly—so suddenly that she was unprepared to resist it—an immense feeling of fatigue of all things, mixed with an infinite yearning for sympathy came upon her. Lewis was not slow to avail himself of what he termed "his chance," and, putting his arm round her waist, he begged of her to kiss him. The way the request was put and a certain awkwardness in the movement recalled her to herself, and, turning, she half coldly, half laughingly answered him.

"I wonder you dare ask me such a thing; I am not in the habit of kissing people."

Lewis felt a chill rise up through him, but he said as firmly as he could:

"Why do you speak like that? You kissed me before in Claremont House, I don't see why you shouldn't do so again."

This answer somewhat embarrassed Mrs. Bentham, but she got out of her difficulty by telling him that a man should never reproach a woman with what she has done; and this led up to an interminable argument in which all sorts of questions were discussed, particularly the morality of women. On this subject Lewis held the most liberal views, and in the hope of converting Mrs. Bentham to his opinions cited many fashionable liaisons, and darkly hinted that if she did not care for him he could do nothing better than drown himself at once in the Seine.

Mrs. Bentham listened frightened to this part of the conversation, but she grew more interested when he spoke of the pleasant life they would have together in Paris, "If she would only love him just a little." His manner both charmed and softened her: she allowed him to hold her hand, and standing on the balcony in the warm twilight, they watched the sky fade, and saw the carriages pass out of the green avenue and roll swiftly across La Place de la Concorde towards the Rue Royal. Then, towards seven, the servant came to lay the cloth for dinner; but the sitting-room, with its tasteless hotel furniture, *ennuied* them, and Lewis proposed they should dine downstairs in the *salle-à-manger*. There the brilliantly-lighted room and the small white table, which only separated their faces by a few feet, amused them beyond measure. It was their first *tete-à-tete* dinner. Lewis forgot for the moment to tease her "as to when she would really love him," and they chattered of light things: of Paris; of the people about them; of the *salon;* referring, *en passant*, to how happy they were, and how nice it was to be together.

Never had Lewis appeared to her so graceful, so delightful; she forgot her doubts and fears again, and abandoned herself joyously to the pleasure of the moment. It was not until they rose from table that a shade of uncertainty crossed her thoughts. How were they, she asked herself, to pass the evening? Not surely alone up in that sitting-room?

Yet she could not send him away. That was impossible. His presence at once fascinated and oppressed her like the dream that the dreamer would willingly, but cannot for some unexplained reason, throw aside. She had told him twenty times that she thought she would have to go and sit with Mrs. Thorpe, but he had pleaded so piteously to be allowed to stay with her, that she remained uncertain. At last, ashamed of her resolution, she decided she would go out to drive. The night was fine, and the evening air would be infinitely preferable to a hot, stuffy hotel sitting-room.

Lewis had counted upon a *tete-à-tete* upstairs, but he was too wise to show his disappointment; and, drawing up close to her in the captivating ease of the victoria, he endeavoured to attune his conversation to the spirit of the hour. And what a delightful hour it was! The tepid air was as soft and luxurious as silk on their faces, and the swing of the swiftly rolling carriage treacherously rocked to quietude all uneasy thoughts. Never had Lewis felt so happy; from time to time so intense a consciousness of pleasure rose up within him, that with a sense of sweet suffocation he caught for breath. He did not look backwards or forwards; his nature allowed him the feminine luxury of burying deep his face in the present beyond reach of the past and out of sight of the future.

This precious quality, possessed by most women and by all men who exercise over others that magnetic influence called love, was in the large lips and voluptuous eyes plainly written upon Lewis's face: he was the perfect lover who could forget all but the adored mistress. To be this lover is no more in every man's power than it is to become an immortal poet; it is as difficult to command an earthly as a heavenly inspiration. This latter, however, Lewis could wholly control, and he now realized nothing but Mrs. Bentham; she was a part of him as entirely as the waves of sound floating around an instrument are the emanations of the musician's soul, and rise and fall controlled by it. Now and again a fitful thought of failure crossed his mind, but he thrust it from him with an almost savage ardour. It appeared to him impossible that fate could be so cruel as to deny him the attainment of his life's desire.

They had told the coachman to take Les Grands Boulevards, and the victoria was now passing through the wide and mournful Place Vendôme into the brilliantly-lighted Rue de la Paix. Upon a vast plain of moonlight blue sky was stretched the façade of the opera house; with its rich perspectives extending down the shadow-filled Rue Auber and Meyerbeer. On each side and atop of the highest roofs two gold figures spread their gold wings, whilst below in the blanching glow of clustering electric lights, the passers went like an endless procession of marionettes marching to the imagined strain of an invisible orchestra.

Lewis, who had till now scarcely spoken, ventured a few remarks on the beauty of the building, and they arranged to go there as soon as Mrs. Thorpe had got rid of her cold. But as they passed into the Boulevard des Italiens, they saw by the bill that *Faust* was being given that night. This coincidence interested them beyond measure; it brought to their minds a thousand pleasant remembrances, and gave them opportunities of playing and fencing with an infinite number of little reproaches and tendernesses. Then, again, they would relapse into silence, so that they might muse over the fatality that had guided them together. Mrs. Bentham had on her side forgotten all resolutions; Lewis no longer thought of himself, and both were united in the sensual moodiness of the moment.

At this hour the Boulevard was full of carriages. Crowded omnibuses, drawn by immense grey horses, often stopped the way. Now and again a victoria containing a gaudily-dressed woman, her tiny feet resting on an embroidered cushion, would speed past; the lady casting amiable glances to the right and left, until perhaps two young men would tell their coachman to touch up the high-stepping bay, and follow in the wake of the reclining beauty. Then would come a *fiacre* with a party of English tourists; three sitting down, whilst the fourth screamed at the coachman, who did not understand him. The footways, too, were encumbered with idlers come to enjoy the evening air. They crowded round the kiosques to buy the evening papers; stopped each other on the edge of the roadway, and entered the brilliantly-lighted cafés arm-in-arm. There, in the great squares of light that the glaring plate-glass windows threw over the pavement, sat groups and single figures drinking, talking, or watching the crowd as it surged past. Women, too, were not wanting, and a gleam of white petticoat or the elegancy of a lace stocking relieved the monotonous regularity of trousers and men's boots. Out of this seething mass of life the tall houses, built in huge blocks of grey stone, arose and faded into darkness, whilst the Boulevard, with its immense grey *trottoirs*, and its two interminable lines of gas-lamps running out and into a host of other lights, extended until lost in what appeared to be a piece of starry sky.

The beauty of the city acted on Mrs. Bentham and Lewis as a narcotic; and, in spirit, they had already stepped into the pleasures which Paris, in her capacity of fashionable courtesan, holds open to all comers.

The measure of expectant waltzes beat in their feet, the fumes or uncorked champagne arose to their heads, and the light wings of unkissed kisses had already touched their lips. Lewis held Mrs. Bentham's hand, and their thoughts and bodies swayed by the motion of the carriage, they watched deliciously the flashing and gleaming of the thousand lights that moved around them, seeing nothing distinctly but the round back of the coachman as he sat, his shoulders set, steering faultlessly through an almost inextricable mass of whirling wheels.

They did not awake from their reveries until they had passed into the darkness of the Boulevard St. Denis. The huge archway of the Porte St. Martin had attracted their attention; they had even attempted to criticise the style of the architecture. But now the honest plain look of the quarter proclaimed that they had passed from the regions of pleasure into those of work. The darkness and sobriety of the streets dimmed their spirits as breath dims a glass, and they told the coachman to turn and go back. The drive home was not pleasant; an irritating feeling of unrest seemed to have come over them. Lewis told Mrs. Bentham that he loved her, that her love was to him something that stretched beyond life, and that death would be powerless to extinguish. Occasionally she would lift her eyes and look at him caressingly, but her manner was vague and uncertain. Lewis noticed this, and in fear he redoubled his protestations of affection. At last, not knowing well what to do, he said:

"But is it not strange that the first opera we should hear of in Paris is the very one we sang together? I always loved the music of *Faust*, but I love it a thousand times better now, for it was in singing the page's song that I first told you I cared for you."

"I wish we could go and hear it tonight," Mrs. Bentham replied, dreamily.

The idea enchanted Lewis, and after a few moments' consultation they told the coachman to drive to the opera house, and they affectionately discussed the possibilities of getting places. When the carriage stopped before the steps they were surrounded by a crowd of *marchands de billets*, who, gesticulating wildly, told Lewis that they could sell him something. Without having very clearly understood what, he pushed past them and made his way into the vestibule. There he found the *bureau de location* shut, but after some conversation carried on in broken French with the officials he learned that every seat was let, but that he could obtain from the *marchands* tickets which would give him the right of visiting the house. He would have liked Mrs. Bentham to have heard the music, but as that, as he put it to her, was not to be, they would have to content themselves with admiring M. Baudry's decorations and M. Garnier's architecture. This Mrs. Bentham declared was all she wanted, and they passed up the staircase.

It was in light-coloured marble, and, according to Lewis, branched to the right and left as white as a woman's arms. The beauty of the place astonished them, but Lewis, not wishing to appear ignorant, argued that the whole building was wanting in style, and he compared it to a huge cake. This made Mrs. Bentham laugh, although she did not quite understand what he meant. In the *foyer*, however, the pictures interested them vastly; even Lewis, who was always disposed to find fault, found himself forced to admit that, as a decorator, Baudrie was the greatest artist of modern times; the immense amount of gold on the cornices and mouldings likewise astonished them, and they wandered until they lost themselves in the great passages which encircle the different tiers. Then they descended again to the *foyer*, and for a time it amused them to watch the fashionable crowd that talked, smiled and bowed as they walked up and down the glittering floors during the *entr'acte*.

But Mrs. Bentham and Lewis were ill at ease. The publicity and agitation of the place wearied them, and they both longed to be sitting again in the carriage under the quietude of the skies. Lewis suffered from an intense anxiety. He felt that his future prospects were to be decided that night. On one side he saw a life full of brilliant *fêtes*, women and gratified vanity; on the other, an existence clouded with misery, made wretched with heart-breaking struggles, and in the end a gradual blotting out, a trampling down by a crowd against whose force he felt he would not have the force to wrestle. Mrs. Bentham was on the contrary calm, and collected; only a slight twitching of the lips betrayed the emotion which she hid under an indifferent manner. For sometime they had been speaking of trifles, but the conversation had become more and more artificial, and at last they walked in silence.

The *entr'acte* bell had rung, and the public had made their way back to the theatre. The evening toilettes were the first to go, the morning coats still lingered. These people had come to gaze at the pictures, the gilding, the parquet floor; the opera was to them a matter of secondary importance. Nevertheless, they gradually by twos and threes wandered back to their places in the upper circle, and Mrs. Bentham and Lewis found themselves almost alone in the glittering gallery. Not a note reached them of the music that was being played deep down in the vast building. A tourist or two passed by, the white capped *ouvreuses* sat in the transparent obscurity of the circular passages or with a tinkling of keys let some late comer into a box.

At last, after a long silence, Mrs. Bentham said, "I think we have seen everything. I think we had better go, it is getting late."

To this proposition, Lewis was delighted to agree. He was sick of the place. They were not alone under these high roofs; any change could not but be for the better; but each change marked the passing of the hours, and he feared the time was now drawing nigh when he would have to bid Mrs. Bentham goodnight. This seemed to him as dark and as miserable as a sentence of death, and he thought frantically of what he should do to keep her with him. He asked himself why he had not made love to her more pointedly—he cursed himself for the want of decision he had shown, and he felt that it might turn out to be the fatal mistake of his life. Resolving, however, this time to retrieve his error, he begged of her, when she told the coachman to drive to the hotel, to take one turn in the Champs Elysées before going in. Mrs. Bentham demurred to any further delay; it was eleven o'clock, but Lewis pleaded—urging as a reason that, on her way back she could leave him at his hotel.

The excuse was a paltry one, but when hand is laid on hand and the breath of amorous words stirs the light hair on the neck, "No" is a difficult word to say. Then Lewis triumphantly gave the order: "Aux Champs-Elysées" to the coachman.

Then as the victoria whirled along the boulevards, the lovers re-found their old dreams. Overhead all was dim, the windows and roofs of the great houses were simplified by the shadows of a lowering sky to one tint; along the street there was a floating mass of light. The shops were closed, but the broad glare of the cafés and the round grey spaces thrown by the gas-lamps on the dark asphalte remained. Women's skirts flashed from shadow to light; the black body of the crowd hustled, and sometimes there was seen in the twilight of a passing brougham a man's hands raising an unshrinking face to his lips.

Ah! what was there in this beautiful city that drew beyond resistance Lewis and Mrs. Bentham together? Pleasure and light love sparkled in every ray of light, seemed blown forward by a million invisible fans, and it gushed and went up towards the stars in the foaming champagne.

GEORGE MOORE

The victoria had now passed the Madeleine. Not a glance did they bestow on the long lines of cold Greek pillars. The stately and rigid perspectives were not in harmony with their thoughts. It was a false note that jarred ever so imperceptibly. But opposite was Durand's restaurant, and Lewis watched the windows of the *cabinets parti-culiers* and a vision of Mrs. Bentham seated at supper by his side, rose to his lips. Would she accept? he asked himself frantically, and he felt in his pocket for money although he knew he had come out without any. This was terribly vexatious, and after a moment's hesitation he determined that it would look too bad to let her pay for the supper. But as they ascended the Champs-Elysées he redoubled his pleadings. His arm had slipped round her waist, and he had drawn her quite towards him. She struggled faintly, hating him for offering her a temptation which she could not combat. He strove to kiss her. Then half determined to resist, half fearing the coachman would turn round, she struggled more resolutely, but by placing his hand on the other side of her face he held her still, and put his mouth to hers. She trembled violently; consciousness slipped from her, and she clasped his lips with hers. The kiss was silent and passionate, but soon recovering herself, she, with a strong effort of will, dragged herself from him and said almost angrily:

"I wish you wouldn't Lewis—you have no right—and—" Then, words failing her, she settled her bonnet which had become disarranged in the struggle. Frightened at his own temerity, he remained quiet; his heart was full of a throbbing delight, but when he saw that she was not going to turn him out of the carriage, he attempted to renew his caresses.

"For goodness sake don't," said Mrs. Bentham, in a very low voice, "he will hear you—you are disgracing me."

Yielding to her entreaties Lewis withdrew his arm, and gazing at the round back of the coachman, they both wondered if he had heard anything. And as they mounted the long green avenue, Lewis told Mrs. Bentham again and again, how life without her would be intolerable, how he had fallen in love with her from the first hour—the first minute he had seen her. Delighted as she was at being assured of the reality of her dearest dream, she had nevertheless to beg of him to speak low. The coachman was to them a perpetual source of fear.

It was a midnight full of stars and dreams; the air was warm and tender, and in the mild and luscious light of a moon swimming up through an illimitable expanse of blue, the gardens on the right and left seemed to realise even more than their name implied. But they were not in the least Greek. They were too fantastic, too weird, too encumbered with trivial strangenesses of form and colour to be anything but modern.

Along the glancing leaves of the chestnuts were long garlands of lamps, looking like chaplets of luminous pearls; these marked the lines of the *trottoirs*: others deeply buried in the woods formed mystic circles: they were the boundaries of the different *cafés-concerts*. Above these strings and clusters of lights the foliage took a greenness as unreal as it was charming, and from time to time the gasmen with their wands bade fairyland depart, whilst a band of hunters playing their *cors de chasse* awoke unearthly echoes in the sonorous gardens.

The big round circus had long ago been closed, and it stood lonely and stupid-looking nearly opposite the Palais de l'Industrie: there a pretentious angel held out both hands as if to welcome all comers. After this came the desolate *rond point*; a dell of dark asphalte in the midst of sylvan fancies: miserable bits of dim water and gloomy avenues breaking off to the right and left. But as they passed they could see a circular archway made of glowing lamps, from which issued suddenly a tumultuous crowd of gaily dressed women. They got into the cabs noisily, sometimes with men, sometimes they drove away alone, and the plumes of their hats could be seen for a long time glimmering over the hoods of the *fiacres*. Mrs. Bentham asked Lewis what was the name of the place. He declared he didn't know, for fear she should think he had ever been there. It was the Mabille.

Mrs. Bentham now lay back in the carriage; dreamily she held Lewis's hand. She had fallen into that delicious state of semi-oblivion which drapes reality in gossamer robes, blots out the hard lines and gives to the present the languid tenderness of a well-loved recollection. Lewis was near her, his presence penetrated her with a sense of mutuality; his arm supported her, and then, mysteriously, with the softness of a warm bath, the phenomenon of the transfusion of blood was imperceptibly accomplished: their eyes gazed deeply, in each ray their souls went forth, and so was consummated the double marriage of the spirit and flesh. For a long while not a word had been spoken; they were both mad with love, the moon, and the fervour of the night. The swaying of the carriage had rocked their bodies as their thoughts to one sweet glowing sensation—a sensation that can best be described by likening it to the moment when sea and sky are united under the wings of the twilight.

But that such dreams may endure, no change must take place; the slightest shock awakes the sleeper; and when the coachman pulled his horse into a walk, Mrs. Bentham's conscience returned to her, and she saw in a moment how hopelessly she was losing herself. She begged her lover to give the order to drive home. She spoke of what Mrs. Thorpe would say if she were to hear that they had remained out till twelve o'clock. Lewis, who thought of nothing now but the time she would bid him goodnight, insisted on driving round the Arc de Triomphe. Mrs. Bentham for peace's sake yielded, and when this détour had been accomplished, they descended the avenue towards Paris.

The chaplets of lights that glowed through the leaves of the chestnut trees were now all extinguished; but Paris blazed at the bottom of the great wide road. Far away lay the Place de la Concorde, the terraces of the Orangerie—the dark running Seine with its bridges and beautiful buildings, lay extended like a lover-awaiting courtesan, and Mrs. Bentham watched the city becoming distinct as they descended the long incline. Chameleon-like it changed with every hour, now it appeared in her eyes like an infamous alcove full of shames and ignominies into which she was being dragged; she would fain have shut out the sight with her hands, she longed to fly from it; but she was whirled in a current which she could not combat, and wearily she wished to sink to sleep, and then to awake to find that all was over, that all had been decided for her.

But Lewis did not give her time to think much, for the feeling that if he did not succeed now he never would, forced him to be explicit. All hints were now laid aside; putting away the childish pretext of marriage, which he knew was impossible, he boldly urged her to be his mistress. Pleading in passionate tones he swore that no one would ever know, or even suspect their secret, that he would never cease to love her. Remembering what he had read in books, he did not neglect to assure her of the slight estcem in which virtue was held in modern society, and he insisted that it would be absurd, nay mad, of her to waste her life in remaining faithful to such a person as he had always heard Mr. Bentham described.

This led to an infinite digression; and all sorts of subjects were discussed, the injustice of the marriage laws, the certainty that, could you look into the lives of the noblest ladies, you could find lovers; and, when this was done with, the eternal question, the brevity of man's love and the durability of woman's, was anxiously argued.

Lewis talked methodically, hoping to persuade Mrs. Bentham that her life would not be worth living if she did not accept him as her lover. At last, losing all patience, he exclaimed:

"But surely you aren't going to sacrifice me for a little wretched pride! Is my love worth so little? I would give up the world for you." He whispered passionately, "You are driving me mad; I would sooner go and drown myself in the Seine than—than—lose your love," he added, seeing that another hundred yards would bring them to the door of his hotel.

But Mrs. Bentham did not look frightened; the mention of suicide did not startle her as it had Gwynnie Lloyd, and Lewis saw that the threat which he had uttered half involuntarily, half with a vague remembrance of its success on a former occasion, had in the present instance failed. Mrs. Bentham only smiled sorrowfully, laid her hand tenderly on his, and as the carriage stopped said quickly:

"Now you must bid me goodnight, I have been very good, I have driven you to your hotel."

"Oh! no—no—no—no—I cannot go in yet, I have something to say to you, let me go with you to the Hôtel Meurice and I will walk home afterwards."

Mrs. Bentham looked despairingly at the round shoulders which remained as impassive as an obelisk. The two buttons in the middle of the maroon coloured coat glistened in the light of a gas-lamp, and a fat hand held the whip as steadfastly as Osiris might the wand with which he rules the world. Lewis continued to plead, again Mrs. Bentham began to lose her head. "What was she," she asked herself, "to do?" Lewis decided the question for her by telling the coachman authoritatively to drive home. The horse sprang forward, and the protestations of affection began again. At the Hôtel Meurice, Mrs. Bentham got out of the carriage wearily, she asked Lewis if he wanted it to take him back, and on his declaring that he preferred to walk home, she sent the coachman away. Time and place were now bringing the argument to a close, although the arguers had gone back to the beginning and were again discussing the morality of the question. On the pavement's edge the lovers remained, stared at by the different people who passed into the hotel; she refusing, and he pleading to be allowed to come upstairs for a few minutes.

Lewis was worn out with fear and expectation; Mrs. Bentham was tired and heartsick. For the last four hours they had been talking, and were now apparently no nearer an agreement than before. At length, at the end of a long silence she said, and with more determination than she had hitherto shown:

"You must let me go in; what will the people think of me for remaining outside all this time?"

Twenty times he had prevented her from ringing the bell, but now before he was aware of it, she passed her arm behind him and rang. Clearly the die had been cast; the *concierge* would pull the string in a moment: they stood looking blankly at each other with disappointment written on both their faces. Then the sharp click came, the door opened, and putting out her hand, she said:

"Now you must say goodnight."

"Oh, I cannot," he replied, with the courage of despair, "do let me come upstairs, I promise—"

"No, no, it is impossible; do go away I beg of you."

Lewis still kept his hand on the door.

"If you don't go the *concierge* will come out to see what the matter is," she said with desperation.

The moment was a critical one. There was no time for further words. Mrs. Bentham pushed past him; but determined not to be beaten he followed her. It was the bravest act of his life.

XIV

A Holiday

Henceforth Lewis and Mrs. Bentham spent whole days together. They breakfasted generally at the hotel with Mrs. Thorpe; but afterwards they were free to go where they pleased. They made the most delicious excursions. They dined at St. Cloud, St. Germains, and even up in the great tree at Robinson. Encouraged by their successes, they extended their travels as far as Enghien, and in a month there was scarcely a suburb they had not explored.

The only drawback to this life of pleasure was that they could not persuade Mrs. Thorpe to accompany them to the theatres, and Mrs. Bentham did not like to go alone. But the evenings passed so stupidly in the hotel drawing-rooms, and the streets looked so bright and gay, that she found herself at last obliged to break through her scruples.

This concession opened up a new world of pleasures; and every evening they found a new place of amusement. Opposite the "Gymnase" there was a café, where everybody went to take chocolate after the theatre, and for a week they never missed going there.

Then there was the "Cascade," hidden far away in the woods of Longchamps, and they loved to drive there in the soft stillness of the summer night, and sit under the porch for an hour or so, watching the carriages arrive.

Very often they saw the same faces. There were two ladies who amused them particularly: one was fair and thin, the other stout and dark; and they spoke to a young man who drove up, sitting between a black pony and a little groom; pony, groom, and master all looking equally vicious. Then there was a *parvenu*, who spoke in a loud voice, and whose manner seemed to say, "That carriage is mine, I paid for it, and could have a dozen like it if I wanted." He was always with an old lady, plastered all over, and dressed in a very shrill dress; he seemed so proud of promenading "the old pastel," as Lewis used to call her, that Mrs. Bentham used to die with laughter when he handed her out of the carriage.

And so they idled the weeks away, until the cold skies of October brought the Parisians back to Paris, and then Mrs. Bentham and Lewis went out shopping every morning. She intended going into society that winter, and was determined that no one should reproach her with dressing like an Englishwoman.

Breakfast was no sooner finished than off they went, in the blue silk-lined brougham, all cushions and looking-glasses, scouring Paris from the Boulevard Bonne-Nouvelle to the Arc de Triomphe.

Mrs. Bentham had a hundred things to buy, to see; and, as she wanted to receive her friends, if not to give parties, it was necessary to find a furnished apartment. At last they decided on one in the Rue de Galilée.

Then Worth occupied a great deal of their time, and Lewis, whose artistic talent lay in designing, electrified that gentleman by the way he made suggestions.

One day he scored a veritable triumph: Mrs. Bentham had asked to have a court dress, expressly made for her, and they had a special appointment. Liveried footmen announced them, and they were shown through the wide, square show-rooms, into the great man's private consulting room. It was wainscotted in light oak. Worth rose from a dark green velvet divan, where he had been reclining, to receive them. At both ends of the room were two large mirrors, one that could be moved about at discretion, the other fixed into the wall; on the right was a high desk where a clerk stood waiting to take down the inspiration, as it came from the master's lips.

After a few preliminary questions, the great man said, sinking back on the green velvet divan:

"Will you kindly walk this way, so that I may catch the character of your shoulders."

Mrs. Bentham passed across the room and stopped. Worth did not speak, but motioned her with his hand to walk back again, and after some moments of deep meditation, he murmured:

"Florentine, bronze tinted, falling over a bouillonné pleating of pale moonlight blue"; then, after a pause, he added:

"The front breadths also blue, closely gathered up more than half-way down."

The inspiration seemed then to have left him, and he moved uneasily on the divan of dark green velvet. The assistant waited at his desk, pen in hand, and the silence was full of much uneasy solemnity. After some moments the master murmured about flounces, and his brow contracted like that of a poet. Mrs. Bentham and Lewis approved of the flounces, but Worth shook his head, and, with the candour of genius, admitted that there was something to be found, which for the moment he could not think of. He pulled his hair, and grew excited, but it was of no use, and he was on the point of asking Mrs. Bentham to call another day, when Lewis hinted that the top might be partially concealed by some handsome bronze and gold bead trimming.

Casting a look of undisguised admiration at Lewis, he added, with an expression of triumph:

"Forming a garland of fringed leaves."

Then three-quarters of an hour were spent in discussing the shape of the body, also in brown satin; but eventually the great man, after listening to their suggestions, decided that it was to be cut in the shape of a heart.

Since Mrs. Bentham had come to Paris, an obvious change had taken place in her character. When Mrs. Thorpe, ten years before, agreed to live with her, she found her suffering from the most intense despondency, declaring that she had neither husband nor child to care for, and that if she were a Roman Catholic she would retire to a convent.

Gradually she got over this melancholy, and her natural tastes for society came back to her; but the many friendships she had formed had added to, rather than detracted from, the reputation she had gained of being a very cold woman.

Now, all this was changed; she laughed, talked, and smiled, with the excitement of a girl of twenty, not only in manner, but in face, she seemed suddenly to have grown ten years younger. There was not a fashionable novelty she did not procure, and her bill at Worth's alone was twelve thousand francs. All her tastes seemed to have changed; she was no longer an Englishwoman, either in dress or manner; she took a prodigious interest in all that belonged to Paris; she read all the newspapers, and soon knew the names of all the actors and actresses. She loved to know the jokes of the boulevards; she learned the tunes of all the operettas. She could not remain still a minute; she became, as it were, possessed by a craving for pleasure; theatres, cafés, balls, turned in her head in a gorgeous and confused dream. Her friends were limited to three or four English families, but she soon found that in the *monde étranger à Paris* it is not only easy to make acquaintances, but impossible not to do so. Soon her salon was crowded, and she found herself adrift in that cosmopolitan element which is gradually taking Paris to itself;

and in this exotic society she and Lewis enjoyed themselves immensely. The arrival of a young man so singularly beautiful as he, was to this circle of pleasure-seeking Russian countesses, and brilliant Americans, a matter of no small interest, and invitations to dinners, balls, parties and theatres flowed in.

At first Mrs. Bentham used to dread meeting her husband. On entering a theatre, the first thing she did was to look along the lines of fauteuils to see if he were there; and, when she went to balls, she was always in a state of terror that in his cool, cynical way, he would come up and ask for a waltz, or if he might take her down to supper.

But as week after week passed, her fears wore away, and at the Marquis de Maure's ball she danced the whole evening without once looking into the corners of the rooms to see if he were watching her.

The marquise was one of her new friends; she was a great admirer of Lewis, of whom she had bought a picture. Mrs. Bentham was a little jealous of her, but that did not prevent her from enjoying herself immensely. She was beautifully dressed in clear muslin and black velvet. Never had she looked so handsome in her life; and as she passed through the groups of dress coats, all eyes followed her superb white shoulders. She danced the cotillon with Lewis, and at six in the morning they were both covered with favours; every woman had wanted to dance with him, every man with her. For both of them it had been an evening of triumph; and in the brougham, for Mrs. Bentham had offered to drive him home, they admitted that they had never enjoyed themselves better in their lives.

Mrs. Bentham was glad that she had been admired, for many reasons; and, not being a jealous woman, it flattered her to see that the man she had chosen to help was as successful in the ball-room as in the studio.

At the door of his hotel she bade Lewis goodbye. The dawn was just beginning to break, and, delightfully tired, she leaned back in the little brougham, never dreaming that the same hack cab that had followed them to the Quai Voltaire was now following her back.

The Champs-Elysées were deserted; the raw green masses of the chestnut trees grew rawer under the cold sky, and the carriages seemed like two crawling insects, lost in a wide plain of interminable grey.

As the brougham turned into the Rue Galilée, a tall thin man jumped out of the *fiacre* that could no longer keep up, paid the driver, and, catching up his long overcoat, ran at full speed up the *trottoir*.

It being no uncommon thing for two inhabitants of the same house to meet at the door, Mrs. Bentham paid no attention to the gentleman in evening dress, who walked rapidly towards her, and who followed her into the house as soon as the *concierge* pulled the latch.

They passed up the wide staircase, and it was not until she had begun to ascend the second flight of stairs that she thought of looking to see who was following her.

It was Mr. Bentham!

She gave a little scream, and leant against the marble painted wall, both hands trying to grasp the polished surface.

"Pray don't make a noise," he said in a cold, distinct voice. He then added, with a little clear laugh: "They might mistake me for your lover."

"I do not know what you mean," returned Mrs. Bentham, who, in her fright, did not catch his meaning; "but you must go; you have no right to follow me into my house."

"Perhaps not; but if you have me turned out, you shall be a free woman in a year, then you can marry him." The diffused light of the dawn came through the window over their heads, and with fatigue and fear, Mrs. Bentham's face grew ghastly on the wide marble-painted wall. The rose was faded in her hair: a few petals fell on the carpet.

"I want to speak to you about a little business; and I warn you, that if you refuse me a hearing, I shall apply at once for a divorce."

"And on what pretext?" asked Mrs. Bentham, indignantly.

"You surely don't suppose I am ignorant of Mr. Seymour's existence? Of course you are innocent," he said, interrupting Mrs. Bentham, who was going to protest; "that is not the question; I want to see you on business; will you give me half-an-hour of your time?"

"I fancied all business between us had been concluded long ago; if not, you should have applied to your solicitor."

"There are things which cannot be confided to a solicitor. Will you lead the way?"

"Why not say what you have to say to me here?"

"First, because I am tired and would like to sit down; secondly, because *cela blesserait mon amourpropre;* thirdly, because someone might come downstairs, and then you would be compromised, for I should be taken for your lover, or for another lover, and that would be too stupid. You see how careful I am of your honour."

Without answering, she went wearily upstairs. She opened the large mahogany door and passed through the ante-room into the drawing-

GEORGE MOORE

room. It was one of those large, modern French salons, with white painted walls, polished parquet, covered in the centre with a Smyrna carpet, and furnished with large armchairs and sofas, all in a rich brown yellow tint. Two large mirrors reflected the opulent ceremoniousness of this apartment, about which seemed to hang an indescribable souvenir of formal phrases.

Mrs. Bentham, broken with fatigue, threw herself down on one of the sofas. Mr. Bentham drew off his glove, and looked mockingly at his wife. After a pause, he said, very slowly and quietly:

"He's not bad looking, 'pon my word; a little effeminate, but that is the fashion, *il parait*; but I hear he costs you a great deal of money."

Insulting as were these words, the cold, sarcastic tones in which they were uttered rendered them doubly so; and Mrs. Bentham started as if he had struck her with a whip across the bare arms. Mild and motherly as her nature was, she grew red with the keenest passion, and at that moment would have given her life to trample him to death under her feet. But, catching sight of his sarcastic smile, she stopped short, and said as calmly as she could:

"If you have only come to insult me you must go, for I will not bear it."

"I congratulate you on the importation. I hear he is a great success in Paris; and that, owing to your generosity, he is enabled to make many pretty little presents to the Marquise de Maure."

"That is not true," exclaimed Mrs. Bentham, turning red for an instant, and then going back to her blank paleness. "You know—"

She did not finish the sentence, for her husband's cackling little laugh told her how she had betrayed herself. Then, losing her self-possession, she cried:

"How dare you insult me! Oh, you beast! how dare you insinuate what you do! Look here," she said, advancing towards him appealingly, "I swear to you I am as innocent now as when—"

Her husband's cackling little laugh again took the words out of her mouth, and she stopped and looked at him in amazement, as if doubtful of his human nature; then, bursting into tears, she fell across the sofa, hiding her face in her arms.

He was a tall, well-built man, with a handsome, wicked, implacable face. He was bald over both temples, and a squarecut brown beard hid the lower part of his face. The eyes were set close together, and were overshadowed by the prominent but narrow forehead and strongly marked eyebrows. His fur overcoat was open, his shirt-front glared in the grey light, and he put on his gloves as if he were vaguely thinking of going.

"My dear Lucy, I wish you would not cry in that way," he said, after a pause; "you must know that tears have no effect on me. Besides, you are delaying me—I have to talk to you about business."

The cold intonations of his voice fell into her soul like drops of iced water, and froze her passion into calm hatred.

"If you have insulted me as much as you intend to, perhaps you will tell me what you want with me?" she said, brushing her tears from off her face.

"I was about to tell you when you stopped me, and I assure you that I only asked you whether you found Mr. Seymour's friendship expensive, because I wished to lead delicately up to the subject I have come to speak to you on. It is curious," he added, as if carried away by his thoughts, "that not only are husbands more compromising but more costly than lovers in this advanced age; for, according to your own confession, you have spent a good deal of money on this young man, and since the last—well, we won't say how many years—I haven't cost you a farthing."

"Ah! so you have come to beg, have you?" said Mrs. Bentham, with the air of one who plays a trump card.

"My dear child, when will you leave off thinking me so childish?" he answered, getting up and looking at her with his hands in his pockets. "I knew it would not succeed, or I should have tried it long ago."

"Then why try it now?"

"Because now it will succeed."

"I beg your pardon, but I would sooner die than give you a penny."

"Well, if you don't mind, I'm sure I don't; but I warn you I shall have to apply for a divorce. But, by-the-way, I have not told you about it. It is the greatest joke in the world. There is a rich widow who loves me. *Je n'en puis te donner aucune idée. Elle me trouve gentil, sentimental, nous parlons toujours de choses éthérées, elle veut cueillir la petite fleur bleue, et c'est moi qu'elle a choisi pour l'aider á la chercher. Ma parole d'honneur c'est à crever de rire, tout bonnement à crever de rire; mais voyons, ne me regarde pas comme cela, je me rappelle que toi aussi tu m'as trouvé très-sentimental, autrefois. Tu ne te souviens pas quand tu me faisais la cour sur le balcon, au clair de lune.*"

Mrs. Bentham shuddered a little, and looked with a kind of mingled horror and curiosity at her husband. He seemed to live in a world beyond the atmosphere of human sentiment. "But you will not be able to obtain a divorce," she said, coldly, catching a little of his manner; "you cannot prove anything against me."

　　　　　　　　　　　　　　　GEORGE MOORE

"That I don't know; I haven't gone into the question; but I can establish the fact that you picked a young man out of the gutter; that you took him down to paint pictures for you; that you kept him there six months; and that you are now running about Paris with him, dining and even supping alone with him in cafés. I don't know whether you would like to have all this gone into, sifted and argued backwards and forwards; but if not, we had better come to some arrangement; for if we don't, I assure you I shall have to marry the widow, and to do that I must have a divorce."

"What arrangement do you propose?"

"Now, my dear Lucy, I knew we should very soon agree; we should have always agreed if it hadn't been—"

"For goodness sake, spare me your homilies!" exclaimed Mrs. Bentham.

"I am sure I don't wish to prevent you living the life that pleases you. Really, I don't see that there is any harm, so long as appearances are kept up."

"I don't care to hear your theories on the goodness and badness of things. Let me know in the fewest possible words what I can do for you."

Now that he had shown his cards, Mrs. Bentham recovered her presence of mind, and for the moment she had the advantage of him. He was obviously trying to reconcile two contradictions—to occupy a dignified position, and to demand hush money.

"Well, since you put it so plainly," he said, resorting to swaggering as a last resource, "I should like to have a thousand pounds."

"I regret to say that, for the moment, I have not so much money at the bank. Besides, I should like to know what you will do in return if I give you the sum you demand."

"You mean what will I *not* do," he replied, jeeringly.

"There is nothing to prevent your coming tomorrow and trying to extract another. No, your plan is not a good one," said Mrs. Bentham, feeling that now she had got on equal terms with him. "No; I will not give you a thousand pounds and have a sword hanging over my head; but I will give you five thousand if you will give me new reason to apply for, and will not oppose my petition for, a divorce, and then you will be free to marry whom you like."

"*Oh, très-bien, très-bien, alors tu veux te débarrasser de cette grosse bête pour prendre un petit mari qui t'aimerait toute la journée. Oh, que c'est vilain, que c'est vilain.*"

Mrs. Bentham's heart sank within her; she had hoped that he would not see through her intention. But her whole hope was in the project, and affecting indifference as well as she could, she tried to persuade him to accept her proposal.

Husband and wife stood looking at each other; they had not met for more than ten years. She was standing with one hand laid on the yellow armchair, her large pale shoulders floating as it were out of her white, cloud-like dress. Her husband looked at her steadfastly; but although his face never changed its cold, metallic expression, with a woman's instinct she guessed what was passing in his mind, and to turn the current of his thoughts, she said:

"Well, is it to be a bargain? We have no time to lose; for I do not want people to see you coming out of my house, as I cannot say you are my husband."

"You have improved," he murmured, staring at her with his glassy, fixed look. "I retract what I said just now about your personal appearance; for, 'pon my word, I am not sure that you are not a handsomer woman now—if it were not for some wrinkles round the eyes and a little puffiness about the cheeks."

"Come to the point," she answered, stamping her foot, resolved that he should not again succeed in making her lose her temper. "Will you accept my offer?"

"Well, no, I think not," he said, twirling his moustache, and trying to answer as if he were asked whether he would take port or sherry. "You see it is against my principles; I am like the virtuous woman of the nineteenth century, I never compromise myself. No, I think I would sooner stick to my first proposition—a thousand pounds."

"Well, then, I shall not give you a penny piece," she said, furious at seeing her last chance of happiness in life slipping out of her reach.

"Then it will be I who will apply for the divorce. But you had better give in, Lucy," he said, moving towards the door. "Give in," she ground her teeth at the words; but when she thought of how every fact would be distorted, of the infamous accusations he would make against her, she felt that she would have to accede to his terms.

Then, with a resolute effort to keep her temper, she said:

"And what security have I, if I give you this thousand pounds, that tomorrow you will not come and ask for another?"

"This: I'll give you my word of honour that I will in no way interfere with you, say till this day twelvemonths; we shall both then be free to enter into another engagement."

Mrs. Bentham looked at her husband at a loss to understand. He read her thoughts with a sensation of pleasure.

He was thoroughly satisfied with himself; he felt he occupied an almost unique position, that he was experiencing a rare and curious sensation, one above all the conventionalities of society, something monstrously fantastic, which not one person in a million would ever understand. He felt he had found an occasion of being more than ordinarily wicked, and he was determined not to lose it; the money was almost a secondary consideration. He looked at his wife: her ball-room beauty attracted him, and for a moment he thought it would be an end worthy of the commencement to finish up with a love scene. But on second thoughts he remembered, with regret, that he would never be able to get his wife to view it in the same light as he did, and that a quarrel would spoil the dignity of an interview which, thanks to him, had till now been strictly maintained.

"Well, my dear Lucy, then we are agreed," he said, taking up his opera hat.

"Be it so," she replied, awaking for a moment from a reverie into which she had fallen. "But you said just now that we would have to enter into another arrangement next year; how shall we meet? You cannot come to my house."

"Quite so, my dear, you did well to remind me. We are now in the beginning of March, the fifth, is it not? Yes, it is the fifth. Well, this day next year you will see an advertisement in the *Times*, which will tell you to travel by a certain train on a certain day; do so, and I will meet you further down the line, *et nous arrangerons nos affaires en chemin de fer*. But I hear a noise in the street; I must be off; will you show me the way?"

Mrs. Bentham conducted him to the door; he bowed ceremoniously, saying that the legend of the Wandering Jew and the woman would henceforth have "*une signification tout-à fait moderne*."

When the door closed, Mrs. Bentham stood staring like one in a dream. Then she traversed the drawing-room, gained her bedroom and undressed in broad day-light. She drew the curtains close, but the light came in in spite of them, and sleepless she tossed, or lay, looking blankly into the coming day.

XV

Jealousy

That morning Mrs. Bentham did not appear at breakfast; and when, late in the afternoon, she got up, it was only to lie, pale and haggard, on the sofa in her boudoir.

Mrs. Thorpe pestered her with questions, and wearied her with offers of remedies. She longed to be left alone, and refused to see anyone.

Lewis, however, insisted; and for an hour they talked together. He was very kind, very sympathetic; but, not being able to tell him what had occurred, his company irritated her, and she sent him away, on the plea that it fatigued her to talk. Fortunately she had no engagement for that evening; but, two days after, she was obliged to go to a large ball, where she had promised Lewis the cotillon.

The same people were there as at the Marquise de Maure's; everybody enjoyed themselves but she.

As the weeks went by, this feeling of dejection grew stronger instead of weaker, and she found she could not get rid of the gloom that had settled over her life. The flaring windows of the cafés, as she passed along the boulevards, now repelled instead of attracting her. She grew too tired to dress in the evening.

Even the Bois ceased to interest her, and after one turn she would tell her coachman to drive home.

At the operettas she only smiled painfully.

She had always been a little bourgeois in her tastes, and now, once awakened from her dream, all her natural instincts asserted themselves with redoubled force; the elegance and fashion around her wearied as much as it had before fascinated her. The eternal perfume of pleasure which seemed to hang round the city sickened and irritated her, and she could but long piteously for the peace and tranquillity of Claremont House.

The interview with her husband had produced a change in her feelings; had robbed her of her taste for pleasure. But this was not her only grief.

A woman is never really unhappy so long as she is sure of her lover; and Mrs. Bentham now perceived the friendship and intimacy which had existed between her and Lewis to be fast fading away. He no longer seemed to care to spend an evening alone with her, in the twilight of the spring fire-side; he now only spoke of the Marquise's portrait, which he had a commission to paint; of balls, parties, theatres, of everything except herself—all seemed changed.

She often cried bitterly, harassed by a thousand regrets and desires. In turn she impeached and defended her conduct, and, certain of nothing, suffered from a sense of discouragement, even to the point of wishing to throw herself at her husband's feet and demand forgiveness. In all sincerity, and with an earnest desire to know the truth, she would ask herself if it were her fault? If she were really to blame? Had not her desire always been to do her duty? Had she not married her husband because she loved him? Had she not gone to the altar, hoping to be a good wife to him, to make his home happy, and be a good mother to his children? And she would have done all this, she was convinced, if he had not mocked at her love and innocence, destroyed her illusions, falsified her ideas of truth and virtue, and driven her, stripped of everything, to face the world alone.

Then her thoughts turned seriously to consider the question of divorce; and she wondered if she were to offer ten thousand, instead of five, would her husband come to terms with her? But she knew very well that such hopes were vain; it was not money he wanted; it was an implacable desire to do evil that made him act as he did. Passionately she thought, by means of a divorce, of taking the world into her confidence, and explaining what her motives really were. But a moment's reflection showed her the impossibility of this; and thinking, in terror, of the brutal examination her life would be subjected to, of how those sentiments which she held the dearest would be branded not only as shameful but as ridiculous, she renounced the idea with horror.

Still, so great was her discouragement, that if Lewis had not shown himself so utterly foolish, so trivial, she would have probably made even this sacrifice for him. But, unable to restrain himself any longer, he had abandoned himself to the temptations of Parisian life, and was enjoying himself prodigiously. He got up late, breakfasted in a restaurant on the boulevards, painted in the afternoon, or paid visits, and generally had a ball or dinner party, which enabled him to pass the evening. The sparkle and effervescence of Parisian life suited him exactly. And to serve as a peg whereon to hang all manner of tinsel and firework sentiments now seemed to be his only ambition. And he realized it. He afforded the excitement of a rendezvous, of a letter to be written, of the difficulty of getting rid of someone else, of the thousand little surprises and disappointments which are as dear to the Parisians as bon-bons to children.

As he could always dine and breakfast with Mrs. Bentham and Mrs. Thorpe, he had no expenses but his room at the Hôtel Voltaire. But his money seemed to burn a hole in his pocket; he bought clothes he didn't want, particularly dressing gowns; knick-knacks in ivory, brushes, scent-bottles, and all kinds of slippers; his room was so littered with such things that the coats seemed out of place. He squandered also a great deal of money in his *menus plaisirs*, and when he got into full swing of Parisian life, it pleased him immensely to drive about in a *voiture de remise*, imitating, the *petits crevés* of Grévin. He rarely knew a lady a few days without sending her a bouquet, or a *loge* at some theatre, and in this way he got through, on an average, comfortably, forty francs a day. In a word, Paris had completely demoralized him, and he no longer knew nor cared to think where folly was leading him.

Mrs. Bentham suffered agony; but mere selfishness was not the whole cause of her grief. She determined that Lewis was to be a great artist, that she should be his protector; and that this would be her excuse, her glory, her consolation. It was therefore with anger as well as jealousy she watched the evil influence of the Marquise undermining what had been done.

She begged of him to remember that he had to work his way in life, that it was wicked of him to throw everything aside. All the arguments which people use on such occasions were without avail. He reasoned with her, told her that the Marquise had given him a commission, and that it would be absurd for him not to accept the work that was offered him, etc. The discussion was carried on day after day, until at last Mrs. Bentham saw that the only way to save him was to tell him plainly that she was leaving Paris, and leave him to decide whether he would stay, or go with them.

Lewis received the announcement with consternation, and tried vainly to persuade Mrs. Bentham to change her mind; and the giving up of all the little dinner parties that had been arranged, seemed to him too utterly cruel.

But as it had been decided that Mrs. Bentham should lend him the money to get a studio in London, his instinct of self-preservation forbade his throwing her over for the Marquise de Maure. Never had

GEORGE MOORE

he displayed, never had he felt so much sentiment; his heart felt like bursting, when, one still night, he stood on the deck and bid goodbye to *La Belle France*. He couldn't think of another phrase, and it seemed to him inexpressibly beautiful. He murmured it over and over again until Mrs. Bentham came up and spoke to him. Then he helped her to wrap a woollen shawl round her shoulders.

She told him of the magnificent artistic future he had before him; and they sat on deck till they arrived at Dover, watching the dark, wide circle of rolling waters.

XVI

SCANDAL

The bustle and excitement of looking for a studio was quite to Lewis's taste, and there was scarcely a corner of London he did not visit. But nothing pleased him. Some were too far away; some were too barn-like; some were not sufficiently private; he did not want the whole neighbourhood to know who came to see him. It seemed almost impossible to find what he wanted, and he was beginning to doubt its existence, when one day he lighted on something with which he could scarcely find a fault. It was at the end of Fulham, a cottage with a garden that an accident, in the nick of time, had preserved from the advancing ocean of brick and mortar. Like a little island it stood waiting to be swept away by the next wave of a hesitating flood. Nothing could exceed the *bourgeois* appearance of the surrounding neighbourhood. There were the usual plate glass windows, the commodious areas, the balconies supported with grey stone pillars. Orchard Cottage was its only bit of romance.

What charmed Lewis was its solitude and quaintness; a high wall shut it out from the street, and the passers could only see the top windows through some thin trees, whose overhanging branches cast their shadows on the pavement.

The doorway of Orchard Cottage was built in the form of a porch, and its little bit of front garden was concealed from the balconies on the right, and the top windows opposite, by a green-latticed verandah reaching to and resting on the boundary wall. Lewis was enchanted with the green softness of the interlacing leaves, and he thought of how he would fill it with rocking chairs and cushions, and of the delightful tea-parties he would give there.

The first floor of this quaint nook was taken up by the studio and its ante-room, the kitchen, and a small room which served as a pantry. The door on the left led to the studio, which consisted of what might be called two rooms, that is to say, there were two ceilings, one much lower than the other. The studio proper, square and lofty, reached to the roof, whose beams gave it a picturesque appearance. It was lighted by one enormous window on the north side, whilst the greater portion of the eastern wall was taken up by a gallery, some twenty feet above the eye, reached by a flight of stairs concealed in a panelled case; this was the only means of reaching the upper story, which consisted of three comfortable bed-rooms.

Next day he brought Mrs. Bentham and Mrs. Thorpe to see his treasure-trove. Mrs. Bentham found no fault, she thought it charming; but Mrs. Thorpe considered it a tumble-down old place, and was certain the walls were damp.

Lewis answered her objections, and explained his plan of making the house habitable: he would hang two large, rough serge curtains across the lower ceiling, and thus transform the second room, or alcove, into a dining-room. The staircase, which Mrs. Thorpe declared to be hideous, he proposed to cover with rose-coloured drapery tied with twisted cords; and as for the anteroom, he would arrange it with a few Japanese draperies, fans, and lamps. The place wanted a little doing up, he admitted afterwards to Mrs. Bentham, a couple of hundred pounds would, he was sure, settle all that.

During the days the workmen had it in their hands, Lewis and Mrs. Bentham ran about London from morning till night, buying furniture, and in the excitement of the perpetual discussions as to whether an oak or a black-stained cabinet would be the better, or whether a Turkish or Japanese lamp would be the more artistic, Mrs. Bentham forgot her husband and the jealousies which had so distressed her. Her only grief was that this delightful companionship would soon have to cease. It was now the beginning of April, and she felt, unless she wished to compromise herself conspicuously, she would have to leave Lewis and go and live at Claremont House, at least for a time.

And she did not come to this decision too soon, for people were already beginning to criticise her conduct; and the echoes of their words, faint and indistinct, had reached Mrs. Thorpe's ears. Unobservant as the old lady was, she could not help noticing that people smiled when Mrs. Bentham's name was mentioned, and that they invariably spoke immediately after of Mr. Seymour. Having lived all her youth in retirement, out of reach of such scandals, she did not catch the full meaning of society smiles and inuendoes; they only troubled and disturbed her. But one day a visitor called, and the servant, forgetting that Mrs. Bentham was out, showed her in, and Mrs. Thorpe had to receive her. The visitor was a Mrs. Collins, one of those women who haunt the drawing-rooms of their friends, who come at three, and remain, for no earthly reason, till half-past five; who are not clever, nor young, nor pretty, nor amusing, nor charitable; who have apparently no quality except that of an emigrant mollusc, who, having no rock of its own, sticks to everybody else's.

Mrs. Collins had long passed the age at which women are admired, and had therefore thrown herself half into the arms of religion, half into those of scandal. Her conversation invariably turned on one or the other, and she glided backwards and forwards with an eel-like dexterity. She would begin with religion, as a means of introducing scandal, and when, finding that she had gone a little too far, would cover her retreat under a fire of pious precepts, never stopping until she had clearly proved that it was only in the interest of God that she spoke of such things. Now, she had just come from Mrs. Herbert's, and as Mrs. Thorpe did not know Mrs. Herbert, Mrs. Collins had to explain: a dear, good woman, who spent her life in works of charity, who, of course, as everybody knew, had once been—well, everybody knew all about that—but, who was now trying to make amends for her past life. At first, Mrs. Collins would not admit that there was a word of truth in the accusation, and defended her friend vigorously; why, Mrs. Thorpe did not clearly understand; for, as she had never before heard of Mrs. Herbert, it was not possible she had ever, even in thought, called the purity of the poor lady's past into question.

The world, according to Mrs. Collins, was horribly unkind; and after an infinite number of digressions, she declared that no one escapes, that it was positively only the other day she heard Lady So-and-so sneering at Mrs. Bentham's friendship for Mr. Seymour.

"I just say this to show you how wicked the world is," she added, in a weak and conciliatory voice; "for of course we all know that Mrs. Bentham is actuated by the best of motives; Mr. Seymour and she have the same tastes."

Mrs. Thorpe had never heard the accusation put so plainly before, and she now determined to get to the bottom of the mystery. Leaning back in her chair, she stopped her knitting and said:

"It is very good of your friend to interest herself in Mrs. Bentham's affair; and what did she say?"

Mrs. Collins always retreated before direct questions; but, after having refreshed herself with some pious reflections, she plucked up courage, and gave an account of what society said, the sum of which, relieved of anecdotes and comments, was, that it was very foolish of

Mrs. Bentham to be seen so much with a young man so handsome, and so much younger than herself.

Mrs. Thorpe listened patiently; her crooked hands trembling a little on her black dress.

"But what do they say?" asked Mrs. Thorpe, determined to arrive at the truth.

Mrs. Collins started at the abruptness of the question, just as if her modesty had been suddenly shocked by the sight of an improper picture.

"Oh, my dear," she said, when she recovered herself, "they make no accusation; people only do that in the police courts." Mrs. Collins could not think Mrs. Thorpe anything but vilely hypocritical, and for sometime continued to preserve the demeanour of a person whose feelings have been shocked. Mrs. Thorpe was a poor hand at playing the traitor, but, unwilling to let an occasion of arriving at the exact truth escape her, she rang for some tea and pressed Mrs. Collins to stay. The conversation was then resumed on more amicable terms; and, after much difficulty, Mrs. Thorpe learned definitely that there were many people who believed Lewis Seymour to be Mrs. Bentham's lover. This was a terrible accusation, and long after Mrs. Collins had left, Mrs. Thorpe sat thinking. She did not doubt her friend's innocence for a moment, but although she hated the world for its injustice, she could not help recognising that Mrs. Bentham's conduct laid her open to suspicion. She remembered how Lewis had looked at Mrs. Bentham on such an occasion; how they often ceased talking when she appeared; a thousand little things, which at the time she had only vaguely noticed, flashed through her mind. Believe her friend guilty she could not; but after much hesitation she determined to tell Mrs. Bentham plainly what the world said, and ask her directly if it were true. She considered she was in honour bound to do this; for the very idea of remaining in the house to screen her friend's sin filled her with shame. She was harassed with doubt the whole evening; and, as the minutes slipped by, she grew so nervous that she was obliged to lay aside her knitting; she was dropping every second stitch. At last eleven o'clock came, and the two women bade Lewis goodnight, and walked upstairs to their bed-rooms.

Mrs. Thorpe's heart beat fast when Mrs. Bentham opened her door, and it was with difficulty she said:

"Let me come in, Lucy; I want to speak to you for a few minutes."

"Certainly, my dear, come in," said Mrs. Bentham. "Is it anything of importance?"

Then, in short, awkward phrases, Mrs. Thorpe related the substance of Mrs. Collins' conversation, and looked her friend gravely in the face.

Mrs. Bentham tried to laugh it off; she explained to Mrs. Thorpe how no one in society could escape the scandalmongers, and that no serious attention should be paid to their insinuations.

Mrs. Thorpe listened quietly, and it cost her an effort to continue the discussion; but, conscious of the equivocal position she was in, she felt that a straightforward answer to her question was an absolute necessity.

Both women leaned against the mantelpiece, and Mrs. Bentham absently picked the grease of the candle which stood between them, shining equally in their faces.

"But I assure you, my dear Lucy," said Mrs. Thorpe, after a pause, "that the scandal is not a vague one; they accuse you most definitely."

"Of what?" asked Mrs. Bentham, bending her head a little.

"Of being Lewis's mistress," replied Mrs. Thorpe, determinedly.

Mrs. Bentham started, and blushed violently, even her hands grew red. Had anyone else used the words, they would not have shocked her so much, but spoken by that little, thin, black-dressed woman, they seemed to take a bitter signification than they would otherwise have had.

Mrs. Thorpe noticed how her friend blushed, but she did not know whether from guilt or modesty.

"Then you want me not to see Lewis anymore, because these women are wicked enough to calumniate me?"

"Not at all," replied Mrs. Thorpe, to whom the idea of parting with Lewis was as painful as it was to Mrs. Bentham; "I only want you to say it is not true."

"Then you doubt me?"

"No, indeed, I do not, Lucy; how could I suspect you of having been so deceitful towards me?"

"Then," said Mrs. Bentham, taking her old friend's hand, "I give you my word of honour that it is not true."

"I was certain of it," exclaimed Mrs. Thorpe, with something like a flush on her wan face. And Mrs. Bentham kissed the old forehead, just on the silver hair, and the two women bade each other goodnight.

It cost Mrs. Bentham an effort to tell that lie; the words nearly suffocated her as she spoke them, and when the door closed, and she was left alone, her face contracted with an expression of pain. Hers was one of those simple, generous natures who wear their conscience upon all occasions; hers was a veritable Nessus's shirt that burned her to the bone. "Can I do nothing? Will this go on forever?" she asked herself. "Oh! how hateful! how hateful!" The life she saw before her looked like a black waste country, without trees, without flowers, made barren with the ashes of regret; without a star of hope in its murky sky, only a few lurid streaks of passion here and there. And this land she saw she would have to travel in silence, without a friend to whom she could speak of her tribulation, without a friend to murmur one word of solace in her ear. Cain-like, she saw herself forever hurrying forward holding her secret to her heart.

At that moment a whistle was heard in the street. It was the signal between her and Lewis. Grasping a chair, she stood rigid. She was determined to resist the temptation. After a pause, the whistle came again; a thousand projects flashed through her brain; she thought of calling him, of dropping him a note from the window, to explain why she could not receive him, for with a woman's instinct she imagined what his suffering would be. He would walk about the streets all night in despair; asking himself if she were going to desert him.

Circumstances can mould some characters, but it cannot break any. Mrs. Bentham had yielded to Lewis, but she was the same woman after as before. Even when her lover was by her she did not forget her own hypocrisy, when he left her she was tortured by fears, by scruples. But now the temptation to see Lewis martyrised her, and, as she listened to his footsteps dying away in the distance, her heart sank within her like a weight of lead. Everyday, every hour, forced a lie direct or indirect upon her. Give up her lover she could not, and, without that sacrifice, there seemed no help. She turned in her own shame like a captive in his dungeon. At last a thought struck her and she raised her face, radiant, from her hands. She would tell the truth to Mrs. Thorpe. She might leave her, scorn her, but never mind, she would have done the right thing. Then her heart beat lighter and her face softened with happiness, and all seemed well. She would tell her friend everything. Nothing should prevent her from doing that. So determined was she that she even considered if she would go and see Mrs. Thorpe at once. This, however, she did not do. She hesitated to awake the old woman who was doubtless now fast asleep, and next morning Lewis called before breakfast.

He was very excited and angry and he demanded authoritatively to be told why his signal was not answered last night. He affected jealousy, which, of course, delighted Mrs. Bentham, and with many supplications and beseechings the story was dragged forth piecemeal. She said she could not help herself: live to deceive her old friend she could not, would not, and the argument grew interminable. Lewis loudly protested against the dipping of his name into any such scandal. She had no more right to use his name than he had to use hers. Supposing, indeed, he was to come crying to her that he was conscience-stricken, and that he felt absolutely obliged to go and tell the whole story to one of his friends, what, he'd like to know, would she say?

Lewis thought this argument very clever, and he laughed in his sleeve at the way it discountenanced Mrs. Bentham. The discussion was then continued on other lines, tender ones, and eventually he succeeded in forcing a promise from her that she would put off her confession to a future day. Immediately after Mrs. Thorpe came downstairs, and talking of other things, they all three sat down to a pleasant breakfast.

GEORGE MOORE

XVII

WORK

A hundred dreams of success had accumulated in Lewis's mind during his long idleness, and his fingers had grown to itch for brushes and paint. He could think of nothing else, he could talk of nothing else.

While the workmen were making the necessary alterations, he strove to kill the time by buying frames, canvases, and looking for models, he was determined not to lose a moment before setting to work.

As he hunted them up in their poor lodgings, many thoughts came to him of his past life, and often as he mounted a rickety staircase, he paused at the landing, fearing to meet Gwynnie Lloyd.

He had glided into his present life feebly and inertly. At first it had shocked him to allow Mrs. Bentham to pay for his studio, but it was easy to imagine that one day he would be in a position to return her the money.

Of his genius he had no doubt. This year a picture of his had been hung in the Academy; it was a small portrait of Mrs. Bentham. One or two papers had spoken of it, and this was sufficient to confirm him in his belief that he had nothing to do but paint pictures to become an academician. He had found a tall, thin girl, with magnificent red hair, and was certain of being able to do something wonderful with her. Her image, for days, never left him; he had determined to paint her against a crimson curtain: the copper-coloured hair on a poppy red would give a vivid idea of Salome. The idea enchanted him, and he fancied (forgetting that he was only doing in red what Reginault did in yellow) that his genius was above all things surpassingly original.

The studio was perfect; the model was perfect; the canvas, six feet by four, drew the charcoal towards it like a magnet; and as for the drapery, it positively screamed crimson.

Mrs. Bentham was at Claremont House, so there was nothing to distract his attention. He ordered the model for eight o'clock precisely, and he worked till five with only an hour for lunch. He made a sketch of the head, and one of the whole figure; he had even thought of doing a life size cartoon. What he had learned at the "Beaux-Arts" enabled him to make sure of his drawing; all had been measured and plumbed, now he had only to paint the wonderful colour; and for days he strove to model the crimson tinted flesh up to the curtain. It was very difficult; but, on the whole, he was satisfied with his work, and longed to show it to someone, to discuss his intentions, to receive encouragement and advice.

He had now been out of London for a year and a half, and had lost sight of his artist friends. This was a great loss to him; for if there was one thing he needed more than another, it was sympathy. Being essentially an amateur, he required the plaudits and encouragements of eye-witnessing friends; he could not work instinctively in solitude, like the silkworm, which is the true type of the artist.

Thomson he had met once accidently, but the bitter epigrammatic Scotchman showed little disposition to renew the friendship of past years. Seeing, however, that Lewis took it to heart, Thompson promised to try to find time to look him up, and a few days after, he came, with his friend Harding to see the Salome.

Thompson looked rather disgusted at the effeminate appearance the studio presented, but admitted that the picture was better than he had expected.

Harding declared himself delighted, and, lighting a cigarette, and lying down on a large divan under the window, attempted to read the moral character of the occupant, in the external appearance of his studio.

Between ourselves and our surroundings an analogy can always be traced; but in Lewis's case this likeness was singularly marked. For between the febrile forms of beauty he strove to explain in his pictures, and his own feminine face and figure, the general arrangement and character of the furniture, down to the patchouli scented handkerchief, that cast a sharp odour through the room, there was a logical sequence that could not fail to strike so keen an observer as Harding.

"So you think that I have begun well?" said Lewis, looking at Thompson questioningly.

"It isn't bad," said the chief of "The moderns"; "but it is rather conventional."

"Conventional!" returned Lewis, aghast; "where did you ever see a nude figure done in full light before a red curtain?"

"My dear fellow, you surely don't think that originality is gained by such simple means as painting a figure against a very red curtain. I tell

GEORGE MOORE

you, you have improved, but between learning certain rules of drawing and developing originality, I assure you there is a difference."

"But tell me what it is you dislike in the picture," pleaded Lewis, who had expected that his red curtain, in daring, would have taken the wind out of Thompson's sails.

"To begin with," answered Thompson, "does it not occur to you that a woman about to dance doesn't stand in that academical pose?"

Lewis was very much disheartened; and, in despair, he asked Harding what he thought.

The novelist professed to like the picture, but he soon began to talk of Mrs. Bentham, whom he appeared to think of much more importance than the Salome. He seemed anxious to know all about the sojourn in France.

The conversation then turned on women, and Harding encouraged Lewis to recount his experiences.

Thompson was bored; but knowing that Harding was studying Lewis, as a chemist might a combination of gases, he waited patiently till the conversation changed, and Lewis asked again, what he should do with the Salome.

"Would you advise me to alter the pose of the legs?" he asked, piteously.

"No, I don't know that I would do that," replied Thompson, who had at last succeeded in getting to the door. "Try to model it a little more freely; try to draw by the character, not by the masses."

Lewis looked at his Salome, and wondered how he could model it more freely, then if it would be possible to change the legs so as to show that she was going to dance: the whole afternoon he remained a prey to the most dreadful inquietude.

Thompson's counsels were of no use to him, they merely made him discontented with his work, and did not help him to do better; and before he had seen the Scotchman half-a-dozen times, he hated his picture.

Thinking the painting too smooth, he set to work to re-do it; but in a couple of days he had lost all the modelling. The pretty legs which had so pleased him now put him into such a rage that it was with difficulty he restrained himself from kicking the canvas through. In vain he tried different kinds of execution; he painted from nature broadly, and tried to finish a piece at a time. Then he made drawings, sent his model away, and tried to copy them.

He was like a starving man led and tempted by a piece of meat that an invisible hand would not let him grasp. Often he threw down his palette, and holding his head between his hands, tried to solve the problem. He could draw a face; he could catch the movement of a figure; he could model it well enough, and yet—and yet—there was something wanted. He tried to think of new subjects, new effects, but it was of no use; his work ever remained the same, vacant, empty, common-place— he could not create.

Every generation sees the same phenomenon repeated, sees the impotent struggling for the right of creation, which nature has denied them.

In art, an original talent takes the place of the queen bee in a hive. But this simile, although a true one, is an incomplete one; for the great artist, although the king, is but the sublime child of those whom he governs; he is, in a word, the *resume* of the imperfect aspirations which preceded, which surround him; he is born in the barren womb of failure and suckled on the tears of impotence.

Thompson was this ideal, this *resume* of the spirit of his time, and his influence was extending over all; a life-giving medicine to the strong, a death-dealing poison to the weak. Lewis was an example of the latter effect, Holt, who had lately joined the ranks of "The moderns," of the former; for without having the great original talent of his master, he was strong enough to be able to reproduce what came to him at second hand, in a form sufficiently altered to be free of the plague spot of plagiarism. But although "The moderns" were now beginning to be talked of, none as yet, not even Thompson, had succeeded in gaining the ear of the general public. He and Holt had a few patrons who believed in them, the others lived poorly and wretchedly, selling their pictures occasionally, principally to old Bendish, without whom they would all have probably long ago starved.

Frazer, who was encumbered with five children and a wife, lived in a garret, unable to prostitute his talent to the public taste.

Howell had unfortunately blown his brains out in despair.

Again Lewis fell under the influence of these enthusiasts; again he fell a victim to that most terrible of maladies, the love of art for art; again he suffered the pain of the imperious want to translate his thoughts, his visions, his dreams; again he felt come over him the terrible shuddering of art, the emotion of the subject found, of the scene which became clear. He suffered all the pains of this terrible child-bearing without the

GEORGE MOORE

supreme happiness of deliverance. His pains were infinite but fruitless, for the impalpable something which tempted, tortured him, faded into nothing when he attempted to reduce the unapparent reality into apparent pictures.

One day, as he saw a dream vanishing under his hands, he threw down his brushes, and in despair went to see Thompson, to seek for advice and encouragement.

Thompson was at work on the portrait of a lady: she wore a large hat, and was placed against a light brown venetian blind: Lewis looked at it with despair in his heart. There was nothing forced, nothing eccentric about it; it did not show any desire on the part of the painter to exaggerate; it had evidently come to him quite naturally, and it was obviously a new art, an art that was the outcome of the life and thought of today.

It was drawn with the wonderful simplicity of a virgin by Raphael; the face was modelled with a mere nothing. Lewis looked at it again and again: he could not understand how it was done.

"What did you mean the other day," he said, "when you told me to draw by the character and not by the masses?"

"Did they not tell you at the 'Beaux-Arts' to draw the large masses of shadow, to decompose your picture, as it were, into so many pieces, and to construct it in that way?"

"Yes, they did; but what's the harm of that?"

"Only this, that it makes them draw all alike. No matter how different the artistic temperament, after a couple of years in the schools, every student produces the same work. The manual dexterity may vary a little, but their impression is always the same. The clavicle is in the right place; the figure is seven heads high, *ergo*, the people think it good drawing. Oh! I know their theories. What is it they say about the legs? *'Cette jambe ne porte pas,'* isn't that it?"

That night Lewis could not sleep, thinking of Thompson's portrait, and wondering how he could do something like it. He was out of bed at eight, he worked till five; then rubbed out all he had done, and walked about the streets wearied. Day after day the same struggle was continued. He turned upon his thoughts, but he felt as if he were bound and could not get free. Thompson had struck him through with an artistic aspiration, and he writhed on it like an insect on a pin.

For two months this continued, till in despair, remembering that, after all, what Thompson did found but little favour with the picture dealers, he set to work to produce work in his own style. But whether it was he had lost his hand, or whether it was that he knew more now than before, he could not say, but it appeared to him that he painted worse now than ever. Still he managed to finish a head and a small picture, then he invited the dealers to come and see them; some came but none would buy. This was the culminating point of all, for it added to the misery of desire, the fear of not being able to succeed even in the humbler walks of art. In despair he again sought the consolation of "The moderns." He frequented more than ever Thompson's studio. There he met Frazer, who still continued to paint landscapes whose austere character and unconventional handling of pigment rendered them almost unsaleable.

They were now more strange than ever, for the enthusiast, finding that some few amateurs were beginning to recognize serious merits in his works, found it necessary to hurry on a bit, so as to keep out of the crush of popular appreciation.

As he said, triumphantly, "Now they buy my early work, and I remember when it was just as much abused as what I do today. It is the old story; you paint violet this year, and they cry it down, and in three years after you find everybody painting still more violet."

Lewis met Stanley, and was very much struck by his picture of a racecourse. It showed the crowd outside the saddling paddock, with some racers walking down the course, the principal horse's head being cut in two by a long white post. It was, as Frazer said, a vigorous protest against the conventional forms of composition.

Lewis listened to their denunciations of the academical rules into which art had fallen, vaguely conscious of the truth, but quite unable to grasp the general application of the theory. He looked at the work done, and saw that, notwithstanding all its wildness, it was more interesting than the endless repetitions of the same formula which crowd yearly the walls of the academy.

He grew to love art more and more; the hollow, empty look of his own work, when compared with the high æsthetic fervour of what he had seen at Thompson's, drove him to distraction, and he racked his brain trying to think of what he should do. He neglected his drawing, as did Crossley, and sought for the sentiment of the effect; and then again he tried to draw as Thompson did, by the character, and to get rid of the mechanical method he had learned at the "Beaux-Arts."

But it was no use, he battled with his intelligence as much as he

GEORGE MOORE

could; he squeezed it, he wrenched it, but without producing one drop of the wonderful elixir—originality.

This struggle lasted nearly four months; daily his desire sought to take his mind by storm; but the walls of the mind are unscalable, and again and again he fell back exhausted. Still he felt he was not born to fail. He was right.

He had, by a moral something equal in physics to a hair's breadth, escaped Frazer's lot in life. Had he, without an immense increase of artistic power, been able to see an idea more distinctly, poverty and misery would have been his inheritance, instead of pleasure and luxury. Nay, more, had he been less cowardly, less selfish, he would have striven to bear the burden above his strength, instead of taking up the lighter one that was destined for him.

Not his good, but his bad, qualities saved him, and led him out of the labyrinth in which he had lost himself.

Sustained by the example of his friends, his weak nature had borne up bravely, but it had been strained to the uttermost, and it gave way utterly when one morning the servant brought him a letter from a dealer, saying that he could not buy a certain picture Mr. Seymour had sent him. He read the dealer's letter again, and asked himself, despairingly, what he was to do? Where was all he had learned in France? Did it count for nothing? Was it possible he could not do as well as the wretched stuff he saw in the shop-windows? Exhausted and wearied, he felt he could persevere no longer, and yearned piteously for a word of comfort, for the pressure of a hand; then he thought of Mrs. Bentham.

During the last four months he had seen very little of her; she had not come up to London very often, and he had been down only twice to Claremont House, and so tormented was he with his art-fever, that he only stayed a few days.

Indeed, he had latterly done nothing but work; it had so entirely absorbed his thoughts that he had not written to her for three weeks. He had had scarcely time to think of her, and he now started when the servant suddenly opened the door and announced her.

She was agitated; she seemed surprised at finding him alone. Lewis's silence—for they wrote to each other constantly—had at first caused her much wearying uneasiness; but as the letter-less days passed by, she began to doubt, and was soon feverish with fear.

In Paris the Marquise de Maure's flirtations had caused her some pain; but it was not till now that she knew all the terror of losing. She felt slowly, but strongly, and for the last fortnight she had seen nothing but his hands laid on other hands than hers, heard nothing but his voice speaking to phantom women, who passed in endless procession before her. For a time her pride had kept her from coming to see him, and asking for an explanation, but at last her anguish grew so poignant that she could resist no longer, and came up to London.

Her coming was a great relief, and plaintively he told her how he had tried and failed; how art had bitterly repulsed him, and at last, in a burst of hysterical passion, he threw himself into her arms and wept.

In all lives, even the humblest, there is always an hour which, like a picture or poem, stands out from the rest, because it is the hour which resumes the most completely the conflicting desires and emotions of which our lives are made. And this hour was Mrs. Bentham's. This hour when the twilight was darkening, and the figures on the easels began to look like white spots, when her lover surrendered his dreams, and came to her as a child for comfort and consolation.

When the first paroxysm of his grief was over, Lewis told her the story of the mental struggle he had gone through, and he explained how he had not only failed in attaining his ideal, but had not even succeeded in pleasing the picture dealers. He showed her the letter he had just received, and declared that the first post tomorrow morning would bring him another from Mr. Carver, refusing to take the pictures he had sent him in payment of the fifty pounds he owed him. Mrs. Bentham knew nothing about this, for Lewis had always concealed from her the details of his poverty. But now, forgetful of everything, he told her how she had saved him from suicide, how Mr. Carver had lent him fifty pounds to buy clothes to go down to Claremont House. The bill had been renewed three times; it was now a hundred and twenty, and Mr. Carver was threatening him with his solicitor.

XVIII

MOTHER AND MISTRESS

On leaving Lewis that evening, Mrs. Bentham went to call on Mr. Carver. He had left his shop, but it being no time for delaying, she drove to his private house and asked to see him. The servant showed her up to the drawing-room, a pompous room full of pictures and china, all of which, curiously enough, looked as much for sale as if they were still in the Pall Mall window.

When Mrs. Bentham called, Mr. Carver was dining in the bosom of his family; but he came upstairs with alacrity, smiling, and picking his teeth with his tongue. He was delighted to see Mrs. Bentham, he inundated her with a fluent flow of affable conversation, in which he referred to the weather, the triumph of the Tories in '74, French art, and the pleasure it gave him to hear that she was satisfied with the way Mr. Seymour had carried out her scheme of decoration.

During the course of this conversation, Mrs. Bentham, with many periphrases and comments, explained that she wished to enter into some arrangement concerning the two pictures with which Mr. Seymour proposed to repay the money he, Mr. Carver, had been good enough to advance him.

The subject was a delicate one; but Mr. Carver, seeing an opportunity of displaying his tact, helped Mrs. Bentham out of her difficulties in so skilful a manner that it seemed more a pleasure than a pain to take him into your confidence. He saw things from a wide and noble point of view, understood all the delicacies of sentiment, and was delightfully unsuspicious of the existence of baser motives. Then he referred to Lewis's talent; he explained the terrible struggle of all *débutants*; he lamented the indifference of the modern world to art, nay, the positive hatred that existed to all that appertained to art; he deplored the fact that the public would subscribe thousands of pounds for founding asylums for mad dogs, but would not give a guinea to rescue the modern Raphaels that were dying of want. According to Mr. Carver, there were hundreds of Michael Angelos and Shakespeares starving, unknown, in London garrets, waiting for the kind hand of some protector to be extended towards them.

Mr. Carver rose to the situation; and when he hinted that in giving Mr. Seymour the decorations to do, she had saved an eternal talent from an ignoble death, tears rose to her eyes, and her heart expanded with a great and ineffable tenderness.

There was a ring of truth in his words when he asked to what nobler work could a woman devote herself than thus succouring talent? He spoke so warmly and eloquently, that at last he found himself forced to apologise for the emotion he had shown. Then, throwing himself into the Napoleonic pose, he surveyed his battle-field.

Mrs. Bentham looked at him in admiration; he had stirred her to the depths of her being, and she longed, like an antique heroine, to act nobly, to succour the arts, and to save genius from extinction. She felt that these were noble things for her to do, and the only question was how to do them.

A pause had intervened, and the dealer's thoughts had gone back to his *entrée*, which was now cold; but at the sound of Mrs. Bentham's voice he resumed the pose and looked profoundly into space. Mr. Seymour's talent was thoroughly discussed. Again Mr. Carver predicted brilliant success for Lewis; he would meet with opposition at first, but such was the fate of genius.

But the inability of the public to judge between the true and the false took so long to explain that Mr. Carver gave up his dinner and made up his mind to have a hot supper at his club on the strength of these extra business hours.

However, at last, by a series of hints, he contrived to lead Mrs. Bentham up to the idea that it would be an excellent thing for her to purchase yearly eight or nine hundred pounds worth of Mr. Seymour's pictures. This would, as Mr. Carver argued, encourage him to persevere with classic art, and not prostitute himself to the public taste. Once arrived at this, a word solved the problem, and Mrs. Bentham entrusted the mission to Mr. Carver, who guaranteed that Mr. Seymour should remain ever ignorant of his unknown benefactress.

In listening to the details of Mr. Carver's projects, Mrs. Bentham saw the work of her life floating out of the mists of dreamland and taking a palpable form. Joyously she congratulated herself that after all her life would not be a useless one, that she had a mission to perform: and she resolved to perform it completely. Then her cheeks flushed with a feeling of false maternity; she thought of the duties she would have to fulfil, of the sacrifices she would have to make.

GEORGE MOORE

And in her great joy she took Mr. Carver entirely into her confidence; she did not hesitate to ask him if she could do anything else to advance Lewis's interests besides buying his pictures.

Mr. Carver reflected. Remembering he had noticed the influence of "The moderns" in Lewis's latter work, he poured forth his wrath upon them, and, as a personal favour, he begged Mrs. Bentham to do all she could to get Lewis out of their influence. He declared, with sorrow in his voice, that if he had not latterly bought pictures from Mr. Seymour, it was not because he did not believe in his talent, but because he had noticed the ruining influence of these people in his work. He, Mr. Carver, loved the beautiful, the pure; Mr. Seymour's feelings for the old Greek filled him with emotion, and it was with despair that he noticed how the young man was allowing himself to be influenced by that man Thompson, a man of talent, certainly, but quite without good taste.

Next day Mrs. Bentham asked Lewis on a visit to Claremont House. She feared it would provoke much gossip in the county, but she had made up her mind to let nothing prevent her working for his advancement. His success should be her excuse; her very life, if required, must be sacrificed; everything else was nothing in comparison; and she felt that she would not have lived in vain if she succeeded in presenting a genius to the world.

Lewis offered no opposition; he was delighted to get out of London. It had no more attractions for him; he was weary of his studio; he was sick of painting, and sighed for idleness. Even Mr. Carver's letter consenting to take his two pictures in payment of the debt, did not inspire him to persevere; and he thought of the green terrace and the leafy alleys by the river as a weary desert wanderer longs for the palms of a smiling oasis.

Mrs. Bentham told him of her scruples: she suggested he should say he had come to re-touch the decorations. Lewis, however, was of opinion that the best way to avoid suspicion would be to say that he had come to make landscape studies for his academy pictures.

A week after, when he got into the dog-cart sent to meet him at Shoreham, he ordered the servant about with a good deal of swagger. As he shouted to the gamekeeper and whipped the horse, he remembered that it was just a year since he, a poor artist that chance had saved from starvation, had come to Claremont House for the first time. He remembered how he had looked out at the park, wondering where he was going, feeling like one entering into an unknown country; now, he knew every turn; he felt as confident as if he were the owner of the estate. In his over-weening vanity he lost sight of the truth, forgot his miserable failures in painting, asked the coachman questions, and felt proud he knew the names of the horses in the stables.

Mrs. Thorpe was delighted to see him. She said he was looking very thin and worn: she reproved him for working so hard, and declared that the country air would soon put some colour into his cheeks. Mrs. Bentham had told her about "The moderns," how Mr. Carver had said that Lewis would be ruined if he were not taken out of the influence of this new school. Mrs. Thorpe listened without understanding, but she entirely agreed with Mrs. Bentham that the best and nicest possible thing to do would be to have Lewis down to stay with them.

"What does it matter what people think, when we know in our hearts we are innocent?" said the old lady, in answer to her friend's apprehensions that the county people might think it rather odd.

At this time the beauty of the country was endless, and, with a sense of infinite lassitude, Lewis sank into the arms of idleness. His struggle with his intelligence had worn him out.

There was absolutely nothing to do but to rest, to live without knowing that you were living; and the days passed like long sweet dreams. After a delicate breakfast, in a room warm with sunlight, he smoked, strolling about the grounds talking to the gardeners, asking them the most useless questions, or he followed Mrs. Bentham, teasing her with interruptions while she spoke to the housekeeper: and when ordered away, he took a book and walked in the shade of the trees by the river. There was one place he preferred above all others. A great elm lay in the water, over a bed of water-lilies, and here and there drops of sunlight fell on the brown-coloured ground. He used to sit in the branches of the tree and imagine, sometimes groups of muslin dresses, girls pic-nicing with a lot of rowing men with bare arms and throats; then, forgetting "The moderns," he thought of women bathing, some sitting in the tree talking to others in the water; then, remembering the Mediævalists, he saw a mythical arrangement, purporting to be the seduction of life by death.

As he thus regaled himself with fancies that came and went with the smoke of his havannah, he listened for steps; and when he looked up, he often saw Mrs. Bentham coming down the pathway. Sometimes she would read to him, but more often they talked; they had a thousand confidences to make, a thousand projects to discuss, and daily the secret of their love became dearer to them. They chatted of anything and nothing; things that did not interest them; of their friends, of a thousand trifles. One day she spoke of her age, and, with an apologetic air, admitted she was thirty; and at different times she related to him details of her early life, until suddenly she told him how she had met her husband in Paris. The tears started to his eyes; and Mrs. Bentham asked him if it were her fault that she had not been able to live with such a man. Then they relapsed into silence; and it often seemed to them that their happiness must last forever, so inherent was it in themselves. The silence and calm of the wood gained upon them; their thoughts passed as quietly and as lucidly as the river; and when they raised their heads they could see the blue of the sky between the tops of the trees.

He had almost forgotten, but Mrs. Bentham remembered well, that where they were passing these imperishable hours was where she had seen him talking to Lady Helen, where she had recognised for the first time that she loved him. Then, what was bitter became sweet, and she grew to love the place better for the recollection.

In the afternoons they often went out to drive, and in the evenings Lewis sat talking to the two ladies, so quiet and contented that it seemed almost impossible to believe him to be the same man whose ambition, no later than a few months ago, had seemed to be only to outdo the Parisians in frivolity.

The successes he had achieved in that siren city had for a time turned his head, and made him commit follies which had very nearly lost him Mrs. Bentham—in other words, everything he possessed in the world. His blood now ran cold when he thought of his mad acts, of the risks he had run during those last few months of Parisian life. He remembered how in those early days he was so proud of his intimacy with her that it was with the greatest difficulty he prevented himself from getting up in the middle of a ball-room before everybody and kissing her. It was only that acute sense of his own interests, which rarely left him, that had saved him from doing something of the kind. But when the Marquise de Maur took him up, he went, as it were, crazed; and had Mrs. Bentham's love not been almost as much a mother's as it was a mistress's, she would most assuredly have left him to his fate. But now all was different. He had somehow grown conscious of the golden rule, that a man who would succeed with women must of necessity be discreet. Also his recent failures in painting had, for a while at least, killed in him all ambitions, and he now only desired peace, and the continual gratification of his appetites. And Claremont House enabled him to gratify them to the top of his bent. He had become Mrs. Bentham's lover and Mrs. Thorpe's spoiled child. He could ask for nothing that was not immediately accorded to him. From morning to night, from night to morning, he was petted and adored by these two women.

Easily, and without remorse, he had accepted the position Providence had pushed him into. Besides, it appeared to him the most natural thing in the world, and he thought of the matter in this way: Mrs. Bentham loved him and he loved Mrs. Bentham; to love her he had to live her life, or give her up, and as it could not occur to him to do anything so romantic, he consented to remain the family friend. Nothing could have been more perfect than this friendship. So sure was he of his calmness, of his prudence, that he kept no watch over either his actions or his words. In the drawing-room, Mrs. Bentham was to him a woman whom he could not kiss, but to whom he owed much, whose friendship was the thing he most valued in the world, but no more.

She, on the contrary, was constantly obliged to play a a part to conceal the truth from Mrs. Thorpe. Her whole soul was bound up in Lewis. Whenever he moved her eyes followed him, her voice grew softer when she spoke to him, her manner more abandoned when he was near her. He was hers now wholly and perfectly. She possessed him beyond fear or hope. There was no one to dispute her right, she could hold his hands and kiss him, and draw him towards her in loving embraces that seemed to know no end. Lewis was her present and her future—for she had thoughts that were buried deep down in her heart—dreams that no one knew of, that no one ever looked at save herself; and, miserlike, she used to think of these dreams. They were her projects for Lewis's welfare, for Lewis's glory; and, oh, how she caressed these projects! When she was alone in the drawing-room the book would fall from her hand, and she would let her mind wander far away, allowing visions of renown and praise to rise before her. Like a fairy she would watch him, none would see her; but she would see everything, and enjoy the unutterable satisfaction of her work.

Such were Mrs. Bentham's thoughts during the summer of '73. It was the only year of happiness she had ever known. Until then her life had been full of bitter resignation; despair at being ever unable to know the world as she felt that it existed. For she had never despised the world; she had, on the contrary, longed for it with her whole heart;

until now she had seen it only as a beautiful thing that some fate had ruthlessly caricatured. But now every dream had become a reality, and for the moment that reality outshone the pale reflections she had long been watching. Now there was no happiness that was not hers. Indeed, often she had to clasp her face with her hands, for her brain swam with a joy so intense that she could not but believe that she was going mad. And if the days passed softly as fairy tales in the telling, the evenings brought delights acuter and more intense. These were the times when she waited for Lewis, when she heard his step in the passages. A hurried entrance, a kiss, and then they did not separate till the window grew grey in the dawn. These were hours of sensuality, if you will; but by Mrs. Bentham, at least, they were purified by many noble aspirations, by many imperishable confidences.

But for these hours she endured excruciating anxieties and fears. Often she said to Lewis:

"If Mrs. Thorpe should find us out, what should I do? I would sooner die than look her in the face after having so shamefully deceived her."

At these protestations Lewis used to laugh gaily. The idea of deceiving the old lady afforded him a sort of acrid satisfaction, and during the long evenings, as he watched her knitting patiently in the wicker chair, he used to experience a ferocious desire to go and whisper in her old ears: "I am going to kiss Lucy tonight when you are fast asleep in bed"; and he would try to imagine what would be the effect of the announcement upon her. It amused him to think how she would start, how she would scream.

But this was crying "wolf" when no wolf was nigh. When the danger came he did not show himself so very brave. It happened in this way. One night as he was brushing out Mrs. Bentham's hair, a step was heard in the passage. Unfortunately they had left the door ajar.

"It is Mrs. Thorpe," Mrs. Bentham whispered, turning pale.

"What shall I do?" said Lewis, looking frantically round the room. "I'll hide in the *cabinet de toilette*."

There was no time for consideration, in an instant he had disappeared; and almost at the same time Mrs. Thorpe entered.

"Oh, you are not in bed yet, Lucy?" said the old woman walking through the room.

"No; I have been reading, and—and I was now brushing my hair."

"Why, it is past twelve, my dear."

Mrs. Bentham asked herself what could have brought Mrs. Thorpe to wander about the house at that hour. "Surely," she thought, "she can't have taken the trouble to get out of her bed to tell me what o'clock it is?"

During the passing of these remarks, Mrs. Thorpe had strayed between Mrs. Bentham and the door of the *cabinet de toilette*.

"Do you know, my dear, that that stupid housemaid did not leave a drop of water in my room, and I, of course, got so thirsty—the first time in my life it ever happened to me—that I couldn't go to sleep. I have come to get a drink."

With that speech she opened the door of the *cabinet de toilette*.

"Oh, don't!" cried Mrs. Bentham.

"Why not?"

"I'll get you something from the dining-room."

"Oh, it isn't worth while, I'd sooner have a drink of water."

There were then about five-and-twenty seconds of intolerable pain. Mrs. Bentham felt as if a wheel were turning in her brain. She heard the water being poured out. There was another pause, and rigid with fear she turned to look away. But to her astonishment, Mrs. Thorpe continued speaking in her usual tone of voice. Has she then seen nothing? Mrs. Bentham asked herself; and with an effort of will she turned and said over her shoulder, "I hope you have got what you want."

"Oh, yes; but the water isn't very good. Still when you are thirsty—" A few forced remarks were interchanged, and then Mrs. Thorpe bade her friend goodnight, and went away apologising. When the door was closed Lewis entered, looking very frightened, and trailed a blue dressing-gown after him.

"She didn't see you then?" said Mrs. Bentham, almost fainting.

"No, I got into a corner and held this up before me."

"Good heavens! what an escape! Oh, what should I have done—what should I have said? And she is so good, so unsuspecting; it is shameful to deceive her as I do."

Lewis, who had now recovered his presence of mind, laughed at Lucy for her scruples, and gave a jocular account of his impressions behind the dressing-gown.

So the days passed until the first of September, and then the house filled with visitors for the shooting. All the principal county people were there. Sir John Archer, Lord Senton, Mr. Swannell (now member for the county), Lady Marion, Miss Vyner, still on the look-out for Sir John, Mr. Vyner, the Misses Davidson, Mr. Ripple, Mr. Day.

Then the routine of English country life began. At half past nine everybody met at breakfast, and the meal once over, the ladies and gentlemen separated for the day; the latter to go to the stubble-fields, the former to the drawing-room, where they sat and talked of servants, dresses, criticised the gentlemen, listening from time to time to the dull report of the guns which rang through the sultry weather. In the afternoons, the ladies walked in groups about the terraces, or, if any visitors called, strove to make up some tennis matches. Among all these petticoats Lewis spent his time very pleasantly. Fearing to make himself ridiculous, he had declined to go out shooting, much to Lord Senton's vexation, and preferred to make himself agreeable to the ladies. He was the centre of attraction. He flirted with them, wormed himself into their confidences, and had trivial little secrets and rendezvous with them all. The eldest Miss Davidson, who was more determined than ever to get married, begged of him to give her drawing lessons, and they used to go off on sketching excursions.

There was also much jealousy about Mr. Day, who invariably made the biggest bag; and, when not present, that gentleman was bitterly criticised on all sides, and his faults afforded an endless subject of conversation both in drawing and dining-room. But Mr. Day had little care for what was said about him. His mind was filled with graver considerations. He had suffered considerable losses. The Crow's Oak, a fifteen acre field, on which he had spent a hundred pounds in manure, had not yielded the crop of turnips he had expected; two or three young horses had gone wrong; and he owed Lord Senton something like five hundred pounds; consequently, his life was no longer his own. The young lord was now more than ever madly in love with Mrs. Bentham, and it was all Day could do to prevent him from being rude to Lewis. One afternoon, oppressed with jealousy, he left the shooting party and returned to see what was really happening. On entering the drawing-room, he found Lewis seated amid a circle of ladies, who were pensively listening to him discoursing on love. It so happened that Lord Senton had lately bought a picture of Boccaccio reading to a crowd of dreamy-looking women, and the resemblance between his rival and the hero of his thoughts caused him such pain that he had to leave the room.

In the evening, when the gentlemen came up from the dining-room, there was a general movement among the ladies, an almost imperceptible settling of skirts, and a dropping of previous conversations.

By general consent, a place next Miss Vyner was always left empty, and Sir John Archer never failed to take it. He sat, the whole evening, talking to her, trying to slide in a compliment or a sentimental speech between two good slices of information anent the favourites for the Leger.

Mr. Ripple and Lewis talked art with Lady Marion. The former had now, for length of hair, completely cut Lewis out, and, as he had two "pars" in the *World*, describing the shooting at Claremont House, he spoke of himself as the Sussex correspondent of the paper. He affected much pity for the county people, who, he considered, were terribly behindhand. Lady Marion and Lewis were the only two he deemed it worth his while to exchange ideas with. The Misses Davidson talked to the two young men who had come down from London, and thought it a shame Lady Marion, an old woman, should occupy the attention of Lewis and Ripple evening after evening. Mrs. Thorpe knitted in her corner, hidden between the Japanese screen and the fireplace, and listened to Mr. Swannell, who talked politics with Mr. Vyner. At another end of the room, Mrs. Bentham encouraged Lord Senton, even to the extent of walking to the window with him and discussing the moonlight.

So the evenings were spent at Claremont, until the partridges were slain. Then the party dispersed, all but Lady Marion and Ripple. Mrs. Bentham had asked them to stay, thinking that their society would be advantageous to Lewis. He had grown tired of idleness, and was busy painting a new picture in a new style.

Ripple declared that it was beautifully poetic. It represented an autumn wood; a sunset glittered at the back, and in the fading light, with entwined arms, two young girls walked, one raising her hand to catch a drifting leaf, whilst the other watched three old women raking up those already fallen to the ground.

Ripple went into fits of praise, and spent his leisure time reconstructing the descriptive paragraph he intended next year to send to the *World;* and at the end of October, Lewis took his picture up to London, intending to finish it during the winter for the Academy. The journey up to town was delightful.

Mrs. Thorpe wondered if she would be able to supply the poor children of some parish with twenty pairs of stockings, while Mrs. Bentham told Lady Marion of the house she intended to take in Princess Gate; Lewis discoursed of his picture.

GEORGE MOORE

He had already fixed upon Miss Jones, who had sat for the Salome, as the most suitable model he could have for one of the girls in his picture of autumn; and he talked perpetually with Ripple of what he would give for a lot of black wavy hair and a pair of wistful eyes. This the paragraphist promised to find him, whilst he explained the plot of a novel he contemplated writing.

The two young men had become great friends; and during the following winter they never lost an opportunity of singing each other's praises. Ripple introduced Lewis to Mr. Hilton, the chief of the Mediævalists, and daily Lewis's star rose higher in the wide skies of success.

He had now been definitely accepted by society. Every Wednesday he had a reception, and his studio was thronged with ladies and young men of poetic tastes. His pleasant manners had won him many friends; he was beginning to become the fashion. His picture of autumn was not only hung, but well hung, in the Academy; and when he drove back in the brougham with Mrs. Bentham, after the private view, he took her hand in his and kissed it reverentially.

He did not know that she had given a commission to Mr. Carver to buy his pictures; yet he couldn't but recognise her goodness. He was full of affection, and he said, trembling with emotion and with perfect sincerity:

"You are too good, too good for me; what shall I do? What can I do to compensate you for all you have done for me?"

Tears of joy welled into Mrs. Bentham's eyes, and her look was as tender as a kiss.

"You owe me nothing," she replied. "Succeed; that is all I ask; if you do, it will be a sublime recompense."

He pressed her hand, and they relapsed into silence.

XIX

Success

During the next four years Lewis basked in the sunshine of the pleasantest kind of prosperity. He was admitted by everybody, at least everybody he knew, to have talent. His pictures were about good enough to get hung at the Academy. He sold them sometimes to his friends; if he didn't, Mr. Carver bought them. But, although he by no means played the part of a hermit, he showed no disposition to throw himself recklessly into pleasure and dissipation as he had done in Paris. Now and then he lost his head, but on the whole his conduct was praiseworthy. The encouragement he received, and the certain success of his work, forced him to produce.

His friendship for Mrs. Bentham continued the same as usual. Society, having said its worst, had almost ceased to chatter; and now, when the subject was raised, she had more defenders than accusers. As people had before refused to see a possibility that she was not a guilty woman, they now declared that there was very little reason for supposing that she was not innocent. This revolution in Mrs. Bentham's favour had been accomplished imperceptibly. The leaders of fashion had not busied themselves about what they considered private affairs; and the smaller fry, who had been the most loquacious, had come to the conclusion that she gave charming parties, and that, as she had in no way compromised herself, they were bound to defend her.

Mrs. Bentham was thankful for these mercies, and continued to devote herself to Lewis's welfare. It is true that she had found he was not all she had imagined him to be, but on the whole she was satisfied. His progress, if not rapid, was continuous; and, as he was only thirty, there was no reason to despair of his becoming as great an artist as she expected—as Mr. Carver prophesied.

All her thoughts were concentrated on this; she had selected it as the aim and object of her life; and she worked for it patiently, perseveringly, and consistently. Not only did she buy his pictures, but she so contrived that her influence followed him wherever he went. She preferred the country to town, but she gave parties at Princess Gate to enable him to meet people whom it would be useful for him to know.

By a hundred devices she guided him in the choice of his friends; she deprecated their mundane life, she cautiously avoided saying anything that would turn his attention from his work; in a word, she lived exclusively for him. His life had become her life. This unity of existence was neither the result of a romantic nor sensual passion, but of a desire to love and be loved; to live to accomplish something. Her marriage had betrayed her belief in all things, outraged all her illusions; and ten weary years of a purposeless existence had forced her upon the only path that lay through the void desert of her life. She had taken it, knowing well the responsibilities, and conscious of the terrible retribution that awaited her in the future.

She had passed over many barriers, but there is one we can never remove, and daily she saw more clearly how implacably time was pushing her aside. She was still a handsome woman, but after thirty-five the years count double, and she was now forty. As she sat before her dressing table she noticed that her shoulders were beginning to lose their symmetry. She took up the comb and arranged her hair, and saw with regret how the dye had rendered it lustreless. Her complexion had faded, and the brick tints which were increasing on her forehead made her look her age. Her hands, like her face, had lost a little of their whiteness, but were still beautiful. "If I could only remain as I am!" she said to herself. "I should not mind about becoming younger." There was a deep sorrow in the simple wish, a grief known to every woman of forty.

Then Mrs. Bentham sighed heavily, for she felt that the twilight of the night that would close upon her life when she was no more than a friend to Lewis was beginning to fall.

She had been now five years his mistress. They had made an excursion to Sweden, and had visited Holland; art and nature had served in turn as mirrors wherein they had sought to reveal to each other every emotion as it wavered in their souls' depths. Apparently, they had been very happy. The old comedy of mistress and lover had been played, complete in every detail. At a certain hour, he would put down his brushes, send his model away, arrange the room, burn a pastille. Then a knock would come, a tall woman entered,—and how sweet were the first kisses through the veil! Then there was his work to be admired, and a thousand little things to be talked of. It was extraordinary how each trifle interested them. But are we not interested in things in proportion to the amount of ourselves we put into them? When dinner came up the curtains were drawn, and warm and snug amid the Japanese draperies they dined, chattering of the ball they were going to that night. Mrs. Bentham had brought a card for him.

It was an annoyance that they had then to bid each other goodbye: but it would not do to drive up to a Belgravian mansion together. Lewis arrived before her, and when her shoulders, and crossed hands holding a bouquet appeared at the door, she sought with a circular glance for her lover; then with looks of well-bred satisfaction shook hands with her hostess and friends. Half an hour after she was speaking to him.

All the pleasures of the world they had tasted, but a bitterness remained on her palate. Habit had softened her remorse, had shown her how by an effort of will to put away the painful thought that her whole life was a lie. Habit had worn a hole in her conscience through which the gall might drip away, but it had done no more. Lewis's immoral nature had not been able to corrupt her. And this was one of his greatest grievances. He could not overcome the reserve she maintained even in the most passionate moments. She was a cold woman, and had given herself more from sentiment than desire.

Without being very much in love with her, he was very fond of her, and he could marvellously well ape the affection he could not feel. "There is always the chance," he argued, "that I might not find another mistress so convenient, and nobody knows I am her 'boy.'"

And this was the reason of the discretion he had always observed concerning their liaison. He was in reality a little ashamed of her, and for worlds would not have it thought that he was the lover of so old a woman. He always dreamed of being known as the possessor of something very beautiful, very fashionable, someone at the head of society, that everybody admired; and it annoyed him that this desire remained still unrealized. Latterly this feeling had been getting stronger in his mind, and his attentions had relaxed considerably towards Mrs. Bentham. He did not, however, neglect her, as he did in Paris; there was nothing wild nor foolish now about his conduct; it was the studied indifference of the man of the world. He sometimes forgot to kiss her when she came to see him, and he passed whole days without seeing her.

Mrs. Bentham was not blind to his coldness; she felt it very keenly, but strove not to see it, not even to think of it. She knew well that her life rested with him; when he left her she would be nothing, she would have nothing to look forward to; a few miserable years, and then old age. For hours she often sat thinking of the terrible punishment that awaited her; bitterly she regretted her former monotonous life that carried no pain with it. Still it appeared to her impossible that Lewis should cease to love her, but with a sudden thought the time would seem at hand. She knew she would one day have to say goodbye to him; and daily the habit of thinking how it would come about grew upon her. They might quarrel, or she might die. This fancy pleased her inexpressibly. And now as she sat before her glass dreaming sorrowfully, idly, she saw herself holding to him a dying hand, and with dying eyes wishing him well to the last.

At that moment her maid brought her a letter, and said that Mrs. Thorpe was waiting breakfast. It was from Lady Marion. As she read the note, she seemed to despair. She read it over twice, spelling out each word slowly in her mind. "So she has come back," thought Mrs. Bentham, and she instantly remembered the flirtation by the river-side. She remembered how passionately this excitable girl had set her heart on Lewis, and how determined she seemed to win him. Like a black shadow the word marriage flitted through her reveries; and for a long time, until Mrs. Thorpe herself came to fetch her down to breakfast, she stood staring into her glass, conscious that it told her the truth as well as any magician's mirror.

XX

A London Ball Room in '78

When the Conservatives came into power in '74, Lord Granderville had been transferred from St. Petersburg to Washington. Business being urgent he had stopped but a few weeks in England, and had not returned home since. The excitement and pomp of her father's court and the sense of personal importance for a long time satisfied. Lady Helen, and it was not until the autumn of '77 that she began to sigh for the pleasures of home, for the intimacy of old associations.

Once set in motion her desires rolled fast, and the news that each mail brought of English fêtes and festivities contributed to increase her weariness of America. The glittering descriptions fired her with the desire to know this new London, resplendent with professional beauties and dreaming æsthetes—the name by which the Mediævalists were now known. She longed to mix in the conflict, every moment she remained out of this flaming centre of modern desire and thought seemed to her so much of her life lost. It was the time when the government of Lord Beaconsfield like a king star was waxing daily brighter in the heaven of glory, just before the fanfares of the Treaty of Berlin echoed triumphantly through all hearts, hushing even the discontented and distrusting Liberals.

Never had London seen more wonderful fêtes; never even in the old monarchical ages had so many crowned heads passed along the banks of the Thames; for years never had the aristocracy so thoroughly dominated the people: never had the daughters of the cotton-spinners been so anxious to exchange their wealth for the honour of an escutcheon.

A general sense of intoxication seemed to have risen like a mist, and to have penetrated even into the sternest hearts. Women almost ceased to take the trouble to conceal their intrigues: husbands were quickly found who did not mind their wives being written about and photographed for public sale. The trade in beauty waxed high; the wives of unknown county gentlemen were suddenly, in the space of a season, the notorieties of the palace and park. The presents they received were openly discussed in every drawing-room, and the sonnets of a third rate poet proclaimed their beauty to the world.

GEORGE MOORE

Every age is remembered by a word. To organise represents the fugitive empire founded by Napoleon; and Lord Beaconsfield's government will be remembered by the professional beauty of whom it is the eternal apotheosis.

Never for years had women been so powerful; never had their influence been so manifest; it was no longer an occult force, they openly made and ruined reputations. An echo of the moral tone of the court of Louis XV had passed over the upper air of English life. Married women had gradually begun to oust young girls out of rights they had always held. And this was productive of a terrible demoralisation; for the young girls were forced either to give up the liberties they owned, and charge their families with the task of finding them suitable husbands, or to compete with married women in looseness of morals.

Naturally, their first impulse was to adopt the latter means; and it is impossible to say where and how the struggle would have ended if, with the triumph of the Liberals in '80, things had not gone back to their normal condition. Probably, the general profligacy that would have ensued would have forced the French system upon English society, and the young girl would have become the nonentity in England that she is in Paris.

Lady Helen knew she was a beautiful woman, and the accounts that reached her weekly of the triumphs of her sex filled her with enthusiasm, and all her artistic sympathies awakened at the stories she heard of the æsthetes. Day passed after day, but Lady Granderville refused positively to accompany her daughter. At last Lady Helen's health began to suffer from intense home sickness, and it was arranged that she should pass a year with Lady Marion, who offered to chaperone her. The voyage was tedious, but the sea breezes and the certainty that her arrival in London was only a question of days, put fair roses in her cheeks, and when she rushed upstairs to her aunt's house in Queen Street, she was an ideal of health and beauty.

Aunt and niece were the greatest friends, and the girl kissed and questioned Lady Marion tumultuously. As she stepped forward she saw Mrs. Bentham's invitation on the table, and instantly her thoughts went back to the tennis party.

Five years is a long time. She now remembered Lewis but dimly, yet the flirtation by the river remained still the most sentimental of her remembrances. Time had at once effaced and etherealised the memory, till she could not separate it from an abstract ideal at whose shrine she laid the poetry of her heart. She did not analyse her feelings, but she knew she would like to see him again, and she listened, deeply interested, when Lady Marion told her how he had got on; how he was now a fashionable painter.

For the next week Lady Helen's time was completely taken up in discussing the making of her dress, wondering how handsome was the great professional beauty, Mrs. Campbell Ward, whom her uncle, Lord Worthing, so much admired; thinking of Lewis, boring her aunt to explain the artistic formula of the æsthetes, and trying to compose a sonnet in accordance with it.

At last the evening came, and her heart beat as they traversed the immense vestibule, almost chapel-like in its silence, of Princess Gate, and ascended the staircase. It was in grey stone, lined with double balustrades branching to the right and left of a large mirror, and leading to a gallery encircling the first landing.

As Lady Helen walked up the long carpet of the stairs, voluptuously soft beneath her feet, she saw herself rising out of the glass. She looked at her arms and shoulders, and wondered whether any of the beauties she had heard so much of were whiter than she.

She was really divine. Upon a white tulle skirt garnished behind with a flow of flounces, she wore a body of green satin bordered with English lace; a single flounce completed the front of her dress, which was trimmed with bunches and garlands of ivy. The body was cut low, and showed her immaculately white shoulders, now entirely developed and full of exquisite plenitudes and undulating lines. The roundness of her neck, and the richness of her golden hair, which on the neck faded to a saffron tint, and the supple swing of her figure made a complete picture of loveliness.

The servant stood on the left hand as they mounted, and shouted their names.

Mrs. Bentham leaned against the balustrade opposite the door of the drawing-room. She was dressed in pink, and held a large bouquet of white flowers in her hand.

The two women looked at each other. Lady Helen thought that Mrs. Bentham had gone off terribly since she had seen her. Mrs. Bentham saw that Lady Helen was a dream of beauty, and she shivered from a feeling of indefinite apprehension. Lady Helen and her aunt passed into the first room: it was lined with pictures and women. On the right stood a group of men. Lord Senton's narrow head, just covered with thin, fair hair, and Mr. Swannell's large, bald crown, attracted the eye. A waltz was being played. Guests continued to come up the stairs, and the room was filling rapidly with clear toilettes and black coats.

"By Jove, that's Lady Helen; she's come back from Washington," said Lord Senton, disentangling himself from the group round the doorway. "I'll ask her for this dance."

Lady Helen took his arm, and they pushed their way into the dancing-room. Lady Marion seeing an empty place near Lady Archer, sat down by her. Mr. Vyner's dream had been realised, but he still continued, from force of habit, to watch his daughter.

"Did you ever see such skin?" said Day, speaking of Lady Helen; "she's like milk."

"Very Greek, is it not?" replied Ripple, making for Lady Marion, with whom he had resolved to sit until Lady Helen came back. The Sussex families generally tried to come up to town for Mrs. Bentham's ball; and, sitting in symmetrical rows, were the same people who had been at the tennis party five years ago at Claremont House.

There were the Misses Davidson, in blue, chaperoned by Lady Archer; and Mrs. French, who was bringing out another daughter.

The tennis player was still to the fore, but Miss Fanshaw, her former rival, had changed her name to Cooper, and they made quite a little party, led by Mrs. Swannell, the wife of the member for the county.

Mrs. Bentham had moved away from the door, and, surrounded by smiling faces and a murmur of amiable words, was talking to her intimate friends. Most of the people had arrived, but as she was expecting two important guests, Lord Worthing and Mrs. Campbell Ward, the professional beauty, she had not ventured to mix with the dancers.

Mrs. Ward never appeared at a ball till about one, and she always left before three, remaining only for its summer-time. Her husband was poor and vulgar, but he had the tact to keep out of the way until he was wanted to repress a scandal.

"Mrs. Campbell Ward," shouted the servant, and Mrs. Bentham turned to welcome a tall, large woman, with brown hair, dyed sufficiently to give it a golden tinge. She took an offered arm and her husband glided away.

At this moment the shrill notes of the cornet pierced through the softer sound of the fiddles, then half-a-dozen clear notes from the clarionet, a clashing of cymbals, and then the strings, wood, brass, and drums, finished the last phrase of a waltz.

No sooner had the music ceased than a crowd of black coats and white shoulders entered, and the quick movement of the fans wafted forwards an odour of shoulders and sachet-scented pocket handkerchiefs. The delicate profiles of young girls contrasted with the heavy faces of the parents, and the words "ices" and "heat" were heard recurring constantly.

As the dancers perceived Mrs. Campbell Ward, there was a slight hush; the men looked admiringly at her face and arms, the women examined her dress. Then, leaving a wake of black coats behind her, came Lady Helen, obviously the most beautiful woman in the room. Mrs. Ward gave her a look expressive both of fear and admiration, and she went off to dance with Lord Senton, whose vanity and silliness interested her. The room was again pretty clear. Lewis stood talking to a group of artists. He was asking their opinion of his full length portrait of Mrs. Bentham, which hung at the other end of the room. Mr. Hilton praised it unreservedly, but Mr. Holt, who was supposed to have some sympathies with "The moderns," was finding fault. The Misses Davidson were sitting underneath the picture, and he used their shoulders to explain his meaning.

"Just look, Seymour, at the subtlety of modelling there is in that girl's bosom. You can't see the face, and yet it is like her; the neck is half tint, and all the light is concentrated on the shoulders; by Jove, how wonderful it is! Now, on your bosom there is—"

Lewis was much interested in the conversation, but, recognising Lady Helen, he rushed off to ask her for a dance, leaving Holt to explain his theories to a young gentleman of artistic tastes, who was listening in the hope of carrying away some of the expressions.

The Misses Davidson, seeing that the men at the other end of the room were looking in their direction, began to feel flattered.

"I wonder what they are saying about us," asked the younger.

"Oh, they are not talking about us," exclaimed Miss French, pettishly; "they are only speaking of their horrible painting. I wish men would not come to balls who don't dance."

Miss Davidson was disappointed, but she felt that it was only too possibly the truth: and with a sigh she said:

"I think it very unfair to ask people to balls and not introduce them; there are lots of nice men here I should like to know."

"As for me, I never bored myself so much in my life," whimpered a young lady in white, who had not yet danced. "It is quite sickening to listen to those men talking politics." This last remark referred to a group of grave men collected in the doorway opposite to where the artists were standing. Lord Worthing, while waiting for Mrs. Campbell Ward, had consented to discuss the affairs of the nation. His remarks were received with great attention. Mr. Swannell, from time to time, made large and unctuous signs of assent, but did not speak until the peer said the difference that would eternally separate Liberal and Conservative governments was the fact that "*we always have and always will teach men to respect their honour before their money.*" Mr. Swannel shut his eyes, as if to appreciate more entirely the delicacy of the aphorism: he declared it ought to be sent to the newspapers.

At this moment Mr. Campbell Ward came from the cardroom. He wore a vexed and embarrassed air, and he asked Lord Worthing if he could speak to him for a few seconds.

"Certainly," replied Lord Worthing; and husband and admirer walked away together.

In the meanwhile Lewis had been enjoying himself immensely. He had been waltzing with Lady Helen, and had attracted much attention. They were delighted to sec one another, and they both remembered all about the tennis party. Lady Helen told him how she had bored herself in America; how glad she was to get home: she questioned him about the æsthetes and his painting.

They were now sitting by Lady Marion. She was talking with a Mr. Liston, a very handsome but grave man, who wrote on the domestic life of the Egyptians. He never danced, but his wife, who was supposed to be a little mad, did, and wildly. So the poor man was enabled to save the midnight oil, and, in the corner of a ball-room, he ruminated over the problems of the past, while Mrs. Liston careered wildly with all the young men in London over the parquet. She was now looking languidly at Lewis, but Mrs. Collins said it was an unrequited affection.

He not being engaged (a dancer had just come to claim Lady Helen), looked round the room to see whom he would ask. Mrs. Bentham, leaving a group of men, called him.

"Are you engaged for this dance?"

"No, I am not," he replied, timidly.

"Then dance it with me," she said, taking his arm, and they went into the ball-room.

"She keeps her puppy well chained up," said Day to Ripple as he passed. Ripple affected not to understand him, and passed on towards the group of artists, who still stood about the doorway.

The appearance of Mrs. Bentham on Lewis's arm brought the conversation back to the point from whence it had strayed, and the young gentleman with artistic tastes asked Mr. Hilton if he thought Mr. Seymour had much talent.

"Talent! Good Heavens!" broke in Mr. Holt; "just look at that portrait up there! Nasty, greasy, sickly, slimy thing!"

"I can't see that it is a bad picture," answered Mr. Ripple, who defended his friend on all occasions; "because the dress is carefully painted, and the rules of art are not openly defied."

This aroused Mr. Hilton from the torpor into which he had fallen, and he hastened to say a word in defence of his principles.

"I, for my part, quite agree with Mr. Ripple; I deprecate this outcry against the traditions. You will never succeed in proving to me that it shows great talent to disturb the whole balance of a composition by leaving one leg of a retreating figure in the picture; it is original, if you like, but it is an originality that the merest tyro can obtain. Now, I don't mean to say that that portrait is a *chef d'œuvre*, but it is fairly well drawn and modelled, and those are qualities far harder to attain than those you mention."

Mr. Holt was dying to reply, but he thought it would be better not to contradict the academician, and Ripple, enchanted at the acceptance his views had received, was preparing a further development of his theories, when the young gentleman, his friend with the budding artistic taste, said:

"Besides, I hear that Mr. Seymour makes at the rate of two thousand a year."

Nobody answered for a moment, and the young gentleman opened his blue eyes in surprise at the embarrassment he had created. Mr. Ripple looked grave as if an accident had happened, but Mr. Holt, unable to resist the temptation, exclaimed, brutally, that there was no reason why he should not make ten, that it was merely a question of women.

Mr. Hilton said nothing, but being a family man would have preferred that Mr. Holt had put his accusation more delicately.

The conversation then turned upon women, and the question of morality was ardently discussed.

Mr. Hilton believed implicitly in the virtue of all women, at least of those in good society. Mr. Ripple, who was anxious not to have it supposed that he lived a totally loveless life, smiled at this general statement, but defended Mrs. Bentham's honour. As for Mr. Holt, he shrugged his shoulders, and wondering that such credulity could exist, went to look after a partner.

The waltz was just finishing, and a crowd of perspiring dancers passed from the ball to the card-room. Mrs. Bentham was on Lewis's arm. Without knowing why, she suspected that the people about were talking of her; but she did not care, and looked to the left and right defiantly. She longed for something to happen, and vainly tried to assure herself that there was no reason for supposing that Lewis and Lady Helen were going to fall in love with each other. Her excitement was not lost upon Mr. Day, and he went over to where Lord Senton was talking with a thick-set man, who generally spoke of thrashing someone.

"There will be a row tonight," said Day; "he's engaged for the next waltz to Lady Hellen."

"I can't see," murmured Lord Senton between his decayed teeth, "what women like in him; I wonder why Lady Marion allows Lady Helen to dance with him, the effeminate brute, how I should like to kick him!"

The thick-set man grew interested at once, and offered much advice as to how it was to be done. They were joined by their old pal, Sir John, who, having escaped from the eyes of his father-in-law, ventured to ask them to come down to supper. Watching Mrs. Bentham till she passed into the card-room, they assented, and then the four men went downstairs together.

The card and lounging-room was a spacious place hung with dark red curtains, full of low sofas and arm-chairs, and soft shadow. Here and there clear dresses and white shirt fronts glimmered in the purple gloom, and as the whist players raised their heads to play, the lamplight fell on their faces.

"Let us sit down here," said Mrs. Bentham; "are you engaged for this next waltz?"

"Well, I am," replied Lewis, hesitating, and colouring slightly.

"To whom?"

Feeling afraid that she would object to his dancing with Lady Helen, for with the instinct of a woman he guessed that Mrs. Bentham was jealous, and wishing to avoid a discussion, he boldly answered that he was engaged to Miss Davidson.

"Oh, very well then, we'll dance together later on."

"You don't mind?"

"Not in the least; what right have I to mind; you are your own master."

"Well, don't be cross; if you don't like, I won't dance with her," he replied, knowing very well that she didn't care how much he danced with Miss Davidson.

At this moment the music began, and Mrs. Bentham went to talk to Mrs. Campbell Ward and Lord Worthing, who were thinking of going.

Lewis hurried away assuring himself that Lucy might not give it another thought, and that it was ten chances to one she would be detained and would not be able to get near the ballroom. He found Lady Helen waiting for him; the two went off to dance together in almost infantile glee. Lewis was completely under the charm of her beauty. Till now, he had never desired anything but faintly; and this was the first time he had ever been able to particularise a passion. Lady Helen, he had remembered as something extraordinarily white, with saffron coloured hair, and as his recollection of her grew fainter, she had passed into his mind as a type of beauty, the queen of all the blonde phantoms that peopled his dreams. He thought sometimes of the flirtation by the river, in the tepid silence of the woods, and it had remained a bit of purity and grace that the ever recurring tendernesses and treasons which made up the tenor of his life had not been able to destroy.

As they glided over the floor, they passed Miss Davidson, who whispered to her partner, as she danced. They bumped up against Lady Archer, who was going at a prodigious rate; exchanged words with the Misses Sedgwick, Lady Helen's cousins; passed by a number of unknown faces, and then came back to the window to rest.

Mrs. Bentham did not believe Lewis when he said he was going to dance with Miss Davidson. She felt sure he was engaged to Lady Helen, and she resolved to watch. But, fortunately for the lovers, Mrs. Campbell Ward could not be persuaded to stay a moment longer, and as the supper rooms were not yet open, Mrs. Bentham had to go down with them, and when at last, wearied out, she got back to the ball-room, the waltz was over.

Nervous and irritated, but determined to find Lewis, she walked to and fro. Constantly she was stopped by young men who thought it their duty to bore her for a dance, and by women who murmured their teasing common-places.

Never had fashionable life appeared to her so insupportable; the soft, fussy ways of those who spoke to her, and the necessity of answering them politely, provoked her beyond endurance. Getting rid of one with

GEORGE MOORE

a yes, the other with a no, and a third with a mechanical smile, she pressed through a group of black coats that blocked the doorway.

Mrs. Collins was talking to Mrs. Thorpe, and Mrs. Bentham tried to escape, but Lady Marion called her, and asked her if she had seen Lady Helen. The old lady was enjoying herself immensely, and in the excitement of her many conversations had forgotten all about her niece. She had had a long political argument, a literary discussion, and was now contesting the origin of the Irish castles with a man who for many years had given it out that he was writing a book on the subject.

Trembling under Mrs. Collin's searching gaze, Mrs. Bentham said she had not seen Lady Helen, and escaped into the cardroom.

But Lewis was not there, and a whist party that had just risen detained her a long while with the most useless and inane remarks. Then she got caught in a crowd of dancers who were going towards the supper rooms, and, thinking he might be downstairs, she determined to follow. But to do this she had to get a partner, and going back to where Lady Marion was sitting, she looked around the group to see who would be easiest to get rid of if the occasion required. Finally she decided on a very young man who was waiting for an opening to say that he was of opinion that Swinburne was a greater poet than Tennyson.

"Have you been down to supper, Lady Marion?" she said, trying to smile.

Lady Marion replied that she had not, whereupon the poetically inclined young man at once put himself forward; but the antiquarian, remembering an argument that he thought would tell against Lady Marion's theory of the Irish castles, offered his arm, and Mrs. Bentham was left to the Swinburnite.

The staircase was full of clear dresses and black coats, which passed up and down, looking at themselves in the huge mirror. Mrs. Bentham, fearing she was betraying her emotion, tried vainly to answer her partner's questions. As they crossed the tessellated pavement of the large hall, with its high pillars supporting the gallery overhead, the sounds of the music died away in the clatter of the knives and forks.

The supper room was on the right; an immense square, wainscotted as high as the doors in oak, with pilasters dividing the walls; dark green velvet curtains, hanging from massive gold cornices, concentrated all the light upon the table covered with flowers, silver, and cold meats.

Mrs. Bentham could not see at once if Lewis was there; lines of black coats and white shoulders intercepted the view. At this end of the table

Mr. Ripple continued to explain to Mrs. Liston that a married woman was not obliged to love her husband after—he added ingeniously—the third year. His argument did not appear to interest Mrs. Liston, who, probably, had long ago made up her mind on the subject; anyhow, she constantly interrupted him with questions about Lewis, and demands for an infinite variety of eatables. Animal instincts were everywhere visible. Old ladies, with lumpy shoulders, attended by young men, were making up for many hours of misery by gratifying the last passion that remained to them: groups of middle-aged men wearily talked politics, thinking of what they should eat when the ladies were gone.

The noise was a long continuous murmur, punctuated by the popping of champagne corks. Men of all kinds called to servants, who were beginning to lose their heads, for "paté de foie gras," "salmi de pleuvier doré," ham, cutlets, cream, and jelly.

The Misses Davidson, the Misses French, and others had managed to get introduced to some men, with whom they spoke of the floor, the music, the weather, and the last plays, novels, and race meetings.

Mrs. Bentham, under the pretext of looking for a place, passed from where Mr. Ripple sat with Mrs. Liston to the far corner, where a cluster of black coats were supping together.

"I'll tell you what," mumbled Sir John, his lips full of salad; "there's a girl here, a Miss Harrison, I don't know who she is, but upon my soul—" Sir John had to stop to swallow the salad.

"I know who you mean," said the man next him; "never saw such shoulders in my life—splendid."

The two men looked at each other contemplative; and Lord Senton begged to have the young lady pointed out to him.

"Look, look," whispered Day, who was a little drunk, "'pon my soul it is as good as a play to watch the old girl."

"What's as good as a play?" replied Senton, who sat moodily sipping his champagne.

"Why, look at dear Lucy, who has come to look after her chicken. Here's to her jolly good health," he added, lifting his glass. The toast was drunk rapturously.

"Just look," said Day, staring vaguely; "she wont stay; he isn't here, is he? Haven't seen him."

"Bet you a fiver she won't stay if he isn't here," whispered one.

"Done," said Lord Senton, and, holding full glasses of champagne, they watched to see what Mrs. Bentham would do.

Having satisfied herself that Lewis was not there, she was burning to get away, but her partner was so pressing that, fearing he would think it strange, she sat down, and he got her some jelly and a glass of champagne.

"I have won," exclaimed Lord Senton, gladly, and he pocketed the five sovereigns.

"But surely you don't believe it is true?" asked Sir John, who was just beginning to remember that his wife was the intimate friend of the lady upon whose virtue they were betting.

"My dear fellow!" replied Day, shrugging his shoulders.

"I am sure, I don't know what you mean," exclaimed Lord Senton, who began to think that, true or false, it was a great piece of impertinence of a man who was only a Scotch farmer to dare to pass judgment on a county family. However, Day eventually apologised, and the conversation then fell into a long discussion on the morality of women.

Mrs. Bentham drank a little champagne, and asked the young gentleman, who insisted upon explaining to her why he thought Swinburne a greater poet than Tennyson, to take her upstairs. On passing into the hall, they met Mr. Holt and Mr. Hilton, whose insatiable desire to talk of painting had brought them together again. Mr. Holt was enthusiastic on the subject of the ball. Never had he seen anything so artistically fashionable, and, forgetful of Mr. Hilton, he declared that the staircase would make a wonderful picture.

On both sides were huge majolica vases, filled with rare plants; two bronze Venuses upheld magnificent candelabras, set with five burners, whose bright light was softened by coloured globes, and the crowd, superb and smiling, descended into, and rose out of, the mirror, the women white and delicate, the men with quick looks, and the movements of lovers talking of love. Mrs. Bentham hated them, their smiles, their polite manners, their laughter; and in the bitterness of her despair, the whole scene appeared to her as something scarcely more serious than a toy, a marvellous toy, most ingeniously contrived, but only a toy after all.

Most of the dancers had now come up from supper; the ball was at its height. The band played a favourite quadrille, and all were dancing with the fumes of champagne in their heads.

The different couples rocked a little as they advanced up and down. The different costumes came and went in a confusion of bright stuffs;

the rhythm, after having mixed and carried away the colours, suddenly brought back on certain notes the same rose satin skirt, the same blue velvet bodice, next the same black coats. Then, like a shower of fireworks, they all disappeared up the room, and so on hour after hour.

Leaving the dancers, Mrs. Bentham passed along the picture gallery, and searched the windows of the card-room, and then the boudoir at the back, but they were not there. She was now at the end of her patience, and her nervousness and agitation had turned into a sullen anger. Fortunately, the couples seated round the card-room were too occupied to notice her. Her lips and hands moved nervously, and she thought of telling Lady Marion that her niece had disappeared.

She had lost her head; was beside herself with mingled suspense and passion. After a pause she went hesitatingly out of the card-room, towards the gallery, encircling the head of the stairs. The upper parts were reached by two small staircases, one on each side of the stair gallery, and united overhead by a long passage; they were partially hidden by large hanging draperies.

Surely, she thought, they cannot be sitting up there alone, she would not be mad enough to do such a thing. Then, almost frantic with jealousy, she determined to see, and, bending under the curtain, went up the stairs. But they were not there; she stopped for a moment puzzled, then passed along the passage by her room, from whence came a faint odour of verveine, and prepared to descend to the ball-room by the other end.

Hearing the sound of voices, she stopped, and, descending a few steps, she looked over the bannisters, and saw Lewis sitting with Lady Helen.

After the waltz, with one accord, they had sought a quiet place where they could talk; they were both dying to be alone. Lord Senton had chased them from the balcony, they had tried the boudoir, the windows in the card-room, but couples as sentimentally inclined as themselves were already in possession of every available space. At last they had sat down in a far corner, but malicious Mr. Day, under the pretence of flirting with a little girl in pink, had taken the places behind them, and they had been obliged to talk of the weather, and the floor.

This was very annoying, and after a few minutes Lady Helen had proposed to go back to the dancing-room. But as they passed the staircase the temptation was irresistible; it looked so cool and cosy, with its deliciously soft carpet, that Lady Helen could not resist suggesting that they should sit there. She knew it was an imprudence, but she felt she could not waste her life thinking of proprieties. So they went up half-a-dozen steps and sat down. And what a relief it was to be out of the glare and the heat, to be able to talk of what interested them without fear of being overheard.

Each great passion is the fruit of many fruitless years, and today were we to meet, we should not love the persons for whom, later in life, it is destined that we shall sacrifice all things; for what indeed is an ideal if it be not the synthesis of our past lives. Lady Helen and Lewis were enchanted with each other, but, knowing nothing of the occult causes, were both a little surprised that it was so.

Then came the wearisome, yet charming fencing with words, the indirect questions and evasive replies, by which, under cover of a generality or an allegory, each tells the other of the passion burning in his or her heart, till at last, like moths fluttering round a light they fall into the flames of each other's arms.

The staircase was full of a most delicious coolness, and they savoured slowly the idle tenderness which the scent of the flowers and mingling music bring to the souls of lovers. Already they murmured their speeches, more softly overcome by the sweet and insinuating emotion which drew them gently together.

Lady Helen wished to go, but she knew that Lewis was near her, and helplessly she leaned towards him; then, feeling his breath burning her she tried to withdraw, but her strength failed her, and she looked at him almost piteously. Their faces approached, and their souls were visible in their eyes; that moment seemed an eternity; then, with a movement like that of a swaying lily, she fell towards him, and their lips met in one long and passionate kiss, and removed the bar that had till now existed between them, and Lewis told her how much he had thought of her during the last five years; she, in return, reproached him with not having written to her; he defended himself with a hundred excuses. He did not know that she would have liked it; he scarcely knew her, he had not dared. At last the conversation turned on Mrs. Bentham.

Till now Lady Helen had made love to Lewis vaguely, but the kiss and the mention of Mrs. Bentham's name suggested two ideas; one was a distinct wish to marry him, the second an indefinite suspicion that Mrs. Bentham stood between her and the man she desired.

"But you—you love Mrs. Bentham, do you not?"

The words defined her ideas, and she felt that she already hated that woman, who, she was sure, loved, or had once loved, Lewis.

At this moment Mrs. Bentham leaned over the bannisters, and, hearing the question, she listened, as the criminal listens for the executioner's step on the fatal morning.

In brief phrases Lewis admitted that Mrs. Bentham had been very kind to him; that she was a great friend of his; that, indeed, there was nothing he would not do for her. But Lady Helen continued to harass him with indirect taunts and indefinite questions, and she remained firm in her belief, that at one time or another he had made love to Mrs. Bentham.

Already, by a hundred equivocations and insinuations, he had striven to make her understand that Mrs. Bentham did not come up to his ideal of beauty; he had even gone so far as to say that she was a little *passée*, but he had hesitated from expressing himself more definitely. Lady Helen, on her side, was dying to ask him if he had ever kissed Mrs. Bentham, but, not daring, she continued to exasperate him with suggestions. Her persistent questioning irritated him. He felt he could not leave her under the impression that he loved Mrs. Bentham. Momentarily, the feeling got the better of him, till at last he exclaimed, his heart sinking like a stone through the deep well of his cowardice:

"Good heavens! I wonder how you could think of such a thing; why, she is old enough to be my mother: you might as well accuse me of being in love with Mrs. Thorpe."

Each dismal word had been to Mrs. Bentham like burning poison dropped into her brain. The intensity of her pain was so great that, while they were speaking, she was quiet as she was pale, but the silence fell too suddenly, and she uttered a little cry.

The lovers started to their feet and listened. Hearing nothing more, Lewis tried to persuade Lady Helen to sit down; but the charm was broken; she remembered she had been away from the ball too long; a waltz was playing, and she insisted on going off to dance.

Mrs. Bentham staggered; her head felt as if it were empty, everything looked as if it were sliding under her feet; but, by holding on to the wall, she managed to get to her room. She could go no further, and, utterly unable to resist the poignancy of her grief, threw herself on her bed, and sobbed amid the white sheets.

The room was in almost total darkness. The veilleuse, hanging in its silver censer, amid the light brown embroidered curtains of the narrow bed, revealed a white marble chimney-piece, where a Dresden clock ticked amid the unfading flowers; the tall wax candles glistened in the branching candelabra. An odour of damp scent and linen drifted through the door of the *cabinet de toilette*, which was open, and floated upwards towards the red flame of the nightlight.

After the first paroxysm of pain Mrs. Bentham lifted her face, and looking vacantly into space, listened to the waltz. Its long undulating rhythm glided up along the walls from the ballroom and died away on the carpet, amid the shadows of the curtains.

She listened to it for a few moments, and piteously longed for it to stop and leave her in peace. Then a sense of the reality came back to her, and she threw herself on the pillows trembling with grief.

Her face was contracted; her eyes were red, a feverish brown red, and, listening to the sensual waltz, with one hand she tore the lace of the pillow. Her face being turned away from the door, she did not see Mrs. Thorpe, who entered as one would into a sick-room, and sat down on the bed.

After a few moments, moaning piteously, Mrs. Bentham turned round. So great was her pain that she was not startled by the quiet little black figure that had so unexpectedly come and sat down by her bed.

"My poor child," said Mrs. Thorpe, taking her cousin's long white fingers in her brown and crooked hands, "I guessed the reason of your disappearance from the ball-room; I have come to comfort you."

The words fell on Mrs. Bentham's burning thoughts as softly as rain on a desert. She answered them by throwing herself on the old lady's bosom, and for a short space the two women wept together.

"Oh, Sarah," she said, "you don't know what I suffer; if I could only die; I have nothing to live for now."

"My dear," replied the old woman, with tears in her voice, "I suffered as you; I also wished to die; I thought I could not survive the death of all I held dear; and yet I have done so these many years."

"But it was death that took your husband from you; we cannot struggle with Death; there is no jealousy there."

"True, we cannot struggle with Death," returned Mrs. Thorpe, "anymore than we can with Time; sooner or later, both surely overtake us."

The two women clasped each other's hands, and there seemed to be an indefinite allegory in the torn pink ball-dress, and the sombre, loose-hanging serge robe.

At first Mrs. Bentham did not answer; but when at last the meaning of Mrs. Thorpe's words filtered its way through her grief-saddened mind, her lips grew pale, and her eyes turned with a violent contraction.

"You mean that I am an old woman," she said, savagely; but seeing Mrs. Thorpe looking so pityingly at her, her anger melted and again she burst into tears.

The soft murmur of the waltz came up the staircase again, and its coiling voluptuousness seemed to mock her in a curious way.

"Oh, if it would stop!" she exclaimed, hiding her face in the pillow, her feet hanging over the edge of the bed. "It is driving me mad! It is driving me mad."

"My dear Lucy," said Mrs. Thorpe, "to obtain the privileges of one age we have to throw aside those of the last; and our lives are spent in making these transitions. Sometimes we pass gently from one to the other, sometimes violently; but in either case we have to go on; for, alas! there are no halting places on the highroad of Time. The girl in her teens has to part with her toys; the girl of five-and-twenty, with her innocence; a woman of forty, with her love. Perhaps the last may be the bitterest parting, but it is none the less necessary to make. Lucy, I have come to befriend you, to give you counsel. Today, you can bid farewell to the past; tomorrow, Time will push you rudely aside. We both have loved him; you have contributed materially to his welfare. He owes everything to you; continue the good work you have begun; let him marry the girl he loves; be it for you to join their hands."

"Then I must resign everything? So be it. I am now alone in the world; a world of days without sun, of things that have no joy for me."

There was both anguish and fear in her face, and she cast on Mrs. Thorpe a look of utter abandonment, one of those looks with which in terrible circumstances we strive to imprint our soul upon another's.

Mrs. Thorpe trembled for her friend; she understood that the sacrifice of a lifetime was concentrated in those moments. The few words Mrs. Bentham had spoken were the agony of infinite passion, an infinite farewell kissed to all earthly things. Even poor little Mrs. Thorpe, who had so long outlived the life of hope and entered into that of prayer, was overcome by the majesty of human passion, and could scarcely find courage to implore her friend to surrender her love to another.

But it was to be, and, after a pause, she went on to explain to Mrs. Bentham what she must do, not only for her own, but for Lewis's sake. Mrs. Bentham sat still on the edge of the bed; her friend's voice sounded vague in her ears, like a murmur of distant waters. Her thoughts were not like waking thoughts, they were indefinite and diffused, penetrated with the sleepy unease of a nightmare, and the heavy grief of such obtuse sensations.

As she sat looking vacantly into space, unimportant details of her past life crowded on her memory, until at last, startled by some sudden recollection, she uttered a little cry like that of a hare when run into by the hounds.

"No, no," she exclaimed, falling on her knees; "I cannot give him up. No, not yet. Oh, save me! Tell him what I have done for him, and he will—he must leave her!"

She stopped, and moaning piteously she held with her white hands on to Mrs. Thorpe's black dress.

The cold dawn glided along the edges of the curtains, revealing the disorder of the room. A black satin dress, which Mrs. Bentham had rejected in favour of a pink, lay thrown across the pearl-grey sofa at the foot of the bed; the white toilette table was strewed with brushes, combs, and tresses of hair; two or three ivory files and nail polishers had fallen on the carpet, and a bottle of white rose perfume, left uncorked, sent its acrid odour upwards through the heavy air.

Mrs. Thorpe strove vainly to lift Mrs. Bentham, who was almost fainting, from the ground; she would have liked, but she dared not call for assistance.

"Air! air! I am suffocating!"

In a minute Mrs. Thorpe pulled the curtains aside and raised the window, letting in the pale light and chill breezes of the morning, and, white as the dead, Mrs. Bentham staggered to the window.

The sparrows were chirping in the two trees which grew in the deep garden; slate coloured clouds rolled upwards, uncovering a piece of yellow sky whose sides were turning to pink.

The two women shivered in the cold air, and the storm of Mrs. Bentham's passion subsided. Her face was swollen with grief, her hair dishevelled, and her dress torn and tumbled. She appeared ten years older than two hours ago when she danced with Lewis.

The conversation between the women was very painful; it was impossible to speak of any but present things; and both heard with impatience the long sing-song of the waltz, and the tramp of passing feet.

At last Mrs. Bentham crossed the room; and pouring out some water, began to bathe her eyes.

"You had better go to bed, Lucy," suggested Mrs. Thorpe; "I will tell them as they go that they must excuse you, that you had a bad attack of neuralgia, and had to go to your room."

"No, no, not for worlds; I shall be all right in ten minutes. I will go through this trial to the end."

"But your hair is in a frightful state; your dress is utterly spoiled; your face is swollen; you had really better not."

"I have another dress just the same as this, and Marie will arrange my hair in a few minutes," replied Mrs. Bentham, ringing the bell.

Even the French maid, whose first rule in life was to be surprised at nothing, could not help showing her astonishment at this second toilette, but she accepted the neuralgic excuse, and with a thousand little words of pity, arranged her mistress's hair as well as she could in the time.

In a quarter of an hour she was dressed, and a little rouge and powder made her look almost as if nothing had happened. Quite calm, but trembling, she went down to the ball-room.

The yellow glare hurt her eyes, and feeling somewhat dazed, she went over to Lady Marion, who rose to meet her.

"I have been looking for you this ever so long, to say goodbye," said Lady Marion. "I am afraid that Helen has been asking you to keep out of my way, she has been enjoying herself immensely."

Mrs. Bentham with difficulty repressed a look of pain, but she saved herself by entering into a long explanation of how she had had a bad attack of neuralgia, and had been obliged to go to her room.

At that moment Lady Helen came up, on Lewis's arm, looking radiant with pleasure.

"Oh, do wait, aunt, for this one waltz," she asked, pleadingly. Lady Marion was too much a woman of the world to accede to this request, and notwithstanding a weak protest from Mrs. Bentham, she insisted upon going.

Mrs. Bentham felt a little sick when she had to take Lady Helen's hand and smile, as the latter thanked her, and told her how she had enjoyed the ball, but she did so, and flinched but very little.

Lord Senton asked her for a waltz, she refused him, for fear Lewis should fancy she did so from jealousy, but a few moments after she accepted an almost total stranger; it cost her a fearful effort, but she did it.

Then she sat for a long weary hour, watching patiently the whirling of white ankles and shuffling of glazed shoes.

There were the Misses Davidson still smiling in their partner's faces. Forgetful of Lewis, Mrs. Liston was dancing outrageously with Mr. Ripple, while her husband, his head on his hand, pondered on the domestic life of the ancient Egyptians. Lord Senton was dancing with a tall woman who aspired to rank as a professional beauty. Then came Miss French with a lord, Mr. Day with Miss Fanshaw, and Lady Archer with her husband, much to the delight of Mr. Vyner, who watched them from the doorway.

An interminable confusion of bright faces, and clear dresses stained over with black coats, swayed to the music, and Mrs. Bentham watched them with bitter curiosity. She saw them vaguely, like figures dancing in a dream, a blonde and rosy show of puppets acting in merciless pantomime the futility and vanity of human things.

She hated them no more; she watched them dreamily, her ears deaf, and her eyes blinded with grief, and bade them goodbye from time to time like a queen in a play.

Couples one after the other came up with a murmur of mincing words, took their farewells, and the scene seemed to grow more than ever like a stage where a troupe of marionettes, beautiful, rosy, chubby-cheeked, delightful in their silk and velvet dresses and large scarfs tied into puffed-out bows, mockingly made their exits.

Then, when they were all gone, she walked with her old friend through the wide reception rooms where the servants were turning out the gas. The musicians had departed; the flowers were withered; a petal here and there, and a bit of torn lace, were all that remained.

The ball-room looked wretched in the white morning light; it was as blank as her own life, of which it was a perfect allegory. Both had been filled with love, rapture, and delight, and both were now hollow, weary and deserted.

XXI

Farewells

During the next two days Mrs. Bentham won and lost many a mental battle. For two days and nights the struggle continued. It was fought here and there, in the sunny valleys of the past, and along the mist-laden slopes of the hills of the future. The ardours of determination and the lassitudes of hesitations followed each other consecutively, and each brought its tribute of tumult and pain. But at last she came out of the struggle triumphant, and on the third day wrote to Lewis asking him to wait at home, that she would call to see him about two.

The letter frightened him. He asked himself what it meant. He had received a hundred from her of the same kind, but in this there was an acid suspicion of curtness which he could not define. He turned the letter over and over with many feelings of apprehension.

Twice he had seen Lady Helen since the ball, and they were now formally engaged. Lewis would have willingly let matters stand over, have let their engagement remain a secret, but Lady Helen would not hear of it, and insisted that Lady Marion should be consulted at once; but that he need not be alarmed, for that nothing would induce her (Lady Helen) to give him up.

On that score he had no fear; but there were many other considerations to be taken into account, and Mrs. Bentham's letter perplexed him strangely. Was it possible she had heard of his engagement? If so, what was he to say to her? Would it be better to deny it or admit it boldly, he asked himself over and over again.

Lady Helen had told him that she would be in the park about one, with Lady Marion, and it was arranged between the lovers that her advice should be asked. She was, as Lady Helen said, the best person to break the news to Lord and Lady Granderville. It was most important that this matter should be decided. Which assignation was he to keep? He was clearly on the horns of a dilemma. As usual, after much hesitation, he chose the middle course. He told his servant to explain to Mrs. Bentham, if she called before he came back, that he had been obliged to go out on important business; to ask her to wait; and to assure her that he would not be more than a few minutes.

The servant was perfectly trained to such commissions, and when Mrs. Bentham called she was shown into the studio, with many protestations of regret, and assurances that Mr. Seymour would be back directly; that she would not have to wait above three minutes.

Mrs. Bentham was not sorry that Lewis was away, for the interval would give her time to compose her thoughts, to dream a little. It was a bright day at the end of April, and the sunlight glinted on the rose curtains that hid the staircase. Overhead, even the dead flowers in the urns seemed to bend towards the light, and the stove simmered and breathed a dreamy warmth through the room.

She looked at a picture of herself; she thought of the pleasant talks that had beguiled away the sittings: strange it was to think that she would never sit to him again. There was a picture of some gleaners he had painted at Claremont House: she remembered how they had quarrelled over one of the figures, and how, at last, he had taken her advice and changed it: he would never take her advice anymore.

She was dressed quite unaffectedly, in a brown skirt, with a black lace mantle; and the autumn of her beauty still presented many bright flowers of forgotten springs and ardent richnesses of summer.

And without deploring her folly at having sacrificed herself to the honour of a false god, she humbly abandoned herself to the contemplation of the past.

It rose before her eyes like haze on the sunset's line: she let herself drift from reminiscence to reminiscence; and, in the irresolute tenderness of her grief, her memories grew bright, faded, and passed like shadows away.

On a *guéridon* next her hand lay her work-basket. Mechanically she took up her embroidery, but dropped it with a feeling of repulsion; the slippers begun must remain unfinished. The book she was reading lay there too, but with half its leaves uncut.

On the carved cabinet, which reared its slender height against the opposite wall, lay a handkerchief he had taken from her on account of the scent; she took it up but threw it aside, the perfume had evaporated; she looked into the mirror, but it preserved none of the smiles of old days: under the shadow of the curtains she saw the arum lily she had sent him slowly dying in its vase.

In the meanwhile Lewis was having a very pleasant time in the park. When Lady Helen looked at him, her eyes beamed with love, and it was like drinking exquisite wine to see the faint shadows fall over her white skin, and watch the light filling with pale flames the saffron-coloured hair.

For a moment he felt he could sacrifice much, if not everything, for her.

The air was delicious to breathe; the sunlight came streaming through the green leaves, and the cavalcades cantered till lost in a cloud of sunlit dust over the brow of the hill.

They watched with an exalted sense of delight, and they dreamed of plunging, locked in each other's arms, and bathing together in the seductive ocean of fashion and elegance.

They dreamt of parties, balls, triumphs, admiration shared together; and then of the quiet half-hour when, in a narrow brougham, pressed close together in the darkness rendered uncertain by the passing light of the gas-lamps, a tired face would abandon itself to the soliciting shoulder.

Everything had conspired to make them happy; Lady Marion met some friends, and they profited by the circumstance to walk on in front, and they talked just as if they had been alone. Nothing could have been more charming or delightful; their only trouble was how to announce their engagement to Lady Marion. Lewis declined the responsibility. Whereupon Lady Helen declared she did not care what anyone said, that she was her own mistress; that parents always had to give way if the lovers were only sufficiently determined.

Lewis listened, amazed at her impetuosity, but without attempting to oppose it; and as they walked home Lady Helen told her aunt, bluntly, that she was engaged to Mr. Seymour, and that she would like her to write to her father and mother.

Lady Marion said she was never more surprised at anything in her life; which was in all probability the truth. She said Lord Granderville would not hear of it; and advised them to break it off. Lady Helen indignantly asked her why, and this provoked a discussion of love and talent *versus* prejudice, in which Lewis took no part, but waited patiently for an occasion to take his leave.

Lady Helen was a little angry with him for his want of pluck in defending himself; but he afterwards explained that he had been placed in a very delicate position.

The truth of it was, that much as he admired Lady Helen, he could not help thinking she was a little rash, not to say unreasonable; for supposing Lord Granderville refused to make her an allowance, frankly, he did not see how they were going to manage. Besides, he could not forget that, once he was married, women would cease to occupy themselves about him; and such successes had become so dear to him, that he feared their loss would make a great blank in his life. On the other hand, he remembered that he would probably never get such a chance again. Never had he seen anyone who so entirely came up to his ideal, and he had no doubt that if Lord Granderville would only give her a proper allowance, he should be very happy, and love her to the end of her days.

So Lewis thought, and in a very hesitating frame of mind he went to meet Mrs. Bentham.

Apologising for having kept her waiting, in an affectionate but somewhat self-sufficient way, he sat down next her, and explained that he had been obliged to go to the park to meet Mr. Ripple, who—

Mrs. Bentham laid her hand on his arm, and said, very gently:

"To see Lady Helen."

Lewis could never command his face, it always betrayed him, but he could nevertheless tell a lie, and he answered, quickly:

"No, no, 'pon my word; what makes you think so? I really went to meet Ripple, who—"

Mrs. Bentham again interrupted him: it pained her to hear him lie, and she said:

"No, don't say so; I know the truth."

Seeing from her manner that it was useless to attempt to deceive her, he tried to swagger.

"Well, supposing I did, what of it? I suppose I am free to speak to her if I like?"

"Of course you are, Lewis, and it was on that subject I came to talk with you. I noticed at the ball that you seemed to like each other very much, and—and—" here her voice slightly trembled—"I have been since thinking about it, and have come to the conclusion that you should marry her. You will not be able to make a better match, and I am sure I shall be glad to help you in anyway I can."

Lewis had little taste for the unknown; and the idea of leaving a life of pleasantness and comfort gave him a little uneasiness. It was all very well to think that Lady Helen was his ideal, but if he hadn't the money to marry her he didn't see what he was to do. Of course she was far handsomer than Lucy, that was beyond question, but then beauty was not everything. Lucy knew his ways, and he knew hers; they could guess each other's thoughts; they had so many interests in common. She understood pictures, and Helen, although she was not wanting in taste, made stupid mistakes; he had caught her in one yesterday; and after all, if Lord Granderville didn't consent he would have lost both; and that was about the long and short of it.

A hundred such thoughts, mixed up with many pleasant memories, flickered through his mind; under their impulse he began to grow sentimental, and to think that this brusque separation was a great mistake.

"No, no, Lucy," he said, taking her hands; "why cannot we remain friends? You know I love you better than anyone in the world. I owe you everything; it was you who took me out of poverty where I might have died; it was you who spurred me on to work; you gave me all my dreams, my thoughts, all sentiment of life and death; I have become a part of you."

He held her hands and looked beseechingly into her face. Mrs. Bentham felt her throat grow dry, and a weakness come over her. She had great difficulty in not giving way, for although she knew how cowardly and vacillating he was, she could not bring herself to admit that her whole life had been no more than one wretched mistake. She trembled a moment, both morally and physically, but gathering up her strength, she said:

"We have been very happy together; but we have all duties to perform, and this is one of yours."

"To say goodbye?"

"Yes, even so; but I hope that we shall always remain the best and sincerest friends; we shall not see so much of each other, that will be all."

The impressions of the moment were always the strongest with Lewis; and, sincere as he was when making love to Lady Helen, he was equally so now.

"I gave what love I had to give," he said, his clear girl-like eyes filling with tears; "I have no more."

"My dear Lewis," replied Mrs. Bentham, almost choking with emotion, "I am today your mother; my only desire in life is to assist you towards success and happiness in life, and for this end we must say goodbye. I bring you back your letters, will you give me mine?"

Looking utterly wretched, and too weak to cope with the intensity of the scene, Lewis pleaded to be allowed to keep the letters as a link to bind him to the past. The demand assuaged Mrs. Bentham's bitterness a

　　　　　　　　　　　　　　GEORGE MOORE

little, although, in her heart of hearts, she knew that he could appreciate no memory, and that the letters would lie in a dusty drawer, uncared for, though he might never find the moral courage to burn them.

"Old letters read distastefully," she answered, sadly; "I read some yesterday. You had better give them to me."

After a little more argument, he gave her all he could find; there were two large packets.

She looked at them, and tenderly turned them over; they extended back over many years; some were quite faded, others were crisp and new.

She was sublimely sad, and the modern dress seemed to add to rather than take away from the poetry of the subject.

Her feet rested on the fender of the stove that, simmering slowly, burnt itself out in the April sunlight, and her hands, in their long gloves, pensively turned over the letters, the mute witnesses of the past.

She had intended to burn them, to watch the flames devouring each leaf, to read a word here and there whilst they turned from red to black, and faded to senseless ashes; but even this last sad pleasure was denied her. She hesitated a long while, for in the situation there was something at once ludicrous and sinister; it was one of those miserable incidents which degrade without relieving the tragedy of our lives.

Mrs. Bentham still waited a moment, but at last, conquering her fancies, she got up, and pushed the whole heap of letters, as they lay about her lap, into the smoking stove.

"Oh, Lucy, how can you!" cried Lewis, interposing.

"What matter here or elsewhere?" she said, bitterly, picking a letter or two from the ground, and throwing them violently after the others.

Then she bade him goodbye, but when their eyes met she could contain herself no more, and burst into a passionate flood of tears.

He held her hand, but she disengaged herself, and, begging of him not to follow, hurried away. He stood for a moment looking after her, unable to realise the situation. He opened the door of the black stove, but an immense cloud of smoke forced him to shut it. Then, like one awakened from a narcotic-produced sleep, he threw himself on the sofa, and lay staring into the past and future which stretched around him, sullen and lead-coloured, like the long reaches of a stagnating mere.

XXII

Engaged

Poor Lady Marion found herself in a serious dilemma.

Her wilful niece would not even listen to her proposals for an armistice, the terms of which were these: That she, Lady Helen, was not to see or hold communication with Lewis until Lord and Lady Granderville had been communicated with. Pleadingly, Lady Marion begged hard for this cessation of love-making. She explained the difficulties of her position. She had undertaken the responsibility of chaperone, and what would Lady Granderville say? She would never forgive either of them.

Lady Granderville had always had a reputation for being practical; Lady Marion for being sentimental; and the latter felt sure she would have to bear till the end of her days the blame of the adventure. However, there was nothing to do but to write to her sister, and give her a precise account of what had happened.

The lettter was a painful one to write. There were many facts that had to be accurately stated, and Lady Marion found that her knowledge on all points was of the meagrest description.

All she knew of Lewis Seymour was that he was a very handsome, gentlemanly young man, whose pictures were always hung in the Academy, and that he was supposed to be making money.

Mrs. Bentham, who was frequently called in to give testimony, declared that she believed it to be a well-established fact, that Lewis made between fifteen hundred and two thousand a year; but when questioned about his family, her responses grew more vague. She thought she was acquainted with his past life, down to the smallest detail. During the last five years they had talked it over scores of times, but when it came to putting her knowledge into distinct statement, it surprised her to find how little she really knew.

Lady Marion thought the whole matter very strange: but at length, half convinced by Lady Helen's protestations that everything was perfectly clear, she composed a letter, carefully limiting herself to the general facts. But this did not in the least satisfy Lady Helen, who insisted on embellishing it, with many turns of fancy. Lady Marion protested, and each amendment provoked interminable discussions.

But a letter had to be sent, and at once; for Lady Helen would undertake to do no more than to give her mother and father a reasonable time to send a satisfactory reply. As for refusing to see Lewis, she declared she could not think of any such cruel arrangement; and as for being influenced by her mother, that was impossible.

"Were I to listen to anyone, it would be you," she exclaimed, kissing the old lady on both cheeks. "Mamma and I don't get on well together, and there is nobody I love like my aunt; but in a serious question like marriage is we must judge for ourselves. If my family object, so much the worse for them. I shall be obliged to run away with him. I am not going to ruin my happiness for anyone."

Lady Marion argued, but to no purpose; for Lady Helen overwhelmed Lady Marion with citations from the conduct of this person and that person, proving conclusively, at least to her own satisfaction, that it was quite right for engaged people to walk out alone, visit picture galleries, and, on a pinch, drive about in hansom cabs. Lady Marion was at her wits' end; and her disobedient niece caused her for over a month intolerable anxiety. For day by day, Lady Helen seemed to grow more and more reckless; and even the telegram they received from Lord Granderville did not appear in the least to affect her.

Sometimes Lewis called to fetch her, sometimes she went to fetch him at his studio. In fact, to save her from going out with him to dine at the restaurants, Lady Marion was obliged to ask him constantly to dinner. She had appealed to his generosity, but when she complained that he had not acted up to his word, he only answered that he could not prevent Lady Helen calling at his "place." It was therefore with a deep sense of relief that she received a telegram from Lord Granderville saying, that they had arrived in Liverpool, and that they would be in town that evening. Lady Marion threw the despatch across the breakfast table to Helen, who read it as coolly as the first; and went on eating. Her indifference so disgusted her aunt, that she could not help saying:

"My dear Helen, I never in all my life came across anyone so utterly selfish, so entirely indifferent to other people's feelings. I am sorry to say, your mother was right when she told me that one of these days I should find you out."

The bitterness of the words startled Lady Helen, and for a moment she saw how selfishly she had acted, and how indifferent she had been to the pain she had caused her aunt. Tears welled into her blue eyes, and she threw her arms around Lady Marion's neck, and begged to be forgiven. She declared that she really loved her aunt better than anyone, and she was sorry to have grieved her. Besides, she remembered that Lady Marion must be kept on her side; for, although she was determined to marry Lewis, she was fully alive to the fact that it would be much better to do so regularly than irregularly.

"My dear aunt, you mustn't be cross with me," she said, winningly; "I can't help it: you don't know how I love Lewis, and how impossible it is for me to give him up. It is that which makes me appear selfish. Mamma couldn't, but you will understand what I mean, for you have loved and have been loved yourself; you know how you once loved a painter; and, tell me, do you think, after all, you did well to give him up?"

This was a very clever move on Lady Helen's part, and the sympathy evoked won Lady Marion over to her side more than a bushel of arguments.

For many years no one had spoken to Lady Marion of her old love, and this sudden allusion startled her more than Lady Helen had expected.

"I suppose your mother told you that," she said in a low voice, but in a way that showed she was not displeased.

Lady Helen saw that this was her opportunity, and drawing her aunt's arm through her own, the two women went up to the drawing-room, one to talk of the future, the other of the past.

After luncheon, Lady Helen said she had an appointment with Lewis; her aunt asked her to remain in to meet her father and mother. She declared that it was not possible, but promised to be home at half past five; they could not arrive before then.

Lady Marion had to accept this crumb of comfort, and all the afternoon she sat waiting in the large drawing-room.

No one called, and the time went very slowly. Lady Marion tried to read, but her thoughts wandered; she was very fearful of meeting her sister and brother-in-law; and as it drew near six o'clock, she listened, expecting them ever minute.

At last the servant announced, "Lord and Lady Granderville."

"My dear Marion," said Lady Granderville, immediately she had kissed her sister, "this is dreadful news; I am perfectly ill with anxiety."

Lady Granderville, who was as stout as her sister was thin, was certainly not looking her best. Her fat face was sallow, and her eyes haggard and dim, from the effects of her sea-sickness.

GEORGE MOORE

"I don't know how you could let such a thing happen; I really don't. Who is this Mr. Seymour?"

"My dear Harriet, pray be calm, you will make yourself ill," said Lord Granderville, as he helped his wife off with her cloak.

"Let me show you up to your room, Harriet," said Lady Marion; "we will talk of this during dinner; will you have a glass of sherry?"

"I really can't do anything till you tell me where my daughter is," replied Lady Granderville, sitting down on the sofa.

"She is out with Mr. Seymour."

"Out with Mr. Seymour! You must be mad, Marion; how could you permit such a thing!"

"My dear Harriet," said Lady Marion sitting down by her sister, "Helen is the most wilful and disobedient girl I ever knew in all my life. I confess I was mistaken in her; had I known what she was I would never have undertaken the charge of her. Since she contracted this engagement with Mr. Seymour, she has, in defiance of all I could say, been out with him everyday. She says she is three-and-twenty, and intends to do as she likes. I did everything I could, I begged and implored, but it is no use arguing with her; she even hinted that if I tried to restrain her, she would leave the house and live at an hotel."

"Leave the house and live at an hotel!" exclaimed Lady Harriet, aghast; "I never took the same view of Helen as you did, but I must say she never spoke like that to me."

"I knew you would blame me and say it was my fault, Harriet; but if you can persuade Helen not to marry Mr. Seymour, or even to give up a single appointment with him, I will confess that I am entirely to blame."

"Then," said Lord Granderville, who had been attentively following the conversation, "you really think, Marion, that Helen is determined on this marriage?"

"So that I may save you errors in judgment, I will tell you that I am convinced that nothing in the world could prevent that girl from having her way, and the more violently you oppose her the more violently will she carry her point. Now, you have my opinion, you can act as you please."

"But who in the world is this Mr. Seymour?" asked Lady Granderville.

At this moment, hearing the bell ring, Lady Marion opened the drawing-room door and listened. Lord and Lady Granderville looked at each other, piteously seeking counsel.

Lady Marion returned quickly, and said: "This is Helen; take my advice and do not try to bully her."

"I quite agree with Marion," said Lord Granderville; "do not let us broach the subject; we will speak of it gradually during dinner."

Lord Granderville, besides being very fond of his beautiful daughter, knew from past experience that her mother's upbraidings would intensify rather than weaken any resolution Lady Helen might have made. Besides, he did not profess to have that innate horror of art that his wife had, and he could not see that there was anything so very awful after all in the abstract idea of marrying an artist.

Lord Granderville was a kind, easy-going man, and whatever ruggedness there may have formerly been in him had long ago been smoothed down by the pettishness and ill-humour of his wife. No longer had he the strength to quarrel with anybody; and he would submit to anything to preserve the tranquillity of his home. He was determined to use every effort to break off the match, but flying into a rage, he thought, would only precipitate it. He and his wife had agreed on a common plan of action: it was to refuse to give Helen a sixpence if she persisted in disobeying them—on this point he determined to remain firm.

After the general inquiries had been made, the conversation fell to the ground; Lady Marion had made up her mind not to have anything further to do with the matter; Helen was determined to be quiet, but resolute; Lord Granderville was embarrassed; Lady Granderville, who could not conceal her pettishness, began a little lamentation about being dragged all the way across the Atlantic, which, to the relief of everyone, was cut short by the dressing-bell.

All were glad to go to their rooms, and put off the dreaded discussion. During dinner it was introduced; but, partly on account of Lord Granderville's reserve, and partly because on account of the servants, the conversation had to be carried on in French, nothing occurred of particular note.

It was not until they were all sitting in the drawing-room round the reading lamp that the real war began. The opening was left to Lord Granderville, who, drawing his daughter towards him, began to question her seriously about Mr. Seymour.

But she had not got well into the explanation when the high notes of her mother's voice interrupted:

"I never heard of such a thing in my life; a young girl running about

London with a painter, whom she hardly knows! Oh, Helen, how could you? And you, Marion, I shall never forgive you. How could you allow it?"

Lady Marion attempted to explain; Lady Helen replied tartly enough to her mother; Lord Granderville tried to pacify them all. When at last silence was obtained, he pursued his cross-examination. Lady Helen did not mind answering him, for she knew that all she had to do was to remain firm, and the game was in her hands.

Question succeeded question, until the final point could no longer be avoided, and Lady Helen cried, in reply to her father's demand, that she loved Lewis very dearly, and that nothing could induce her to give him up, but that, otherwise, she hoped she would always prove a dutiful child. Lady Granderville could no longer restrain herself. She declared that with so disobedient a child parents were never cursed; with uplifted hands she asserted that she did not envy Mr. Seymour. She went back to the past, and showed how Helen had manifested her real disposition at the age of three, when she positively refused to wear a blue riband with a pink frock. Lord Granderville tried to interpose, but she would not be interrupted. She sat up on the sofa; her face got red and her stupid eyes glittered with passion. She showed how basely ungrateful Helen had always been, how selfish, how indifferent to the feelings of others. Then, having pretty well demolished her daughter's character, she turned round on her sister, declaring that she had acted in a shameful, if not criminal manner. Passing on to her husband, she accused him of having encouraged his daughter in wilful ways from her earliest childhood, illustrating her argument, as she went along, with numerous anecdotes.

Then she paused, like a ratter considering which of the dead was most deserving of a concluding shake. Her husband tried to break in, but she cut him short, and turned back upon her daughter, who sat whispering to her aunt, knowing well that she would annoy her mother more by pretending not to hear her than by any retort.

She was right; Lady Granderville blazed forth again, and repeated all she had said before, only concluding this time with the prophecy that Helen would prove as great a curse to her husband as she had to her parents. Lord Granderville tried mildly to interpose, but the word husband had suggested a new train of ideas to Lady Granderville. She had forgotten Lewis, and hastened to retrieve the oversight. She criticised him as effeminate, as a man that no girl could like, a man that looked like an ugly girl, a soft dreamy creature. Up till now Lady Helen had kept her patience wonderfully, but she could not hear Lewis maligned and sit silent, so a violent dispute arose between mother and daughter.

Lady Helen attacked her mother vigorously; told her how her perpetual discontent and violent temper made life a hell for those who had to live with her; that if her daughter were self-willed she had only herself to thank for it; and that she, Lady Helen, could stand it no longer, and was glad enough to get a home of her own, even if it were by marrying a painter. These recriminations drove Lady Granderville quite beyond herself, and for a moment she did not know how to reply; but collecting herself with a supreme effort, she said:

"And a nice kind of creature he is, this Mr. Seymour; he has been trying after Mrs. Bentham for the last five years, and now that he can't get her, he wants to marry you."

Lady Helen's white face flushed red to the roots of her saffron-coloured hair; she trembled with passion at her mother's brutality; but before she could reply, Lord Granderville interposed.

"My dear Harriet," he said, pleadingly, "really, really you are a little premature in your judgment; remember, you never saw this young man but once in your life, and you have no right to make such accusations against Mrs. Bentham."

Lady Granderville did not answer; her strength was spent, she could say no more; and she lay back on the sofa, her expansive bosom heaving like an ocean after a storm.

As for Lady Helen, her tears overcame her, and for some seconds only the girl's sobs broke the rich and shaded silence of the vast drawing-room. Lord Granderville spoke in whispers to his wife, who eventually rose to leave; but as she passed her daughter, she stopped before her, and said:

"As far as I am concerned, Helen, you shall never have my consent; of course, you are a free agent, and you can go and spend your fortune upon whom you like; but I will never allow your father to add one penny to it."

With that she swept out of the room. Lord Granderville and Lady Marion were so shocked that they attempted to apologise for her; but Lady Helen only shook her head, and begged of her father to tell her about the voyage, how he had left America, anything he liked save the matter in hand, she said; she could not bear to discuss the subject anymore that evening; but they were all so excited that their thoughts

GEORGE MOORE

wandered insensibly to the point they were trying to avoid; so, after a few attempts at conversation, Lady Marion proposed that they should retire for the night. Kissing his daughter, Lord Granderville told her he would go and call on Lewis tomorrow morning; then they bade each other goodnight, and gradually the lights went out in the different windows.

Lady Helen sat on her bed thinking. Her father was going to see Lewis the next morning; she would give worlds to see him for five minutes, just to explain to him what had happened, and tell him how she wished him to act. Without having precisely come to the conclusion that her lover was weak-minded, and could not be trusted to hold his own in an argument, she was sure that it would be advisable to forewarn him of what the family opinions were on the subject, so that he might meet her father on equal terms.

This idea gradually shaped itself in her mind till she became convinced that, by some means or other, she must see Lewis that night. In the morning there would be no time, for doubtless her father would start early, and she never would be able to get out of the house unperceived. Looking at her watch, she saw it was only eleven o'clock, and she suddenly remembered she had not yet returned the latch-key her aunt had given her; nothing, therefore, would be easier than to slip out, a hansom would take her to Chelsea and back in an hour. In a minute she had put on a hat and cloak, and was stealing downstairs. The hall door opened without a creak, and, hailing a passing cab, she was soon driving rapidly towards Fulham.

When she arrived at Lewis's, she saw he was in by the light in the studio. She knocked, but received no answer. This appeared to her strange; she knocked again, and after sometime the door was opened, and by Lewis himself. He was more than astonished, and her presence visibly embarrassed him. But she was too agitated to perceive anything, and she rapidly explained that she must see him, and was preparing to pass into the studio, when he said, hesitatingly:

"I have a model."

"Ah! then send her away, because what I have to say to you is most private."

"Well, then, wait there a minute," he said, leaving her in the ante-room hung with Japanese draperies.

He came back in a minute, and asked her to come in; Lady Helen did not doubt what he said about the model. Briefly she told him what had occurred; how her mother had absolutely refused to give her consent, and how bitterly she had told her that she must not count on sixpence more than her child's portion, which was only five thousand pounds; and how he might expect a visit from her father in the morning.

"But what am I to do?" asked Lewis, helplessly; "I can't say that I won't marry you unless they give me more money."

The answer caused Lady Helen a delicious little thrill of pleasure, for she did not suspect that it was not a perfectly disinterested observation.

"No," she exclaimed, drawing him towards her and kissing him; "but you can talk a little about the money if he mentions it, and tell him that it will be very hard for you to keep me in the position I have been accustomed to unless he assists you. He will have to give way, you know, for everybody has heard of our engagement; and my aunt tells me that there is no doubt but that I have compromised myself in driving and walking about with you. You see what a good manager I am," she murmured, as she kissed him again; "I thought of all that before."

This was not true; but it pleased Lady Helen to take the credit of it when it seemed likely that her imprudence was likely to prove a trump card. Lewis looked at her admiringly.

"Now I must be off," said Lady Helen, moving towards the door; "and mind you be firm with papa tomorrow, and tell him straight that nothing will induce you to give me up."

As they paused in the street to bid each other goodbye, Lady Helen said, laying her hand on Lewis's arm:

"But I forgot; mamma said worse than all I have told you; she said that you had been flirting with Mrs. Bentham for years, and that it was only because she wouldn't marry you that you proposed to me; tell me, is it true?"

Lady Helen spoke as if her heart would break; a pale moon had risen and was whitening the roadway; the street was deserted, and their voices took a strange sonority in the silence.

"I assure you it is false; Mrs. Bentham was never more than a dear, good friend to me."

"Give me your word of honour."

"Upon my word of honour; I can't understand Lady Granderville saying such a thing."

"Well, papa seemed quite shocked, and so did aunt; but I don't think that any man, or woman, or child, ever had such a temper as mamma. I wonder how papa can stand it; but it doesn't matter what she said as long as it is not true. Goodbye; you don't know how happy you have made me; I hated Mrs. Bentham once, but now I feel I love her for having been a kind friend to you; goodbye."

They kissed each other again, and Lady Helen drove away. Lewis looked up and down the street once or twice, and then entered his studio.

XXIII

DIFFICULTIES OVERCOME

A half sterile seed and a half formed talent will both grow and blossom, if especially favoured by circumstances. In Lewis's case the combination had been so extremely subtle that the small grain of original good had been almost cultivated into a flower. He was irresolute, but he had had someone always by him to sustain him; he sighed for pleasure, but he had obtained it with such ease, and in such profusion, that he had been forced, from sheer feebleness, to seek shelter in his art; he was lacking in perseverance, but he had obtained his successes so rapidly that they had pushed him on in spite of himself. Up to the present the medicines used were exactly those required to keep alive this unhealthy talent; but as there are some diseases that will outwear even the most powerful remedies, so Mrs. Bentham's influence had ceased to benefit him: his present life had lost its strengthening properties, and a something else was needed to unclose the hothouse reared bud that was now breaking to flower. Lady Helen came at the right time. Her beauty roused him from the state of apathy he was beginning to fall into, and her love of art at once amused and delighted him. She used to read him her poems between the intervals of love-making. She was the something that was wanted to complete the growth of his talent; for not only did her beauty and enthusiasm awake new dreams and aspirations in his soul, but by family influences she would be able materially to propel him along the road to fame.

During the last five years he had not only made much progress in his art, but he was beginning to be known as a constant exhibitor at the Academy, and was now recognised by the frequenters of fashionable drawing-rooms as a man of talent. He was asked everywhere; he was surrounded by friends; there was no one he did not know, and consequently he was a man that no one could afford to ignore. His pictures were well hung, and formed the subject of much conversation during the season. There was nothing to be said against them; if they did not show much individuality of feeling, they violated in no way any of the recognised canons of art. They were fairly well drawn, well modelled, well grouped, and pleasing in colour. "Then, why not hang them on the line?" said his friends to the other academicians, who had at first displayed some hostility to his pretty effusions in Greek draperies and fashionable dresses. In a word, he was on the eve of becoming a fashionable painter, that is to say, the artist who lives surrounded by grand people, and who rarely speaks to an artist.

Naturally, his friend Thompson had long ago ceased to visit him, seeing clearly that in art he would never do anything of the least interest to anybody. Lewis, on his side, had little inclination to leave the sweet pleasant way of success, to climb the thorny path leading to some far ideal, and he was now foremost in ridiculing what he was pleased to term foolish eccentricity. He deplored the teaching of "The moderns," and he predicted a great decadence in art if the academicians did not resolutely close their doors against the new sect. Experience, he said, had taught him the folly of ideals. He, too, had wasted lots of time listening to their nonsense; weeks, months he had passed, tearing his hair, trying to make possible the impossible; he, too, had spent sleepless nights, but he thanked heaven he had had the force of character to shake off their influence.

With this kind of conversation he entertained Lord Granderville when he called upon him the morning after Lady Helen's midnight visit, and he ventured to suggest that if he were not already an A.R.A. he had only "The moderns" to thank for it. Not only had they made him waste an enormous amount of time, but had so completely put him off the right track that it was wonderful that he had ever found his way back again. However, he had done so, and had now the satisfaction of seeing his pictures well hung and sold. Lewis spoke well, and he was able to show that he now made something between twelve and fifteen hundred a year. Lord Granderville listened, and congratulated him on the result of his labours, but declared, nevertheless, putting all other questions aside, that he did not see how Mr. Seymour could settle even a hundred pounds on his daughter.

Lewis replied that he wished all Lady Helen's money should be settled on herself. Lord Granderville smiled at this suggestion, and remembering his wife's injunctions to come to the point quickly, he told Lewis, with much gravity of manner, that for many family reasons, quite needless to enter into, the marriage was impossible, and that it was better not to think anymore about it.

Lewis bowed, and Lord Granderville took his leave with much formality. He did not know what to do. He felt that Lady Helen, notwithstanding all his wife could say, would not allow her wishes to be set aside: and try as he would, he could not see that, even if this marriage did take place, that it would be anything more than a very bad match, a somewhat unfortunate affair.

That night at dinner, Lady Helen guessed, from her father's face, that Lewis had answered according to her instructions, and that it was now left to her to fight the fight out to victory. Her plan was one of passive resistance, resolute disobedience, and by persisting in this course she knew that in the end her parents would have to give way. Her mother, as she expected, forbade her imperatively to bow to Lewis when she met him, to dance with him at balls, to stop to speak to him in the park. To these orders Lady Helen made no reply: she merely set them at defiance. Then Lady Granderville tried, by turns, threats, and persuasions, until she was, on the failure of both, obliged to beg her daughter, at least not to publicly *afficher* herself with Mr. Seymour. Lady Helen felt a thrill of pleasure, but she answered, quite calmly, that she was quite willing to behave herself properly if Lady Granderville would consent to reconsider her decision, and allow Lewis to come and see her.

This proposition was received with indignation, but as they were discussing it, Lord Worthing, who had just come home from abroad, called. As the head of the family, the whole matter was referred to him. He was a large man, and he listened, majestically, leaning back in an arm-chair.

It was afternoon, and the rays of the setting sun glinted through the Venetian blind. After listening very attentively, Lord Worthing declared that the whole matter required the gravest consideration. On the one hand, he was surprised at Helen's disobedience to her mother's commands; whilst, on the other, he felt bound to say that he could not share Harriet's somewhat sweeping condemnation of Mr. Seymour; he had found him a very nice young man, well bred and gentlemanly. Of course it could not be considered an advantageous alliance, from any point of view; but he was bound to admit that it was possible to cite cases of lovers who had sacrificed all for their love; though, personally, he was not prepared to say that they had acted wisely in so doing. In such a strain Lord Worthing continued, until his sister, who lay tossing with exasperation on the sofa, lost all patience, and asked him to say definitely what he meant.

Lord Worthing did not much like this, but, after a good deal of evasion, he admitted that as Lady Helen could not be made to promise not to go out walking with Mr. Seymour unless he was asked to the house, it might be as well to comply with her request. Lady Granderville was furious, but after some discussion it was decided to ask Lewis to dinner, and Lady Helen said to herself, "Check number one."

That night she wrote a long letter, putting off a rendezvous they had made, and giving him a full account of the conference which she declared to have terminated very satisfactorily.

Three days went by in a tedious way, and then Lewis came to dinner, and was introduced to Lady Granderville. He passed his examination very creditably; Lord Worthing and Lord Granderville spoke to him about art; he replied modestly, but with enthusiasm. He listened deferentially to their views, and when they went up to the drawing-room after the ladies, the brothers-in-law agreed that he was an uncommonly clever, well-bred young man, and that it was a pity he had not a stake in the county, was not a landed proprietor.

During dinner Lady Granderville had maintained a dignified reserve. Determined not to commit herself in anyway, she had measured her words so as just to remain within the recognised bounds of politeness. As Sir John Archer would say, she was making a waiting race of it, and Lewis, seeing this, determined to force the running.

On entering the drawing-room he sat down by her, and tried various subjects of conversation. Lady Grauderville answered only in generalities, but every now and then she raised her eyes to look at him; his softness of manner charmed her as it did everybody, and before the servants brought in the tea she had almost forgotten her animosity.

"Just look, aunt, how mamma is flirting with him," said Lady Helen, laughing; "she is beginning to regret that she is not twenty years younger."

"Hush, hush, my dear," said Lady Marion, trying not to laugh, for she saw that this was really the case.

Lewis conducted himself perfectly, and with a tact that even Lady Granderville was forced to recognise; and when he went away that evening he had won the sympathy of the whole family. The two men had agreed that there was nothing particularly disgraceful in the marriage, but Lord Granderville, urged on by his wife, did all he could to induce Lady Helen to give up the idea. He spoke to her about the settlements, showed her what she would lose, argued from every possible point of view, but to no purpose. Lady Helen replied that she would do anything else in the world to please him, but she could not, and would not, give up Lewis; and, regardless of advice, she continued to meet him, and once even went to lunch with him at a restaurant. When this last escapade reached Lady Granderville's ears, she flew into the most violent of her passions, and, like a prophetess of old time, denounced the tennis party, and the day that Lady Marion had introduced them.

Lady Helen was out, and escaped the first paroxysms, but Lady Marion and Lord Granderville were kept close prisoners all the afternoon to witness the *dénouement* that Lady Granderville said must take place that evening. She was resolved to show them how she could bring an affair to a conclusion. Fifty times did she look at the clock, and fifty more out of the window, holding forth all the while on the mistake of the English system of managing young girls. They should be brought up, she maintained, under their mother's eyes; should come back after every dance; should never speak to anyone alone, and should be eventually married according to their parent's judgment. The liberty they were allowed only encouraged them to ask for more, and led, as in the present case, to open defiance of all authority.

In her youth the traditions were still respected; but now everything was in a state of general revolution, and she deplored the introduction of American freedom into English manners and customs. Lady Granderville hated America, and, once on this track, she soon rambled off into a long dissertation, which called into question the first principles of Republican government, the abolition of slavery, the declaration of independence, Irish disaffection, and the wisdom of Lord Granderville in entering the diplomatic service. Sometimes her sister's theories on the first principles of things provoked an answer from Lady Marion, but at a look from her brother-in-law she would sink back into silence.

When Lady Helen arrived, Lady Granderville looked at her husband and sister as much as to say, "Now you shall see how determined I can be."

Lady Helen was very hot, and her white skin was overspread to the roots of her pale hair with a crimson flush. She wore a large hat which she took off on entering the room, and she threw herself on a sofa.

"It is dreadfully hot," she said, fanning herself with her hat; but seeing grave faces on every side, she stopped, and looked perplexed.

"I hear you have been out to lunch with Mr. Seymour," said Lady Granderville.

"I have no intention of concealing the fact; but may I ask how you heard it, mamma?"

"From people who saw you," replied her mother. "Now, look here, Helen, there is no use arguing this matter all over again; it has been thoroughly well considered by the whole family, and we have decided irrevocably against this marriage. I have forbidden you repeatedly to walk about with Mr. Seymour, but as you cannot or will not obey me, I must take you out of temptation."

"Take me out of temptation?" asked Lady Helen, opening her eyes.

"Yes," replied Lady Granderville, casting a look of triumph on her husband and sister; "we shall leave London tomorrow."

"You may leave London if you like, mamma, but I am afraid I shall not be able to accompany you," said Lady Helen trembling a little, for she felt that they had now arrived at the critical point of the struggle.

"Where will you go then?" said Lady Granderville, whose astonishment for the moment overcame her passion.

"Well, if my aunt refuses me hospitality, I shall go to an hotel and marry Lewis Seymour next week, without any settlement."

Lord Granderville and Lady Marion looked shocked, but, not knowing what to say, remained silent. As for Lady Granderville, she looked from one to the other, quite at a loss how to proceed. She had expected to take her daughter by surprise, force her from her position of lofty disobedience, and so secure a triumph over the whole family.

Lady Granderville's large face for a moment was pale with passion, but as the different sentiments of rage began to break through her thoughts it grew purple, and then she burst out into a wild storm of invective.

Lady Helen sat quite still, and continued to fan herself. At last Lord Granderville thought it advisable to interfere, and then she profited by the occasion to slip out of the room, just lingering at the door to say that mere abuse was child's play, and that she had a right to chose for herself.

Notwithstanding this defeat, Lady Granderville continued the struggle for some days longer. Her husband and sister preserved a strict neutrality. They knew that Lady Helen would not give in, and, wishing to shield themselves from future reproach, they agreed to let Harriet fight out her battle to the end. But the process of fighting the battle out was an extremely disagreeable one for all concerned, particularly the spectators. Lady Granderville refused to speak to Lady Helen, and the latter retorted by refusing to speak to her mother. Lord Granderville and Lady Marion found these hostilities extremely inconvenient, particularly at meal times and when visitors called; the artifices to which they were obliged to resort to conceal the family quarrel were quite heartrending. Mother and daughter cut each other dead on the staircase, and would sit in the drawing-room for hours, so that the one that remained should not think the other was giving way.

This continued for over a week; Lady Marion bore up bravely, but at last she declared that she could stand it no longer, and that if they did not make it up she would leave the house. The threat frightened both parties equally, and mother and daughter were at last persuaded into wishing each other good morning. This was followed by a week of as lively days as the last had been of solemn; scarcely an hour passed without an altercation of some kind or other. Lady Marion would take Helen into one corner, and Lord Granderville his wife into another, and all four would argue passionately under the shade of the window curtains. Then the conversation would become general; and when a scrimmage was imminent they would exchange partners, and discuss it all over again; and so on, and so on, day after day. However, at last Lady Granderville began to see she was occupying an untenable position, and one morning, at the end of a good three-quarters of an hour of expostulation and recrimination, she declared, with the dignity of the Roman Governor, that she would wash her hands of the whole matter; that they were all against her; that they might do as they liked. Lady Marion and her brother-in-law protested that this was not the case; Lady Granderville shrugged her large shoulders; and Lady Helen fixed her marriage for the end of the month.

From that magic morning everything was changed; everything, person, and thought grew bright and gay, and cumbrous Time could not keep pace with the flying feet of Love.

Lady Helen lost herself in a whirl of business: first of all came the important question of the trousseau; there was scarcely breathing time, and often she missed lunch. The carriage was out all day, and before the large plate glass windows of Regent Street the sun glistened on the sleek bay sides of the champing carriage horses, on the cockade, on the coachman's hat, and the white legs of the footman who resignedly sat on a neighbouring bench.

There were dresses to be bought for the mornings; for the evenings, bonnets, hats, tea gowns, and *peignoirs*. The number of new fashions were confusing, and although she had deliberated an hour before she had decided on the blue cashmere the bays had reached the circus when

GEORGE MOORE

she had come to the conclusion that it would be very much better with a pink scarf, and the coachman had to drive back.

Twenty different varieties of this accident occurred daily.

Lewis often accompanied her on these excursions. He was never tired of looking at her in new dresses and hats; and he criticised their harmonies or discords. She fluttered as happy as a butterfly in the sun, and her life was full of delightful little surprises. On one occasion she had missed buying a green felt hat with an immense feather; she could not say how it had happened, somebody had spoken to her, called her away, and she had let it slip. Next morning she went to the shop, but although there before twelve, she was told that they had sold it, but that they would be able to get another in a few days. This little incident was very vexatious, and it spoilt the day. As she drove about, she passionately regretted the green felt. She was going to a flower show with Lewis, and when she told him of her disappointment, she thought it unfeeling for him to laugh; but when at last he confessed that he had seen the hat accidentally, and bought it, thinking it would suit her, she threw her arms about his neck and kissed him. No other man, she was sure, would have thought of doing such a thing, would have known what kind of hat would suit a woman.

She studied the past, and it seemed to be quite wonderful how they had met, how they had remained faithful to each other so many years. She felt sure that there must be some fatality in life. But she had not a minute to herself. There was an immense amount of work to be got through, and her father plagued her with business. He would insist upon explaining the settlements to her; she had six thousand pounds, well, five of that was to be settled on herself, and the other thousand was to be put aside to furnish their house with. To this sum Lord Granderville had added fifteen hundred, and Lord Worthing five hundred, as it was considered that money would be the most serviceable wedding present. She knew all this, and she could not understand why her father would insist on dragging her into his study after breakfast to go over a lot of legal documents, and she was delighted when the servant would interrupt them with the announcement that Mrs.——was waiting to see her about a certain trimming.

Then there was the difficulty to be solved of where they should spend their honeymoon. On this question Lady Helen consulted all her friends; some suggested Paris, some Italy, some were in favour of the Isle of Wight. But it was on the married women's opinions Lady Helen placed the most reliance, and she found no better confidant than Lady Archer. Even Sir John's sporting tastes—and it was said that on his bridal night he had gone upstairs reading the stud book—had not killed her love of sentiment, and she encouraged Lady Helen to come in and out at odd times, and tell her about Lewis. As she listened, sighing, she would tell Lady Helen all about her own honeymoon, and how delicious it would have been but for Sir John's racing calendar.

And the two friends would draw together and talk with the hundred little intimacies which a tea table inspires. Lady Helen had also consulted Mrs. Bentham.

She spoke in a quiet, half friendlike, half motherlike way, of Lewis, which completely deceived Lady Helen, who now felt sure that Lady Granderville's hints were only those vague accusations which she made against everybody. Mrs. Bentham had, after many efforts, to a certain extent, conquered her repugnance, and she was determined to become the friend of the lovers. An opportunity soon offered itself. Lady Helen's maid left her, and Mrs. Bentham proposed to go the round of the agents: Lady Helen, with a profusion of thanks gladly confided the commission to her.

After a great deal of interviewing, Mrs. Bentham picked out of the numbers that applied, half-a-dozen of the most likely ones, and wrote to Lady Helen to come and see them.

When she arrived, the poor girls were all waiting in the dining-room, looking askance at each other, wondering who would be the fortunate one. Lady Helen was out of temper, and she declined four of them without knowing why. The fifth was a short girl, dressed in a poor brown dress, and her boots were terribly worn. She had evidently been out of place a long time. She was about the medium height, with a pretty, plump figure. Her face was disfigured by the small-pox. Even the forehead had not escaped; it was discoloured, and its brick tints contrasted unpleasantly with the light brown hair. The malady had respected nothing but what it could not touch, the clear eyes and the white teeth.

"What is your name?" asked Lady Helen.

"Lloyd, your ladyship; Gwynnie Lloyd."

The candid look of the eyes, and the musical name, caught Lady Helen's fancy; her appearance pleased her, her character Mrs. Bentham had previously gone into; there was no reason why she should not be taken, so, after a moment's hesitation, Lady Helen told her that she might bring her things to Queen Street as soon as she liked.

Her story since she quitted the house where she had sat for Lewis was the simplest. Determined that he should not trace her, that they should not meet for the present, she had left the shop where she was employed and had sought work elsewhere. She had confided her story to no one, and she could not find courage to write to Lewis; she put it off until she was struck down with the most virulent form of small-pox. During her convalescence, which was long, she wrote many letters, but they remained unanswered. Lewis had left no address, and he never called again at the shop in the Waterloo Road.

Gwynnie cried bitterly, and feared for his safety. On leaving the hospital she went down to see Mrs. Cross, who could tell her nothing but that Mr. Seymour had gone away with his pockets full of money, dressed out in new clothes, "and what not," and that she had seen no more of him. This was all she could say, and, mournfully, Gwynnie went away to work for her daily bread. As time went on she grew reconciled to her grief; it became part of herself, and her little life slipped into a sort of stagnating gloom. She lived indifferent to all things, only fulfilling her duties perfectly, and, in a year, was allowed to assist as show-woman in the shop. Her quiet, kind manner made her a general favourite, and one day a lady whom she was in the habit of attending, offered to take her as her maid. The offer was tempting. The bustle of the shop was little to her taste, tranquillity was what she sought; and for four years, until her mistress died, she lived a life of unassuming dependence. Then after so many years of calm, she found it hard to face the world. Still she thought she would not have much difficulty in finding another situation, and having saved a little money, she resolved to wait.

But month after month went by without her finding what she wanted. Some would not have her for one reason, some for another. At length her little resources were nearly at an end, and she had determined to go back to business when Lady Helen happened to take a fancy to her. Hers was a nature that instinctively loved the common-place, and turned in distrust from all that is strange and exceptional; therefore, the gloomy sacrifice she had made for Lewis had fallen with its full weight on her mind; it had rendered her graver, quieter, than she would otherwise have been; it had a little clouded her perceptions and hopes. She did not definitely expect ever to see him again; but although time had effaced her dreams of one day being his wife, there lay at the bottom of her lonely heart a sort of shadowy belief that in some dim, future time her love must surely be requited. This was noticeable in her whole demeanour, for, as her fellow-servants said, "She always appeared to be dreaming." The remembrance of the past unfitted her for the life to which she was born; she could feel no interest in herself nor in others. Her gentle ways saved her from being actually disliked. But when she left the servants' hall a housemaid would often call her a "stuck up little thing." The footmen took her part, and defended her vigorously, although she had always fled in disgust when they attempted to kiss her behind the doors.

XXIV

The Bridal Dress

My dear Gertrude, I did all I could but I wasn't listened to," said Lady Granderville to her sister-in-law, Lady Worthing, as they entered Lady Marion's bed-room. Lady Marion was arranging her bonnet before the glass, and she thought as she heard her sister's voice, "Now I wonder how often Harriet will grumble before we get to the church?"

"My dear, haven't you got any other bonnet than that one? Why, you will be nearly in black," said Lady Granderville, who wore an elaborate grey silk, with innumerable flounces.

Lady Marion made it a rule never to contradict her sister, so she put on a bonnet with coloured strings.

"Do you like this better?" she said, turning towards her.

At this moment, Lady Mary Lowell, Lady Worthing's youngest daughter, rushed out of the next room, where her cousin was dressing.

"A pin! a pin!" she cried, looking hurriedly over Lady Marion's dressing table.

"What kind of pin?"

"A long one, aunt, to fasten the wreath. Ah, here's one," and she fled back again in a glare of cream-coloured ribands.

"How nice she looks in her new frock," said Lady Granderville, speaking of her niece; "she will be a very pretty girl; she is just twelve, is she not?"

"She will be twelve next month. Do you think her better looking than her sister?"

"Which one?"

"The eldest."

"Oh, I don't know; it is a different style."

"Isn't Helen ready yet?" asked Lady Granderville, in her peevish voice. "I declare we shall be late; it is a quarter to eleven, and it's half an hour's drive from here. I never could understand what induced you to come and live here, Marion."

"Number two grumble," said Lady Marion to herself, and she went on arranging her bonnet without replying.

"I can quite understand a girl falling in love with Mr. Seymour," said Lady Worthing sitting down on the sofa; "he is very good-looking."

"My dear Gertrude, I can't understand you talking like that; you surely do not think it advisable to give way to a mere sensual passion," said Lady Granderville, pettishly. "Good-looking! He is so good-looking that he has been the toy of every woman in London."

"Hush, hush!" said Lady Marion, turning, and looking really angry at her sister; "I wonder, Harriet; how you can talk like that in her hearing, really?"

"She can't hear," replied Lady Granderville, somewhat humbly. "You know, my dear," she continued, addressing her sister-in-law, "I have always approved of the French system. These flirtations on the staircases, and private conversations, are to my mind perfectly abominable."

"What you say is very true, my dear," returned Lady Worthing, "but although I agree with you that young ladies carry their flirtations much too far, still I think they should have a voice in the matter; for you know that in France—"

"Oh, aunt, the servant says that they have only brought two bouquets of blue flowers instead of three; so either I, Mary, or Lucy, will have to do with a white one," exclaimed Lady Alice Lowell, entering suddenly, with one tress of hair waiting to be pinned up.

"I can't possibly wear a white bouquet; I must have some Forget-me-nots in mine," cried Lady Mary, pushing open the door of Lady Helen's bed-room, and revealing the bride waiting to receive the body of her dress.

The sisters argued angrily for some moments; presently the lady's-maid came up to say that another bouquet had arrived, that the extra white one was a mistake.

Then the two girls retired to their rooms, and Lady Worthing and Lady Granderville resumed their conversation. "You know, my dear," said the latter, "I was entirely opposed to this marriage, but I was overruled. It is all very well to say that he makes a thousand a year by painting, and will make more; but, I ask, supposing he lost his health tomorrow?"

"I quite agree with you," said Lady Worthing, "the first of all things is health; I would not marry one of my girls to a man with bad health, no, not for worlds!"

"Yes, yes, my dear; but you see it is doubly important in this case, for my daughter has married a working-man."

GEORGE MOORE

"Help! help!" cried Lady Mary, in a high, shrill voice from the next room.

"Good heavens! what has happened now?" exclaimed Lady Granderville; and the three women rushed simultaneously to the rescue.

When they saw what it was, they drew a long breath. It was not Helen, it was the new maid who had fainted. She was lying back on Lady Mary's shoulder, and Lady Helen on the other side, her veil hanging down, was trying to support her.

"For goodness' sake, take care, Helen!" cried Lady Worthing, "you are walking on your veil."

"Oh, how very tiresome this is; servants are certainly the greatest worry in life," exclaimed Lady Granderville.

"I told you not to take one who looked delicate. The girl has fainted, and there's an end of it," said Lady Marion, helping her niece to place the girl in a chair; "open the window and give me your salts."

The reason for Gwynnie's fainting was not physical weakness, as Lady Granderville supposed, but the sudden knowledge that she was dressing her mistress to marry her old friend and lover. Lady Helen and Lady Mary Lowell had been chattering about Lewis, the name had been frequently mentioned; but it only gave Gwynnie an interest in the marriage that she otherwise would not have felt: the name of our first love always remains dear to us. In talking of Lewis, Lady Mary had declared that handsome as he undoubtedly was he nevertheless did not make a good photograph. This the bride was not disposed to admit, and she had asked her cousin to get down an album, and she would see a new one which was quite perfect. Lewis had scarcely altered at all; there was no mistaking the picture, and the emotion had been too much for Gwynnie.

"My dear, we shall certainly be late; she is all right now; let me pin up your veil for you," cried Lady Granderville.

"I am so sorry, your ladyship; I don't know—" said Gwynnie, trying to rise; "I am quite recovered now."

"No, no, stay where you are," said Lady Helen, stooping so that her mother might place the crown of orange flowers on her hair and pin up the soft folds of the veil.

"Mind you must not think of coming to church—"

"Oh, your ladyship, I assure you I am quite well," replied the maid, getting up and helping to arrange the veil. "I don't know what came over me."

"Now I am ready," said Lady Helen, taking up the great white bouquet off the chintz sofa. Then Gwynnie opened the door wide, so that the bride should not catch her veil, and they went down to the drawing-room, where the bridal party were waiting.

When Lady Helen entered the room, there was a cry of admiration; Lord Granderville kissed his daughter, she looked quite lovely in white silk. The skirt was encircled with a garland which passed round and was lost in a rain of white blossoms which covered the train, and, in all this whiteness, her yellow hair and red mouth, set in the white face, came out charmingly.

The big drawing-room was literally filled with bridesmaids. They were mostly cousins.

There were Lady Mary, Lady Alice, and Lady Annie Lowell, Lord Worthing's daughters, three little girls of twelve, sixteen and eighteen, the Honourable Misses Sedgwick, and three school friends of Lady Helen's. They were dressed in clear dresses of Indian muslin, garnished with white lace, touched off with knots of pale blue riband, which echoed the tint of bouquets they carried in their hands.

The wedding presents were of all kinds. One table was piled with jewellery, another with china; there were books, fans, ornaments in gold, silver and ivory; but over all a splendid tiara of diamonds, the gift of Lord Worthing, sparkled in a stream of sunlight which fell obliquely through the windows.

The bridesmaids crowded to see Lady Helen, and Lady Marion drew Lord Worthing aside.

"Has Sir Thomas Towler promised to be there?"

"Yes, yes, my dear, he has; we shall see him probably in church; anyhow, he is sure to be here for the breakfast."

"It will be a great advantage for Lewis to know the President of the Academy," murmured Lady Marion.

"Of course, my dear, of course it will."

At this moment the servant came up, and announced that it was a quarter past eleven, and that the coachman said that he would be scarcely able to get there in time.

Precipitately Lord Granderville gave his arm to Lady Helen, and in a murmur of voices the whole party went downstairs, and passing between a row of street idlers who had collected to see the show, they got into the carriages.

GEORGE MOORE

As they drove away the crowd slowly dispersed, cracking jokes at the splendour of the footman's white legs and red breeches.

Then Gwynnie Lloyd, in her little brown dress, came down the steps, and the red plushed footman put her into a cab, and the four-wheeler drove after the brougham and victorias.

XXV

In Church

A bout twenty minutes past eleven, a small brougham coming from Piccadily drove up to St. George's. Lord Senton and Mr. Day got out. There was a movement among the crowd as the two young men walked up the crimson carpet which stretched between the smoke-blackened pillars down to the pavement. The idlers were in doubt as to which was the bridegroom.

Lord Senton looked annoyed. Having been more than usually unfortunate in his love affairs, he had thought of signalising himself by marrying somebody very lovely; and, after some hesitation, he had fixed upon Lady Helen as the most suitable person. Mr. Day viewed the scheme with positive horror, for he knew that the obloquy of its non-success would fall upon him. However, the sudden announcement of Lady Helen's marriage made an end to his lordship's projects, and the duty of consoling him devolved on Mr. Day. But this was no easy matter, his lordship's self-love had been severely offended, and he fancied that everybody thought that Lady Helen had jilted him. Knowing the uselessness of argument, Day advised him to give her a handsome present, and accept the invitation which he had received for the wedding breakfast.

"Are you sure, old fellow, I was right in sending that bracelet?" he said, as they entered the church; "won't she think it queer?"

"Not in the least, old man," replied Day, who had answered the question fifty times that morning.

It was a dignified and aristocratic looking church. Under the large stained glass windows which filled the end of the chancel, was a brown picture representing the Last Supper, four pilasters, likewise brown, and covered with gold ornaments, enframed this mediocre work of art.

Two deep galleries extended from the organ loft to the altar rails, they were lit with large white windows, through which the white sun streamed, to die away in the stained glass twilight of the chancel. On the right was the pulpit, on the left the reading desk, both rich with crimson velvet and oak carving. The roof and the four columns, which supported the galleries, were painted in light grey. The brown coloured

GEORGE MOORE

pews were in keeping with the rest, for they seemed to be haunted with the echoes of rustling silk and mundane prayers.

"Let's sit here," said Day, getting into a pew about half-way up the aisle.

"He's with Ripple," whispered Lord Senton, sitting down.

"Where?"

"Why, near the reading desk."

"Ah, so he is; I wondered who he would have for his best man; just fancy, Ripple!" and Day smothered his laughter.

"A great deal too good for the fellow; how I do hate him! 'Pon my word, Day, she was a girl I could have loved."

"Oh, you have said that about so many!"

"She was not like the others, I assure you," replied Senton, pulling his little white moustache.

The body of the church had been retained for the bridal party, and the *élite* of Vanity Fair was there, all friends of the Grandervilles and Worthings.

Lewis had very few friends to invite. He had been for the last month trying to work up his acquaintances into the position of friends, and he made the best show he could with them. They consisted principally of young men who came to smoke cigars in his studio, and a few artists. Mr. Hilton, the academician, was there, with his wife and family. Next to them were the Misses Davidson, in new dresses, and they talked together disparaging the marriage.

"It is a terrible come-down for Lady Helen," said the elder.

"Terrible indeed," replied the younger, "but I never thought her so beautiful; and as for the stories of the dukes and princes she refused—"

"All that occurred abroad," returned the elder.

At this moment Mrs. Campbell Ward, magnificently dressed in Scandinavian sky-blue satin, decorated with sulphur-hued lace, passed up the church, attended by her husband.

Mr. Swannell, as the member for his county, had, of course, been invited, and having secured a seat for his wife, he proceeded to finish his explanation of the Government's views in respect to Afghanistan, which he was confiding to a friend. Mrs. Collins came noiselessly up the aisle, looking round for someone to whom she could confide a little budget of information she had for sometime been patiently collecting. Seeing Mrs. French, she sat down beside her, and the two old women discussed the wedding.

In the back benches there were quite half-a-dozen dissolute-looking girls, who had all nodded to Lewis as he passed up the church, much to his annoyance. In answer to a question put by Ripple, he said that they were his models, but that he did not anticipate a scene. Yet every chance rustle of a skirt caused him to start violently. On all sides he saw people whose absence would have been to him delightful. There were ladies whom he had not seen for years, and to avoid their eyes was almost impossible, they seemed to be all round him. At last he caught sight of one he feared more than all the rest, Mrs. Liston; she was sitting in the first row of pews in the aisle, so that there was no possibility of getting to the vestry without passing her.

"Let's sit here, Ripple," he said, looking frightened.

"No, no," replied the best man, "you had better come into the vestry."

"I can't yet, I will in a minute," he replied, sinking into a seat. "But what time is it?"

"Just the half hour."

"Then I must brave it."

Mrs. Liston was in an extreme state of excitement; her pinched up, somewhat vacant-looking face twitched violently, and she scarcely took her eyes off Lewis for a moment. Her husband sat by her; his grave, handsome countenance calm and collected. He stroked his soft red beard as he mused over some analogy between the Government of Socrates and Lord Beaconsfield.

As Lewis tried to pass Mrs. Liston, she stopped him resolutely.

"Surely," she whispered, getting up from her seat, "it is not true that you are going to be married? You will never do this thing?"

Lewis stuttered and stammered; it was on his lips to tell her that she was mistaken, that he had no intention of doing any such thing; but the lie appeared to him too ridiculous, and he faltered and tried to excuse himself.

"Come, I want to speak to you privately; don't refuse me; I tell you I must," she whispered, reckless of appearances. Luckily, at this moment Mr. Liston woke up from his Athenian reverie, and addressed some common-place remarks to Lewis.

His wife fretted and fumed at the delay, and Lewis made a vow, if he once got out of this scrape, never to make love to another woman.

"Look! look!" whispered Mrs. French to Mrs. Collins, "I declare there's going to be a scene; I wish I hadn't brought my daughter"; and

Mrs. French looked at the last of the flock, a wee, dried up, little thing, who was watching Lewis's difficulty with the keenest interest.

Fortunately Mrs. Bentham happened to be coming up the aisle, and not knowing what was going on, stopped to speak with Mrs. Liston.

Lewis profited by the occasion to slip away, and immediately after the organ snored out a song of welcome to the bride, who was coming up the church between the three rows of benches.

The wedding party consisted of about twenty; they were joined by Lady Alice and her daughters, who were also bridesmaids. They passed round where Mrs. Liston and Mrs. Bentham were sitting. The former was sobbing hysterically, much to her husband's consternation, who could not imagine what was the matter. Mrs. Bentham was quite calm, and she endeavoured to reason with her friend, who was attracting some attention.

"They say that every woman in London is in love with him," whispered Mrs. French, who was burning with curiosity.

"So I have heard," replied Mrs. Collins; "we were talking about it last night. You know my son Henry? Well, he tells me that they said at his club that the church would be filled with the women he had jilted."

"So it appears, but I never should have thought that Mrs. Liston—"

"Nor I," whispered Mrs. French, as she told her daughters to move a little higher up. "I beg your pardon, but you know at that age girls are so curious."

"Indeed they are; but do you know how this marriage was arranged?"

"No, I haven't heard."

"I never would have thought that the Grandervilles, who were so proud, would have consented."

"My dear, they were obliged."

"You don't mean it?"

"I assure you it is a fact; Lady Helen would hear of nobody else. Her father and mother did all they could, but when she took to visiting his studio alone, they had to give way."

"You don't mean it; I should never have thought it! And Lady Helen Trevor! Ah, my dear, girls are not what they used to be. I for one don't understand these new-fashioned ways; a great deal too much latitude is allowed young ladies now-a-days."

"I quite agree with you, my dear. But have you heard the last report about Mr. Seymour?"

"No, I can't say I have."

"Well, you know that no one ever heard of him until Mrs. Bentham took him up."

"Between you and me, I never could understand their friendship."

"You mean that you do understand it," whispered Mrs. French significantly; "but what were you going to tell me?"

"Ah, I had lost myself; well, they say that she has spent thousands of pounds buying his pictures, that she employed a dealer to buy them in secret, and that if it were not for that, he would not make two hundred a year with his painting."

"It does astonish me; I never admired his portraits."

"Nor I, very much; but he paints satin very well, I will say that for him. But look, my dear, there is Mrs. Bentham herself sitting beside Mrs. Liston; well I never! You know she had a great deal to do with making up the marriage."

"Impossible!"

At this moment the bridal party left the vestry. The bride, on her father's arm, and Lewis, with Lady Granderville.

The vicar, a large, portly man in a cloudy white surplice, led the way, and opened the gate of the altar rails, passed inside and arranged the whole party in line before him. The organ ceased playing, he began to read the service, and got as far as, "Therefore if any man can show any just cause why they may not lawfully be joined together, let him now speak—"

Here the vicar raised his monotonous voice, trying to silence a commotion proceeding from the far end of the church, which had necessitated the interference of the pew-opener.

A dispute had arisen among some common looking girls; but beyond the fact that they were clamouring noisily about something, and were likely to come to blows, it was impossible to distinguish between them. Everybody looked round, and Mr. Swannell whispered to his wife:

"I hear the church is filled with women he has deceived in one way or another; I hope that nothing will happen."

Mrs. Swannell tried to look shocked at the idea, and hastened to tell it to Mrs. French, who begged of her to speak low for fear her daughter should hear.

Mr. Day seemed highly diverted at the pew-opener's difficulty, and, under the pretext of assisting him, he went to find out what the row was about. Once Lewis half turned his head to see; he was very pale, and with his whole heart wished that the parson would read the service a little quicker. He thought it would not matter what happened if he were once married, and he wondered, trembling with fear, who the girls were at the end of the church; he tried to think which among his female acquaintances would be capable of stopping his marriage by making a scene, and he was so confused that he could not answer the questions.

Lady Granderville tried to catch her husband's eyes; and, failing to do so, she whispered to Lady Marion:

"Did you hear Mrs. Liston sobbing! Did you notice all the women that are in church?"

"Hush, hush!" said Lady Marion, who had seen everything, and was every minute expecting something awful to occur.

Lady Helen alone seemed unconscious of what was going on; and she said, quite distinctly, holding Lewis's hand:

"In sickness and in health, to love, cherish and to obey, till death us do part; according to God's holy ordinance, and thereto I give thee my troth."

The service then proceeded briskly amid the most profound silence. The pew-opener had, by assuring the young ladies that he had a policeman at hand, succeeded in subduing their clamour; and to ensure silence to the end, he had sat down beside them.

The parson now asked Lewis for the ring, but someone had stirred in the benches near, and, without replying, he looked round quite bewildered.

"The ring, the ring," repeated the parson.

Remembering himself, he fumbled in his pockets; a look of consternation passed over his woe-begone face, and he thought for the moment he had forgotten it.

At last, however, he found it, and having laid it on the book, he said, after the minister, the words:

"With this ring I thee wed, with my body I thee worship, and with all my worldly goods I thee endow," &c.

Having put it on Lady Helen's finger, they both knelt down, and the parson went on with the service.

Once the ring was on her finger, Lewis began to feel more at ease. "After all," he said, "no matter what happens now, they can't break off the marriage."

He looked at Lady Helen with admiration, and congratulated himself on his success. "She is," he thought, "one of the handsomest women, and belongs to one of the first families in England, and I hope they will do something for me." Then the minister put their hands together, and said, in a clear voice that echoed through the church:

"Those whom God hath joined together let no man put asunder."

This phrase impressed Lewis so much with the indissolubility of the marriage contract, that he ventured to look slightly round, but, meeting Mrs. Bentham's eyes, which were fixed on him, he turned away, and thought of how bravely she had behaved: under the influence of the thought he grew quite sentimental.

The organ then began playing, and the minister, going to the Lord's Table, sang with the congregation the hymn beginning, "Blessed are they that fear the Lord and walk in His ways." In the excitement of the singing the general feeling of uneasiness that had prevailed during the ceremony vanished, and everybody seemed to forget that anything unusual had occurred. The bridesmaids began to consider how they looked, Lord Granderville examined the picture of the Last Supper, wondering if his son-in-law could do a better one, and the service went on without interruption to the end. Then the bridal party passed into the vestry, followed by a few friends from the body of the church.

The clerk was there with the books; he held the pen with one hand, and with the other indicated the place where they were to sign. The vicar was still in his surplice, but had put off the solemn look which he wore in church, and was now smiling blandly and shaking hands with those of the company whom he knew.

Lady Jane Archer could not restrain her tears, and as for an old lady in purple, Lewis thought that she would never let his wife sign, several times she had interrupted her; at last, however, it was done, and Lord Worthing and Sir Thomas Towler, P.R.A., added their names as the witnesses.

Then Lewis gave his arm to his wife, whom nobody now could take from him; Lord Granderville gave his arm to the first bridesmaid, Mr. Ripple to Lady Granderville, who was beginning to brighten up, and the whole party passed down the church.

There was a murmur of admiration, and more than one woman envied Lady Helen, and more than one man wished himself in Seymour's place.

Lewis had now recovered his courage, and he looked around him, although still a little timidly. Gwynnie Lloyd, who was sitting on one of the back benches, caught his eyes; her face seemed familiar to him, he wondered for a moment if he had ever seen her. Gwynnie's heart sank within her; she would not have cared had he recognised her. "He does not know me, and it was I who saved him!" she thought, as she got up and struggled with the crowd to get out of the church.

"Thank Heaven," whispered Mrs. French to Lady Jane Archer, who was just behind her, "it passed off without a hitch."

But Lady Jane had been so carried away by the sentiment of what she considered to be the most perfect love match since the days of Romeo and Juliet, that she had perceived nothing, and asked what was meant by there being no hitch.

This embarrassed Mrs. French, who murmured something and pressed on. Sir John lingered, trying to get a word with a a man he knew had a large commission to back—for the Derby. Mr. Day made his way in the same direction in the hopes of hearing something he could turn to his advantage, but Lord Senton detained him to point out a little girl in a common black dress and bonnet who was crying bitterly.

"Who do you think she is?" asked Lord Senton.

"Oh," said Day, giggling, "we shall have some fun"; evidently a happy thought had struck him. "I think she is one of his models. Let's wait, and we'll speak to her."

"You'll lose her if you don't make haste," cried Senton.

"No, no, I sha'n't," replied Day, who knew what he was about; "tell your coachman to wait."

The carriages had now all gone off, and as he passed, Lord Senton made a sign to his man to stay where he was.

"Are you sure she's a model?" he whispered, but Day was walking too fast to answer.

"I beg your pardon," he said, as he caught the girl up, "but if I am not mistaken, you sit for Mr. Seymour."

The little girl stopped, and replied peevishly, "I used to, but I sha'n't anymore."

The two men exchanged glances; this was becoming interesting.

"And how is that?" asked Day, in his blandest tones. "Mr. Seymour doesn't intend to give up painting."

"No," replied the girl, looking at him with a vacant stare; "but she is so well made, one can see that through all her frippery."

"Who's well made?" said Day, pretending not to understand.

"Why, the one he has married, to be sure," returned the girl; "but I must make haste. I have a sitting at half-past one. Are you an artist? if so, will you write to me when you want me?" and after some fumbling, she discovered a card in the bottom of her pocket which she handed to Day, and then hurried away. Day was so surprised that he did not call her back till she was half up the court; but she motioned with her hand that she had no time to waste talking.

"So we shall see Lady Helen as Venus next year; that's a consolation for you, Senton."

"'Pon my word, Day, I won't stand it; you are too deuced coarse. I won't stand by and hear a lady spoken of in that way."

"Well, I said nothing," replied Day, still laughing. "It was the girl who said so, not I. But you had better make haste; you'll be too late for the feed. I am not invited, ta, ta."

The friends shook hands; Lord Senton got into his brougham, somewhat wrath at what he thought was d—— coarse. Day walked down the street, twiddling the girl's card.

GEORGE MOORE

XXVI

THE HONEYMOON

The breakfast was a solemn and wearisome affair; everyone had noticed that the congregation had been a curiously composed one, and it was irritating to have to murmur perpetually that the bride and bridegroom were the handsomest couple in London, when there were so many other interesting criticisms to be made.

Lords Granderville and Worthing made two speeches, as dignified and grave as themselves. Lewis spoke charmingly, at least so the ladies said: he referred to Greek art, female beauty, and to the influence of women in modern life; he congratulated the sex on the way they had elevated love, from the coarse passion it used to be, to the delicate emotion it is in the present century. No one understood exactly what he meant, but it rendered them reflective, particularly Lord Senton; and the elder Miss Davidson profited by the occasion to renew an old flirtation. Lewis and Lady Helen looked at each other embarrassed, and longed to be alone. She grew weary of the perpetual murmur of amiable words which followed her round the drawing-room, and sick of the white monotony of her dress, and was delighted when the time came for her to go upstairs and exchange it for a travelling costume.

Then came the farewells; the carriage was at the door, the trunks were on the cab, and Gwynnie was waiting in the hall. Another kiss Lady Helen had to give to Lady Marion, another to her father, another to her mother; some friends stopped her: at last she got into the carriage.

For a moment they both felt uneasy, but her hand lay on the cushion between them; Lewis took it in his; this gave her confidence, and she turned and looked at him. They gazed fervidly into each other's eyes, then, losing all restraint, she put her arms round his neck and set her lips to his.

She had only kissed him once or twice before, and then reservedly; but now he was her husband, now it was her right, hers and hers only, and how delicious it was to lie back on the soft cushions and lean against each other. Lewis put his arm behind her, drew her closer, and he felt her cheek touch his face.

Lady Helen had not decided where and how she would pass her honeymoon in a hurry. She knew that a month of love with him you love is a dream easy to dream, but difficult to realise; that, once gone, neither wealth nor desire can buy it back; that its sentiments, pleasures, and experiences can be tasted but once. She wanted to have Lewis to herself, wholly to herself; she had determined that each minute should be cherished. She had written of love, she had dreamed of it, and now that she was to enjoy it, all other pleasures and desires were to be put aside: all was to be centred in one supreme thought: all things were to be so calculated that they should complete and perfect it.

Having come to this conclusion, she gladly accepted from a friend who was going abroad the loan of her villa at Teddington. She had heard of the high trees where nightingales sang and of the green swards leading to the water side, shaded by willows where one could sit, talk, read, or sleep in a hammock slung from the branches; she had been told that the rooms were papered with the most delicate greens and blues, and hung with choice specimens of art, old Italian mirrors, whose ledges and brackets were covered with quaint china; that the carpets were utterly soft, and strewn with low-cushioned seats; that Chippendale chairs and beautiful majolica vases stood in the corners; that the windows were filled with flowers and surrounded with Virginia creepers, and that a grey parrot talked all day long to an immense Angora cat who slept on the white fur rug.

"What nook in the world more fitted for love?" the fair owner said, as she pressed Lady Helen to accept. Lady Helen's face flushed as she listened to the description, for she now saw her dream becoming real, all her pale imaginings changing to vivid actualities.

Everything had been prepared to receive them, and on their arrival the butler asked Lady Helen when they would like to dine. The lovers looked at each other, and after a moment's hesitation, Lewis proposed that they should have supper about nine instead. The idea enchanted Lady Helen, who felt that a solemn dinner in the presence of servants would be too utterly wearisome. Besides, she wanted to see the garden and the river, of which she had heard so much; so, calling on Lewis to follow her, she asked the way. They passed through the drawing-room, but only stopped a moment to praise the fantastic furniture and shady nooks and recesses. Two windows painted yellow, with rose blinds, opened into a large verandah full of cane chairs and overgrown with creeping plants; and she thought of the bright morning hours she would pass there *en peignoir*, reading and talking to Lewis. On the right were the tall, shady trees where the nightingales sang; on the left was a wall covered with ivy and lined with graceful poplars. The long swards were garnished with flower-beds, a foreign fir added here and there a note of bright yellow, and through the pale green of the willows came the ever-sounding roar of the weir.

Lady Helen felt the godhead of nature, the fragile flowers, the infinite deeps of the skies; she loved the soft grass under her feet, and it was irresistible joy to breathe the large sweet air. She passed her arm through Lewis's; the intimacy of the pressure was enchantment; she plucked a rose and bruised the soft leaves against her lips, and then gave it to him, that he also might be possessed of its fragrance.

"It is here that the nightingales sing," she said, "and we shall listen to them here when the moonlight is clear, and a light wind wafts the scent of the roses towards the river."

With eyes full of dreams Lady Helen looked round. She felt an immense love for the place rising in her heart. Every tree, every flower, became endeared to her by a thousand expectations; she saw not the mundane swards and flower beds, forgot the rose blinds; in her eyes the garden lost its artificial air, and became an Eden, where the purpose of her life was to be accomplished.

Lewis, too, was full of joy. He put his arm round her and kissed her at once passionately and reverently. She trembled in his arms, and hoarse with emotion, he said:

"Is it not wonderful to think, Helen, that we are now man and wife, that life extends before us, that we shall share it together?"

"I fought hard for you, darling, did I not?" she replied, flinging her arms round his neck, and they both sank on a garden bench. Their emotion was akin to the perfume that floated in the air warm with sunlight; and above them there was a manifold twittering of birds. Sitting side by side, their thoughts drifted: and oppressed with tired passion, she put her face to his and sighed. And, in silence sweeter than speech, they dreamed, until the monotonous roar of the unseen weir throbbed in their ears, and they grew glad to go to the water's edge. Leaning on the iron railing that passed behind the willows, along the circular stone embankment, they looked out into the sky. It was a vast sheet of grey out of which the sun sank, a vague and luminous patch. The rays glittered along the water, bathing in sickly sunlight fleets of skiffs and canoes coming up from Twickenham. On the reedy banks of the weir island, among the tall poplars, pic-nic parties spread their luncheons and shouted at barking dogs that swam after drifting sticks.

"What gaiety! what life!" said Lady Helen, dreamily; "it is quite wonderful."

"Yes, isn't it?" Lewis replied, mechanically, "and those are the scenes 'The moderns' like to paint."

Lady Helen did not answer; she thought for a moment of asking something about "The moderns," but she was too weary to do so, and she continued to watch the continual gliding, rowing and sailing of the boats as they came and went. Sometimes they stopped under their wall, and Lady Helen was gazed at long and curiously. Once a man tried to make a sketch, but the boat drifted away too fast. Lewis wondered if the man could draw, Lady Helen was too listless to pay any attention. The magic-lantern-like appearance that the boats presented as they passed down the barge stream amused her. Only the occupants could be seen: the men in white flannel, bending backwards and forwards; the women, gathered together in the stern, shading their faces with red parasols that stained the green of the opposite bank. The tide was beginning to fall, and the water poured boisterously through the coarse, red piers, whilst from the long, grey rail, leaning figures fished in and about the white line of foam.

The warm May afternoon that had sent the young men and women out of town, the latter in their summer dresses, threatened to turn a little chilly. Lady Helen shivered slightly, but more from lassitude than from the light breeze that shook the drooping willow leaves. She was dressed in pale mauve, fitting very close to the figure, and garnished at the bottom with large plaited flounces. Her saffron-coloured hair was scarcely hidden under a wide hat ornamented with a large plume.

"Do you feel cold, dear?" said Lewis, pressing her arm; "shall I fetch you your jacket?"

"Oh, no, not the least. But are you perfectly happy, Lewis? If this time could last forever!"

Lewis murmured something to the effect that nothing would ever change, but Lady Helen did not appear to hear him, for as she continued to gaze at where the sun sank, her heart grew larger, and she felt as she had never done before the ineffable persuasiveness of nature.

At last, at the end of a long silence, she said:

"Supposing we go out on the river; it is not much after six, and we have not ordered supper until nine."

Lewis approved of the idea; he was beginning to feel very tired of watching the passing boats, and the wide extent of grey sky.

"Do you know how to row?" asked Lady Helen.

"Yes, a little," he replied, "but I don't much care about it."

"Then what shall we do?"

"Sail, of course," he replied, smiling; and they went to the house to get someone to show them the boat-house and to fetch some rugs, for Lewis declared that the evening would be colder than she expected, when the sun was down.

She put on a little grey cloth jacket trimmed with mauve velvet; Lewis found a large wolf-skin rug in the hall; the gardener got the boat out for them and hoisted the sail; then, leaning back in the stern, their hands laid on the rudder, with wind and tide they sailed down the river.

Knowing nothing of the beauties of the Thames, every moment was to them full of charming surprises. On the left was the Anglers' Hotel, with a wide fleet of skiffs drawn up by the black painted wharf. Bronze-throated rowing men walked towards the garden, flaring with long beds of red flowers and cosy with laurels, under which sat girls in clear dresses making tea.

"I suppose the people who live here never think of anything but rowing," said Lewis, astonished at the number of boats.

Lady Helen smiled dreamily; she was very warm, covered over with the wolf skin rug, and, penetrated with a feeling of comfort, she dreamed slowly and indefinitely.

On the right the high bank intercepted the view, but the tops of occasional trees growing blue in the twilight suggested long waste meadows. On the left, as they passed on, villa succeeded villa in uninterrupted succession, some common-place as London houses, some as fantastic as Chinese pagodas, and all hidden or partly hidden in bouquets of large trees. Green swards extended to the water's edge, guarded either by iron railings or by balustrades lined with vases of geraniums. A woman's figure, passing round the balcony of a turretted building, came out against the pale sky; amid the willows, a little boy stopped in his play to watch a passing boat, and amid the universal greenery, a yellow boat-cover struck a singularly sharp note.

"How delicious life is when we love! Oh, Lewis, you don't know how wearisome the years were to me since we talked to gether by the river side in Sussex. I did not know why I could take no interest in anything, but now I know—I was in love with you."

"But I always knew I loved you," he answered, striving to put passion into his words.

"I cannot believe that," she said, tenderly, but with a suspicion of dissatisfaction in her voice; "you have loved lots of women."

"That is not true; any fancies I may have had were but dreams; you are the reality."

She smiled softly with pleasure; the sentiment pleased her, and then, as they sailed through the twilight, they continued to talk in undertones of infinite passion. Lewis spoke fluently, but she only replied occasionally, and continued to watch the landscape which faded before her eyes. It was almost night, the shadows fell like dust; and in the daylight, which still lingered on the water, the Thames glittered and turned like an immense sheet of tin. The reflections of the willows and the studied curves of the swards trembled in the waters with all the strange delicacy of a Japanese water colour, whilst at the back confused heaps of foliage lay piled against a very pale blue sky. Only a few streaks of colour remained to show where the sun had set, and out of the fast paleing heights there fell a calm—tender, vast and delicious; the evening died, gently, without an effort, wrapped in a winding sheet of soft shadow.

The river was rapidly becoming empty of boats; sometimes, like a phantom fish, a long outrigger shot past, the thin sculls flashing tremulously. The skiffs still lingered, the young ladies helping at the oars, whilst the sharp puffing of a pleasure launch broke the silence of the deep distance.

Neither Lewis nor Lady Helen knew anything of sailing, but the breeze blew so gently and steadily that they had nothing to do but to keep in the middle of the stream, and, talking of love and poetry, the time passed imperceptibly.

They had left Twickenham behind before the gathering gloom startled them, and they thought of returning home. Then there was a long delay, and Lady Helen grew irritable as one suddenly awakened. She hated to have her dreams thus rudely dispersed: Lewis had to ask her to change her position in the boat, that he might get off the mud bank, where they had run aground. At one moment they were nearly upset by a false movement on the part of Lady Helen, but Lewis moved to the other side, and the boat righted herself. It was nothing, and he could not help laughing.

"Supposing we were drowned now," he asked, looking at her very seriously.

"I wonder how you can say such a thing," she replied, angrily; "if you loved me, you couldn't speak so unfeelingly."

Seeing that he annoyed her more than he intended, he apologised; and having got the oars out, he toiled on till they reached Twickenham; then, resting on his oars, he proposed that they should get a man to row them home.

"I am perfectly sick of this work," he said, turning the boat's head towards the pier.

"And I am tired of sitting here alone," replied Lady Helen, tenderly.

The night had not turned out so cold as he had anticipated; yet he was glad to resign his place to a boatman, and wrap himself, with Lady Helen, in the large fur rug.

The landscape lay dark beneath the wide heavens, whose hollow, speckled with a few stars, opened larger and deeper; the river faded on either side into darkness, and the boat followed the stream of crystal light that fell from the mounting moon. On the right a sea of shadow rolled over the gardens, and the black masses of the trees stretched across the sky. On the left all was solitary, and violet, and grey. Along the sedge bank a boat passed with someone asleep in the stern: far ahead, over the bending shoulders of the man towing, a red cap appeared, the last point of colour that remained in the gradual effacement.

Lady Helen lay back on the cushion like one in an invalid chair, and listlessly twisted the hair of the wolf-skin rug. She was very warm in her jacket, and, watching the lights darting through the dark trees, she sought for the windows of their house. Her thoughts and his faded into a sensation of glowing numbness; and slowly they savoured the voluptuous idleness which overtakes lovers rowing dreamily throught the moonlight. Lewis held Helen's hand in his, and touching the silken skin, slightly moist and delicately soft, he felt her life mingling and becoming one with his.

The green swards were as bright as day, the alleys were filled with blue shadows, and amid the river reeds the monotonous chant of the frogs continued unceasingly. From the distant fields a landrail answered a nightingale that sang in a tree close by, and the light winds that passed seemed to shudder with kisses and warm breaths.

XXVII

The Honeymoon Continued

Next morning she was down a few minutes before Lewis. As she lingered in the breakfast-room she noticed, with surprise, that it was only laid for two, and then she smiled at her mistake: she had forgotten that they were living together. As she passed through the drawing-room she stopped to look at the pretty furniture. The Italian glass over the chimney attracted her; she examined the tiny cups and vases with which it was covered, and catching sight of herself in the glass, she wondered why she had done her hair that way. She was in a grey *peignoir*, and her pale hair was tied into a knot upon her neck. Then she blushed, remembering that it was Lewis who had wished it so. The *peignoir* amused her, she had never come down to breakfast so before, and she thought she had never looked so handsome.

Her eyes were clear coloured as the morning skies, but around them the skin was rimmed with a somewhat deeper blue—her lips looked like flowers of blood. Elated with a thousand thoughts, she passed into the garden, and breathed the sweet air with *gourmandise*. Picking a red rose, she placed it in her bosom; she started back, frightened by a chattering blackbird that dived into a thicket on the other side. The weir roared loudly; she caught sight of the river glittering through the leaves of the willows, and the garden tempted her on; but the cold dew, which lay heavily on the grass, pierced the satin shoe. Then, hearing Lewis's voice, she hastily plucked a rose for him and ran back.

The servant had brought up the tea and coffee—and she took her place at the head of the table. Feeling a little nervous, she cast a rapid glance to see that the butler was not looking, and asked Lewis with a sign which he would take. The man seemed to her to fidget about the room an interminable time, but when at last he did go, it was delightful to attend to Lewis, to coax him, to talk, to ask him a hundred times if he loved her, and to hear him say that he did—fifty times more than ever.

The morning was passed dreaming in the verandah. Lady Helen lay back in a long cane chair. A light air floated through the garden, the shadows of leaves trembled on the pavement, wings were heard vaguely in the trees, and the lovers murmured for hours the softest words and phrases.

And yet it was not for a few days that she appreciated the whole luxury of living *en ménage.* At first there was a slight sense of strangeness, but this wore off; every hour brought new pleasures, little surprises, which offered her the most exquisite delight. Once, it was running from the housekeeper's room to the verandah, where Lewis was smoking his morning cigar, to ask him which he would like better for dessert, a cream or an ice. Another time, it was sewing a button on his glove; but, above all, it was an exquisite satisfaction to write "my husband" to Lady Marion. "Yes," she thought, as she paused after she had written it, "it was I who won him away from all the others. Yes, I am his little wife, whom he loves better than all the world, and he is my little husband, whom I love better than all the world." Smiling, she repeated the words over, half conscious of but fascinated by their childishness, letting, all the while, her thoughts drift back to some little remembrance of a day or two, or perhaps only an hour or two old; something she had said to him, something he had said to her of their love, or of love in general, was sufficient matter for an hour's reflection.

In the afternoon they would go for long drives, or else they would take the boat and row to some shady place, where Lewis would sketch, while she talked or read.

Lewis had a knack of rendering himself so wonderfully intimate that she soon had no secrets from him, and was less reserved with him than with her mother or aunt. These intimacies fascinated her. Quite naturally, he would take up the dress she had taken off, turn it inside out, and hang it up; he could lace the body of her dress far better than her maid, and, as if by instinct, his fingers divined the use of the pins and the hooks and eyes.

As the days went by, Lady Helen grew to love him more and more; hourly his companionship grew more necessary to her. She felt that to lose him would be like losing part of herself, so completely in unison were their tastes and sentiments. Yet, notwithstanding, Fate managed to extend her crooked hand, and tear away some of their illusions before the end of the honeymoon.

One evening it was a little chilly, and for sociability they had ordered a fire in the drawing-room. Lady Helen was glad of this, for she had often thought how delicious it would be to sit dreamily looking into the embers, with Lewis's head resting against her knees, and she had almost hated the fine days for what they deprived her of.

The lovers were sitting in this much-longed-for position when the dressing-bell rang for dinner. They had just come in from a long drive, and to sit in a cold dining-room, just as they were beginning to feel comfortable, and exchange their sweet words of endearment for a lot of conventionalities would be detestable. Lady Helen felt her heart sink at the thought. Guessing what was passing in her mind, Lewis proposed that they should have dinner brought up to the drawing-room. The tea table would be quite big enough for their two plates. It was just what Lady Helen felt she would like, and she kissed him for the idea; she wondered how he always thought of things so utterly fascinating.

The dinner passed off delightfully. They waited on each other, and they had exchanged glasses a dozen times.

The *sole au gratin* Lady Helen declared was the most delicious she had ever tasted; the cutlets were perfect; and not to be bothered by servants, they had had the dinner brought up at once. There was a *riz de veau* inside the fender, and behind Lewis's arm-chair a bottle of champagne stood in its silver bucket of ice. The windows were shut, and the roar of the river was only heard vaguely.

Lady Helen slowly picked the bone of the lamb cutlet with her white teeth; and her yellow hair, which had fallen down her back, glittered in the light of the reading lamp like corn under a setting sun. Both their faces were flushed with the glare of the fire.

"Well, Helen, what do you think of being married? 'Tis nicer dining like this than with my mother-in-law, isn't it?"

Lady Helen replied with a superb gesture of disgust, and Lewis helped her to some strawberries and some more champagne. They had finished a bottle between them.

"Oh, Lewis, you don't know how my mother annoyed me at times; it was quite impossible to live with her."

"I hope it wasn't for that only that you married me; you are not complimentary," he said, laughing.

She squeezed his foot in reply. The table being small, they could not move without kicking each other, and to prevent anymore accidents, Lady Helen held Lewis's foot between hers. Then for a few moments the lovers ate their strawberries in silence, until Lewis, amused at the idea of a *tete-a-tete* dinner with Lady Granderville, burst out laughing, and said he would make a sketch, but Lady Helen held his foot, declaring that he should not spoil their *tete-a-tete* with his tiresome sketching: she complained that she could not say a word but that he wanted to illustrate it. At last, on his promising not to fetch a pencil, she allowed him to get up and get the coffee. They had no cups, and hating to ring, they chose a couple from the Venetian mirror, and after rinsing them in the champagne bucket, they resumed their seats.

Their little dinner had been a complete success; it had had a quaint charm of its own, and was a refinement of pleasure as subtle as it had been unexpected.

Helen looked at her husband, her eyes were luminous with love; and, as her thoughts detached themselves, she remembered the time when she did not possess him: she wondered how she had lived through those bleak years full of febrile aspirations and irritating deceptions. She recalled everything, from the first waltz to the time when they knelt at the altar together.

"You don't know how hard I fought for you, how difficult my position was with my mother."

"Well, I hope you are not dissatisfied with your bargain," he replied, laughing.

It irritated her to hear him laugh; he constantly did so at the wrong times; but she pretended not to hear him, and continued to sip her coffee; her white cheeks blazing with two red spots. Then, after a pause, she continned:

"You don't know how afraid I was of losing you; I thought the days would never go by; even in church I thought something might happen to take you from me."

"Not half so much afraid as I was," thought Lewis, and he chuckled inwardly.

"But, suppose anything had happened, and we had been forever separated," she murmured, looking at him intently; "what should we have done? Do you know it frightens me?"

"What a foolish baby you are to think of such disagreeable things."

Lady Helen had finished her coffee, and, absently, they listened to the weir, which enveloped the windows with a murmur of vague sound. The light of the lamp fell on the long grey *peignoir* and Lewis's upturned face, whilst out of the large deep of purple shadow which filled both sides of the room there seemed to rise a dreamy languor, a desire for infinite rest. They remained silent until, at last, Lady Helen said, speaking very slowly:

"You know, Lewis, I have never seen such beautiful hands as yours; I can scarcely look at them without trembling."

Lewis laughed softly, and blew his cigarette smoke into wreaths. Neither of them spoke again for some moments, and Lady Helen continued to caress Lewis's hand which she held between hers. At last the glitter of a diamond awoke her from her reveries, and she examined a ring he wore. Then, seeing it was a lady's, she drew it off his finger before he was aware.

"Why, Lewis!" she said, in a tone of voice indicative at once of surprise and suspicion.

Lewis looked up puzzled. It was a ring that Mrs. Liston had sent him, and having found it that morning in one of his pockets, he had slipped it, without thinking, on his finger. Lady Helen's eyes were beginning to flash with anger, and fearing a scene, he told her that he had bought it for her, and had forgotten to give it to her. The lie was not ingenious, but he had no time to think of a better one. Anyhow, it seemed to answer as well as the best, for Lady Helen, remembering how he had bought her a hat in a similar way, brightened up, and the look of distrust faded from her face. Seeing that the story succeeded, he resolved to brave it out; so, putting his arm round her waist, he said, in his most coaxing voice:

"I thought it would please you, baby, and that it would be sweet on those white, oh, the very whitest of fingers in the world."

There were some words engraved on the inside, but he trusted that Lady Helen would not think of examining the ring that night, and that he would be able before long to find an opportunity of stealing it. Lady Helen smiled with pleasure, and she leant over the table, holding the ring under the lamplight. He kissed her, and whispered in her ear softly, trying to attract her attention. But suddenly, as she turned the ring over, she noticed there was something written inside. Lewis saw the movement, and turned pale. It was all up with him; the truth must come out.

Thinking it was one of the little surprises he was so fond of playing upon her, Lady Helen eagerly held it closer to the light, and read:

"From Lily to Lewis."

In the silence of the room her astonished voice sounded like a bell. She did not understand, and she looked to her husband for an explanation, but seeing his embarrassed look, the truth began to strike her.

"So, then, this is some woman's present to you; and you are wearing it even now," she said, through her teeth.

"My dear Helen, just listen, and I'll explain."

The scene was very short. Her white skin grew ghastly white with rage; she stammered for lack of passionate words to express her disgust; he pleaded to be heard, but, unable to contain herself, she threw the ring in his face, and walked upstairs.

So taken aback was he, that he did not at first attempt to follow, but stood looking into space; then, suddenly darting forward, he hurried after her: he was too late, she had locked herself in her room. He knocked at the door, but receiving no answer, went down to the drawing-room and walked up and down excitedly.

"What cursed luck!" he thought. "Just because I took it off her finger once, and said it was a pretty one. I never made love to her!" And with a grave look he concluded with this phrase, full of unconscious cynicism:

"That's just the way people get into rows, not for what they do, but for what they don't do."

He looked round vacantly, and his eyes fell upon the ring; it lay in the fender amid the fire-irons. He picked it up, and not knowing what to do with it, put it in his pocket. Then, after cursing Mrs. Liston and her presents, he got up, drank some wine, pushed the *débris* of the dinner out of the way, lit a cigar, and waited for his wife. The hours went by slowly; he sat smoking, inventing excuse after excuse, trying to think of the best way out of the difficulty.

At last the clock struck eleven, and the servant came to take away the lights. Lewis dismissed him, saying that he was going to sit up a little longer, but that he had no further need of him, that he would turn the lights out himself before going to bed. The man offered to remove the plates and dishes, but Lewis, who was irritated to the last degree, told him he could not be bothered by the clattering, that it could be done in the morning. The butler went out wondering. Lewis smoked on. The lamp burned out, and in the gathering gloom the crimson ash of his cigar made one fiery point, which at every respiration illumined the thinking face. He still expected his wife to come downstairs, and he waited listening nervously to the footsteps that approached, and then died away at the end of the passages, to the locking of doors, the shutting of shutters, and the different noises attendant on the fastening up of a house for the night.

At last the servants ceased to go to and fro, and he ventured to creep up the dark stairs and knock again at his wife's door. Once, twice, he knocked, but got no answer; he pleaded and grew seriously alarmed, and wondered what Helen intended to do. Then he went down to the drawing-room, lit some candles, and thought the matter over, after which he unbarred the window and took a turn in the garden. He watched his wife's window, and called her by name, and wondered if he could climb to her window by the ivy that glistened in the moonlight; then he went back, piled some more coal on the fire, smoked a cigarette, abused Mrs. Liston for having dared to send him the confounded ring, and finally went upstairs and pleaded piteously again for admittance. But his prayers were unheeded, and seeing at last that there was no chance of obtaining even an answer, he got a rug out of the hall and went to sleep on the sofa in the drawing-room.

When he was awakened by the arrival of the housemaid with the dustpan, he mumbled something about having overslept himself, fetched his hat and went down to the river. The time went dreadfully slowly; everything was unpleasant. The grass was dripping wet, the willows were weeping in every sense of the word, and he wandered about feeling most wretchedly miserable. He considered the desirability of packing up his easel, and going off to paint. It would be, he thought, an excellent way of paying his wife out; but his courage failed him at the last, and he loitered about waiting for the time when Lady Helen would ring for her maid.

At last his patience was rewarded, and, seizing the opportunity when Gwynnie was going down for some hot water, he pushed passed her, rushed into his wife's room and locked the door after him, determined that she should at least hear him.

Lady Helen had just taken her hands out of the basin and was drying them slowly with a towel. Lewis saw that she had been crying.

"Oh, Helen," he said, "you must listen; I can explain everything if you will only hear me."

She said nothing, but stood waiting. This somewhat disconcerted him; he had expected her to assail him with indignant words, and to push him, with her long white hands out of the room. He hesitated a moment, then volubly explained the story of the ring, adhering strictly to the truth, which for once in a way he was unable to amend.

Lady Helen looked at him fixedly, and the tears glistened in her eyes.

"Is this really true?" she murmured.

He advanced towards her, and strove to take her in his arms. She resisted a moment, and then suddenly he felt warm tears on his cheek, and moist hands clasped round his neck. The lovers kissed, vowed, pleaded, and were reconciled. She loved him again, and more passionately than ever, not because she either believed him or disbelieved him, but because she had been miserable, and felt that she could not live without his love.

XXVIII

Passing a Page

After this, their first and last lovers' quarrel, Lewis and Helen again took up the course of their honeymoon, and the days passed like long, sweet dreams in the peace of the fair river-side villa, in the midst of the odorous deaths of flowers, whose soft leaves falling on the marble tables scanned the almost imperceptible passing of the hours. There they sat side by side, their hands' flesh melted together, and their thoughts lost in a *far niente* of happiness; words often seemed an effort, and they could but exchange soft pressures of fingers, and smiles of languid adoration.

Then, again, they would awake from their reveries, and go for excursions into the country. The soft days of June were delicious, and they grew, as it were, spiritually drunk with the delicate air. But it was the garden they loved best. There was not a tree they did not know, not a corner that had not its own particular memory. Under the great shady trees on the right they used to sit when the moonlight was warm. In the summer-house they took tea in the afternoon. There was a rose tree there, and they used to bet kisses about the buds that would blossom during the night, and in the morning they ran across the wet grass to see who had won. Then, after breakfast, they went to lie in a large, dreamy place under the laurels, where they could see nothing of the outer world, and hear nothing but the silence humming above them in the trees. They went with books that they did not read, but which suggested long and delightful conversations; and when tired of talking, or teasing some crawling insect with a cane or a parasol, their souls filled with summer-sleepy idleness, Lewis would ask her to sit: he made sketches of her while she wreathed her hair with flowers, or read poetry, lying full length on a garden bench. They were never at a loss for occupation; for being both artists, a ray of light, a bit of perspective, a passing figure, were to them subjects of endless interest.

Lady Helen had her poetry to write; they worked in collaboration; she planned a volume of verse to be entitled "Flowers of Love and Sadness," and, as they talked, Lewis composed a frontispiece.

But at last came the final week of the honeymoon, when their thoughts had begun to drift away from the garden, when the present could no longer hide the future from their eyes; and these last days were full of infantile sadness. It grieved them to leave the garden where they had been so happy; they visited each nook; and even when the carriage came to take them away, Lady Helen ran back to pluck a rose from the kissing-tree. She gathered two, a bud and a blown flower; and quarrelling as to who should wear the former, the lovers drove to London.

They went straight to Lady Marion's, where they were to stay until the house she had chosen was ready to receive them.

There was little time to lose, for, as said the whole family, "He is married to her now, and the best thing to do is to put him into a house and get him as many orders as possible." Lord and Lady Granderville, who had just come back from Paris, where they had been staying with some friends before returning to America, begged of him to work hard, for they could do nothing more for Lady Helen than they had already done.

It was Lady Granderville who had insisted on this explanation. She foresaw all kinds of money difficulties in the future, and she declared that the young man should be properly warned, and if after that he chose to run into debt, why, nobody could help him.

Then came a large dinner-party at Lord Worthing's, to which the leaders of the Conservative party had been asked, so that they might bid goodbye to Lord Granderville, who was to start on the following day. It was a very formal affair. Lewis and Helen peeped at each other between groups of grave men over the large shoulders of dowagers, and she took that evening her first lessons in the art of touting for orders.

The next day Lord and Lady Granderville bade their children goodbye. Lewis was pensive, Lady Helen careless, Lady Granderville hysterical, and Lord Granderville sincerely affectionate. He shook his son-in-law's hand and wished him success, kissed his beautiful daughter, and begged of her not to be extravagant.

But as she was now the wife of an artist, and was received in artistic as well as fashionable society, she had determined, at all costs, to live up to the latter. This she found somewhat difficult. Her life had been spent abroad in the society of diplomatists, and beyond the construction of a sonnet she knew nothing. However, remembering that in St. Petersburg she had heard a great deal of French taste and fashion, she resolved, after some hesitation, to make her drawing-room an exact copy of a French salon. She thought it would be a novelty, and, without confiding her project to anyone, spent her mornings, not only in looking at French poufs and long sofas in the style of the Empire, but, what was worse, in buying them.

The house Lady Marion and Mrs. Bentham had chosen suited them admirably. It was in Kensington, towards Fulham, and Lady Helen learned with satisfaction that that was as artistic a neighbourhood as any in London. The rent, with the studio, was only three hundred a year, which was not much, considering the difficulty of getting both together, and Lady Helen would not for worlds have her husband paint anywhere but in her house.

"It would be perfectly wretched," she said, "to see him going off every morning, and would destroy the whole charm."

Lewis having declared himself satisfied with the light, a lease was drawn and signed, and Lady Helen occupied herself more than ever in choosing the furniture. It was left entirely to her. Lewis had to go off to his studio early in the morning, for his marriage had brought him some orders, including two portraits.

Lady Helen was, of course, delighted, and yet it was very tiresome to see him always at work. She would have liked nothing better than to trot about with him from shop to shop, asking his advice; but, on the other hand, she hoped to surprise him by a display of good taste; and already she congratulated herself on the success of her French salon. She had confided her project to no one except Lady Marion, who offered no opinion on the subject. The old lady, although strong on the origin of the Irish castles, was weak in modern æstheticism.

Time went by very quietly; Lewis painted all day at his portraits of the two dowagers, who, he said, wearied him, both with their conversation and their lumpy shoulders. In the evening he asked his wife how the furnishing was getting on, but she answered him evasively, determined to surprise him.

This continued until one day, catching sight of her in a shop in Regent Street, he went in, and found her buying two vulgar, gold candelabras. He endeavoured to dissuade her, but believing in her own judgment, she argued the point with him, and gradually the truth came out.

Lady Helen was dreadfully disappointed. She had spent the better part of two hundred pounds, and felt very mortified.

Lewis consoled her; he assured her it was not her fault; she had lived out of England all her life, and could not be expected to understand the developments artistic tastes had taken in the last few years.

As luck would have it, they were going that evening to dine with the Hiltons, and Lewis said that she must see what an artist's house was, before she could think of furnishing one. There she met the most distinguished of the Mediævalists. Lewis showed her Morris's most artistic wall papers, chairs older than Chippendale, dados, the finest Worcester, Derby, Bristol, and Chelsea. She listened in amazement, believed at once, and strove vainly to grasp the meaning of all that was said to her. Having been thus baptised and received a convert, she asked to be taught. She implored Lewis to come with her, feeling, as she said, "hopelessly at sea." For the present, he said, he could not possibly spare the time, and he advised her to ask Mrs. Bentham, whom he declared to be a far greater authority on such matters than he. Mrs. Bentham consented readily to this arrangement, and at eleven o'clock every morning Lady Helen went to fetch her; and then till lunch, in Pall Mall, or Bond Street, they discussed furniture.

As the days passed, the two women became dearer and firmer friends. After shopping, Mrs. Bentham would take Lady Helen home to lunch, and then, later in the afternoon, they would go to drive in the park, and as they leaned back, shading their faces with their sunshades, they talked together, and not unfrequently Lewis was the subject of their conversation. And Mrs. Bentham did not attempt to conceal her affection for Lewis, but the most careful observer could not detect in it anything that was not both motherly and friendly. Great as her passion had been, she had been able to subdue it. She went to balls and dinner parties dressed as a woman who wished to please, and no one except Mrs. Thorpe knew of the great change that had come upon her friend's life. Sometimes she regretted that the past was the past; but time soothes us with hands which, although they may be murderous, are yet most merciful.

As for Lady Helen, she enjoyed herself immensely. Under Mrs. Bentham's instructions she soon began to see the beauties of Wedgewood, to distinguish between Japanese and Worcester, and to pooh-pooh the new Saxony, which at first she thought as good as the old. The red French curtains were replaced by pale blue, and the poufs by Chippendale chairs. Mrs. Bentham was glad when her pupil had made sufficient progress to be trusted to rummage about and make purchases on her own account, for she naturally soon grew tired of this perpetual bric-à-brac hunting. But Lady Helen was indefatigable, and she grew daily more infatuated with the charm of collecting. Trouble she thought nothing of, and she extended her search for old chairs and china to thirty and forty miles round London. On these excursions she was always accompanied by her maid, Gwynnie Lloyd, to whom she had become greatly attached.

Gwynnie's kind, gentle nature was very sympathetic to Lady Helen's ardent and impulsive disposition. Gwynnie's calm, quiet little ways interested her, and when she caught sight of her in the glass, as she humbly twisted flowers into the pale hair, Lady Helen wondered what the girl's past had been. Once or twice she had asked her; but Gwynnie only looked shy, and answered in generalities. But if Gwynnie did not speak much of herself, she tried in her timid way to get Lady Helen to talk to her about Lewis. Her head was full of vague surmises, and night and day she wondered how he had managed to succeed so thoroughly. She especially sought to find out who Mrs. Bentham was, and in the hope of hearing something about her, Gwynnie consented to walk out with the footman on many a Sunday afternoon.

The man was glad to tell her all he knew, which amounted to this, that it was common talk that Mrs. Bentham had bought Mr. Seymour's pictures, and helped him in his "beginnings"; this was not very precise, but with Lady Helen on one side, and the different ladies' maids on the other, Gwynnie succeeded gradually in piecing together the greater part of Lewis's past life. She did this from the interest she felt in him, without any other motive; and even when she arrived at what she believed to be the facts, she failed to draw any conclusion from them. For years his memory had exercised a dim and indecribable influence over her, and she was unable either to blame or praise him. She accepted him as she had always done, as the guiding power of her life, and she could not disassociate their meeting, and living under the same roof, unknown to each other, from some strange fatality. Every link of the chain that bound her seemed to have been forged in mystery.

At first she fancied he would recognise her; but when he passed her on the stairs unheeding, she stole away to her room in bitter disappointment, tears flowing down her pock-marked cheeks. Her name, too, had been changed to Westhall, that of Lady Helen's former maid, so there was no trace of her past left, and she felt too weak to struggle against what seemed fated to be. She would have given worlds to tell him she was the Gwynnie Lloyd who used to walk with him on the London Road, but the grandeur with which she was surrounded had so impressed her with a sense of her own insignificance, that she could not bring herself to the point of making herself known. Besides she had very few opportunities of doing so; once or twice at Twickenham she had been very near it, but, when the words were on her lips, something had occurred to remind her so forcibly that she was only his servant, that her courage had slipped away from her. She supposed he would be glad to see her, but when she felt the most tempted to reveal herself she remembered that she would have to tell how she had sat for him—then she paused trembling. Lady Helen, she thought, would most assuredly grow to dislike her, and feeling that the end would be dismissal, she resolved to keep her counsel, and wait for something that would "put it all right." She hoped he would some day recognise her; and as the time passed she grew to feel the poetry of her position, and the sadness of living near him, unknown, was not without its charm: often she would escape from the servants' hall, and, deaf to the footman's entreaties, would go upstairs and read a sentimental romance, striving all the while to trace a likeness between the characters described and Lewis and Lady Helen and herself.

The "Last Days of Pompeii" especially delighted her, and after reading a favourite passage, looking out into the summer night, she saw herself as the blind girl, and Lady Helen as Iona. The vague sentiment which had impoverished her life, and rendered her incapable of appreciating what fate had given her, still held its mastery over her.

XXIX

Married Life

Meanwhile everything went well with the Seymours. Contrary to their expectations, their house was finished before the end of July, and they were enabled to give a ball. Everybody came, and Lords and Marquises jabbered of art as well as they knew how. Lady Helen was much admired; and when the bills came in, they found that they had spent nearly three hundred pounds. Three hundred pounds for one ball, Lewis said, was a great deal, and yards of canvas waiting to be covered with dowagers shoulders rose before his eyes. He looked a little frightened, but his wife threw her arms round his neck. "My dear," she said, "you had to give something, you know, and it was as well to do it well. Never mind; you will get it back with a portrait or two."

Lewis hoped that it would turn out as she said, but confessed that three hundred pounds for one ball was not reassuring as a first experience of domestic administration. For a couple of days the incident threw a gloom over their happiness. However, Lewis was the first to weary of unpleasant foreboding, and he consoled Lady Helen with the assurance that it was an acknowledged fact, that to make money one had to spend money, and since they were going to stay with the Sedgwicks in Scotland, they would be living on nothing for the next two months. A week after, in the Highlands of Scotland, they had forgotten all about their lost three hundred. The house was full of nice people, and as a newly-married couple who had sacrificed everything for art and love, they were the centre of attraction. People were asked from far and wide to meet them; and they enjoyed themselves immensely.

Lewis painted a portrait or two, made a few sketches of Highland scenery, and talked a great deal of the picture of Clytemnæstra he was going to paint. She was to be represented in the full moonlight watching for the beacon fires that would announce the death of her son.

Lewis thought highly of the subject, and decided that neither time nor money were to be spared. He declared that this time he would fire a broadside into the whole lot, Moderns and Mediævalists, that would oblige the academicians to elect him an associate at once. For a long time he had been cherishing this idea, and had come to the conclusion that it would be as well to give the R.A.'s. an opportunity of doing him this act of simple justice. He declared that a sound classical picture, of undeniable merit, was sorely needed, for it would give many the long-desired opportunity of dealing a death blow at "The moderns," whose influence, he regretted to perceive, was daily increasing.

Holt, who had lately been made an R.A., had entirely espoused their cause; and there were others among the forty who secretly sympathised with the new sect. "The mediævalists," it was true, out of hatred to "The moderns," made common cause with "The classics"; but it was known that they cared little for the trailing white draperies of the heroes and heroines of ancient Greece; and this, Lewis said, was the worst feature of the case. He declared that Mr. Hilton was the only one of the lot that could be depended upon; and he was often asked to dinner, for the purpose of calmly discussing the best means of resisting this modern vandalism, which, they agreed, was sapping the very base of English art. In the studio, after dinner, the conversation was continued in front of Clytemnæstra, whom Mr. Hilton was expected to criticise gently and admire vigorously.

In reality he cared but little for Lewis's pictures, but he was obliged to support him in the Academy for three reasons: The first was his hatred of "The moderns"; the second that Lord Worthing was an extensive purchaser of his mediæval pictures; and the third, that Mrs. and Miss Hilton, received certain invitations solely on account of their friendship with the Seymours.

It was now spring; the pictures had all been sent in, and Lewis profited by the temporary absence of Lady Helen, who was staying on a short visit with Lady Marion, to ask a number of artists to dinner, with the intention of formally talking over the prospects of the exhibition. It had been rumoured for sometime past, in artistic circles, that Thompson, who had now a party behind him, was going to send a very large work, which might not only be considered as a final exemplification of all his latest theories, but as a direct challenge flung to "The mediævalists and classics." It was also known that Mr. Hilton had for a long time been preparing a large picture, to be called "The Land of Hesperia"; it was already spoken of in the art world as the rival picture; and everybody was busy wondering if the hanging committee would take cognizance of the matter, and place Modern and Mediævalist side by side. Mr. Hilton himself, when questioned on the subject, took a very lofty air. He declared that his opinions and tastes were well known; that he was not aware that Mr. Thompson had painted his picture in any spirit of rivalry; and, he affirmed, loudly, that as far as he himself was concerned, such an idea had never entered his head; that he had painted, and would exhibit, "The Land of Hesperia," just as he would any other picture he might be pleased to paint, without reference to any other artist's work. When questioned more minutely, he did not deny that the "Hesperia" was, as far as size went, of about the same dimensions as Mr. Thompson's picture; but said that he would strenuously object to their being hung in the same room; and that if, after that, the public still insisted on attaching any particular significance to the size of his pictures, he could not be held responsible.

Everyone listened deferentially until the academician had finished speaking; and Mr. Ripple, who had been all the while elaborating a compliment, said:

"The interest the public take in such controversies is quite too contemptible, and you may be sure that before the first of. May the newspapers, no longer contented with a duo, will be demanding a trio, and that our friend's Clytemnæstra will be put forward as the watchword of 'The classics.'"

A sweet smile of approval, with various fragments of the word "appropriate," went round the table, and inwardly blessing Ripple for the suggestion, Lewis fondly hoped that the paragraphist would not delay a minute to indite a par. for the *World*. But Mr. Hilton had great difficulty in looking amiable. Much as he might hate Thompson's work, he knew the suggestion of rivalry would secure for "The Land of Hesperia" an amount of notice it could not otherwise possibly obtain; but to have the Clytemnæstra dragged into the competition would, he thought, only throw ridicule on the whole thing. Lewis murmured that the honour assigned to him was too great, and asked Mr. Hilton if he had yet seen this picture of Thompson's.

"Oh, yes," replied the academician, "I saw it today."

"And what is it like?" asked several voices from the top of the table.

"It is, of course, very objectionable," suggested Mr. Ripple.

"Naturally," returned Lewis, as he bent forward to listen.

The butler ceased to ask the guests which they would take—sherry or Madeira, and a deep silence came over the dinner table.

"Mr. Thompson's Academy picture this year," said Mr. Hilton, emphatically, "represents a very dirty maid-of-all-work, in a dirty print dress, cleaning a dirty doorstep, or, rather, idling in her work, and talking to the milkman."

A look of horror went round the table, and everyone laid down his soup spoon.

"You must be joking," said Lewis, in a voice of mingled incredulity and disgust.

"I assure you such is the fact," replied the academician, going back to his soup.

"You don't mean to say you have hung such an abomination on the walls of the Academy?" exclaimed an artist from the top of the table.

"I protested, but we can no longer close our doors to this man. Holt has several supporters, and he insisted that it should be hung on the line at the end of the long room. I assure you it is not an edifying spectacle, but we had to give way."

Lewis shrugged his shoulders.

"But, my dear fellow, look at the success he would have had, if we had not given way," continued Mr. Hilton. "Holt threatened to resign, and if that happened the public would have flocked to see Thompson's picture, no matter where he exhibited it." Lewis did not answer, but Mr. Ripple said he would use all his power to get the picture "slated"— that the *World* could be counted upon.

Then "The moderns," and the influence they were beginning to exercise on the public taste, were passionately discussed. Mr. Hilton declared that it was perfectly shameful that—thanks to the undisguised patronage of Holt, and the secret sympathy of someother R.A.'s—not only Thompson, but the whole of his tribe, Frazer, Stanley, &c., had made a regular descent upon Burlington House. Stanley had a picture of two washer-women, one ironing and the other yawning; Crossley, a pic-nic party—a flare up of blue and pink dresses; Frazer, a railway junction; and as for Holt, his picture was neither more nor less than a group of peasant women bathing, and Mr. Hilton declared that he could give no idea of its abominable coarseness. "Soon," he said, "it will be impossible for us to take our daughters to the Academy; and I should not be surprised if we found ourselves boycotted by the givers of school treats; these people have to be considered. Then Lewis explained that he had entertained hopes that "The moderns" would respect the sanctity of the nude, but that now the last sacrilege had been committed.

During the next fortnight, everyone was on tip-toe with excitement. The news of the coming contest between "The moderns" and

Mediævalists had—thanks to the paragraphists—been spread through the regions of Mayfair and Belgravia, and it already formed one of the ingredients of fashionable table talk.

Ripple had written and re-written the "par." stating that Mr. Seymour's Clytemnæstra was to do battle for "The classics" in the impending contest—now so much talked about—but he could not get it printed anywhere, except in a wretched rag called *Fashion*, that no one ever read. He had begged the editor of the *World*, for the sake of all the descriptions of scandals and weddings he had supplied him with, to insert the "par." but to no purpose—the man in the leather arm-chair had obstinately refused. Lewis was in despair, and Ripple was mortified; he said he would give up journalism. But notwithstanding the threat, the days went by, and one grey morning about ten o'clock, a group of men, talking excitedly, crossed the courtyard of Burlington House.

XXX

A Private View

It was private view day at the Royal Academy. The doors had just been opened, and in another hour or so the *elite* of London would be there. But for the moment the galleries were quite deserted; not a soul was to be seen but one little old man, who moved silently along the lines of pictures, stopping every now and then to make entries in his pocket-book.

"By Jove!" exclaimed Stanley, "we aren't the first after all; there goes old Bendish; he must have been waiting outside before the doors were opened."

"So it is," said Crossley; "well, it is good of the little beggar to take so much interest in our success; let's come and speak to him."

"Take interest in our success," growled Thompson; "considering he has hundreds of pounds' worth of our pictures in his possession, all of which he bought for a tenth part of their value."

"Yes, but he did not know that when he bought them; let's come and speak to him, anyhow," replied Harding, interested in the fact that it was principally a silly old man, knowing no more about art than a child, whom fate had selected to keep alive the most important artistic movement of the present century. And the novelist proceeded to explain how the cursed *dilettanti*, who for the past ten years had done nothing but mumble about the traditions, would, in a week hence, be nodding their heads suggestively, and softly murmuring of a modern art, the outcome of our present civilisation.

"So, Mr. Bendish," said Thompson, accosting the old man, "you have come to see us; well, this time, I think we are going to have a success."

"Oh, splendid, Mr. Thompson; I have just been looking at your picture. I wish I had bought it," replied the old man, in a thin voice.

"Why, surely you don't want anymore of our pictures, do you?" returned Thompson, laughing; "you must have some hundreds."

"Yes, yes," said Mr. Bendish, "I think I have a fine collection. I have been very busy sorting them since I heard of your success. You must come and see them, they cover two whole walls of the big room."

"Very well, I will," said Thompson, shaking hands with the old man, who immediately continued peering at and taking notes of the different pictures.

"What a strange old beggar he is," said Crossley; "you know he wouldn't part with anyone of his pictures if you offered him ten times the price he paid for it."

"Marvellous," replied Harding; but at this moment they caught sight of Thompson's picture, and they rushed forward simultaneously.

"By Jove, there's no doubt," said the novelist after a pause, during which the whole party gazed in speechless admiration, "there's no doubt but that we have let the Mediævalists have it this time!"

If letting the Mediævalists have it meant staring them out of countenance, there was no doubt that this at least Thompson had achieved. It was impossible to see anything else in the room but the housemaid and her print dress. The picture represented a pretty but dirty girl whitening the steps of a house. Red geraniums flared in the window, where a large card announced that there were lodgings to let. The girl sat on her heels, with one red hand resting on her bucket, talking to the milkman, who had put down his cans.

Thompson looked at his picture quietly. The hour of dawn was nigh upon him, the hour long desired, the hour long dreamed of, but now that it had come it seemed an ordinary, if not common-place, event. For what, after all, would it bring him? Had not his victory long been won? What cared he for the praise or blame of the *dilettanti?* He had to thank them for nothing. In his case they had acted as they have done since art began to be; they had striven to retard the taste of the age, and, having failed, would now, when their praise or blame was valueless, join in the chorus of applause. He knew well enough that today they would wag their heads knowingly, forgetful of the fact that they had jeered only a few months ago; forgetful that he had been the same man seven years earlier as he was now. What were their praises to him? He had worked and laboured, not for them, but for his own heart's praise, and for that of the little band of artists that surrounded him; what were these gilded saloons, subsidised by the state, to him?

It was not there he made his *debut*, as Harding said afterwards in an article, but in the dusty garrets of Chelsea. It was not the wealthy *dilettanti* that had found him out and recognised his great talent; it was some dozen or so of poor unknown artists and writers who had fought for him, and forced an unbelieving public to believe, and it was of them, and not of the praises of an uncritical public, that Thompson thought as he looked at his picture. He was not dreaming now of the brilliant drawing-rooms to which he would soon be invited, but of the cold lodging where he had evercome hunger, and, what was worse than hunger, cruel lassitudes and yearnings for rest; where, at the point of his iron will, he had driven himself to his work, scorning respite and comfort. He thought of the past; there it lay before him, concentrated into a few yards of canvas, but of the cost and the worth, who could speak but himself? What could his friends tell of? A few years of perseverance and privation, but only he knew of the terrible drama of abdication, of the life that might have been, of the life he had let lie in the limbo of unborn things, of the love, the dreams, the joys and sentiments that he had ruthlessly torn out of his heart and flung like flowers under the resistless wheels of the chariot of art, that most implacable god, that most terrible of all Juggernauts.

"By Jingo," said Stanley, "I don't believe that anyone ever was so much in the open air before; I can't imagine, Thompson, how you managed to model the hands and arms in that pure cold light."

"It is the positivism of art," exclaimed Frazer; "at last we have got an art in concord with the philosophy of our age."

Stanley and Crossley looked disposed to laugh, and Thompson turned for an explanation, positivism of art he had no idea when he painted the picture.

"Yes, quite so," said Harding; "I know what he means, it is the positivism of art, for it is an art purely material and experimental. Bravo, Frazer! you have given me a title for my article"; and the novelist repeated the phrase which had suggested to him a whole host of ideas.

At this moment they were joined by Holt, the academician. Thompson shook him by the hand warmly.

"We owe it all to you," said the red-bearded Scotchman, with tears in his voice.

"You owe me nothing," replied Holt; "if I have gnawed through a few threads of the veil of folly and prejudice, which stifles all artistic aspirations, I have done good work, and am amply recompensed. But you have no idea what a fight I have had for it. They knew that they could not well turn you out; they would probably only have hidden you up there, but when they saw that I was making a stand for the whole school, by Jove, I can't describe it! Hilton stood by his maidens, and said that he would defend beauty, poetry, and grace, and the rest of it, to the last. However, I was successful, let's say no more about it. Come, and I'll show you the rival picture. It is at the other end of the gallery; we'll see all our own things on the way down."

Although not apparent to the general public, the walls of the Academy in '79 offered the interesting spectacle of a contest between two rival schools of painting, one purely material and experimental, the other wholly ideal and subjective.

The extreme note was struck by Thompson on one side, with his maid-of-all-work; on the other by Mr. Hilton; but on every wall there were pictures which showed, both in execution and sentiment, the influence of either school.

The galleries were now gradually filling. Frazer, Crossley, Stanley and Holt had gone different ways; but Harding, who had an important review article to write, remained with Thompson. They walked up and down together, talking seriously and examining the pictures. At last, stopping before Lewis's Clytemnæstra, Thompson said:

"Did you ever see anything so piteous? You remember the fellow, he began with us."

"Yes," said Harding, "he was one of those creatures who exercise a strange power over all with whom they come in contact, a control that is purely physical, yet acting equally on the most spiritual as on the most gross natures, and leading us independently of our judgment. How can we blame the women for going mad after him, when even we used to sacrifice ourselves, over and over again, to help him?"

"Quite true," replied Thompson, reflectively; "I took a lot of trouble about him; and, although I knew in my heart he wasn't worth it, but I'm damned if I could help myself!"

"Marvellous," said Harding; "and he married the most lovely girl in London. In fact, he succeeded through women; he never had a half-penny worth of talent. But, by Jove! he is just the man I want. I must have someone to hold up to ridicule; let me see, how can I describe his picture?" Then the novelist's face grew more than ever cynical in its expression as he searched for a scathing criticism. After a pause he said:

"'To show how utterly outworn is the classical formula, I cannot cite a better example than Mr. Seymour's picture of Clytemnæstra. Here we have a figure, drawn, I will admit, with tolerable correctness, the modelling is fairly well executed, and the composition is well balanced, and yet it excites as little emotion as a design for a chair in an upholsterer's catalogue.' I will then, you know, go on to explain how, in the academies, a pupil is taught that that is right, and that that is wrong, that good painting is this, and bad painting that, and I shall sum up by showing that an emotionless art is the inevitable result of such training."

"What you say is true enough," replied Thompson; "but, after all, is he worth attacking? Wouldn't it be better to say that Mr. Seymour has painted a picture, which, doubtless, all the ladies in Mayfair will declare to be utterly fascinating?"

At that moment, two fashionably dressed women stopped before the picture.

First fashionable lady.—"Sweetly pretty, is it not?"

Second fashionable lady.—"Charming; what lovely arms she has got."

First fashionable lady.—"Lovely! I believe he did them from his wife."

Second fashionable lady.—"Delightful man is Mr. Seymour. How very handsome he is, and what good manners; 'tis a pity all painters are not like him."

First fashionable lady.—"It is, indeed; how beautifully he paints satin."

Second fashionable lady.—"He always shows such taste in the arrangement of his dresses, and, above all, he doesn't make one look ugly, and that is the principal thing."

First fashionable lady.—"Of course, what's the use of having an ugly picture?"

"And it is to be known to such people that we sacrifice our lives," murmured Harding, as he linked his arm into his friend's, and walked with him out of their hearing.

The fashionable world had now begun to arrive, and the rooms were already thronged with artists, praising and abusing each other's work, and showing their pictures to their friends and relations.

Lady Helen passed through the crowd talking to Sir Thomas Towler, the president; Lewis followed, walking between Lady Marion and Lady Worthing; Lord Worthing had just stopped to speak to Lady Ann Sedgwick. Mrs. Liston, who had left her husband in the first room examining a couple of pictures of ancient Egypt, one of which profoundly interested him, was laughing with Mr. Ripple. He was telling her about "The moderns" and Mediævalists. As he hurried her forward to show her Thompson's picture, they bowed to Mrs. Campbell Ward. Mrs. Bentham was with Mrs. Thorpe, and Mr. Carver, magnificently dressed in a new pair of white and black plaid trousers, gallantly proposed to take her to Thompson's picture, an offer which was politely declined.

Everyone talked of the maid-of-all-work. Mr. Swannell, who had lost his seat at the last election, declared that it was a picture of great political significance; it appeared to him to represent the tide of Radicalism which was carrying away the bulwarks of our entire social system. Mrs. Bentham thought it very coarse, but admitted its power. Mrs. French and Mrs. Collins agreed that it was immoral, but refused to give their reasons for thinking it so; it suggested an epigram to Mr. Ripple; and Lady Helen, finding that the general opinion was against the picture, declared herself in its favour; but, on her husband calling their love into question, was induced to modify her opinion. As for the critics, they never ceased talking; they passed through the rooms to and fro between the two pictures, rapidly asking each other what they thought, and discussing the meaning of the phrase, "Positivism of art," which was now in everybody's mouth.

Thompson still walked about with Harding, and, as he passed, everyone who knew him pointed him out to their friends.

Lewis was absolutely frantic. He had hoped that the paragraph in *Fashion*, describing his Clytemnæstra as representing the classical interest, would have attracted some little attention, but it had been entirely passed over, and people seemed to have no eyes or ears for anything but the rival pictures.

As he edged his way through the crowd, throwing civil words to the paragraphists as they passed him, he met Lady Helen and Mrs. Bentham, and they asked him to bring them to see Mr. Hilton's Hesperia. Biting his lips with vexation, he assented. Thompson's picture was the most talked about, but Hilton's was certainly the most praised. All spoke in raptures of its poetry and passion. Mr. Ripple declared that it was the "pain of unassuaged desire," and, enchanted with his phrase, he went about recklessly repeating it.

The picture was hung at the end of the galleries, just opposite to Thompson's maid-of-all-work. It represented a band of maiden's in rose-coloured draperies, pink, white, yellow, and purple, dreaming amid rose-crowned, and sea-begirt rocks. Some sat on high crags, some lay on the low shore, all seemingly overcome by the perfume of the flowers, and the intense glory of the sunset, which flamed around them.

Lady Helen, notwithstanding her general inclination to abuse what other people liked, grew quite enthusiastic, and leaving her husband with Mrs. Bentham, she walked down the galleries, and explained to

Mr. Hilton the emotions it suggested to her, and the poem she intended to write immediately she got home.

It was now mid-day, and all who had been able to obtain invitations were within the walls of Burlington House. Grave men with pocket-books edged their way down the lines of pictures, taking notes; now and then they exchanged ideas with their friends, but it was easy to see that they were performing their daily work. Chaperonless young girls, in terra-cotta, or sage-green dresses, with puffed sleeves, passed in great numbers—they criticised the pictures energetically. Occasionally a stylish dress struck a clear gay note here and there, but the fashionable world remained distinct from the artistic; only a few youths who seemed to belong equally to both passed from one to the other. Among these the most remarkable was a tall young man, dressed in a long, dark green frock-coat; his flaxen hair fell on his shoulders; and as he passed he spoke affably of art in general terms. Every now and then was heard the phrase: "Positivism of art."

Mrs. Bentham and Lewis walked about through the crowd, looking at the pictures. It was the first time he had found himself alone with her since his marriage, and now in this hour of bitter discouragement, her sympathy was the solace he needed. Lady Helen's impetuous enthusiasm wearied and irritated him. She passed over his faint-heartedness as if it did not exist; but Mrs. Bentham understood him, and he told her of his troubles and sorrows, and she pacified him just as she used to do in the old time. Then they went together to see the Clytemnæstra, and she spoke of it in a tenderer way than Lady Helen had ever done. She condoned its faults, pointed out its merits, reminded him that after all it was only the first day of the exhibition, and that he really did not know what the critics would say of it. Lewis brightened up at her words, and he talked with the gaiety of a convalescent who has been brought out into the sunshine after an illness. He praised her, he thanked her, and he scolded her affectionately, "You never come to see us," he said. "Us" was an awkward word, but he slid over it, and continued to tell her how lonely he often was, how much he missed her advice.

As they walked through the rooms, they were stopped from time to time by artists, critics, and friends, who told them what they thought of pictures, and repeated the stray fragments of gossip that were going the round of the galleries. Most of this was idle verbiage, but, nevertheless, one bit of startling news reached Lewis's ears. It was to the effect that Harding was doing an important article on the

Academy. This was quite enough, and Lewis found no difficulty in imagining the terrific shaking he would receive. His first idea was to renew his acquaintance with Harding, ask him to dinner, and persuade him, as best he could, not to be too hard on the Clytemnæstra. But this, on second thoughts, seemed to him a very simple way of proceeding, and it struck him that it would be far more ingenious to introduce Harding to his wife and leave her to speak for him. Full of the idea, he bade Mrs. Bentham goodbye, and looked round for Lady Helen. After some little difficulty he found her talking to a whole group of people under the "Land of Hesperia." He signed to her that he wanted her, she nodded assent, and, profiting by an occasion that offered itself, said goodbye to the people she was with, and walked up the galleries with her husband.

Lewis explained to her in brief phrases his fears that Harding was going to "slate" his Clytemnæstra, and proposed that he should introduce her to the novelist. She readily consented, and he told her what she was to say.

"You know he is a very clever fellow, and will be able to tell you far more about your verses than I can."

Lady Helen had read many of Harding's novels, and she thought at once of the advice he would be able to give her on certain questions of versification that interested her.

"Of course, my dear, I shall be delighted to know him, and you can depend on me to make it all right."

"I wish I knew where to find him," repeated Lewis, looking about him anxiously, and nodding rapidly to his acquaintances so that they should see that he didn't want to be interrupted.

"If he is writing about 'The moderns' we may probably find him near their pictures," suggested Lady Helen.

"Not a bad idea; come, I'll show you Frazer's Railway Junction," replied Lewis, plucking up courage.

The picture was not difficult to find; it was surrounded by a jeering crowd; ladies, critics, and artists pressed forward smiling and curious to see, and then retired shaking with laughter. Frazer watched from the other side of the room, and his long, sallow face showed no trace of either anger or disappointment.

"That's Frazer," Lewis whispered to Lady Helen; "did you ever see anything like it. If my picture were laughed at like that, I think I should die."

"What a curious man he is," replied Lady Helen, looking at the enthusiast with interest. "I should like to know him."

"Oh, impossible," returned Lewis; "he says the most extraordinary things, but I'd give anything to show you his studio. He used to keep a raven that he had taught to say, 'Frazer is a great painter:' he used to call the bird his art critic. He's the most curious card you ever saw in your life. But, come and look at his picture."

Frazer's picture represented a railway junction seen from above, probably from a railway bridge. Through clouds of steam three or four engines loomed indistinctly, their yellow wheels glaring horribly.

"Well, do you know," said Lady Helen, after a long pause, "it doesn't seem to me to be as bad as you say it is. The wide, grey track covered with a network of lines is very real, and it is like no one; you can't say it isn't original."

"What's the use of being original and bad?" said Lewis, pettishly; "I'd sooner be like someone, and do good work."

The argument perplexed her, and she was annoyed that she could not answer it.

"But," said Lewis, stopping suddenly, "there's Holt's picture; did you ever see anything so shockingly coarse?"

The last phrase was whispered softly to Lady Helen; and then, in the hope of being overheard, Lewis talked loudly and extravagantly in its praise.

Holt's picture showed a group of peasant women bathing in a shady pool. Overcome with heat, they had left the glaring cornfields, indicated here and there through the opening in the trees, and were plunging about in a way that clearly showed that bathing was to them a novelty. Both in conception and handling, it was undoubtedly a very powerful painting; and being a sort of compromise between "The classics" and "The moderns," mightily pleased the *dilettanti* and critics, who prided themselves on their impartiality.

Lewis continued to point out the merits of the picture, and, as luck would have it, his words were not wasted; for Harding, who was passing at the time, stopped to listen. At first the novelist did not intend to speak, but he was so astonished at hearing Lewis praise Holt's picture, instead of abusing it, that he could not help saying:

"I shouldn't have thought that you would have cared for anything so modern as that."

Lewis turned round at once, surprised at the success he had so quickly achieved. He shook Harding warmly by the hand, and declared he was delighted to see him. Then, after these expressions of good will, Lewis said that the peasant women were simply magnificent; and that he wasn't in the least opposed to "The moderns" when they took the trouble to draw correctly. This opinion being very much Harding's own, he felt already disposed to take a more lenient view of the man whom he intended to "slate"; and an introduction to Lady Helen helped him, in a few minutes, to believe that Lewis was not half such a bad fellow after all. She congratulated him on his last novel, mentioning certain details which obviously pleased him. Then she questioned him about the new phrase "Positivism of art," and laughingly declared that she was sure he was the author of it. For the moment, Harding forgot to pry into the truth and falseness of things; and, blindfolded, Lady Helen led the analyst away to talk to him of her poetry.

The excitement of introducing his wife to Harding being over, Lewis began to grow dejected, and to think again of Mrs. Bentham. Looking about for her, he passed from room to room, until he found himself opposite his Clytemnæstra. Now and again a small group would form round it, but it suffered from the presence of a large landscape on the right, which was much admired, and Crossley's pictures of race-horses, which attracted a good deal of attention.

Lewis examined his picture with painful curiosity. As he did so he remembered his hopes and expectations; they rose before him a pale vision of folly and weak imaginings.

He felt quite disgusted with himself. Clytemnæstra appeared to him the most wretched and ludicrous thing he had ever seen; and a cruel temptation rose up in his mind to take a penknife from his pocket and cut it down from the walls. A cynical smile curled round his lips as he thought of what a scene there would be were he, quite politely, to ask one of the people about to oblige him with the loan of a knife. Then, one—two—three, and the whole thing would be finished. Such foolish fancies afforded him for the moment a sort of bitter amusement; and, allowing his thoughts to wander, he examined unconsciously the different women that passed. A certain green dress interested him, and he followed it with his eyes until he was suddenly startled by a voice speaking behind him:

"Well, Mr. Seymour, which of us do you give the apple to?"

It was Mrs. Campbell Ward. By her side, with dyed whiskers and hair, his portly stomach tightly buttoned in a superb new frock coat, was Lord Worthing.

"To whom am I to give the apple?" said Lewis, smiling gaily—a woman always brushed sorrow from his heart—"Am I Paris, then, that I have the apple to give?"

"Certainly," said Mrs. Campbell Ward, flashing her large eyes. "Have you not won Helen?"

Lewis laughed lightly, and his face became grave as he thought of a reply. Lord Worthing had moved aside and was looking at the Clytemnæstra. Lewis watched him a moment, and then said, with obvious satisfaction, for he prided himself on his *esprit*:

"Yes, but if you were Eve, and I were Adam, would you give it to me?"

"It is quite possible that I would," replied the professional beauty, with a quiet glance. Lewis was in the habit of deciphering such glances, and he said to himself: "By Jove! I wonder I didn't guess it before; there's no doubt but she has a fancy for me." But at this moment Lord Worthing, who had finished his examination of the Clytemnæstra, addressed himself to Lewis. Mrs. Campbell Ward listened to his twaddling talk impatiently. At last she could stand it no longer, and, determined to get rid of him, she said:

"Have you seen my husband lately, Mr. Seymour? I promised to meet him about half-past one; it must be that now."

Lewis replied that he had not seen Mr. Ward for the last hour or so.

"Oh! how very tiresome; he will be looking for me everywhere. I wish, Lord Worthing, you would see if you could find him. I'll wait here; Mr. Seymour will take care of me."

The old gentleman hesitated a moment, but there was nothing for it but to go and seek for husband.

As he disappeared in the crowd, Lewis and Mrs. Ward looked at each other; it was a look that meant a great deal. "Thank Heaven," it seemed to say, "now he's gone we can talk at our ease." After a moment's pause, Lewis said:

"I am glad you like my picture, Mrs. Ward."

"Oh, I think it perfectly lovely, the arms are so sweet."

"They don't quite satisfy me. Ah! if I had had your arms to draw from."

"You have never seen my arms: they mightn't suit you at all."

"Never seen your arms? I think I have had the honour of feeling them on my shoulders—at balls."

"Oh, yes; but a Greek dress shows more of the figure than a ball dress."

"Yes, but I can judge of a rose by the bud. . . You must come. . . and sit to me. . . I am sure I could—"

"And what would your wife say?"

"What could she say?—a mere question of art. You would be doing me a great service. A picture of you by me would be talked of everywhere."

"And my husband, I don't think he would consent. You know you have such a bad reputation. They say you make love to every woman."

"There is very little love I would care to accept were it offered me—nothing less," he murmured with a sigh, "than a supreme desire is worth gratifying."

Mrs. Ward laughed nervously, and Lewis congratulated himself on the way he had spoken, and thought how nicely he had hinted at things without saying anything that could by any possibility be turned against him. Mrs. Ward puzzled her brain to think how she should arrange a rendezvous.

After a pause she said, "What a long time Lord Worthing is away; I wish he'd come back. I want my husband to take me to lunch, I'm dying of hunger."

"And is that what you want your husband for?" replied Lewis, laughingly. "You do surprise me. Really if you had told me you wanted him to kiss you, you could not have astonished me more."

This remark both of these professional beauties considered excruciatingly funny, and, with a great deal of laughter, Mrs. Ward said:

"Oh, you mustn't make me laugh so" (she burst forth again), "you are really too shamefully wicked."

Enchanted at the success of his joke, Lewis thought of sending it to *Punch*; and they walked down the galleries, conscious of no one but themselves, penetrated and tickled with many pleasurable feelings. The pictures they did not even see; and when they got entangled in a group of artists, their only thought was how they could quickest rid themselves of such hum-drum bores. After many twists and turns, Lewis contrived to ask Mrs. Campbell Ward if she would like to go out to lunch with him.

"But how shall I come back here? It would look quite awful."

"But you won't come back here," said Lewis, gaily. "I will put you in a cab and send you home, and I can tell Lord Worthing and your husband that you were so tired looking at the pictures that you could wait no longer, and that will be the truth, for you have had enough of this place, haven't you?"

Mrs. Campbell Ward raised her eyes; words were weak to express her weariness of the place, and they walked out of Burlington House together.

"There are even occasions when it is unpleasant to be well known," said Lewis, as he followed Mrs. Ward into a cab, and told the driver to go to the Café Royal. There was a side door, he assured her, in one of the back streets, a little back passage, the most convenient thing in the world, not a particle of risk.

After some difficulty this luxury of modern life was explained to the dull-headed coachman, and five minutes after Lewis Seymour and Mrs. Campbell Ward, these two representatives of fashion and art, were passing up a black back stair, smelling of beer and grease.

"It's dirty but it's safe," said Lewis, referring to the back way as they were ushered into a private room—a snug little nook with a glaring look of public vice. There was a chair and a divan, both covered with red velvet, and the table was laid for two. The ceremonious Swiss waiter closed the window, and took the order for lamb cutlets and a bottle of champagne. When he left the room there was a slight hesitation, but, taking Mrs. Ward's hand, Lewis said: "And when shall I see these beautiful arms in a Greek dress?"

The professional beauty answered, "If you are good, one of these days."

"You promise me I shall see your arms in a Greek dress, or, the equivalent?"

This sally provoked much laughter, after which Mrs. Ward gave the required promise.

"And now give me a kiss to seal that promise with."

They bent their heads and kissed each other.

It being the first occasion he had betrayed his wife's trust, he was for a while in an ephemeral sort of a way conscious of his own baseness. Somewhat frightened, he asked himself how he could have done such a thing. He had often acted equally vilely, but was nevertheless now ashamed to find that he had accepted a woman whom he did not love, whom he did not even remotely desire, because her viciousness had enabled him for an hour or so to forget his disappointments. With characteristic treachery and cowardice he turned on the woman, and in his thoughts denounced her as a vain fat creature, with the airs and caprices of a macaw.

It was the suddenness of the sin that had discovered in Lewis Seymour this thin streak of conscience, or, rather, of nervous irritability. Many events had happened, and it was the combination of these that had produced this unique result. For above other things he could not help recollecting how he had left his wife working in his interest, and he thought, with some tenderness, how good she was, how much she had given up for him. There was no subject of reflection that pleased him so much as to think of the women who had loved him, of how they had sacrificed themselves for him. Naturally, Gwynnie Lloyd and Mrs. Bentham came uppermost in his thoughts, and his sensibilities being on this day strung to a keen pitch, it dawned upon him, in a vague, glimmering way, that perhaps some part of the success he had achieved in his life was owing to the assistance he had received from women. He did not quite reach this most certain fact, he grazed it as a ship might a rock, for his vanity came to his assistance immediately, and floated him into dreams where he could luxuriate at ease. A hundred pleasant memories of the compliments he had received thronged on his mind at once, how that dealer and this amateur had come into his studio, and been perfectly dumbfoundered by the grace and beauty of his work, how they had given proof of the genuineness of their admiration by paying their money. And then it was not difficult to find reasons for Thompson's success and his own failure. It was easy to think that Thompson was surrounded by a lot of friends, Holt and the rest, who hated Lewis Seymour, for he had succeeded by legitimate means, which they couldn't do. He had never descended to painting bar girls and housemaids. He had stuck to the nude, and he was the only person who could sell it; and if his pictures did sell it was not because they were the fashion but for the good work that was in them.

In this way Lewis's thoughts ran on until he arrived at Burlington House. Indeed, so occupied was he in considering the shameful neglect that had been shown him that he had almost forgotten his own treachery. His remorse was already a phantom of the past; and, assuring himself that he had far more important things to think of, he dismissed the subject forever from his thoughts.

In this frame of mind he ran up the stairs, and passed through the turnstile into the galleries. The first person who caught his eye was Thompson. He was surrounded by a crowd of journalists and artists. A bitter feeling of envy rose up in Lewis's mind, and now he hated his former friend with all the strength his weak soul was capable of.

Nevertheless, he wished to be seen speaking to the hero of the hour. This was not easy to do, for he had been in the habit of cutting Thompson for a long time past. Thinking how he could deny these affronts he approached the great man, and reminded him obsequiously of their friendship of old days. Thompson looked at him contemptuously, and, without troubling himself to ask him why he had not spoken to him before, bowed and accepted coldly the congratulations that were offered.

This embarrassed Lewis not a little, and he inwardly wished himself miles away from the artists and journalists who stared so rudely at him; and had it not been for Frazer, who insisted on explaining some new dogma, Lewis would have fared badly. The interruption enabled him to put on his haughtiest air, and, with a sarcastic remark, he strolled off after Mr. Campbell Ward, whom he recognised in the distance.

The husband was walking pensively in company with his little boy, to whom he was much attached. Both father and son inquired anxiously after Mrs. Ward, and the latter declared that Lord Worthing wanted particularly to see her.

"Well, he'll find her at home," replied Lewis, indifferently. "But, by-the-way, have you seen my wife?"

The husband looked steadfastly at the lover, and after a pause answered, with a deep sigh, "Oh, yes, she is walking with Mr. Harding."

Lewis wondered for a moment why Mr. Ward should sigh so profoundly; but, catching sight of Lady Helen's narrow back in the crowd, he rushed after her.

"I have been looking for you everywhere," he said, with an air of affected annoyance.

"And we have been looking for you," replied Lady Helen, smiling. "But Mr. Harding has been very good, has shewn me everything, and has promised to take a poem of mine to one of his papers."

"That is very kind of him," said Lewis, taking his arm in an affectionate manner, "and I must tell you, Harding, my wife is one of your greatest admirers. For myself, you know—of course I see the power—but the beauty—well, that's the old argument."

As her husband spoke, Lady Helen could not help wishing that he would not begin to discuss the beauty question again. She was beginning to realise that his criticism on this and all other subjects was shallow and common-place. For the last hour, while Lewis had been away at lunch, she had been unconsciously weighing him in the balance with Mr. Harding. His logical views and methodical judgments awoke a new fire in her heart, and she had already begun to long for the intellectual comfort and advice he could give her. She had already begun to tire of her husband's caresses and superficial attainments.

The conversation then returned to the pictures, and dwelt on Thompson's success, which Harding declared was undoubted. Lewis said he was delighted, that it was deserved; at the same time expressing fear for the traditions, so that he might not appear too conciliatory.

The novelist accompanied them to the turnstile, and then in the clearest tones of her flute-like voice, Lady Helen said:

"Goodbye, Mr. Harding, I shall expect you tomorrow; we lunch at two."

Harding bowed, and continued to watch the slender neck, fluffed with delicate lemon coloured down, till it was lost in the shadow of the lower hall. When he turned he saw, much to his irritation, Thompson and Frazer examining some bas-reliefs. Accosting them familiarly, he took Thompson's arm, and they walked again through the galleries, and agreed that no better title could be found than "Positivism of art" for the article he was about to write.

Thompson did not mention Lewis's name even when looking at the Clytemnæstra, a fact that somewhat disconcerted Harding, but he still congratulated himself that his walk with Lady Helen had passed unperceived, until the Scotchman said to him as they parted in the street:

"By-the-way, Harding, I nearly forgot to tell you; I think, on the whole, you had better not make an example of Seymour in your article, he isn't worth it."

XXXI

Looking Back

After the Academy, like an immense flowering tree, London blossomed into dinner parties, balls, garden fêtes, race meetings. Lady Helen and Lewis went everywhere, for them were all pleasures and delights, until, at the end of July, they watched the season dragging itself to its end, marvellous and common-place, like a hundred other seasons.

Mrs. Bentham had guessed from Lewis's manner that he had not wholly forgotten her; and with an exquisite thrill of pleasure she saw that her place had not been entirely taken; that there was still a spot left for her in his life. This being so, she asked them to come and stay with her on a visit, and in the beginning of August Claremont House united the three women, who had worked so lovingly and successfully for Lewis's welfare, under one roof. Unconscious of each other's rights, they continued to love him, with loves as different as were their ages and positions.

But of these three women Gwynnie Lloyd, who had possessed the least, was the happiest. Lady Helen was devoured with jealousy, and the pleasure that Mrs. Bentham experienced in having Lewis near her, was saddened by the memory of the past. Had it been anywhere but at Claremont House, the pain would not have been so defined; but there the whole place was so filled with memories, that the smallest incident sufficed to raise from their dust the dear, dear days, complete in every detail. Sometimes a chance word, the falling of a leaf, a sunset, a particular *entrée* at dinner, would bring back to her the exact image of some past happiness. Sometimes she thought of their life in Paris, and of the many pleasant voyages she had made with him; but often of the first six months, when Lewis came down to decorate her ball-room, when her love had been a pure and sweet illusion.

But to her the sadness of the present was not untinged with pleasure; for although Lady Helen hung upon her husband as if haunted by his hands and lips, Lewis was often anxious to escape from her, and talk to Mrs. Bentham. They understood each other so perfectly; they had so many interests in common, that they were always glad to be together. They were bound together by the indissoluble chains of five years of love and intimacy. At first they were embarrassed when they found themselves alone, and avoided alluding directly to the past; but gradually their constraint wore away, and involuntarily they sought for opportunities of idly dreaming in the cool shade of bygone joys, and the sweetness of half-forgotten kisses. Mrs. Bentham did not deny herself these sad pleasures; for she regarded the past as all hers, as the present and future were all Lady Helen's.

Daily the yearning for the memory of old times grew stronger upon them, and Lewis sought Mrs. Bentham's society more and more. One afternoon, after lunch, he asked her to go out for a walk. Lady Helen was lying down with a sick headache, and Mrs. Thorpe was laid up with a cold. Without knowing why, he was burning with curiosity to talk to her of the past, and he intended to take her to some of the places they used to love in old times.

It had been raining, the trees glistened with wet, but it was now fine. Towards the sea the sky was a dull heavy grey; and the clouds were collecting overhead. They walked through the pleasure grounds towards the river, but before they had got far large drops of rain fell on the moist gravel; the sky darkened, and the thunder rattled along the horizon. It was too late to go back to the house, so they took refuge under a clump of beeches, which grew in the hollow below the terrace, and just within view of the bridge.

"How tiresome this rain is," said Lewis, wondering how he should lead up to the subject of their dead love. At last he said: "Do you think we should be more in shelter over there?"

It was a spot they both knew well. The brown water rushed round a flat island overgrown with tall trees. Lewis had painted it several times, with figures and without. Mrs. Bentham did not answer, and, after a pause, he continued: "Do you not remember the big landscape I did there, and I was so busy that I did not come to lunch, but used to ask you to bring me a sandwich?"

"Yes," she replied, "I recollect, but I thought you did not think such things worth remembering."

"I, not remember! I have forgotten nothing; I never was so happy as when I was with you."

Mrs. Bentham's heart throbbed as she listened to the words, and a delicious sigh of pleasure passed through her lips.

"But you," he said, "why are you not the same as you were? All things seem so altered."

It was a great joy to Mrs. Bentham to see that in some ways he missed her, but at that moment, remembering how cruelly he had acted, she could not help saying:

"Of course it cannot be the same as it was; how could you expect it?"

The phrase somewhat disconcerted him, and he did not speak for some moments. He wondered that she dared say such a thing; and she began to regret that she had expressed herself so clearly.

The rain now pattered heavily on the foliage overhead, and the large drops which fell on the bare brown ground at their feet rustled amid the red leaves that remained from last year. The day grew darker, and the thunder rattled rapidly.

"I wish we could get away," said Mrs. Bentham, who was beginning to feel afraid.

"It is a dreadful day, is it not, and is well suited to the bitter sadness of—"

"Ah!" cried Mrs. Bentham, nearly blinded by a vivid flash of lightning, and they waited for the answering peal which, in a few seconds, burst forth and seemed to roll quite round them. Then Lewis thought of the past, and seized with a vague and undefinable regret for what had gone from him, he put his arm round Mrs. Bentham and tried to draw her towards him. She looked at him with surprise. In this instance, his tact had failed him. It was a sweet sad pleasure to her to talk of their past life, but his sentimentally sensuous nature prevented him from seeing that any renewal of love-making was impossible.

"Oh, Lewis! How could you? I thought you loved your wife better than that," she said, looking at him rather sadly.

Lewis stammered, equivocated, and entered into a long explanation: he referred to the happiness of days gone by, Mrs. Bentham's great goodness, and Lady Helen's irritability. He told her how wretched it made him. Then her desire to protect him overpowered all other thoughts, and she consoled and advised him. They talked for a long half-hour under the beeches, every now and then stopping to listen to the thunder, which they vaguely feared was threatening them. At last, however, the storm ceased; the sun shone brightly out of a large piece of blue sky, and they walked towards the house through the warm, gay rain which sparkled in the luminous air.

Lewis was in high spirits, and he kissed Lady Helen rapturously when he got up to her room. His vanity had been gratified; he could congratulate himself that there were at least two women in the world who would lay down their lives for him; and, like a cat in the sun, he basked in the warmth of the idea.

Mrs. Bentham was not so well satisfied. Her faith in her *protégé* had been shaken, but it was built on too stable foundations to be overthrown at the first shock. Her life had been too intimately bound up with his. She had done too much, sacrificed too much, for him, to allow her belief to be cast down without a struggle. To acknowledge him worthless would be to admit that the work of her life had been wasted; and now, when she heard or read of his successes as an artist, she felt all the joys of a kind of adopted maternity, which has grown since their separation, daily more and more inexpressibly dear to her. He belonged to Lady Helen, yet she often said to herself, and always with exquisite pleasure, that he owed everything to her. But if jealousy could no longer touch her, it was not so with Lady Helen. She could never quite understand Mrs. Bentham's affection for her husband, and she often, like the rest of the world, suspected her of having been her husband's mistress. A hundred times she had passionately dismissed the idea, because it pained her, because she felt that she had no right so to accuse her friend; but, struggle as she would, it always came back, and at each return buried its sting deeper in her heart.

Little things constantly occurred which were irritatingly suspicious, and she grew to hate Claremont House; it seemed filled with ghosts. In one room there was a sketch of Mrs. Bentham, by Lewis; in another a book, a present from Lewis to Mrs. Bentham; on the piano she found old songs they used to sing together; and the ball-room seemed to her little more than an emblematic record of their love. Then her husband and Mrs. Bentham had so many subjects in common that interested them, and of which she knew nothing. They were always talking of past times. Sometimes it was when Lewis was at the "Beaux Arts"; sometimes a summer they passed in Sweden. They laughed over one adventure, grew serious over another, or disputed some minute fact which was at last referred to Mrs. Thorpe, who sat, as usual, knitting by the fire-place.

Lady Helen bit her lips with vexation; she often complained bitterly to her husband, but he only laughed, and told her she might as well suspect him of being in love with his great-grandaunt. This assurance appeased her wrath for the time, and as these bickerings always took place in the silence of their room, a few kisses ended the matter happily. Nevertheless, the feeling of jealousy remained, and an explanation seemed more and more imminent.

GEORGE MOORE

At last it came, and more naturally and quietly than might have been imagined. One day the ladies left Lewis at home to finish a landscape he had begun; and they drove over to Coleworth to see Lady Marion. As they talked, under their parasols, of different things, the conversation suddenly turned upon friendship. This was the opportunity Lady Helen wanted, and, determined to come to the point, she declared, after a little hesitation, that she did not believe that friendship could exist between a man and a woman.

Mrs. Bentham looked at her, and Lady Helen returned the look, and then the former said:

"I should have thought, Helen, that you would have been the last person to think so; for you ought to know better than anyone that such friendships are possible."

This was a direct reproof, but Lady Helen was determined to see what Mrs. Bentham would say when taxed with having been Lewis's mistress.

"You know, I have heard people say that your liking for Lewis was more than mere friendship."

Lady Helen expected either an angry retort, or blushings and tremblings, but, to her surprise, Mrs. Bentham answered her quite quietly.

"My dear," she said, "I must forgive you for your accusation; for I must admit that it is not easy for you to understand the friendship which has existed so long between me and your husband. You are too young, and you are too much in love to suppose that any other sentiment but love is worth prizing. Under such circumstances it is difficult to close one's ears to scandal, even when it is a question of one's friends."

This calm reply at once astonished and discountenanced Lady Helen; but when she reflected that, notwithstanding the fine words, Mrs. Bentham had not answered her question, she grew angry, and put the question in all its brutal simplicity.

"Yes, but were you, or were you not, ever Lewis's mistress?" Mrs. Bentham looked at her in silence for a moment, and then said:

"No, it is not true."

"You swear it?"

"Yes, I swear it; it is not true."

The women continued to look at each other fixedly for a moment, and then Lady Helen, unable to contain herself any longer, seized her friend's hand, and, with tears in her eyes, said:

"Oh! Lucy, you don't know how happy you have made me! It would kill me to know that Lewis had ever loved any other woman but me."

Mrs. Bentham laughed a little nervously, and said:

"Of course it isn't true; Lewis never had a chance of making love to me. I knew him under circumstances which would not have permitted of it."

Then she went on to say how she had met him, telling the truth as far as she could, and mixing in the narrative the sorrows of her own matrimonial life, explaining how utterly it had disgusted her with all love, forever and ever. The tale brought tears into Lady Helen's eyes, and she asked, with much commiseration, many questions concerning Mr. Bentham. The conversation deeply interested her; she pitied Mrs. Bentham with her whole heart, and she assured her that all men were not like Mr. Bentham. With Lady Marion they passed a charming afternoon, and during the drive home Lady Helen, who was in a confidential humour, initiated Mrs. Bentham into the secrets of her wedded life, dwelling particularly on all the delicacies of Lewis's character—and she was too much wrapped up in her own happiness to notice the pained expression on her friend's face.

XXXII

Bills

In the last week in September the Seymours went back to London; they had been married now nearly two years, and were just beginning to perceive that the money was going out far faster than it came in. Not only did Lewis not get so many portraits to do as he had expected, but Mr. Carver, to whom he had been in the habit of selling seven or eight hundred pounds worth of pictures a year, had lately died, and his business had been broken up. This deprived the Seymours of a large portion of their income, for Mrs. Bentham was unable, for the moment, to find a dealer to whom she could entrust the task of buying Lewis's pictures. Lady Helen's questions had frightened her, and she now dreaded every breath of gossip. Besides, Lewis's brag of what he made deceived her. He talked a great deal of the prices he received, and the social position of his sitters, and complained despairingly of how he was pressed for time. He had received a letter from Lady X, saying that she would be in town in a week, and would then be able to sit to him.

This was cheering news, and he soon forgot all about Mr. Carver.

Lady X was a handsome woman, and it would be both amusing and profitable to paint her picture, and not long after this piece of good luck came two more portraits. This looked promising indeed, but when the bills came in at Christmas, they found that they had not only spent the thousand pounds which had been taken out of his wife's fortune, but were at least two thousand to the bad. A weekly dinner party, and a small dance or two, and the quarter's rent, had got through six hundred pounds in four months and a half.

It was clear that they were going a little too fast, but Lady Helen consoled herself with the assurance that expenses were always very heavy at first: when they had once settled down, things would come right. She wrote to the upholsterer, that it would not be quite convenient to pay him just yet, but that she hoped to settle the matter during the course of the summer.

"There will be no difficulty about this," she said to Lewis, as she stamped the letter; "you are sure to get five hundred for your picture of

Sappho; and we will give the wretched man three hundred out of it. I thought the critics would like it. Has Harding seen it yet?"

"No, I have not seen him lately; have you? You know it would be as well to keep up the acquaintance."

"No, not for sometime; but I shall ask him to dinner one of these days," and she passed her arm through her husband's and went down with him to the studio. It was large and sumptuous, and only recalled his former ways of life by a few stray touches, a coquettishly arranged bunch of flowers, a glove, or a solitary fan. A few pictures and a piece of tapestry decorated the walls; a large divan covered with dark green velvet, a few arm chairs to match, and a table covered with paints: the view was everywhere intercepted by portraits of fashionable women.

"Heavens! how the sun does come in here at ten; but it is gone in half-an-hour," said Lewis, drawing the blind.

The picture of Sappho stood on the easel; it was nearly finished, only bits of detail here and there remained to be added. It showed the poetess seated amid her attendants, who were engaged in completing her toilette. One of them had just handed her a lyre, and, resting it against the porphyry table, strewn with silver boxes and vases containing odours, she had begun to sing. It was decidedly Lewis's best work.

"I think I shall score a success this time," he said, looking affectionately at his work.

"I am sure you will; but you have made it so like me that everybody will recognise it."

"The arms are not quite right yet; take off the body of your dress, Helen, and let me have another go at them." Nothing Lady Helen liked so much as sitting to her husband. They used to spend the happiest days together, all alone in the big studio. She had not only sat for Sappho, but for the hands and feet of the attendants.

Now she put herself into the necessary light and position, and as Lewis squeezed the paint out on his palette, he bitterly deplored Carver's death; he declared he would never find another customer like him.

Lady Helen grew interested, and eagerly demanded the details. He told her how Carver had been in the habit of buying of him nearly a thousand pounds' worth of pictures yearly. The story made Lady Helen thoughtful, and she wondered why this man had been such an extensive purchaser of Lewis's pictures.

"I never had so bad a year in my life," said Lewis. "It is a fact that I have made only seven hundred pounds this year, and I used to knock off twelve hundred, and did not work half so hard. Had it not been for the portraits, I don't know what we should have done. I wish I could get some more orders."

The conversation here ceased. Lady Helen continued to think, and from the expression on her face it was clear that she was annoyed. Little things were constantly occurring which kept her suspicion always on the alert. She could specify nothing; indeed, when she tried to examine any particular bit of evidence, it faded from her like mist; but yet, in the distance, the clouds of mistrust maintained their sinister appearance. The uncertainty irritated her, and she now suspected every second woman she spoke to of having been a former admirer of her husband.

These suspicions had rendered her extremely jealous, so much so, that Lewis was often puzzled how to act. If he came home five minutes after she expected him, she would turn away her face from his kiss, saying, "No, thank you, I don't care for the leavings of others." He, of course, would protest, plead, and swear that it was not true; but it made no difference; Lady Helen remained in the sulks for hours.

So little sufficed to create one of these scenes of jealousy, that Lewis fairly lost his head. He positively dreaded to walk in the park with her; for if she caught a woman looking at him, which they all did, he found it impossible to persuade her that he not only had no appointment with, but had never seen, and had no knowledge whatever of the lady who had just passed. To go to a ball with her was positive torture, for it did not matter with whom he danced, Lady Helen declared all the same that he had been flirting and amusing himself the whole evening. Lewis hated scenes, but in his heart he bitterly resented these continual recriminations, and he often said to himself that it was beastly hard lines that he should be badgered about his unfaithfulness by the only woman to whom he had ever been true.

"You know, Helen, it is somewhat your fault, if I have not had as many orders as I might," he said, as he modelled Sappho's arm with short strokes of the brush passing rapidly backwards and forwards.

"My fault!" exclaimed Lady Helen, turning round, regardless of the pose. "How do you mean?"

"Well, you know, dear," he answered, putting away his palette and brushes, and sitting down at his wife's feet on the edge of the throne, "you are so jealous."

"But what has that got to do with orders?" returned Lady Helen.

"You don't know how people get their orders; one has to make oneself agreeable to people, and persuade them gradually into it."

She looked at him in astonishment; but the ice being broken, he went on more boldly. "And you are so jealous that I am always afraid to say anything agreeable to anyone; for if she were sixty you would never believe that I was not in love with her, and—"

Not knowing how to go on, he kissed the white arms that encircled his neck like a garland of roses.

"Then you mean to say that you must flirt with women to get them to give you orders?" returned Lady Helen, as she withdrew her arms with a feeling of disgust.

"I don't mean to flirt with them, I only mean to be agreeable with them; surely there's a difference," he said, kissing her in spite of herself.

"I would sooner starve, live in a garret, than have you flirt with anyone, Lewis."

"I don't mean to flirt with anyone, you silly little puss; but one should be attentive and polite; ladies like it."

Lady Helen looked at him tenderly; she could not resist his caressing ways, but inwardly she felt that he was cowardly and false.

"What would you think of me," she replied, "were I to flirt with anyone to get you an order?"

She looked at him passionately, speaking in a hesitating way; she had something to say, and didn't like to say it. Lewis did not know at first how to answer; but recovering his assurance, he said, laughing:

"Flirtation, after all, is nothing; it only means making oneself agreeable."

He could not have summed himself up more completely. The whole man was in the phrase. It was like a sketch by Daumier, and it gave the mental and physical character of this most modern of lovers.

Lady Helen laughed; but she learned afterwards to understand the phrase at its full value. Nothing was said again for sometime, but her face twitched nervously.

At last she decided she would.

"You promise not to be angry if I tell you something?" she said.

"I promise," returned Lewis, looking up from his palette.

"Well, then, you never noticed it, but that fool, Lord Senton, is always trying to make love to me."

"You don't say so?" said Lewis, laughing, and trying to appear surprised. He knew it well enough. "That fellow," he continued, "is the biggest ass I ever met. Do you know that he makes love to every woman, and no one will have him. Tell me what he said to you; it amuses me."

"Amuses you!" said Lady Helen, looking at her husband rather sternly. She had expected that he would be furious.

"Well, why should it not? Nobody pays any attention to Senton; he's a perfect fool; every woman amuses herself with him."

"It does not amuse me, I assure you," replied Lady Helen, smiling, in spite of herself, at the recollection of something too utterly absurd he had said to her; "you have no idea how idiotic he is."

"But what does he say?"

"Oh, nothing, only that I am looking well, and that he admires me, and little things like that."

The conversation here dropped; but Lewis could see from the expression on Lady Helen's face that she thought the idea of flirting with Senton for a portrait irresistibly funny. He did not speak, but left her to consider the matter. After a minute or two she said:

"I wouldn't mind dancing with him once or twice of an evening, but I really don't see how that will get him to give you an order."

"Won't it, indeed!" replied Lewis; and he explained how the trick was to be done. "First of all, be civil to him, smile at him, speak to him in the park, and ask him to call on you."

"And then?" she asked, quite interested in the intrigue.

"Why, when he is a little in your confidence, you must tell him to make himself agreeable to me, and come and see me; I will see him once or twice, and show him my pictures; then he will be only too anxious to sit for a portrait; it will give him an excuse to hang about the house."

Lady Helen laughed; and, seeing that she had accepted the idea, he added, brutally, "And I will charge him two hundred pounds for the portrait and one for the flirtation."

A knock came at the door, and a servant announced that Lady X had arrived. Lewis told him to show her into the drawing-room. Lady Helen put on the body of her dress hastily, and they went up to see their visitor. She was a two hundred guinea one.

XXXIII

More Treachery

To make love to Lady Helen stretched beyond Lord Senton's wildest dreams into a dim region inhabited by his divinities the Lovelaces, the Buckinghams, the Duc de Morny.

On receiving his first encouragement, he rushed down to Sussex to consult his friend Day.

Lady Helen had ridden with him in the Row; told him when she would be there again; danced with him three times at one ball; asked him to call. He felt sure that this time, at least, he had inspired *une grande passion*. He followed his adviser about from room to room, questioning him as to what he thought of this fact and of that. Day had a suspicion of the truth, but he knew better than to hint it to Lord Senton. Long were the discussions, and profoundly philosophical the remarks on the passions and desires of women.

Day sometimes felt bored to death, but he thought pleasantly of his banking account, as he settled himself down to Lord Senton's long-winded anecdotes.

"What is the use of telling him the truth?" thought the farmer; "it will only make him unhappy, spoil Lady Helen's prospects, and mine too, for the matter of that. Much better advise him to be cautious, and do everyone a good turn"; and with this kindly intention, Day listened, and advised Lord Senton to the best of his ability.

Nothing could have succeeded better, and everybody seemed to be perfectly happy. Lady Helen drew Lord Senton on beautifully; she chatted, and smiled, and joked, until he grew delirious with excitement; and then, choosing an appropriate pause in the conversation, she counselled him to make friends with her husband.

The two men had never quarrelled, and whatever ill-feeling had existed between them was of Lord Senton's seeking. Their reconciliation was, therefore, a matter of no difficulty. It was done in a trice; he came to see Lewis in his studio. Lewis flattered him, talked about women, chaffed him about his successes, and Lord Senton went away quite astonished to find that Mr. Seymour was such an agreeable fellow. This visit had profoundly interested him. For a few days he thought of nothing else, until, suddenly remembering that he had forgotten to ask if it were better to pretend to neglect a woman or to pay her unremitting attentions, he determined to call again and discuss the matter thoroughly. This time, however, Lewis, although still studiously agreeable, did not fail to let Senton see that he was engaged, and really had not the time to devote to him. But Lady Helen pressed him to return, and before a week he was back again. Lewis received him pleasantly, entertained him with long discourses on the tastes and habits of women—interlarding them carefully with so many allusions and references to his work, until at last Lord Senton perceived that the only way to become Lewis's friend, and to have the run of the house, was to give him an order for a picture. Then, like a bird that flits about before entering a trap, he talked about having his portrait done; then tried to retreat; then advanced again, and finally asked Lewis how he would do him. Lewis at once began a sketch just to show him, and when that was done, Senton, not seeing the way out of it, gave the order for a full length, and asked the price.

When they were alone, Lewis described the interview in detail to his wife, and they both laughed over it: he with a vain, empty laugh, which showed how indifferent he was to all sense of honour; she with a light laugh, indicative of discontent and irritation. In truth, she was ashamed of the whole affair, but, although possessing the stronger will of the two, she was more affected by the influence of his company than she was aware of. His soft nature, although it yielded at the slightest pressure, was as difficult to escape from as a sensuous thought; it depraved with warm water-like treachery, corroded like rust, and soon the fine steel of Lady Helen's character lost its temper and became tarnished.

In due time, the Sappho was sent to the Academy. It encountered a great deal of opposition, and had it not been for the President, Holt would have succeeded in having it turned out. He denounced it vehemently—partly because in his heart he loathed Lewis's painting, and partly, it was whispered, because he considered Lewis a representative of that section of society which had persistently refused to receive Mrs. Holt. When Lewis heard this, he took a hansom and drove home, determined to ask his wife to be civil to Mrs. Holt if the occasion presented itself. He knew Lady Helen would not like it much, but he hoped that when she understood how important it was to him to have Holt on his side in the hanging committee, she would not refuse. He approached the subject carefully, but at the very first suggestion Lady Helen flared up and said:

"Oh, impossible! I cannot know such a woman as Mrs. Holt."

"Mrs. Holt is as good as anyone else," Lewis exclaimed, getting angry. "I just ask you to consider the consequences: supposing he had succeeded in getting the Sappho kicked out, I should like to know what I should have done; whereas, with a civil word or two, you can bring him over to my side. I tell you it is most important."

"But, surely, you would not like me to know a woman who has sat for a model for half the artists in London."

Lewis seldom got into a passion, but every now and then he tried to prove that he was not as weak-minded as you might suppose, by answering rudely, and pretending to lose his temper.

"That is not true; she never sat for any artist but Holt," he said, walking up and down the room violently; "and now she is his wife, as much as church and law can make her. If you only married me to push me down, instead of up, I am damned if I don't wish you had left me alone."

Lewis knew that this would wound Lady Helen's feelings as acutely as anything he could say, and he said it with that intention.

"You have quite sufficiently degraded me by making me flirt with Lord Senton to get you a portrait to do, without wishing to introduce me to such a woman as Mrs. Holt."

Lady Helen could not restrain her tears, and she went out of the room, sobbing bitterly. But she had no sooner gone than Lewis began to regret what he had said—not, however, because he was sorry he had hurt his wife's feelings, but because he remembered the disagreeableness it would cause him personally. The dinner bell was going to ring, and of all unpleasant things a sulky face was the worst. As he considered the question, it occurred to him that, after all, perhaps Lady Helen was right. It might do them harm with other people if they were to try to drag Mrs. Holt into society. Still, he didn't see why it should; she was not half as bad as Helen wanted to make her out; lots of nice people knew her, and why shouldn't they? Then, thinking of what an escape the Sappho had of being turned out, he resolved to let his wife stay in the sulks as long as she liked.

This was their first real quarrel. Eventually Lewis apologised for having been rude, and Lady Helen promised to inquire into Mrs. Holt's case.

This decision was arrived at afterwards, as they were looking through some very unsatisfactory accounts, which proved to him, at least, that it would be impossible for them to give another ball. Nevertheless, they went a great deal into society, and gave many dinner parties. Lady Helen liked it, and Lewis said that otherwise he could not hope to get orders. He knew, in reality, very little of picture trading. Mrs. Bentham's commission to Carver to buy from him yearly several hundred pounds' worth of pictures had blinded him to the wants of the actual market, and to his own position as a painter. His instinct was to make acquaintances, flatter and cajole, until they gave him an order. His persuasive manners enabled him to do this with some success, and he did not hesitate to push his wife forward, and make her do the same. It was he who gave her the tips. If he heard that they were to meet a sporting man at dinner, she was to talk to him of hunting and racing, and ask him if he had ever been painted in scarlet; if there was a lady at the table who was fond of riding, she had to suggest a portrait in a riding-habit. In fact, Lady Helen had to keep her eyes open, and do the business of a tout. Mr. Ripple also lent his aid. He hung about the editorial offices of the society papers, and pestered the editors into accepting "pars." describing what Lewis had done, and intended to do. Having no occupation and five hundred a year, he got up at twelve, tossed off a "par." or two, and spent his afternoon talking of literature wherever he went, and of his artistic acquaintances, and his intimacy with the Seymours, of which he was very proud. He had a "have a drink, old man" acquaintance with the tag-rag and bob-tail of Fleet Street, and these gentlemen were very glad, in consideration of a five bob loan, to help him crack up Mr. Seymour, in whose genius he firmly believed. He took much trouble, but in the end was recompensed, for, after a series of interviews and beating about the bush, he at last persuaded the editor of the *World* to let him do Mr. Seymour at home.

This was the literary event of Ripple's life; hitherto his contributions had not exceeded a six-line "par.," and an article, in his eyes, took the proportions of the "Decline and Fall." The morning it was to appear he was in a fever of excitement. He had sent the servant out at least a dozen times to see if the paper was out, and, at last, when she brought it, with what trembling fingers he tore the pages! But, alas! the number contained no "Mr. Seymour at Home."

For days he had been describing this article to every young lady of his acquaintance, and, pale with fear, he thought of what excuse he would make. To dress was the work of ten minutes, and a hansom took him to the offices in five, but those five seemed an eternity.

"Why is not my article in?" he asked the editor, in an agitated voice.

"My dear fellow, I really couldn't print it as it was; you really should be more careful. You confused the tenses so dreadfully."

"Shall I rewrite it for you?" asked Ripple, hoping against hope.

"Oh, there is no necessity for that; I have asked Jones to set it straight; it will be all right for next week."

Mr. Ripple's face lost its painful intensity of expression. The article was going in, that was all he cared about, and he assured himself that no one he knew would ever be likely to hear that it had been touched up.

The result of this and sundry other puffs, written by or at the instigation of Harding, who was a great friend of the family, was that Lewis's picture of Sappho got so well talked about that he finished by selling it for three hundred pounds; two off the original sum, but still a fair price, and the money came in very handy, for it paid the Midsummer quarter's rent, which was just due. Nevertheless for him, the season did not turn out very successful; and one morning, after breakfast, instead of going to his studio, he went upstairs with Helen to her boudoir to look into the books.

Drawing down the blind to keep out the sunlight, Lady Helen sat down by her work-table, and telling Lewis to bring his chair up, she proceeded to look through the accounts. A little examination showed them that they were enormously high. The butcher's bill was thirty pounds; the poulterer's, forty-two; the grocery, twenty; the greengrocery, seventeen pounds seven shillings and elevenpence; and the butter merchant, sixteen pounds and sixpence; the fishmonger, thirty-three pounds seven shilling and fivepence; and the wine merchant's, fifty-five pounds. After reading the figures out, they looked at each other nervously. This was a terrible result to arrive at, after two years' housekeeping. It was clear that, at the lowest computation, they were living at the rate of three thousand a year.

However, as Lady Helen said, there was no use crying over spilt milk, the only thing for them to do was to retrench. Fortunately they were going now to stop with Lady Marion for two months, and that would be an immense economy.

"But after all," said Lewis, "if it had not been for those confounded dinner parties we shouldn't have done so badly. I was adding it up the other day. I have made nearly twelve hundred pounds since Christmas. If it goes on, this will be the best year I have had."

Lady Helen waited to see if he would recognise what she had

done to help him to this sum of money, but he did not say a word of thanks, and she watched him with irritated eyes as he walked up and down the room admiring himself physically, whenever he passed the glass, intellectually, as he repeated the words, "nearly twelve hundred pounds"; yet notwithstanding the twelve hundred, Lady Helen found herself obliged to write to her dressmaker for time, and apply the thirty which she drew quarterly from the funds to paying these bills.

She made this sacrifice without grumbling; she still loved her husband passionately and tenderly, although she had heard many stories which had considerably altered her faith in him. Lord Senton, who had become one of their most intimate friends, had told her a hundred tales of Lewis's bachelor days. Although they stabbed her like daggers, Lady Helen encouraged these confidences, and Lord Senton, blind to every consideration but his own flirtations, would probably have given her date, name, and address, had he been able. He had lately bought, besides his own portrait, two pictures from Lewis; nevertheless, she was at home to him less frequently, and unflinchingly discouraged all allusions to the tender passion. She could not forgive him for having awakened without having satisfied her doubts, and her life now became one prolonged agonising question. Lewis still held his empire over her, she still trembled neath his touch, but when he was not near her she almost hated him. Now his little feminine ways exasperated her, and very often the merest trifle, even a remark about her dress, would provoke a violent scene of tears, anger and recrimination. She never knew for certain whom he had and whom he had not loved; and she fancied every second woman she shook hands with had flirted at sometime or another with Lewis. Even Gwynnie did not escape her suspicion, and remembering the anxiety the girl had shown to see his picture in the Academy, Lady Helen, in her exasperation, often thought of getting rid of her maid.

XXXIV

FRIEND OR WIFE

The baby that was born in the beginning of the third year of their marriage patched up the differences which had spoiled the last six months of their married life. There was little that was paternal about Lewis; but the pallor and languor of Lady Helen's convalescence touched him with its poetry, and in the pleasures of home life she forgot her jealousies, and remembered only that he was the father of her child.

But as the months passed by full of delicate tenderness, their affairs grew daily more embarrassed. Debts grew pressing, and it became clearer than ever that they were living beyond their income. Last year had been a good one; Lewis had made nearly two thousand pounds, but the upholsterers had been only paid three hundred on account.

And there were hundreds of other bills: Lewis owed his tailor a hundred; Lady Helen had not paid her dressmaker for the last year and a half. This was a very gloomy look out; and Lewis declared that, at his present prices, he did not see how he ever would be able to meet his engagements. He said he could not work more than six hours a day, even that was killing in the hot weather; and as for his portraits, he began to loathe the sight of a satin dress. To have half-a-dozen perpetually before your eyes, in various stages of completion, was sickening. So long as the ladies were there, the time passed pleasantly enough, and the painting of the faces and hands was, of course, always amusing; but then there were the long hours in the afternoons, all alone in the studio copying a bit of lace hung on a squat, lay figure. Besides, everything seemed to be urning out badly. His Academy picture was not sold; it had not been too well noticed; and he had only a few orders in hand. Lady Helen urged him to work, but as their difficulties increased, he grew idler instead of more industrious. But this could not go on forever, and one morning he received a packet of very disagreeable letters.

Lady Helen was more resolute than Lewis, and after reading the letters she said:

"It is clear that we are living beyond our income, we must see how much we owe, clear off our debt, and live within our means, whatever they are."

"I quite agree with you, my dear," said Lewis, who was quite sick of work, and would gladly have exchanged his fine house for a cottage where he could idle.

The duties of motherhood had wrought a change in Lady Helen, and the necessities of the situation rapidly developed the clear logical intelligence which her passions had obscured.

After having gone into the accounts carefully she found that they owed three thousand pounds. Lewis was perfectly aghast.

"What shall we do?" he exclaimed, pale with fright.

"There is only one thing to do," returned Lady Helen who had carefully considered the matter from all points of view.

"I must see Worthing, tell him the truth, show him the accounts, and ask him to let me sell out of the funds sufficient money to pay off our debts; then we must give up this house, it is too large and expensive for us, take a cheaper one, and live within our means."

Lewis had nothing to say against this proposition, and to avoid further annoyance, he left his wife to work it out her own way.

Lord Worthing was dreadfully shocked when he heard of the difficulty his niece was in, and, of course, reproached her with her marriage, and reminded her how she had been warned. She let him have his say, and then showed, by means of the accounts with which she had come armed, how much Lewis had made, that, in point of fact, he had even done more than he said he could do; and that it was her extravagance that had got him into this trouble.

Lord Worthing looked surprised. He had never suspected her of so much decision of character.

Lady Helen explained that if he would not allow her to sell three thousand out of the funds, there was nothing left for them to do but to go through the Bankruptcy Court, "And that will ruin us every way," said Lady Helen, "both socially and financially, but it can't be helped."

The threat of bankruptcy seemed to frighten Lord Worthing, who at first had refused to listen to her proposition of drawing upon her capital.

Lady Helen explained how she had already arranged to give up her house, and had her eye on another which would suit them just as well, and was a hundred and fifty a year cheaper; that she had determined to put down her carriage; and how she not only hoped, but had reason to believe, that instead of living above her income, they would then be living within it, even if Lewis's artistic position only remained what it was, a thing which she said was highly improbable, for his pictures were yearly being more and more talked about.

"Ah," said Lord Worthing, in answer to Lady Helen, "you remind me of something I was going to write to you about. Have you heard that Stevens, the A.R.A., is dead?"

Lady Helen had not heard it, and then Lord Worthing proceeded to explain that the thing to do would be to use all their influence to get Lewis elected. As for the President, they were sure of him. He would at once put Lewis's name down, if he had not already done so; and then they would have to work up the other men. Lady Helen's face flushed with pleasure. He was her husband, and it was her duty to help him.

Lord Worthing then began to count up the names of the academicians whom they thought could be depended on to vote for Lewis. Together they reckoned up about half-a-dozen, and their faces beamed until Lady Helen spoke of Mr. Holt. This was clearly the rock on which they might split. Holt had a lot of friends who believed in him, and who would follow his vote.

"When does the election take place?" asked Lady Helen, suddenly.

"Two or three months hence, probably in October; we have time, but we must not let the grass grow under our feet; I will call on Sir Henry today."

"Thanks, very much, uncle; but what about the three thousand?" asked Lady Helen.

"Well, you know, I can't do anything without the consent of the other trustees. I will write to your father; he will be awfully annoyed, but I will put the matter to him in the most favourable light."

"Be sure you don't say it is Lewis's fault."

"I will forward him a copy of the accounts, which will prove that your husband is not to blame."

Lady Helen remained sometime longer, explaining and repeating her story, so that Lord Worthing should make no mistake. Then they again discussed the chances of Lewis's election, till the servant announced that lunch was ready.

But Lady Helen would not stop, and bidding her uncle goodbye, she got into her carriage. From the expression of her face, it was clear that she was thinking out the details of some project.

For sometime her uncertainty was evident, but at last with an effort she made up her mind; the struggle was over, and, determined to act before her resolution cooled down, she put her head out of the window, and told the coachman to drive to Orchard Villa, Grove Road, St. John's Wood.

Mr. Holt was painting when the servant handed him Lady Helen's card; he looked at it, and wondered why she had come to see him. "It is impossible," he thought, "that Seymour's not aware that I oppose his pictures whenever I get a chance; in fact we haven't spoken to each other for years; what, then, can his wife have come here for?"

Mr. Holt was a timid man, and when the servant ushered Lady Helen into the studio, she saw that so far the advantage was on her side. He asked her to sit down, but she declined, begged him to go on painting, and asked to be allowed to look at the pictures.

"Surely," thought Holt, "she hasn't come here only to see my pictures."

Lady Helen talked volubly of things in general, but Mr. Holt was not a conversationalist, and after having tried vainly to lead up gradually to what she wanted to say, she found herself obliged to come straight to the point.

"I dare say, Mr. Holt," she said, "that my visit surprises you, but I have come to see you with a very definite purpose."

Mr. Holt bowed, looked embarrassed, and tried to mumble something about the honour.

"I have come," said Lady Helen, "for neither more nor less than to ask you to vote for my husband at the next election."

Mr. Holt's face expressed so much astonishment that, notwithstanding the gravity of the situation, Lady Helen could not help smiling. But the academician's feelings of surprise soon gave way to that of anger, and he answered curtly that his vote was promised. Never in all his life did he remember having felt so indignant. For years his dream had been to get Thompson elected; it had been talked over and discussed, until it took in his mind the force of a hobby. For years "The moderns" had laughed at him for even dreaming of the possibility of such a thing, and since. Stevens's death he had been secretly thinking what a surprise it would be if he could succeed in getting a sufficient number of votes to carry the election. Consequently Lady Helen's request appeared almost in the light of a joke, or an insult. He looked at her, and wondering when she would take her leave, said:

"Besides, I thought it was known that, in art, my tastes are so diametrically opposite to Mr. Seymour's that—"

"I am well aware," interrupted Lady Helen, "that you have not many sympathies in common, but in this case I hoped you might promise me your vote."

Mr. Holt's look of anger now gave way to one of complete bewilderment.

"I really don't see what you mean," he answered bluntly; "why should I in this case promise you my vote?"

"Because there are services I could render you in return," replied Lady Helen, nervously; "social services; do you not guess what I mean?"

Lady Helen blushed, and trembled. She knew Holt hated her husband's painting, but she had often heard that it was the sorrow of his life that he could not bring his wife into society; she hoped that the latter would prove the stronger motive.

Mrs. Holt used often to tell her husband that she was quite happy as she was, and that it was silly of him to trouble about introducing her to a lot of people she had no wish to know. This was partly true; but although she never complained, Mrs. Holt often regretted her isolation, and her husband knew it.

Lady Helen had therefore been rightly informed: the sorest point in Holt's life was his wife's position; he loved her, he was proud of her, and the certainty that she could make herself liked, were she to get a chance, rendered every snub she received doubly annoying.

He had understood Lady Helen's proposition, and his face for a moment had flushed with pleasure, for he knew that if once his wife were taken up by the Grandervilles and Worthings, there would be an end to all the petty slights from which he so perpetually suffered. He felt he would give anything to avail himself of this chance; but his antipathy to Lewis's painting, and the treachery of throwing over Thompson, made him irresolute.

He did not answer Lady Helen at once, but remained thinking. She saw that he was struggling between desires so evenly balanced that the smallest word or thought might decide him either way. To vote for Lewis was the bitterest sacrifice that he could make. His whole soul was bound up in the new school, and he looked to Thompson's election as one of the achievements of his life; to give up the man whose talent, perseverance, and courage he admired more than any other, for this wretched creature with his women, and his licked-up painting, seemed to him the basest of treasons. But, on the other hand, he loved his wife, and to see her fêted, courted, and admired was the dearest wish of his heart.

"What you ask of me is a very serious thing; you must know that Thompson is my dearest friend."

Lady Helen feared to say a word, and Mr. Holt hesitated, and was on the point of telling her that he could not throw over his friend, when he remembered that if he didn't, he would be throwing over his wife. He was on the horns of a dilemma, and after some consideration he resolved to put it to his wife and to vote which way she liked. "After all," he thought, "she is one of the parties most concerned in the matter, and should be consulted: if she asks me to behave dishonourably, I will; but not for anybody else." Having come to this resolution, he was just going to ask Lady Helen to give him a day to think over her proposition, when the door opened and Mrs. Holt entered.

"Will you come upstairs, dear, and have some tea?" she said, but seeing Lady Helen, she stopped, confused.

This was an opportunity not to be lost: seeing her advantage, Lady Helen asked Mr. Holt to introduce her to his wife.

Mr. Holt did so, not knowing whether it would be better to give right out the reason of Lady Helen's visit. Half because he thought it would humiliate his wife, half because it was a most embarrassing explanation to make, he waited, and in a few seconds the two women were chatting quite affably. He had lost his chance.

Lady Helen could be extremely fascinating when she liked; she said pleasant things, praised the portrait Mr. Holt was doing of his wife, asked Mr. Holt's assistance for a charity bazaar, and with the most perfect assurance explained that that was the reason of her visit. There was not a grain of malice in Mrs. Holt; when she liked a person she showed it. Lady Helen she thought charming, and at the end of five minutes asked her up to tea in the drawing-room. Mr. Holt remained behind, feeling sure that the women would settle it between them. He saw that his wife liked Lady Helen, and he thought what a good wife she had been to him, and of the pleasure it would give her to be received by nice people, and to wipe out once and forever the memory of an unpleasant past. He remembered what a difference it would make to his little daughter when the time came to bring her out, then he came to the opinion that it was his duty to vote for Lewis Seymour, and throw over his old friend. It was most abominably disagreeable, he thought, but he felt sure it was his duty; and, firm in that belief, he went upstairs.

He found Lady Helen and his wife delighted with each other; and when he conducted the former downstairs, she said:

"Have I your promise to vote for my husband?"

"You have."

"Thanks, a thousand times; but you have a great deal of influence with the other academicians, can I count on that also?"

"I never do things by halves, Lady Helen; I will do all I can to secure Mr. Seymour's election."

"Thanks, it is so good of you, Mr. Holt."

Three days afterwards Mr. and Mrs. Holt received an invitation to dine at the Seymours.

XXXV

Veils Fall from Their Eyes

The twenty-ninth of October, 1882, was the day on which the academicians would meet at Burlington House to decide if Lewis should be admitted as an A.R.A.; on account of the condition of the two parties, the president's and Mr. Holt's, his election was considered almost a certainty. The news that not only was Holt going to vote for Seymour, but was using all his influence to get him votes, fell like a thunderbolt on artistic London.

At first every kind of conjecture was put forward to account for his extraordinary change of front; but gradually the truth began to be suspected, and the wiseacres predicted that if Seymour were elected, Mrs. Holt and Lady Helen would be seen driving in the park together.

Holt knew that it was useless to try to convince his friends that he liked Seymour's work better than Thompson's; and he remembered with regret that it was no later than last year that he had spoken of Seymour's Academy pictures with disdain. He told his embarrassment to Lady Helen, who in turn explained it to Lord Worthing, who in turn communicated it to Sir Thomas, who very kindly solved the difficulty by taking Thompson's name off the list. This materially facilitated matters, though Holt still felt himself in a very awkward position; but his friends, guessing the truth, made it easy for him, and without questioning him as to why and how he had so suddenly changed his opinions, promised to vote for Lewis Seymour.

As for Lady Helen, she patiently waited the result of the election; there was a great deal to do, and everything devolved upon her. She had to write innumerable letters to her father, explaining the necessity of allowing her to sell three thousand out of the funds, so that they might pay their debts. Lord Granderville had written in a very alarmed strain to Lord Worthing. Then Lady Granderville wrote, denouncing the whole thing, and declaring that they had better go through the Bankrupcty Court. All this was very harassing, and she had to keep her uncle up to the mark, and insist on his taking her view of the matter. Finally her father put it into Lord Worthing's hands, who, of course, did not like to bear so much responsibility. At last it was done, and the money placed in the bank. But even then her troubles were not nearly over. She had to look into all the bills, make them up, and when this was done, she had to decide how she would distribute the money, for she found she was three hundred short. Then she had to look out for a new house, and see how much it was possible to get for two hundred a year, she was resolved to give no more.

She had scarcely been out of town during the summer; all through the months of August and September she had driven from house agent to house agent; and, not satisfied with consulting their books, had rummaged St. John's Wood, South Kensington, Fulham and Chelsea, from end to end.

Lewis irritated her beyond bearing; he seemed as inert as a log of wood. Even when she had noted down a house that might suit, she could scarcely get him to come and see if the studio would please him, and his want of energy sickened her.

But the final shame was reached when, on entering the studio suddenly, after a hard day's work, she found him kissing a wretched little model. She felt too sick at heart and disgusted with his weak treachery to lose her temper. She had long suspected that he was unfaithful to her, now she was sure of it; and, miserable as the truth was, she felt that it was better to face it, than to be half tortured and half deceived. Still, he was her husband, and the father of her child, and she would have to make the best of it; and after the first few days she spoke to her husband just as if nothing had happened. Congratulating himself that it had passed off so easily, Lewis devoted his whole time to his election, and to admiring his pictures. Never did they appear to him so good; and so great was his vanity that he did not seem to see that, even if he were elected, it would be owing to extraneous influences, and not entirely to his own merit.

He alluded to what Lady Helen had done, but only as if her aid were one of those little stepping-stones which an admirer lays at the foot of a great man, that he may take his place on Parnassus; and he spoke of his election as a tardy recognition of his genius.

The election was within a week of the day when they would have to get into their new house, and Lady Helen was very busy looking through papers and books; cataloguing the furniture, and getting everything ready for removal. Lewis did not attempt to assist her; he let her see the tradesmen, and make all the arrangements, even down to the removal of his pictures. Not only was he of no use, but he very much hindered her in her business, for he was too excited to sit still, and he followed her from room to room, asking her what Sir Henry had said when she saw him last, what Mrs. Holt had told her, and such like inanities. And what annoyed her the most was that he only appeared to wish to gratify his vanity. After having hung about the place looking at the various clocks, and wondering if the election were already decided, he walked down the street so that he might get the news from some model.

Thankful at having got rid of him, Lady Helen continued, with the housekeeper, to catalogue the different articles. They were in a top room where a lot of books had been put away. As the housemaid turned out the contents of a press, they came on one of Lewis' old dressing-cases, out of which fell a bundle of letters. She saw at a glance that they were from women; and then there rose up within her an irritable curiosity to know, to read, the story of how she had been deceived. Her sentiments were more those of anger than of jealousy; she wished to place herself on equal terms with her rivals; and, unable to control her desire to learn who they were, she walked into the next room, her hands clutching the little delicate missives.

Sitting in a chair next the window, she read through half a dozen letters without stopping. The first began with, "Darling Lewis, just a line to tell you that it is impossible for me to see you tomorrow," etc. It was from a young girl whom she knew—whom she met every Sunday in church—the last person whom she would have suspected of such infamy! The second was written in a strange and vulgar style, and ended, "Your own ducky little sweetheart, Alice." The third letter accused Lewis bitterly of loving his wife better than anyone in the world. The fourth was from one of Lady Helen's most intimate friends, a married woman, who was supposed to adore her husband. The following phrase is sufficiently characteristic: "I think that perhaps you were wrong in stating that 'a letter means nothing,' as it proves at least that one was thinking of you while writing; but, as your letter was not very long, you need not feel any qualm of conscience for making me *too* vain."

Smiling bitterly, Lady Helen opened a fifth letter. It was one of her own, and as she read its wild declarations of love, her last illusions withered and fell, like the autumn leaves that rustled against the window panes. It seemed to her that she could never be happy again, that she had measured the heights and depths of all human baseness, that there was nothing more for her to learn. What did it matter to her who were her husband's mistresses—he was for any woman who chose to make love to him.

She compared her letters with those of her rivals, and was astonished to find how similar they were; her anger melted and for a moment she pitied those who loved him, as she pitied herself. She wondered what there was in this man that so irresistibly attracted every woman to him, until, with a savage burst of cynicism, she asked herself aloud whether love were not only sensuality in disguise. Then, without attempting to find an answer to this delicate question, she got up and threw the letters from her into the fire-place. But, as she did so, another packet became undone, and she recognised Mrs. Bentham's handwriting. Smiling bitterly, she thought, "At last, I shall be able to solve this wonderful platonic mystery."

There were there letters of all sorts; some long and tenderly solicitous for Lewis's welfare, full of kind encouragements. Others, merely warnings that she would not be at home on certain days, others giving rendezvous, and written in a more compromising manner. Her first impressions were those of sullen anger, for she felt that Mrs. Bentham, from the tone of some of the letters, must have been her husband's mistress, and the deception that had been practised on her all these years rose up before her eyes in all its hateful cruelty. Angrily she asked herself if their *liaison* still continued, but a moment's reflection showed her that her supposition was absurd. Then, looking at the letter again, she was forced to recognise that the tone, though affectionate, was not incompatible with that of a dear friend; and that, though suspicious, the letter was not conclusive.

"After all," she thought, "what does it matter? Why should I trouble myself about what occurred before my marriage, when he betrays me even now, and with a model!"

Little by little her anger changed to curiosity, and she felt a violent desire to know if this woman, whose hair was now grey, had really been her husband's mistress, and, if so, whether she had loved him years ago, as she herself had, only a few months since.

Then Lady Helen thought with pity how Mrs. Bentham must have suffered when she found that she had to give him up, she imagined a whole little romance, some of which bore a striking likeness to the truth; and she wondered what there was in this man that had not only fascinated her, but so many others.

Having pursued her thoughts to the end, she again referred to the letter, and the sense of curiosity predominating over all others, she felt she would give anything to know the absolute facts.

At that moment one of the servants announced that Mrs. Bentham was waiting in the drawing-room.

"Nothing could have happened more fortunately," thought Lady Helen, as she ran down-stairs; "I shall show her the letter, and I shall be easily able to tell by her face if it is true or not."

When we voluntarily give up anyone of our delights, it becomes a joy that nothing can dispossess us of. It was thus with Mrs. Bentham. Her love remained a mirror of unchanging purity, in which her whole life lived. Others might forget Lewis, might turn from him, but she could only love him.

She had come up from Sussex, so as to be one of the first to congratulate him if he were elected.

"Have you heard yet?" were the first words she said.

"No, we are expecting to hear every minute; but will you look over this letter?"

Wondering at Lady Helen's coldness, Mrs. Bentham took the letter, and at the first glance recognised it.

It was a letter she had written to Lewis, encouraging him to persevere, now nearly six years ago; it was full of tenderness and exhortation. Her eyes filled with tears as she read it, for almost every word recalled some well-beloved memory. Her hands, which were just beginning to wither to those of an old woman, trembled. After forty the years count double, and if grief and disappointment be added, the sum may be doubled again. Mrs. Bentham was only forty-five, but she certainly looked fifty-five; her hair was quite grey, her lips were almost colourless, and the wrinkles were creeping from her eyes down along her cheeks.

"So I married your cast-off lover!" Lady Helen said, affecting a bitterness which she strove to feel, but could not.

"I admit," said Mrs. Bentham, "that this letter seems to justify your accusation, but I assure you now, as I have always assured you, you are mistaken."

Lady Helen, in the confidence of her youth and beauty, looked at Mrs. Bentham pityingly.

"Was it possible," she asked herself, "that this woman with the iron grey hair had been, no later than a few years ago, her husband's mistress?" And yet she loved him enough to come from Sussex to congratulate him, who had deserted her for another; if so, how she must have suffered when she (Lady Helen) won him from her! Anyhow, what did it matter? what was the use of raking up the dust of the past? and she began to feel sorry for what she had said.

"I take your word; but, if you weren't, a hundred others were, so it comes to much the same thing."

Then the memory of how Lewis had deceived her and lied to her over and over again, getting the better of her, she exclaimed, savagely,

"All I know is that it is disgusting, and I loathe him when he comes near me; for I know now that every word of love he utters he has said a million times before, and every kiss and caress he has learned, if not in yours, in somebody else's arms. It is perfectly beastly!"

"You have no right to look into a man's past," said Mrs. Bentham; "the most you can expect is for him to be faithful in the present and the future."

"And do you think that he is faithful to me?" exclaimed Lady Helen, passionately; "not a month ago, when I was moving heaven and earth to get him votes, when I went to Holt and promised to get his wife into society if he voted for Lewis, why, I found him one day kissing a little model—a dirty little model, who sits to him for a shilling an hour!"

Mrs. Bentham did not answer, and Lady Helen, unable to contain her emotion any longer, burst into tears and sobbed convulsively on the sofa.

But it was over in a minute or two, and drying her eyes, she said:

"I beg your pardon, Lucy, for what I said to you just now, but it is very hard to bear; I declare I would sooner have a cripple, a hunchback, anything you like, and have him to myself, than this wretched creature, whom every woman I know has loved, or will, if she gets the chance."

Then, after a pause, she passed her arm through Mrs. Bentham's, and the two women walked up the drawing-room into the boudoir.

When they opened the door, Gwynnie Lloyd turned round. There was a photographic album on the table, and a carte de visite, which she had evidently just abstracted from the book, fell from her hand on the floor. Lady Helen picked it up; it was Lewis's portrait, and she said, in a look, to Mrs. Bentham, "You see, what I told you, even my maid is in love with him."

"What does this mean, Westhall?" asked Lady Helen, savagely.

Poor little Gwynnie looked quite bewildered, and she began to cry. At last she said:

"I'm sure I didn't mean any harm, your ladyship; but I knew Mr. Lewis years ago, when we were very poor."

"When we were very poor," said Lady Helen, sneeringly; "and you followed him into my house. I don't want to hear anymore."

The shock bruised her till she was conscious of nothing but one immense feeling of sickness, horror, and disgrace; and an infinite desire not to know who the man was whom she owned as a husband, but to hide herself out of his sight forever.

"Oh, don't think that, your ladyship," cried Gwynnie; "he does not know I am here; it was an accident that I came here, and, being called Westhall instead of Lloyd, prevented him from recognising me."

A cool and grateful sense of relief passed through Lady Helen, and she looked at her maid without speaking.

"What is your story?" asked Mrs. Bentham, gently.

Lady Helen and Mrs. Bentham listened to Gwynnie Lloyd's story. She told it so simply and so unaffectedly that it carried with it an air of truth that no one could fail to recognise. But just as she was telling how she never knew who her master was going to be, till she saw his photograph in Lady Helen's hand on her wedding-day, Lewis burst into the room.

"I have been looking for you everywhere," he exclaimed; "it is all right, I am elected!"

His weak, soft face was flushed with the excitement of his triumph, and for a moment he did not notice that anything particular was happening. Time had changed him but little; his figure was as slim, his eyes as sweet, as they were ten years earlier. He was the same beautiful, soft creature, bad only because he had not strength to be good.

But at last, seeing that Gwynnie was crying, and that Mrs. Bentham and his wife did not congratulate him, he asked what the matter was, looking from one woman to the other in a vague and apprehensive way.

"Nothing is the matter," said Lady Helen; "I am sure we are delighted at your success, for we three have all contributed something towards it, no one more than Miss Lloyd."

Gwynnie looked at her mistress, then at Mrs. Bentham, then at Lewis, and the three women saw, but not one so clearly as the wife, that it was they who had worked for this man's happiness, that is was they who had made him.

Lewis looked wonderingly, first at one, then at the other, quite at a loss to understand.

At last, Gwynnie seeing that Lady Helen wished her to speak, said:

"Don't you remember me, sir? I am Gwynnie Lloyd." The name seemed to recall something to him, but after a moment he shook his head.

"I am sorry to say I can't remember," he said, in an embarrassed way. He did remember her, but, as was his fashion, he still hoped against hope that she was not the person, who had sat to him in the garret in the Waterloo Road.

"Don't you remember, sir, when you lived in Waterloo Road, and when I sat to you?"

Then, seeing it would be utterly useless to pretend any longer not to know her, he seized her hands, and squeezing them tightly, exclaimed, with a great deal of fervour, that he was enchanted to see her. But he did not waste much time over her, and at the earliest occasion began to speak of his election, and of everybody's jealousy.

Gwynnie took this opportunity of slipping from the room. The conversation immediately went back to her, and Lewis, seeing that his election had dwindled to a matter of very secondary importance, went off in a huff to the club, where he would be sure of being able to talk of himself.

XXXVI

Conclusion

Lady Helen redeemed her pledge to Mr. Holt as thoroughly as he could desire; she made his wife her intimate friend, and eventually forced even the innermost heart of Vanity Fair to accept her. The task was not so difficult as Lady Helen first imagined. Mrs. Holt's agreeable little ways and pretty manners covered many defects, and eventually her sins were both forgotten and forgiven. Her first bow into fashionable life was on the occasion of a great dinner, given by Lady Helen to celebrate her husband's election. Everyone was there, Lord and Lady Worthing, Lady Marion, the Sedgwicks, Mrs. Bentham; the artistic world was well represented, the President of the Academy, Mr. Hilton, Mr. Holt, and in watching his wife's triumph, the latter was almost compensated for his desertion of the man to whom he owed everything, James Thompson.

Mrs. Bentham wept tears of joy at Lewis's success, apparently forgetting how it was obtained. Her love only seemed to see no change. Lady Helen was discontented, and petulantly regretted the past. Even Gwynnie Lloyd, simple and quiet as she always was, realised her mistake in a vague way. Naturally, on her part, there was no definite reasoning, but gradually her memories and prejudices and illusions wore away, and in the spring of the next year she left her place to marry a small tradesman, who had a greengrocery business in the neighbourhood.

As for Lewis, he remained ever the same. He was now three-and-thirty, but he did not look more than six-and-twenty, and he grew daily more delightful and seductive. Experience and necessity had perfected the social talents with which nature had endowed him. Better than ever he knew how to interest, how to move. He knew the words that touched, the words that caressed, the words that tickled; and, smiling and graceful, he continued to persuade ladies to sit for their portraits. His election had done him a good deal of good. He got more commissions, and he put a hundred on his full, and fifty on his half-lengths, and in that way, without much trouble, made a very fair income.

Lady Helen, although she no longer loved him, lived on the best possible terms with him. Their Thursday evenings were considered most interesting; everybody who did anything or pretended to anything met at their house.

Lady Helen received them graciously, asked them about their novels, poems, pictures, plays, and, eventually, she herself published a volume of verse entitled, "Flowers of Love and Sadness," the proofs of which were corrected by Mr. Harding. The book was considered a success, it was seen on every drawing-room table, and the following sonnet was much praised by the press:

> *When faded are the chaplets woven of May,*
> *Unto the shadow of the deepening skies*
> *Goes forth a train of human memories,*
> *Crying: the past must never pass away.*
>
> *Yet, in this time of ruin and decay,*
> *The fragrance of an unborn summer sighs*
> *Within the sense, before my dreaming eyes*
> *Passes the spirit of an ideal day.*
>
> *Then, fervid hours of sunlight and repose,*
> *The warm delights, the tears that true love knows,*
> *Are mine, are thine; until in sweet belief*
>
> *We dream, beside our broken prison bars,*
> *Of love exceeding joy, defying grief,*
> *And higher than the throbbing of the stars.*

A Note About the Author

George Moore (1852–1933) was an Irish poet, novelist, memoirist, and critic. Born into a prominent Roman Catholic family near Lough Carra, County Mayo, he was raised at his ancestral home of Moore Hall. His father was an Independent MP for Mayo, a founder of the Catholic Defence Association, and a landlord with an estate surpassing fifty square kilometers. As a young man, Moore spent much of his time reading and exploring the outdoors with his brother and friends, including the young Oscar Wilde. In 1867, after several years of poor performance at St. Mary's College, a boarding school near Birmingham, Moore was expelled and sent home. Following his father's death in 1870, Moore moved to Paris to study painting but struggled to find a teacher who would accept him. He met such artists as Pissarro, Degas, Renoir, Monet, Mallarmé, and Zola, the latter of whom would form an indelible influence on Moore's adoption of literary naturalism. After publishing *The Flowers of Passion* (1877) and *Pagan Poems* (1881), poetry collections influenced by French symbolism, Moore turned to realism with his debut novel *A Modern Lover* (1883). As one of the first English language authors to write in the new French style, which openly embraced such subjects as prostitution, lesbianism, and infidelity, Moore attracted controversy from librarians, publishers, and politicians alike. As realism became mainstream, Moore was recognized as a pioneering modernist in England and Ireland, where he returned in 1901. Thereafter, he became an important figure in the Irish Literary Revival alongside such colleagues and collaborators as Edward Martyn, Lady Gregory, and W. B. Yeats.

A Note from the Publisher

Spanning many genres, from non-fiction essays to literature classics to children's books and lyric poetry, Mint Edition books showcase the master works of our time in a modern new package. The text is freshly typeset, is clean and easy to read, and features a new note about the author in each volume. Many books also include exclusive new introductory material. Every book boasts a striking new cover, which makes it as appropriate for collecting as it is for gift giving. Mint Edition books are only printed when a reader orders them, so natural resources are not wasted. We're proud that our books are never manufactured in excess and exist only in the exact quantity they need to be read and enjoyed.

Discover more of your favorite classics with Bookfinity™.

- Track your reading with custom book lists.
- Get great book recommendations for your personalized Reader Type.
- Add reviews for your favorite books.
- AND MUCH MORE!

Visit **bookfinity.com** and take the fun Reader Type quiz to get started.

Enjoy our classic and modern companion pairings!

Printed in the USA
CPSIA information can be obtained
at www.ICGtesting.com
JSHW022210140824
68134JS00018B/971

9 781513 291017